The Valkyrie in the West

by

Alaric Araya

DORRANCE
PUBLISHING CO
EST. 1920
PITTSBURGH, PENNSYLVANIA 15238

Dorrance Publishing Co
585 Alpha Drive
Pittsburgh, PA 15238
Visit our website at *www.dorrancebookstore.com*

ISBN: 979-8-88925-021-0
eISBN: 979-8-88925-521-5

CHAPTER ONE

The air was blisteringly hot, and not even the streams of sweat lathering her skin cooled Kindra's body as it drips off the tip of her nose. She lay on the ground on all four limbs, trying to control her heavy breathing and steady her heart that was ready to erupt from her chest. Her long brown hair, once tightly braided, loosened into a jumbled mess and clings to her forehead and neck. Dirt coated her hands and plastered any exposed skin due to her excessive perspiration.

"Finished already?" Hildr said with a whimsical tune as she hovered above Kindra, elegantly flapping her feathered wings. "You are only hours away from reaching the final steps of your training, and you stop to take a break?"

Kindra's heart was engulfed in a roaring flame. Her muscles were tight and burning intensely at every simple movement, causing her to dare not to stutter a piece of her. All her joints felt like they would rupture at any moment. She had been cutting down trees since dawn with no food or rest and barely enough water to keep her going. Only at sunset, when the light behind the rocky surface of the mountains, would she be granted the right to end her day. As far as Kindra could tell, she cleared over a kilometer-long path through the forest on her own.

For Kindra, this was not the first time she had been pushed to her physical limits. This was also not the first time she had worked extensively for days, but not continuously without adequate rest in between sessions. For the past week, Hildr subjected Kindra to numerous physically demanding activities to signify the closure of her training. Yesterday was a full day of gymnastics and flips. The day before that was an uninterrupted sparring session with Hildr, who did not pull her punches. Before that was a solid day of running through grassy plains with her shield and spear. And before that was nothing but swimming in the sea till nightfall when the shore blended with the sky. There were numerous times Kindra vomited, even with an empty stomach, but she did not let that stop her.

Kindra had become accustomed to the searing pain accumulated after a long day of training and had even found enjoyment in it, but not to this magnitude. As she kept her body moving, there was growing concern she would spontaneously collapse to the ground. Doing so would end her life goal of becoming a Valkyrie.

Grasping the bronze ax on the ground before her, Kindra pushed against the dirt doing her best to keep a tight grip on the handle. Unfortunately, due to her weary body and tender hands that turned raw, the weapon's weight was starting to feel a hundred times heavier than it usually did.

"I … am not done . . ." Kindra said exhaustedly. She stepped towards the next tree in her path, her feet shuffling through the dirt. The ax raised over Kindra's right shoulder, glistening in the orange sun with the gleaming blade ready to cut down another standing oak.

"Good. Now finish strong. There is no weakness here," Hildr said.

Kindra stood in front of the large tree in front of her, staring into the thick brown bark. She swung the ax down, cutting halfway into the trunk. Then, yanking the blade out, she delivered another strike, completely passing through the tree. Kindra watched as the tall piece of timber slowly tipped over and slammed on the ground, sending a soft quake through the earth before moving on to the next oak tree to be brought down.

The sun finally vanished from the sky, taking with it the heat and leaving the cool night to prosper in the woods. Kindra sat on a freshly cut log in front of a small bonfire, wiping the dirt, tree sap, and grime of her sweat off the ax with a black cloth. The ax belonged to Hildr as her signature weapon and was loaned to Kindra for today's task. She held Hildr's mighty ax many times before and trained to employ it in battle. Still, whenever she wielded the heavy weapon in her hands, Kindra succumbed to the fascination of the fine artwork etched into the metal. Numerous stars were imprinted on the blade in a horizontal zigzag pattern. Lines and swirls covered the metal, appearing like tree branches with the handle as the trunk. Even after extensive use in cutting down hundreds of trees, the blade was still amazingly sharp, like it was freshly filed.

Hildr floated down onto a log adjacent to Kindra with the fire between them. Her broad gray feathered wings magically retracted as she sat on the log.

"How are you feeling, Kindra?" she asked softly.

"I am doing quite well," Kindra lied as she wiped the ax, feeling her eyelids too heavy to hold up.

Hildr removed her bronze helm, set it gently on her lap, and let her long dark red hair drape over her broad shoulders. The Valkyrie was much older than Kindra chronologically by hundreds of years, but in appearance, looked no more than ten years older than her. Hildr's slim figure and gentle personality were unique among the Valkyries, as most of her compatriots were gruff and eager for battle. Though that did not mean she was any less of an elite warrior. The woman's eyes spoke more of the many conflicts and stringent years she had overcome than the smooth skin on her face. Only on certain occasions did Hildr bring up her past adventures, typically as an example for Kindra to learn from and grasp how a Valkyrie conducts oneself.

"Do not hide your feelings, child."

"I am tired, but I can keep going," Kindra replied. "I should not let exhaustion slow me down."

Hildr gave a warm smile. "Well, I sure do hope so."

Kindra kept her eyes on the ax withholding a question to ask. Her eyes glanced at Hildr, who was gazing right at her knowing there was something on Kindra's mind. She knew there was no reason to keep her query to herself as, one way or another, Hildr would draw it out of her, followed by a lecture

3

on honesty and openness. Keeping a secret from Hildr was impossible, but she was always willing to discuss anything with Kindra as long as it did not detract from her training.

"Do you truly think I am ready?" Kindra asked Hildr.

"I have trained you up to this point, giving you the tools and the strength to mold your own path. In my eyes, I believe you are ready. Now, it will be up to you to claim what you desire. Do not hold doubt in your heart; otherwise, your actions will spiral out of your control, and you will accept defeat."

"Would chopping trees help in my resolve? Perhaps if I was challenged in collecting lumber, I would feel more confident."

Hildr placed her helm beside her on the log and said, "There was more to it than just chopping down trees. You have to expand your mind to more than what lies before you. The trees you cut down will be used as lumber to build homes and farms for people to thrive. Even though the Valkyries are to lead people after death, it does not mean we are prohibited from helping the living."

"Then maybe … I am not ready … ." Kindra whispered, pausing in her wiping motion.

"Kindra, bring me my ax." Hildr calmly ordered.

The young woman stood up and walked around the fire with the bronze ax in her hands. She held out the weapon in front of her for Hildr to accept. Retrieving the ax with one hand, the bottom of the handle touched the ground, with Hildr holding it like a walking stick comfortably at her side. When Kindra was young, any time she laid a finger on Hildr's ax, she made Kindra wipe it all down, leading Hildr to conduct a thorough inspection once she was done. She would have thrown the ax in the dirt if there had been a minor blemish and made Kindra clean it again. This time Hildr did not bother to give the ax a second look. It had become second nature to wash Hildr's weapon and her own after its use for the day. One may never know when the next battle would be, so it was imperative to keep one's arms ready.

Hildr placed a hand on Kindra's shoulder and said to her, "You will do great." She could feel Kindra's body relax while nodding to Hildr's words.

There were not many people Kindra trusted, but Hildr was among the best individuals, if not the only person to believe. "Now eat something and get some rest for your big day tomorrow. And if you fail, we will pick up where we left off and get back to training. It will certainly be harder the second time. So, use that as motivation."

Kindra smirked, saying, "On your lead, my master."

CHAPTER TWO

The morning finally arrived, far faster than Kindra would like, so she could have more time to recover from the previous week. The sky was gray, with a thin layer of mist hovering above the surface. A perfect day like any, to achieve victory. She stood on a plateau surrounded by water where several thrones were carved in stone and placed in a half-circle. The thrones were uniquely crafted to represent each Valkyrie and stylized to their taste. Hildr's chair had a large four-point star in the center of the backrest, along with red leather covers over the armrests.

This was the Court of the Valkyries. This was where Kindra would make her claim to live among them. Or perish.

Kindra stood at the edge of the circular pad opposite the Valkyrie thrones, carrying the wooden spear in her left hand and the shield in her right.

Each Valkyrie took her seat, ready to begin the trial. Their former pupils, who were now Valkyries themselves, stood beside them to spectate today's event. This was an honored event, though there was more to it than just a spectacle. The Valkyries present for the trial halted their duties to witness whether a candidate would join them in their cause. A few of them began their training after Kindra and became Valkyries before she had the chance. The leader of the Valkyries, Herja, glided elegantly from the heavens through the parting clouds, taking her seat in the center of the formation. Herja was a goddess sent down by Odin to train, lead, and supervise the Valkyries to ensure they honored their oath to him. Her armor and helm were gold plates, and her dress was pure white, almost blinding if caught in the right angle of light.

"Hildr, I see you have brought your apprentice for trial," Herja said calmly.

"Ah yes, finally," the Valkyrie Kara cut in, "Hildr has finally brought her prized candidate to be tested."

"Do you think she is ready? Perhaps you would like to spend a little more time training her just to be sure," Sigrdrifa also commented.

Kindra knew the audience would be making jokes at her expense as she was the oldest apprentice trained by a Valkyrie to undergo the trial. Her peers faced the challenge much earlier when they were fifteen or seventeen years old. At the age of twenty-five, most of the Valkyries questioned Hildr's intention, including Kindra herself, for delaying the process. When Kindra turned eighteen, she thought she was doing something wrong in Hildr's eyes. As the years passed, Kindra was worried that Hildr would abandon her in the middle of training since Kindra may not be the right candidate. But Hildr never left her, and now Kindra was here to face the Valkyrie Trial.

"Sisters." Hildr calmly began, settling the surrounding commentary and commencing the trial, "Today, I conclude my extensive training of Kindra and present her to face our trial."

"Do you believe Kindra is ready to take on the mantle of a Valkyrie?" Herja asked Hildr, sounding more like a scripted ceremonial question than genuine curiosity.

Hildr stared at Kindra, standing alone in front of the court, who had not moved a muscle since she stepped into place. "I am strongly confident in Kindra's capabilities of not only joining our ranks and accepting the responsibilities of a Valkyrie, but deeming her a worthy successor."

Kindra tightened her grip on her spear as she had never heard her mentor recommend her as a successor. None of the other Valkyries spoke highly of their apprentices in such a manner when Kindra witnessed her peers go through the trial. This raised the expectations of Kindra's performance for her to meet.

"Those are certainly bold words, Hildr," Herja replied with intrigue, equally shared with the others.

"Yes, they are, but I believe it should be Kindra's responsibility to tell you that she is ready." Hildr held out her hand toward Kindra.

On cue, Kindra took one step forward and kneeled in front of the court, paying her respects to some of the fiercest warriors in all the nine realms. Her heart beat loudly in her chest, nearly making Kindra deaf to her surroundings. "The Great Herja, I, Kindra, declare myself to be ready to prove I am worthy and welcome the opportunity to become one of the Valkyries."

"Are you aware that once you begin the Valkyrie Trial, there is no backing down, and you willingly put forth your life in your own hands where you may perish at any moment?"

"Yes, your majesty. I am willing to die for the opportunity."

"Then let us not waste any more time to meet your destiny." Herja scanned the Valkyries seated beside her and said to them, "Who here amongst this counsel wishes to face the brave Kindra to see if she deserves the title of Valkyrie?"

There was silence among the ranks as they waited for one of them to volunteer to partake in the trial. Kindra's heart continued to beat rapidly while she also waited for her challenger to identify themselves. She did her best to remain calm internally and in appearance to represent an unshakable warrior ready to face death. This was not the time or place to falter. Kindra needed to be fully committed and faithful to her word.

"I will accept her challenge," Rota stated, sitting two seats down from Herja's left side.

"Very well," Herja said in a calm tone. "Kindra, step forth and prepare to be tested in combat."

Kindra stood with pride, approaching the center of the platform where the trial would take place.

Okay, this is it. I can do this.

Kindra tried to keep her spirits high for the upcoming battle she had prepared for her entire life. The goal of this trial was to best a Valkyrie in one-on-one combat or survive long enough until Herja considered the match a stalemate and decided based on the outcome. Unfortunately, only some people who participated in this trial were victorious. Only a few times had Kindra seen an apprentice die during their attempt in a trial. Some were even maimed to the point where they no longer had control over parts of their body and had to be cast aside to whatever fate awaited them. The masters who witnessed such a calamity sat in silence, as there was no changing what happened, and quickly accepted the fate of their apprentice. It was a cruel way to go, but it was their way.

This stone platform had experienced much bloodshed, and it was almost a death sentence to be standing over it.

Rota picked up her large mace leaning against her stone throne and made her way towards the platform to meet Kindra. The Valkyrie had a rather large, muscular build that even trumped most men. Yet, she had a beautiful round face that did not look like it belonged on her body or on a battlefield. She maintained a constant scowl even when she smiled.

Kindra placed her shield across her heart and bows to the powerful Rota as she approached. "Thank you for granting me the honor of engaging you in battle," she said, sounding confident without wavering.

"Let us see if you have what it takes to become a Valkyrie and determine if Hildr's efforts were not wasted." She replied in a gruff manner.

With a subtle nod, Kindra raised her shield and took a defensive stance. Rota gave a soft chuckle, holding up her mace and swinging it toward Kindra. The first strike was to force Kindra to react irrationally, pushing the fight in Rota's favor. Instead, Kindra backed up, letting the mace sweep past her and maintaining a defensive posture. She did not want to fall into Rota's trap which could end this battle quicker than anticipated.

Observe and study, just like how Hildr taught you.

Rota swung the mace again; this time, Kindra moved in closer, diverting the blunt object with her shield to avoid direct contact and reduce the impact. However, the sudden touch of the mace gave Kindra some insight into the sheer power Rota possesses. Pushing the mace upward felt like she was lifting a falling tree with only one arm. Kindra had to use the strength of her whole body to move it.

Kindra thrusted the spear forward at Rota's legs to throw the Valkyrie off balance. She shuffled back but quickly discovered Kindra's intention and swung her free hand at Kindra's head. Ducking beneath Rota's giant fist left Kindra vulnerable to another attack; Rota exploited the opportunity and kicked Kindra in the chest. For someone so massive, Rota was quite agile.

Knocked backward, Kindra controlled her movement and rolled over the ground to continue the fight. As painful as it was to be kicked by Rota, Kindra did find some minor enjoyment in taking the hit. Hildr advocated seeking pleasures in a dull—even painful—situation, including the battle to keep her motivation up. After taking her first hit, there was no doubt that Kindra was not performing at her greatest. Although she spent several days undergoing intensive physical training, that should not be an excuse. Kindra should have seen that hit coming. She needed to be faster. Better.

"Are you really going down so easily?" Rota antagonized. "I thought you would be more impressive after the extra time Hildr has been training you. She might have thought you were ripe for the moment, but instead, you have rotten in your age."

"I still have a lot more in me. So, swing away!" Kindra said to Rota.

Rota lunged forward, swinging down her mace. Kindra spun to the left, letting the mace crash into the earth where she once stood, and used the momentum garnered to strike Rota in the face with her shield. The impact was thunderous. The sensation felt like hitting the side of a mountain. What a shocking moment for Kindra to experience delivering a successful hit to a Valkyrie. She heard the spectators gasp from Kindra's counter maneuver, yet she did not allow it to distract her. This was no time to celebrate and not a moment to make a fool of herself in front of Hildr.

While the hit felt satisfying, all it did was cause Rota to take one step backward. It certainly did not land a knockout victory, but it was a step in the right direction. As long as Kindra could hold her own against Rota, she would make it out of this alive.

"Now, *that* is what I was expecting. For a moment there, I thought maybe Hildr had selected the wrong person. Let alone someone, she claims to be her successor," Rota said with a wide grin, touching her cheek where Kindra's shield struck. There was no bruise or thin scratch on Rota's pale skin.

Rota swung her mace wildly at Kindra, attempting to throw her off balance and take control of the fight. Kindra let the enormous Valkyrie maneuver forward while carefully observing each mace swing and studying Rota's movements. As the bludgeoning weapon pounded the ground at Kindra's feet, she used this opportunity to leap and thrust the spear at Rota's upper torso. The attack was far from slow, yet Rota snatched the tip of the spear in one hand, where it was only a few inches from touching her throat.

"Is that all you got?" Rota questioned before yanking the spear down along with Kindra grasping the handle.

Kindra crashed onto the stone platform, hitting the ground with her left shoulder at full force. The already sore muscles in her arms were screaming, and Kindra was doing her best not to do the same. However, spending too long recovering on the ground gave Rota a chance to slam the mace on top of Kindra. Quickly rolling on her side, the weight and force of the mace collide against Kindra's shield, sending a powerful tremor to travel through her forearm.

The pain was an intense shock to her nerves that Kindra unintentionally yelped out of pure instinct.

Don't get pinned down! Find a way out of this. Turn this around.

Kindra rolled on the ground from under Rota's mace into a low crouch with her shield and spear pointed outward. The discomfort in her arm was set aside as she maintained her attention on the hulking Valkyrie. It was easy to tell that Rota held back on her swings as a hit from her at full force would have quickly shattered Kindra's wooden shield and crushed her underneath. If Rota had delivered the mace a tad harder, it would have indeed broken Kindra's forearm on impact. After a hit like that, Kindra needed to change tactics to avoid being beaten to death and not taking the chance to go on the offense.

Twirling the spear overhead to thwart Rota's advances, then whipping it at her, both ends slapped Rota's arms and legs. The stings were mild, but they kept the Valkyrie at bay and prevented her from making an attack. Kindra pushed forward to provoke Rota to counterattack while looking for an opportunity to strike. Growing agitated from the constant barrage of hits, Rota swung her mace wide, giving Kindra an opening. With the flat side of the spearhead, it slapped against Rota's face on the left cheek.

Rota growled from the audacity of being slapped as if it were a joke. But, since Kindra was close to her, the mace slammed over the young woman. She quickly dodged to the right, letting the weapon swipe beside her body. Once it touched the ground, Kindra rammed the shield's edge against Rota's hands.

Instantly, Rota screamed and released her grasp of the mace.

Yes! Now it is time to make my move.

With Rota separated from her weapon, it was now up to Kindra to keep up the momentum. Swiping the spear along the midsection, the tip made a narrow incision on Rota's left bicep, effortlessly slicing through the skin.

"First blood has been drawn!" Herja announced with surprise amongst the court.

The minor inflicted wound did not settle well with Rota; for one, it mocked her abilities as a warrior against an unenhanced mortal. Clenching her jaw and producing a menacing stare that would intimidate even the vilest creatures in Hel, Rota snatched the spear's tip with one hand. Then, without effort, she snapped the end of the spear off, tossing it aside.

"Enough games!" Rota quickly grasped Kindra by the throat in one hand, lifting her off the ground. Her strength was incredible, almost like her muscles were made of stone. Kindra struggled to breathe in Rota's grasp, trying to pry her fingers apart, which seem tougher than iron. "Show me you are worthy. Show *me* Hildr made the right choice!"

Rota yanked Kindra forward, headbutting her right in the crown, where she blacked out for only a second before the daylight entered her eyes. The impact put Kindra in a heavy daze, with her fighting to maintain consciousness more so than breathing. The world spiraled in Kindra's mind as her head throbbed in the same rhythmic pattern as her rapidly beating heart. A trail of blood poured down from an open wound on Kindra's forehead, passing over her right eye, and clouding her vision. She was thrown to the ground, rolling over the surface on the opposite end of the court. Droplets of blood from

Kindra's mouth tapped on the platform beneath her. She spit a wad of the crimson fluid to free her airway and finally took a deep breath of the misty air.

Get up! Do not show weakness in front of Herja and the Court of Valkyries ... do not let Hildr down ...

Kindra stumbled to stand on her feet, feeling the blood rush to her head with nausea settling in her senses. After a glance at the broken spear in her hand, there was no point in using it for battle since it was nothing but a large stick trying to defeat a mountain of a woman. Bellowing a loud roar, Rota charged toward Kindra while she was still recovering from the previous headbutt. The relatively calm, stoic demeanor Rota once wielded shifted into a feral animal with the desire to kill. This time leaving the mace behind, she intended to tear Kindra into pieces with her bare hands.

Taking a deep breath to soothe her nerves and think clearly, Kindra briefly assessed her situation. Unfortunately, there was not enough time to develop a decent plan, meaning Kindra would have to be reactive, which was what Rota wanted. The broken spear was held up near Kindra's head as she took steady aim at Rota. With the lack of the metal head, the spear would be off-balanced, with reduced accuracy, and travel a much shorter distance. To be effective, Kindra would need to have Rota get closer to the point where there would be no escape from her stampede.

Kindra stared into Rota's eyes which were burning with rage, probably from having her patience tested and seeing her blood for the first time in possibly centuries. At this point, Kindra did not know nor wanted to try to see if she would still pull her punches for the rest of the fight. However, once Rota reached within a dozen feet, the spear was thrown straight into her legs. The pole was not nearly strong enough to stop her, breaking in half with her powerful legs, but it did cause her to stumble.

As Rota leaned forward off balance, this opportunity allowed Kindra to strike by swinging her shield upward as hard as she could with both arms, clobbering Rota under the chin. The impact was fantastic, probably the most significant yet, putting the large woman on her back. As surprised as Kindra was for performing such a feat, there was no time to relish a minor accomplishment as the battle was yet to be won. Leaping over towards Rota while she was on the ground, the shield was drawn back to deliver another heavy hit, maybe the final blow to this trial.

A powerful force struck Kindra in the ribs on her right side, throwing her off Rota and onto the ground. The air was forced out of Kindra's body, with a burning sensation at her side.

"Kara!" Hildr shouted in disbelief, standing from her seat.

"What is the problem, Hildr?" Kara replied cheekily. "If Kindra is as good a warrior as you propose, then surely she could face another Valkyrie in combat."

Hildr turned her attention to Herja for an answer to Kara's intrusion along with the rest of the court.

"I understand your concern, Hildr. I do," Herja began calmly, "but I, too, am curious about the child's skill. She must be a great combatant if you have spent a fair amount of time training the young one. However, you can withdraw your candidate from the trials at the sign of doubt."

Gasping for the lost air, Kindra looked for a response from Hildr, who had a conflicted expression on her face. Only for a second did it take for Hildr to decide on the condition of the trial. Kindra nodded to Hildr, who returned it and said to Herja, "I hold no reservations and wish to proceed with the trial."

"Very well. Kara and Rota continue the trial until I have reached a verdict or Kindra succumbs to her wounds during the event. There will be NO further interruptions. Is that understood?" Herja said aloud with a bold command voice. Every Valkyrie, including Hildr, tapped their weapon once against the stone floor to signify their acknowledgment of Herja's order. Hildr sat back down as the trial resumed, carefully watching Kindra.

Never in Kindra's tenure had she witnessed or even heard of an apprentice facing off against two Valkyries at once. The anxiety built up to this point had transitioned into fear as she must fight for survival, let alone for a seat on the court.

"Come now, young Kindra, enlighten me of your training," Kara instigated with a smirk.

Compared to Rota, Kara was slimmer with a lean athletic build and stood an inch or two taller than Kindra. Her bright blonde hair was braided neatly behind her head thus to prevent interference during a fight. It was efficient in eliminating distractions and avoiding cutting the strands due to her swift movements. Kara drew the two short swords from her leather belt. Even with the sun blocked by the expansive formation of clouds, the swords shone like brand-new, untouched silver.

Taking two steady breaths as Kindra's body began to settle from Kara's kick, she slowly stood up, instantly feeling the sharp pain erupt along her abdomen. She was unsure if her ribs were broken, but this was not the time to make that determination. All Kindra could do was try her best to ignore the pain and not let it interfere with her execution.

"Let me make this simpler for you." Kara flipped both swords in her hands with the blades facing backward and flat pommels forward. "Now, you won't have to worry about dying too quickly."

The energetic, playful attitude of Kara's personality was a ploy to draw out an enemy to attack first and have them underestimate her capabilities. However, Kindra knew not to fall into her trap and instead considered partaking in Kara's fun.

"Then show me how a *real* Valkyrie fights," Kindra said to Kara, whose grin widened from her words.

Kara darted forward, thrusting the pommels at Kindra's face. She nearly missed hitting her cheek, though Kindra knew that if it were the blades out, it would have been over for her. Kindra would need to be faster in dealing with Kara than in her confrontation with Rota. She did her best to dodge every attack thrown at her, yet it did not seem fast enough to break away. There were multiple times when Kara could have easily made contact. It appeared she was similarly toying with Kindra to Rota either to prolong this battle to test Kindra or to have fun during this trial.

While using the shield to block some of Kara's direct attacks, the weight of the wood and iron that constructed it were wearing down her body to keep up with Kara's speed. The soreness of the muscles tearing in her right arm caused Kindra to lower the shield, allowing Kara to strike precisely in the opening of her defense. A quick jab at the tissue between Kindra's shoulder and chest shot an excruciating burning sensation across her body, making Kindra drop the shield on the ground.

Wide open with her guard down, the large Valkyrie, Rota, re-emerged on Kindra's left, swinging a giant fist into her face. It was the most potent punch Kindra had ever felt, far greater than any hit delivered by Hildr. Rota's fist was solid and unwavering once it hit Kindra's skull, feeling like a stone clobbered her instead of flesh and bone. The force was powerful enough to knock Kindra flat on her back.

No ... no ... do not stop now ... stay awake. Keep fighting ... even if it means it will kill you!

"It is in your best interest that you stay down," Rota told Kindra, cracking her knuckles. "Not everyone is meant to become a Valkyrie."

With her right arm numb, ribs on fire, vision blurry, and head throbbing fiercely, there was little Kindra could do to turn the tide. The lack of a stellar performance was already making Kindra concerned that she would not be declared a Valkyrie. Of course, Kindra's primary goal was to be alive once this was over, but if it killed her, so be it. She would rather die trying and receive such a glorious death against two Valkyries than live as a broken failure.

Barely balancing herself on all four limbs, the world in her mind shuttered and swayed while Kindra tried to hold still. Sweat dripped from her face, and blood seeped out her mouth. Kindra was exhausted, and the court knew it, yet they remained silent about her anguish.

"Then how ... are *you* a Valkyrie?" Kindra taunted Rota, almost too exhausted to expel the words out of her mouth.

The frustration in Rota erupted with a deep growl into the sky, then a leap into the air to stomp on Kindra. But, right before Rota could crush Kindra, she rolled out from under the Valkyrie, where her foot slammed through the solid stone floor. As Kindra got back on her feet, Kara performed a lateral kick into Kindra's stomach, forcing her a few steps back.

The tender muscles in her abdomen desperately begged Kindra not to move, but those cries were ignored. Clenching her teeth, Kindra pressed forward to face Kara.

Kara is too fast. There is no chance for me to keep my distance. But maybe that is what she wants. Kara is trying to get close, but how close can she get before her agility is inadequate? With my body in so much pain, I can take the hits and keep going.

Kindra allowed Kara to approach her to deliver a hit. Kara threw her left arm forward towards Kindra's head, to which she canted her head to the side, letting Kara's left arm slide right past her body. Immediately, Kindra hooked her arm around Kara's bicep, moving closer to Kara's body. The Valkyrie's eyes widened in surprise as she was not expecting Kindra to close the distance between them.

Now that Kara was locked in place with nowhere to move, an elbow was thrown into her face. A loud crunch was heard on impact, along with a high-pitched squeal from Kara. As satisfying as it was to deliver such a hit, Kindra was not done with her opponent and followed up by punching Kara in the throat with only her knuckles. The squealing abruptly stopped, and Kara tried to clutch her throat to breathe.

"I am not done with you!" Rota shouted, sprinting towards Kindra.

Without putting much thought into her next move, Kindra spun Kara around. At the same time, she was preoccupied and tossed her into Rota. The large woman uncaringly swung her arm into Kara, knocking the sister out of her path. Again, Rota grasped Kindra by the throat, but this time she began clenching her hand to crush Kindra's windpipe. Lifting her off the ground to dangle freely, a fist was driven into Kindra's abdomen, causing her to expel the remaining air held inside her lungs.

Everything in Kindra's eyes dwindled into black as suffocation grew near. She tried to break free of Rota's grip, but comparing her strength to the Valkyrie's own was useless.

Fight it! Don't succumb to the darkness! Kindra ordered herself. *This is my last shot.*

Kindra swiftly brought up her knee, smacking Rota in her bruised chin. When Kindra's knee made contact, Rota released her grip on the woman. Kindra kicked as hard as she could with both legs against Rota's chest, sending her to the ground. Rota fell on her back like one of the many logs brought down yesterday. Kindra's landing was not as elegant as she tried to land on her feet but ended up collapsing on the floor due to the overall fatigue and air deprivation.

After briefly cursing at herself for not sticking the landing, a stone shard was picked up from the cracked platform. Kindra moved at her best speed, approaching Rota with the stone in her hand. The fragment was raised, ready to slam into Rota's neck and remove her from the fight. She did not know if it would kill or even have any effect on her, though there was no time to consider another option.

Flying with an immaculate speed that Kindra barely caught a glimpse of the reflective surface, one of Kara's swords pierced Kindra in the left shoulder. Her body seized in an instant, with her collapsing back against the ground. The fight in Kindra vanished in a flash, leaving her to lie on the floor, panting and staring blankly into the clouds. She did everything in her power not to break down and cry in front of the court, not out of the excruciating pain, but because her chances of becoming one of them were gone.

The remaining strength mustered by Kindra was used to grip the sword's hilt and frantically try to pull it out. The blade was a couple inches deep yet barely moved, despite Kindra's efforts.

Kara approached, placing her foot on Kindra's chest to keep her down.

"Do not move," she ordered, holding out her other sword with the tip of the blade, staring down at Kindra inches from her face. The playful mentality Kara once wielded shifted into resentment. Still, Kindra tried to remove the sword embedded in her shoulder. "That was a warning. I will take your life if you continue."

"I-I cannot quit … a Valkyrie never quits . . ." Kindra said in an exhausted voice.

"You are not a Valkyrie! Do not be foolish, child. You may be willing to forfeit your life for a just cause, but are you not thinking about your master? How humiliating would it be for Hildr's protege to die from a sparring match?"

Sparring match? My life was endangered. I was fighting for my life!

Kindra turned her head towards Hildr, noticing her fingers clutching the edge of the stone armrests on her seat. Much restraint was applied to hide the tension bubbling in Hildr.

Fear roamed inside Kindra that if she said a word, the cries of failure would be released from her mouth, and she would not be able to hold her composure any further. With nothing to say, she let go of the sword handle to signify that she yields.

"Kara." Herja said, "Lower your weapon." Without hesitation, Kara sheathed her sword in silence. "Rota, bring forth Kindra."

Approaching Kindra on the ground while rubbing her chin, Rota grabbed Kindra by the right arm and lifted her to her feet in one pull. In such a weakened state, Kindra could not stand on her own and had to be supported by Rota all the way to Herja's presence.

Kindra felt entirely unfit to be presented in such a fashion, preferring execution with some honor intact than experiencing the shame of being seen like this.

"Kindra, I know you waited a long time to reach this point, and I am certain Hildr had good reason to withhold your evaluation in the trial. I trust her judgment in her methods and reasoning. Now your performance today was questionable at best, I will admit, yet I was surely intrigued by how you adapted to the conditions of this fight. While you did not defeat or at least reach a stalemate against your opponents, the verdict would be undeniable. If this were a traditional trial with a single Valkyrie, I have no doubt you would have succeeded." Herja turned her attention to Hildr, who hid her anxiety about the final verdict. "Hildr, you must be proud of Kindra, and I applaud you for making the right choice." Standing up from her throne, Herja held her right hand forward and said, "Kindra, you have truly lived up to your namesake to endure and battle against the odds to become an exceptional champion. With great honor, I declare you to be a Valkyrie."

The words slipped through Kindra's ears, with the only word "Valkyrie" repeatedly ringing like the clanging of swords against each other until everything else drowns.

"What . . ." Kindra muttered. Tears rushed down her face as she slowly processed Herja's decision.

Kara ripped out the sword still lodged in Kindra's shoulder while she was distracted, causing a short-lived scream to burst out of her mouth.

"Welcome aboard, sister." She whispered to Kindra sincerely, then softly kissed her sweat-covered cheek.

"You did well, little sister." Rota also complimented Kindra, shaking off the belligerent trait and producing a smile that had never been seen before.

"I … I am sorry for—"

"There is nothing to be sorry about." Rota gave her a gentle squeeze with the arm supporting her. "You were relentless, reminding me to never underestimate my opponent. It has been a long time since I have taken a hit like that."

The Valkyries enthusiastically cheered loudly that they caused the foundation of the court to quake, raising their weapons to the sky to congratulate their new member. It was surprising not only for Kindra to earn the title of Valkyrie but to every court member. It was a rare moment to witness Herja overrule her own mandate.

The crowd instantly went silent as Hildr stood in front of Kindra.

"You are no longer the little girl I trained. You are a Valkyrie. And in time, I know you will be a great one. One to surpass me." Hildr said to her now-former apprentice.

"Thank you … thank you . . ." Kindra cried.

Hildr placed a hand on Kindra's cheek to calm the newly christened Valkyrie and then leaned forward, kissing her forehead.

"You were magnificent."

CHAPTER THREE

Moving from the Court of the Valkyries, Hildr brought Kindra to a small lake beside a mountain to wash and recover from her glorious day of battle. It was a perfect spot to bask in her victory. The gash in her shoulder and multiple cuts and scrapes were packed with herbs and bandaged with a healing rune inscribed over the cloth. Unfortunately, the compass rune tattoo on her shoulder was sliced on the side, thanks to Kara's sword, meaning she would have to retouch it once the skin mended. However, she was in no hurry to get it attended to. Most of the pain had subsided partly due to the rune, leaving only the bruises and overall soreness.

Kindra's bare body was halfway inside the lake as she rested against the bank, letting her muscles finally relax after several days of intense labor and strain. It felt amazing to feel the warm water against her skin, allowing it to wash away all the sweat, dirt, and blood.

"Enjoying the bath?" Hildr asked, walking towards Kindra at the edge of the lake.

"It is glorious, master," Kindra replied soothingly.

"Please, Kindra, you can forgo the formalities. You are a Valkyrie now. A sister." Hildr sat on the lake's edge, dipping her feet in the clear water.

"Yes ... Hildr . . ." Kindra said, sounding nervous to call her former master only by name.

"I know it will be odd at first, but you will get accustomed to it as you work with your sisters as equals. The only one you must address with honors is the goddess, Herja."

"I still cannot believe I am a Valkyrie. A title of repute. It is completely surreal to earn this status. I have always dreamed of this moment ever since I was a child, but I never knew what to expect or how to feel once the time came."

"Yes, it is an undertaking to live up to and uphold our reputation but remember that your journey has only begun. What you have trained for does not come to an end by merely becoming a Valkyrie."

"I understand. You should not worry; I will work as hard as I always have."

Hildr smiled and nodded, saying to Kindra, "I know you will. You have made me so proud to see you join our ranks."

"Then I have just one question," Kindra softly said.

"What is on your mind?"

Kindra pursed her lips, nervous to ask what had been harbored inside her for years. "Why did you have me wait so long to attend the trial?" she asked softly yet respectfully.

While maintaining her smile, Hildr said, "Ah, yes, the question I have been waiting to hear for a very long time. The reason I waited was that I wanted someone different. You know that all the Valkyries, including myself, were indoctrinated at a young age when we were still children. While this has many advantages, I sought to tackle the disadvantages of molding a warrior to fill these shortages. With time comes maturity, the biggest thing I wanted for you. When you are declared a Valkyrie at such a young age, you miss the opportunity to develop and think methodically. Today, you analyzed your opponents and did your best to defeat them despite your heavy exhaustion and facing two much more powerful beings. I have never been more pleased to see you utilize your training during the trial. You may have become a Valkyrie later than you expected, but you are ahead of your peers from when they—we—started."

Kindra took a moment to think about everything Hildr said. She had been curious about Hildr's justification for many nights and finally hearing why after all these years brought an unprecedented sense of relief to Kindra's soul.

"Did you ever think you may have picked the wrong person to be your apprentice?"

Hildr gently moved her legs through the water before answering Kindra's question.

"I am not going to lie by saying I did not have any doubts because I did, but it was not from you or what I saw in your training. I doubted myself in making that call. However, when the day comes for you to select your apprentice, one who will follow in your footsteps, do not cast doubt in yourself, as it will bleed into your pupil. Believe in what you feel is true and believe in the ones that follow you. You cannot go wrong."

Kindra smiled upon hearing the wisdom from her mentor and hoped to continue to learn more from Hildr as she ventured into the life of a Valkyrie. A glorious and adventurous life.

"Now, if fate had changed and you had died during any point of your training or the trial, I would not hesitate to resurrect you and work you harder until you got it right." A chuckle burst out of Kindra's mouth before her sore abdomen extinguished it. "Now, do you understand what needs to happen next?"

"Yes, I do," Kindra said carefully. After an apprentice is declared a Valkyrie, they are sealed inside a mystical tree known as the Tree of the Dis, granting them the gifts of a Valkyrie. It will also accelerate the healing process for the damage inflicted during the trial. This gave a person enhanced strength, agility, recovery, stamina, and durability, as well as other properties that Kindra had only heard rumors of and not seen herself. Once the infusion was complete, the new Valkyrie would be given their armor and escorted to Asgard to pledge their oath to Odin himself. That was when they received their wings. From there, they set off to the nine realms and fulfilled their duties. "Do you know how long it will take?"

Hildr rubbed her chin to ponder a reasonable answer. "For simple injuries, it would only take a day or two, but for a stab wound such as yours and the broken ribs, I would say about a month at the most."

"That is not so bad. I can handle a month."

"There is no need to worry. You will be in a deep slumber for all of it and reawaken as a new person. It will surely be the best sleep you will ever have."

"Ah, sleep. That is what I have been waiting for, for days now."

Hildr removed her feet from the water, standing up by the shore. "Once you are done here, meet me by the fire. I have something to show you."

Gradually, Hildr departed from the lake walking into the woods facing the mountain. While wishing to bathe in the soothing water longer, perhaps even through the night, Kindra was wondering what Hildr had to show her now that she is a Valkyrie. Kindra had always been curious but managed to control her curiosity and reason to avoid a problem. It was best not to get into trouble now, especially after achieving her new profession.

Dunking her head beneath the surface of the water, the sense of weightlessness was pleasing to Kindra's body, where her muscles could relax and freely move in the water. To her, this was what flying must feel like, though she would know the true sensation soon enough. For the time being, Kindra relaxed in the calm waters as her body mended itself in peace.

You did it, Kindra. You beat the odds and overcame years of training to get here.

She was at peace with her thoughts, which had felt like a hefty burden.

Even though she had reached this particular class of warriors, it was just as Hildr had said, and this was only the beginning of her new life. She could not afford to fail or embarrass her mentor as she progressed from this point onward.

Kindra rose from out of the water letting the cool breeze from the mountain blow the moisture off her. She walked towards her old armor that rested on a log, examining the scuffed metal plating over the torso and worn, cracked leather layered underneath. Hildr had Kindra construct her own armor set when she was a child and had to modify it as she grew. Her fingers slid over the rough metal. In her youth, the metal plates were heavy and cumbersome that did not fit her small frame. But over time, Kindra became so accustomed to them she would forget they were there. Strangely, this armor was a part of her as her own flesh, and it would be difficult to trade it for the glamorous armor of a Valkyrie.

A dark blue tunic was worn as it was the closest thing Kindra owned to casual wear, with her light brown hair tied back in a ponytail still soaked from the water. She followed the narrow trail through the forest left by Hildr. Aside from the rustling of leaves caused by the wind, the forest was silent, though not in an eerie sense, more like natural tranquility. The trail led Kindra to a small encampment where stone blocks surrounded a smoldering fire. Hildr sat on one of the stones, prodding the fire with the blade of her ax.

"You know, child, when I first saw you, I always knew you were meant for greatness. Valkyrie or not. Your mentality and devotion will lead you to success, but it will be up to you to determine what success means." Hildr said, drawing back her ax and leaning it against the stone.

Kindra sat on one of the blocks beside Hildr, putting her hands up against the fire to dry her moistened skin.

"Hildr . . ." Kindra began, still hesitant in referring to her directly by name, "did you ever have any trouble fulfilling your duties as a Valkyrie?"

Hildr held a smirk on her face yet did not immediately respond to Kindra's question. "There will be days in your role as a Valkyrie where you have to make difficult decisions, especially when leading the souls of the dead. You can lead them to the magnificent halls of Valhalla, Vanir's majestic realm, or Hel's horrendous, empty valleys. I do not want to delude your mind of what we are meant for, but you must stick with your gut on the choices you make or intend to make, even against the minds of others."

"I see . . ." Kindra whispered, hoping she did not overstep her bounds. "Well, I will face whatever lies ahead of me head-on."

"In that, I have no doubt. Now, let me present you with a gift."

"Gift?" Kindra questioned, watching Hildr stand up from the block and retrieve a wooden chest beside the stone block she sat on. The crate was not large, only a tad wider than Hildr's shoulder width, with markings burned into the walls. One of the markings was recognized as Hildr's symbol, but Kindra was unsure about the others.

She placed the chest on the stone block with the lid still closed. "I have been waiting to give you these for as long as you have been my apprentice.

These were to be presented to you once you have awakened from your time in the Tree of the Dis, but I thought I should give you a break and hand them to you early." Hildr lifted the lid, revealing two objects crafted from polished silver; one was a dagger no longer than Kindra's forearm, and the other was a spiral disk. The engineering and craftsmanship were beyond anything Kindra had seen from a mortal blacksmith on Midgard. "After your battle today, it seemed fitting for you to receive your new arms to replace the ones lost in your trial."

Kindra approached Hildr, hesitantly picking up the dagger from the chest. The sun's light reflected off the blade's mirrored surface. It was amazingly polished to the point that she could see her reflection perfectly. There were runes along the edge, one of them being Kindra's name, followed by the same mysterious symbol on the crate. The other runes translated to *indestructible*, meaning the blade was enchanted and impervious to damage.

A dagger would be a slight change to Kindra's fighting technique, not entirely something new for her to train on. However, she was curious to know why she was given a dagger, not a spear similar to her old one. The spear had been a weapon she had been trying to master for over a decade. As she fixed her grip on the handle, the pommel shot out, extending the telescopic segments hidden inside, reaching the same length as Kindra's old spear.

"Wow . . ." Kindra whispered.

Her eyes glanced at Hildr, whose vast smile was full of excitement. "What? Did you honestly think I would just give you a dagger?"

Kindra slightly blushed with embarrassment for even having the thought in her mind. She retracted the spear into its dagger form and retrieved the disk. On one side of the disk was a metal band that Kindra believed was where it would fasten to her arm. The row of blades rotated in unison to expand the size of the disk to double its original diameter. And similar to the dagger, each segment had an invincibility rune inscribed into the metal.

"Is this my new shield?" Kindra asked, still fascinated by the components.

"Indeed, it is. Much lighter, more robust, and compact. After lugging around your old shield for so many years, you earned the right for an improved shield to match your skills and make you a much more devastating opponent."

Kindra's mouth trembled for the right words to say and how to properly arrange them. "I … Hildr—" she said.

"Kindra, it is all right." Hildr placed a hand on Kindra's shoulder, settling the young woman's sentiment towards the gifts. "You deserve this. These are tools that will help you through the start of your journey. Besides, you need to look presentable in front of the Allfather."

Once again, the sun was close to setting behind the horizon, except this would be the last time Kindra would witness it as a mortal. The ritual that would embed Kindra with the physical attributes of a Valkyrie took place within the heart of a mountain, the closest one to the Court of the Valkyries. The hike from the forest to the snow-covered entrance was hardly challenging, even in Kindra's physical state. Kindra would have preferred to run up the mountain the entire way. Still, Hildr insisted on moving at a casual pace, refusing to use her wings to ascend the rocky terrain. She assumed that it was because Hildr wanted to savor the moment until it was time for them to part ways.

The mountain cavern was carved into a dome containing statues of all the Valkyries to have existed placed along the curved wall. Those currently sitting on the court were the ones Kindra recognizes. However, some lived years before she was born and only knew of them from the stories told by Hildr when Kindra was a child.

Those who perished in battle wore a blue sash over their statue with a valknut medallion around their neck. The death of a Valkyrie never plagued Kindra since she knew their journey did not end once their mortal life is expended.

Kindra approached Hildr's statue of her posing with the ax held horizontally in both hands in front of her waist. The face of the figure depicted a young Hildr as a teenager when she was indoctrinated into the Valkyries. It was a strange sight to see an image of Hildr at such a young age when for the past sixteen years, Hildr had been the same woman in appearance. The ax was almost as big as her when she started as a Valkyrie and eventually grew into it.

However, it must have been a relatively long time. Even as a young woman, Hildr was remarkably beautiful.

"Seems like a lifetime ago when I was in your place," Hildr said, standing beside Kindra to gaze at her statue.

"For a normal person, I believe it has been many lifetimes," Kindra said.

Hildr grinned and replied, "True. Time certainly passes by when you live past your normal lifespan."

"It was the start of greatness. I only hope I can be as good as you."

"I think you will be better. Do not strive to live in the shadow of my statue. Stand tall as your own." Kindra faced Hildr staring into her soft eyes for a second before hugging the woman who had helped get this far. Neither of them said a word while they briefly held each other. There was so much that Kindra would want to say to Hildr, but she thought it best to keep it to herself for now since it might not be the appropriate time. "Now, let us begin with turning you into a Valkyrie."

"Yes, let us begin." Kindra smiled and followed Hildr to the center of the cavern.

The Tree of the Dis trunk stood slanted with a hollow opening in the middle for the selected individual to enter. Carved into the bark were numerous runes, magical inscriptions, and artistic depictions of the qualities of a Valkyrie. This tree had produced all the Valkyries before Kindra, making great warriors better. A humbling sight to see in person. Kindra shed her clothes, placing them neatly beside the base of the tree. The only items she would carry with her were the spear and shield. She could finally see the large purple bruises scattered across her body, appearing more prominent than the tattoos on her arms. Taking a deep breath, Kindra slowly stepped inside the trunk, facing the opening to see Hildr standing outside the tree.

"I will see you in a month," she said softly to Hildr with a wavering grin.

Hildr returned the smile and said, "Sleep well, and I will see you when you are ready."

The bark from the tree grew, covering the opening in the trunk to seal Kindra inside. The last thing she saw was Hildr's face which held an expression of gratification. As the outside world was cut off and the light no longer touched Kindra, she stood in the darkness, waiting for the process to begin. The inner walls of the tree secreted a sweet-scented sap and a liquid that felt like running water. But without any light, Kindra could not see what it truly was that covered her. Vines crawled over Kindra's limbs and around her waist, securing her to the tree's interior. The fluids gradually rose to cover her entire body. A soothing warmth inside the tree trunk was relaxing, like a hot spring.

Kindra's eyes grew excessively heavy, and her breathing became slow and shallow. An overlapping desire to sleep smothered her senses. It was a collection after everything she had gone through, not just from this morning but for the years Hildr had been training her. She wanted to know what was happening or would happen to her body as she inhabited the tree, yet it was a fight that she could not win, no matter how hard she tried to keep her eyes open.

It soon became difficult to differentiate the darkness from her sight.

This is it. Once I come out of this, I will be a Valkyrie ...

CHAPTER FOUR

Taking an aisle seat on the second row before the stage, Eric McCullough waited for all the so-called "honored guests" to return from their brief intermission to restart the auction. In between the fingers on his right hand was a glass of sparkling wine that he had taken sips during the break. He wished to have taken a second glass for how the night had been going. Eric was not one to walk away from an auction empty-handed and had either been outbid or presented with uninteresting items. While displeased, he tried to maintain his composure and professional appearance. For him and everyone else here, this was just a costume.

The second half of the auction may hold more surprises, though he would not hold his breath.

"Honored guests, if you may, please return to your seats. The auction will resume in two minutes," said the auctioneer standing behind the podium.

Eric fixed his stance, tightening the front of his tuxedo while running his game plan through his head. There would need to be a considerable cost to maintain his image among the crowd. He figured he could assume the loss and come back from it. Money needed to be spent to continue to be invited to such events. Those who showed up without bidding were eventually barred from future events to allow those willing to spend money on the finer things in life that boost social status.

Tonight's auction was for artifacts and ancient artwork from various ages and cultures worldwide. Eric did not have much affinity for art pieces. Most people present did not care for them, only that they were expensive, a conversation piece, and something no one else in the world would own.

"Ah, still here, Eric?" said Frederick Grunberg, an acquaintance of Eric who was also a frequent visitor to these social events. The man must've been twenty years older than Eric, reaching his sixties.

"I can say the same about you. Didn't you throw away enough of your money yet?"

He smiled through his trimmed beard that was turning grey down the middle.

"It is merely an investment into the fine qualities of life. Heh, when you're my age, you begin to appreciate things in a certain light. What's the point in keeping a bank account full if you never get to spend it?"

"I'll take a quick note of that," Eric said.

With a quick clear of the throat from the auctioneer, he banged his gavel to garner everyone's attention for the auction to begin.

"It is pleasing to know that many of you have yet to run away with your wallets," he mildly joked, which sparked a peal of mild laughter from the crowd. "Now, we will begin the second half of the auction with this broad sword and scabbard believed to be dated back to the sixteenth century from Spain."

Eric watched as the weapon enthusiasts eagerly fought to claim any instrument meant for killing. It was futile to outbid them as those collectors were willing to drop everything they had and their trophy wife to claim such an item. Instead, Eric patiently waited and was even amused seeing this particular set of individuals duel with a wave of their number or unique call to the auctioneer.

Once the weapons inventory had been sold, the excitement settled as the auction shifted to the presentation of miscellaneous items. This was near the end of the auction, with only a few things up for sale. Some of the guests had already vacated the auditorium as they were not interested in throwing away money for trinket items.

"Up next, we have a unique item recently discovered in Mount Kerling in Iceland." The staff members wheeled a cart onto the stage with a large chunk of petrified wood, possibly the largest Eric had seen, still intact. Along the surface were various symbols finely etched into the rough exterior, almost like they were recently carved. "What you see here are remnants from the Viking age, where it is believed that the tales of the Valkyries are carved into the stone surface."

Eric scanned the item on display, holding a slight interest in the historical relevance. However, since the auction was reaching a close, there were not many options left to make an offer. The sheer size of the petrified wood had Eric considering passing this one up. Although he had yet to see the remaining items, they were probably nowhere near as large as this one. It was better to shovel money into a prominent item than a dainty piece, which could be easily overlooked. Well, Eric had been meaning to add something to his atrium.

"The bid will start at fifty-thousand dollars."

Eric raised his number and began his bidding war.

Victorious and somewhat pleased with his purchase, Eric shipped the chunk of stoned lumber to his mansion. A work crew waited to offload and place it inside his empty atrium. He wanted to see how it looked first thing in the morning before making additional arrangements. If Eric liked what he saw, he may consider changing the front exterior aesthetics into a Viking theme. This could mean another trip to an auction house, which with this recent purchase, gave Eric a ticket to the next auction.

Utilizing a small forklift, the crew moved the petrified wood from the delivery truck. They were cautious not to drop or cause any damage to the piece; otherwise, they would be repaying Eric for the full price. Erecting the stone like a flagpole, the natural artwork was left standing on its own in the center of the atrium, where guests would immediately see it as they enter. The other artwork he had lying around was a mixture of different cultures that range from Egyptian relics to traditional Vietnamese art. The petrified wood did clash with the assortment of artifacts in his collection. However, this could be the start of a change in scenery.

As the working crew vacated Eric's mansion, he took a moment to stare at his new decoration. Seeing it up close in person was different than on stage under the bright lights. He could see the natural age of the stone and the fine lines of each symbol. It was astonishing how defined they were by the tools of early man.

I could invite a couple of the college girls to come over and translate them for me. But unfortunately, Eric had no genuine interest in their true meaning nor in Norse mythology but thought it could be a clever way to get laid. It was a unique item, after all.

"You know, you're not a bad purchase. Perhaps you could pay yourself off one day," Eric said to the petrified wood. He left the atrium, shutting off the lights and making his way to bed.

CHAPTER FIVE

The peaceful night sky rapidly changed as powerful gusts of wind swiftly passed through the earth. Clouds formed a mass, blocking the crescent moon and all the dimly lit stars. Electricity stirred inside the formation, waiting to burst. A powerful bolt of lightning shot from the sudden storm straight into the petrified wood, instantly causing it to explode.

Shards jettisoned in every direction, and Kindra fell flat on the ground as if she were a corpse. The cool draft from the storm touching her skin awakened Kindra in an instant, letting her take a deep breath of air as if it was her first. The viscous fluid encased with her in the tree slipped through her mouth like saliva, where it pooled on the flat surface.

W... what happened ...

Kindra's brain was still trying to awaken and piece together her senses that were on overload. She pushed off the ground to get her bearings. Strangely, she ended up hitting the ground so violently and without anyone to greet her as she awakened from her slumber.

No ... this cannot be right—no, it is not right!

As her eyes quickly adjusted to the low light, every object, surface, and color around her was a mysteriously bizarre sight. The structure Kindra found herself standing in was beyond anything she had seen before and was certainly not the cavern in the mountain where she was encased. Hildr's absence imposed fear in her heart, with Kindra begging for answers to the buzzing of questions on her mind. She would not have missed the moment Kindra would be released and expected her to be the first person to welcome Kindra's return.

Looking up towards the sky through the opening in the roof, the storm that freed Kindra from her confinement quickly dissolved, and the gibbous moon shed its light over the darkened world once again.

The sound of footsteps nearby caught Kindra's attention, prompting her to hide from whatever was coming her way. She positioned herself against the wall that would lead the unknown entity to her for an ambush. If it was a person, Kindra would question her whereabouts. But if it turn out to be a monster, she would slay it. No matter what it was, it would be no match for a Valkyrie.

Waiting anxiously for something to appear, the grip of the dagger was clenched tightly close to Kindra's body, ready to lash out and earn its first kill. A figure walked past the corner of the wall, appearing to be a man holding a small object out in front of him. Kindra pounced towards him from the shadows, pinning him against the wall with ease. The blade was held against his throat as an incentive to keep him from moving or screaming.

"W-what-who the fuck are you?" he quivered. The man's accent was strange, one she had never heard before. A sweet aroma resonated off him that masks his natural scent. Although Kindra could not see his eyes clearly in the dark, she could feel them scanning her naked body. Through his nervous shaking and stuttering, she could sense his fear.

"Who are you? Where am I?" Kindra demanded.

"Who am I? You broke into my fuckin' home!" The man shouted. "Who the fuck are you?"

"Answer!"

There were heavy bangs against the front door, startling Kindra.

"Mister McCullough, are you okay?" Another man from outside asked. "A freak storm passed by, and we saw lightning hit your mansion. It knocked out the power, so I called the police and fire department to check for damage."

"There is no escape once the police get here," the man, referred to as Mister McCullough, sputtered. His threat was meaningless through his lack of conviction; however, she should not jump into a fight, especially with un-known opponents.

Kindra tossed him off the wall since he avoided answering her questions and dashed towards the nearest window, breaking the glass where she landed on a small grass field. Then, without stopping, she vaulted over a brick wall taller than her and entered the brush surrounding McCullough's property.

The air was cool and moist, feeling entirely different from her home's air. Even the vegetation was new to Kindra's eyes, with the trees shooting straight up and standing incredibly tall. The bushes had long, broad leaves at her level, and some plants had strange prickly trunks. Kindra kept moving through the brush, hoping to get as far away from the stranger's home as possible and figure out what had happened to her.

Only after a few minutes of running, Kindra faces a body of water in front of her. What truly caught her attention was the view of a large city filled with tall structures made of stone emitting a copious amount of light. Such a sight was unfathomable, putting her in awe with her jaw dropped. The light was far more significant than any fire. This city was unlike any other she had come across and did nothing to help identify her location.

"What is this place?" Kindra whispered to herself, utterly aghast at what she was seeing.

The powerful lights from the city reflect off Kindra's skin, and she noticed the tattoos on her body were now a different color. Initially, they were all de-tailed in dark blue ink; now, they were silver. The wound she received from Kara's sword was completely healed, and there was not even a scar on the skin. Only a gap between the tattoo remained as a reminder of what happened. It was irrefutable that the Tree of the Dis was the cause of her restoration. To Kindra's knowledge, no other Valkyrie had silver tattoos.

I need to find the Court of the Valkyries. I need to find … Hildr … but how? I need answers, but I can't trust anyone here. At least not right away.

Kindra was conflicted on how to progress from where she currently stood. She could stay put and do what she could about her situation. However, she suspected that eventually, someone would find her here, leading Kindra into an unwanted battle. Or she could head towards this strange city and find someone willing to offer assistance. Again, this could lead to a conflict, but Kindra could try to avoid it by not being confrontational.

"What would Hildr do in this situation?" She asked herself.

No! Do not think like that! I am a Valkyrie, and I should not rely on someone else to guide me. I need to settle this on my own. Besides, Hildr told me to go with my gut, and my gut is saying … go to the city.

Closing her eyes for a moment and taking a deep breath, Kindra sprang forward into the murky water submerging her entire body beneath the soft current. All senses ignited the instant the cold seawater touched her skin. To her surprise, it was pretty refreshing after being housed with tree sap. She began propelling herself through the water towards the city shore, effortlessly battling the waves as they tried to divert her course. A swim such as this was nothing in comparison to the times Hildr had Kindra tread through the powerful storms spawned from the mighty Thor's wrath or the frigid seas during the harshest periods of winter. Even as painful as those moments were, Kindra would prefer them over where she was now.

It did not take long for Kindra to cross the body of water. She felt like she was moving faster than in her previous swims, where she reached a shore of metal and stone in only minutes. She did not see anyone nearby and quickly hops out of the water onto land, her feet lightly padding over the flat surface. A glance at Kindra's surroundings shows that the area was clear and quiet for a large city. Moving in between the buildings while blending in the shadows to avoid detection, Kindra worried that the first person she came across would be hostile, which would progress to the rest of the population. Kindra was an outsider, and most tribes did not treat outsiders too kindly.

The environment was a drastic contrast to the natural elements Kindra was accustomed to, which would take some time to adjust to the new setting. Even the air itself tasted different. To her, something seemed wrong about this place. The further she traveled through the gap between buildings, the stranger the area became. Near the end of this trail was a large green metal container producing a putrid smell.

While the scent was foul, it was nothing like a decaying body or excrement, more like spoiled food. Kindra lifted the container's cover to examine the contents, hoping to find something useful inside. The crack of the container lid released the fumes at full force, making Kindra wince but not provoke her to vomit or divert her actions. Pushing around black bags made of unnatural material, there seemed to not be much she could gather about these people except for their disposal of strange objects. Underneath the top layer of bags, she discovered a used red coat. Pulling it out of the container to give it a thorough inspection, the quality and construction were unlike the clothes she had worn. The garment did not offer any physical protection aside from the elements. It appeared to be more for casual wear, not combat. There were only a few stains on the front. Some fraying on the sleeves and abrasion marks along the back, yet it may be suitable to blend in for the time being.

Kindra slipped on the coat that was too large for her frame, with the bottom surpassing her waist and the sleeves extending a few inches over her hands. At least she could conceal her weapons more easily and not draw attention to herself. Hugging the coat to keep it closed, Kindra continued to walk through the alley, staying within whatever shadows she could find.

Let's just take this slow. No need to run into an issue.

Casually following the sidewalk through the city, enjoying the silence only offered at night, Anna Park took her time to reach her apartment. After moving to Seattle three years ago, she had gotten used to the heavy vehicular and foot traffic, but it was nice to have a break from it and see the city on its own. This was why Anna opted for evening classes to focus on her studies and not be disturbed by the crowds roaming the streets during the day.

Anna's evening schedule had her go to class at eight o'clock, which went on for about an hour and a half. From there, she stopped at her favorite coffee shop midway between the classroom and her apartment. It was a treat to enjoy a vanilla latte while working on her assignments for a couple of hours until the city's nightlife had died. Everything for Anna was clockwork which was how she liked it.

Her apartment was only two and a half blocks from where she currently stood. By the time she got settled at home, she was considering putting on Netflix and watching a couple of episodes of whatever she found interesting. Maybe something comedic to end her night on a positive note.

A slight gust of wind blew between the structures, producing an instant shiver to travel through her body. Anna pulled down on her black beanie to cover her ears and zips up the collar on her jacket. The cold, wet climate of the region was also something she had slightly become accustomed to, though cold weather was not something she was fond of. However, as they dived into winter, she would soon have to brace for the incoming cold front.

Footsteps were heard moving in Anna's direction from behind her. They were not moving fast to catch up to her, but it was strange as she did not notice anyone as she was walking on the sidewalk. Anna widened her stride while also trying not to appear to be avoiding the person trailing her. She wanted to look back and see who was following her but was worried that the person would immediately run after her once she makes eye contact.

The backpack straps were cinched tightly over Anna's shoulders in preparation to run, though should she run straight back home was the question that plagued her mind. It would be a horrible decision to lead the person to where she lives.

Anna took a right on the next block to see if whoever was behind her was in pursuit. As she walked out of view, Anna moved quickly to gain some distance before she resumed her previous pace. Anna listened for the sound of footsteps to return. They moved quickly in her direction but were trying to mask their signature.

"Fuck!" Anna muttered under her breath. She could try to run, but she knew she would not get far.

Reaching the end of the block, Anna was now faced with the decision of what to do next. If she kept going in the same direction, eventually, Anna would meet the shore. Going left would guide the stranger closer to her home, and going right would indicate her suspicion.

Christopher, maybe I can get help from him … if he is not on shift tonight …

Christopher Miles was her neighbor from across the hall, a police officer for the Seattle Police Department. It was risky to bring her pursuer close to where she lived, but right now, she had no one else to get in contact with. Her hand slipped into her right pant pocket, gripping her cell phone.

At the corner of the block, a man stepped around the side of the building. He wore a black hoodie over his head and a black cloth covering his face. There was only a narrow opening for Anna to see his eyes which were focused solely on her. Anna darts across the street to get away while simultaneously trying to draw out her phone. But the person behind her quickly caught up and snatches her by the waist, lifting her off her feet.

Anna could only produce one scream as the arms around her waist squeeze her too tight to breathe and cry out for help.

"C'mon, get her in the alley!" said the man that stood in front of Anna on the sidewalk.

"I'm trying! She just keeps moving," replied the person carrying her.

Their voices were youthful, sounding between late teens to mid-twenties. They forced her into an alleyway far enough from the street to be seen. The man threw Anna against the brick wall, where she hit her head and fell to the ground.

"Hurry up and get her shit." They both rushed to remove Anna's backpack off her shoulders but struggled to get the straps loose. The man in front of her abandoned any attempts to free Anna's backpack; instead, he started rummaging through her pockets. In doing so, he felt every bit of her along the way.

"No. No!" Anna screamed once a breath was drawn.

She tried pushing them away, but they were already on top of her and too close to gain leverage.

"Move away from her!" shouted a new feminine, powerful, and stern voice.

The two men were startled by the sudden intrusion in the alley. Turning to face the origin of the unknown voice, they only saw a figure further down the passage wearing nothing but an oversized red coat. Oddly enough, the person was not even wearing shoes. The unknown woman stood with her arms crossed over her chest, sticking close to the shadows to partially conceal herself.

"Get the fuck out of here!" the man in front of Anna shouted back.

"Fuckin' hobos, man," the second man commented. "They're all over the place."

"Move away," the cloaked woman growled. The men refused, with one even flipping her the middle finger out of spite. Such an act did not tread well for the woman.

She uncrossed her arms, loosening the coat revealing only a sliver of bare skin through the narrow opening. The sleeves were drawn back to bring out her hands. Her face was still obscured in shadow by the hood, but judging from her figure, it seemed to be a young woman.

"Woah . . ." the man in front of Anna said in astonishment. None of them, including Anna, expected to see someone, a woman, of this magnitude in their presence.

"Forget this bitch. Let's go after her!"

There was no argument as the two men sprint toward the woman, who seemed to be more of a prize than a threat to them. The woman shifted her legs to some form of boxing or martial arts stance, showing no fear as they approach her with gross desire. The first man to get in close tried to wrap his arms around her; however, before he could even touch her, she struck him straight in the face with an open palm. The impact was so loud that even Anna could hear it from where she was sitting, and the man quickly tipped backward and was knocked out cold on the ground.

The second man did not have time to make another decision other than to start swinging his fists clumsily at her. A right hook was thrown toward the woman's head without any remorse. Not flinching a single muscle, she raised her left arm, halting the man's arm from moving further. Anna had seen numerous videos of martial artists on the internet blocking incoming strikes, but the way this woman moved was astonishing and put those people to shame. Her reaction was almost too fast for the human eye to see; it was merely a red blur from the coat. The man could not move her arms once she blocked him. It was like he wrapped his arm around a telephone pole rather than mere flesh and bone. With a flick of her wrist, she ended up gripping his arm and twisting it rapidly. A loud snap erupted in his arm, causing Anna to shiver from the grotesque sound.

Screaming in the narrow confinement, the woman grasped the man's throat and then effortlessly lifted him with one arm pinning him against the wall. Anna's jaw dropped as she had never in her life seen someone do such a thing, man or woman. The man's demeanor transitioned from an aggressive young adult to a whimpering child in seconds, and he no longer put up a fight against his opponent.

"If you lay your hands on another person in such a vile manner, I *will* break your other arm and then rip it off!" she said in a bold voice.

The threat was loud and clear.

The man could only nod, and that was all she needed before she released him to collapse on the ground, cradling his broken arm. While the pain was undoubtedly intense, he dared not cry out for help or be confronted by the woman again.

The mysterious woman walked over to the first guy she took down without a care, making her way to Anna, who did not get up or move from where they left her. It was not until she was a few feet from her that Anna tried to crawl away. She held out her hands to calm Anna and let her know she was no threat. Kneeling in front of Anna, the woman pulled back the hoodie draped over her head, unveiling her identity. The first thing Anna noticed were her honey-brown eyes and smooth complexion. Anna was unashamed to admit that this woman was beautiful and not from any clever manipulation of cosmetics, which did not appear on her face.

This woman was naturally beautiful.

"Are you hurt?" she asked Anna, loosening the threatening tone to one of genuine concern. There was an accent to the woman's voice, though Anna could not put her finger on the origin. Sounds European, albeit from the northern countries.

"Uh … no. I … I think I'm fine," Anna replied, still shaking from her encounter. She gently pat the spot on her head where she hit the wall during the scuffle. Fortunately, no bleeding, though she could feel a welt begin to form. "Thank you for, uh, saving me. This has never happened before."

"Your gratitude is appreciated," she said, helping Anna back onto her feet without any visible strain. "But I need your help."

"Oh, um, okay … ."

"Where are we? What realm is this?" the woman asked.

Anna stood completely confused about the question. The first thing that popped into her head was that this woman was insane or disturbed. There were many crazy people out in the world, and this may be one of them.

"Realm?" she questioned.

"Yes! Are we in Niflheim, Vanaheimr, Jötunheimr? This cannot be Midgard."

The only word that made a connection in Anna's brain was Midgard. She was referring to realms depicted in Norse mythology.

CHAPTER SIX

"Please, I need to know where I am. I need to get home," Kindra pleaded, trying to get something from the woman she saved. She was different in appearance from the type of women Kindra had seen. The woman's age was close to Kindra, maybe a few years younger, with a round face and light complexion.

"Okay, um … I don't know what kind of drugs you're on, but please let me go," the young woman quivered.

"I just need to get back to Midgard." Kindra tried to speak softer to get her to cooperate and not feel coerced.

"Midgard? That's Earth, right?"

Kindra gave a bewildered look on her face, then quickly shook it off, saying, "Midgard is where I'm from. I need to get back there."

"And that is here, don't you understand? This should be Midgard or whatever. It's all the same place."

There was a pause between them as Kindra took a second to digest the words spoken to her.

This cannot be Midgard … What happened when I was asleep? Where did everyone go, or where did I go?

"Odin. Where's Odin? The Valkyries?" Kindra quickly asked.

"Odin? As in the god, Odin, of Norse mythology?"

"Mythology?"

"Yeah. Norse mythology, the ancient religion of Scandinavia. You do re-alize that it was folklore, not real."

Kindra shook her head, "No-no, it is real."

"Well, I'm sorry I can't help you," the woman slid her back against the wall, trying to slowly slip away from Kindra. "Maybe someone else can come along and give you some advice."

As the young woman tried to break free from the conversation, Kindra quickly positioned herself in front of her, preventing her from going anywhere else. It was not the best idea to pressure this young, obviously frightened woman, but Kindra had no other option. Not when she had more questions to ask about this realm. "Please ... I beg you ... can you help me with some information?"

While the woman tried to avoid making eye contact, the small glances that did connect happened to hold some empathy towards Kindra's disposition. A deep sigh was emitted from her mouth with a subtle nod.

"Fine. Since you did save me, I guess I should return the favor."

Kindra took a step back, placing a hand over her heart, and said, "I whole-heartedly appreciate your assistance. My name is Kindra."

"Oh, well ... hi, -uh-Kindra? I'm Anna. Anna Park," she said, with a weary smile and simple hand wave, doing her best to act polite. "Let's just get out of here before anyone else shows up and makes a mess of all this."

Anna immediately took the lead out of the alley, hoping to distance herself from the muggers. Kindra wrapped the coat around her body and followed Anna. In comparison, Anna was shorter than Kindra by half a foot and had a slimmer build, and that was only based on what she saw, not what lies beneath the thick clothing. She had a knitted cap over her head, covering most of her short black hair.

There was an awkward silence between them, and it was evident that Anna felt uncomfortable being followed. So Kindra stepped up to walk beside her and offer protection during their trek through the city.

Anna did what she could to maintain her cool in the presence of this mysterious woman. Kindra carefully observed the woman's hardened demeanor as she walked beside Anna. Her walking posture spewed confidence, even if she was barely clothed in public, with only an old coat covering her body. This was also surprising in how she could handle the cold without discomfort or hindrance. There was not even a shiver in her limbs as the breeze brushed by them.

"So," Anna began, trying to stir a conversation and break the silence between them, "Kindra? That is an interesting name. Does it mean anything?"

"It is means greatest champion or champion who is the greatest," Kindra replied.

"Oh, that's cool. I never heard anyone with that name, so I just thought I'd ask."

"And what about your name?" Kindra asked Anna.

"My name? I'm not quite sure. I never looked into it. My parents only named me Anna because of a famous actress from the Sixties."

Kindra cocked an eyebrow, appearing puzzled by what she just said, and instead remained quiet.

Anna was still determining where she was taking Kindra. This woman could be playing a trick on her to ransack her place or scope it out for later. Kindra was obviously physically strong enough to overpower Anna. However, she had not attempted to steal Anna's belongings despite having the opportunity to do so.

Stop it. Kindra saved you from being mugged. Be thankful that she was even there, or else things could have worsened. I just can't believe what I saw her do to those men. There is no way some random homeless person could be so strong that it was enough to lift a full-grown man with one arm. That feat of strength is frankly abnormal and is beyond my scope of expertise.

She wished this were just a regular night but noticing Kindra's eyes glance at the flashing signs they passed, Anna believed they want the same thing. A typical person would pay no attention to the everyday sights found in the city. Kindra, on the other hand, was intrigued and not on the level of a tourist. Kindra genuinely looked stunned at everything, like she had never seen it before.

Maybe the police can help her because I surely can't. What can I do to help her?

This world is strange, Kindra thought as she scanned every detail of all the objects that go by. How *could anyone build such things? This can't be the work of man. The unique masonry of these structures is incredible. Standing at the base of one to see how they extend upwards into the sky like a mountain is mesmerizing, to say the least. If the phenomenal Valkyries did not possess such architecture, how could mortals dwell in such a lavish city? A place like this would certainly be a prize for Midgard. Though it is not exactly a paradise based on some of the people she came across that still prey on others. I guess every place, no matter how grand, has its own set of wolves lurking about.*

"What is this place called?" Kindra asked Anna.

"This is Seattle, Washington. Are you really not from around here?"

"I can assure you I'm not," Kindra replied sternly.

"What am I doing?" Anna muttered, trying to keep her voice low enough for Kindra not to hear. "I need to take her to the police or a hospital to get some real help."

Kindra halted in her tracks, to which Anna immediately turned in confusion.

"Who are these police that you speak of, and what kind of help can they offer me?"

"Wait … you understood what I said?"

"Well, of course, you were not exactly discreet when you spoke it."

"No-no, that's not what I meant. It's that you were able to understand Korean."

"What is that?" Kindra bluntly asked.

"Korean. You know, from Korea." Anna observed Kindra's blank stare and knew she was serious. "Are you sure you can't speak Korean?"

"Yes, I do not know what Korean even is."

"You just did it right now!" Anna said in shock, "I spoke to you in Korean, and you not only understood what I said but also spoke it back to me."

"I ... I did?" Kindra quietly said, completely unaware of her speaking a different tongue and understanding it clearly as if nothing had changed. "How can this be? Wait . . ." she paused, resurfacing a rumor she remembered hearing from her peers during the training. "It is the Omni speak ... it truly does exist."

"The 'what-speak'?" Anna asked.

"The Omni speak. When I was a child, there was a rumor that all languages could be heard and spoken through the all-speak. I must have received it from the Valkyrie enhancement process."

Anna's mouth remained open with no words coming out, completely baffled to hear such a wild concept. Now she appeared just as confused as Kindra about what was going on.

"Okay ... um, maybe we can figure something out that doesn't involve the police. There are a lot of questions that I have about you, and this is not the place to ask. I can take you to my place to discuss some things." Anna said, sounding hesitant yet willing to invite Kindra.

"I am truly honored to receive your generosity and will be in your debt," Kindra said sincerely.

"Yeah, uh, no problem. Just follow me," Anna said, unsure how to respond and slightly embarrassed by the compliment.

She abruptly changed her direction on the sidewalk and directed Kindra to her place.

Chapter Seven

Anna brought Kindra to one of the many tall structures in the city, where she initially stared into the night sky to see the tip of the building. Then, pausing before the double glass doors leading inside, Anna curiously watched the young Valkyrie.

"You live here?" Kindra asked while keeping her head tilted up to the heavens.

"A room here, yes. Along with about a hundred other people." Anna moved towards the entrance, but Kindra remained there in place, entranced by the tall building.

"Are you coming in?" she asked Kindra.

"Uh, yes," Kindra immediately replied, breaking the spell that held her attention and following Anna.

As Anna approached the double glass doors, they automatically moved aside in her presence. Kindra instantly took a defensive stance holding out her dagger. "What is this!" she exclaimed.

"It's okay-it's okay!" Anna tried to calm her down. "They are just doors, nothing to be alarmed about. Now please put that away before someone sees."

Kindra slowly lowered her weapon and carefully stepped through the doorway. Once inside the building, the illumination from the lights nearly blinded her eyes, taking her a moment to adjust. It was pure white light, unlike the dwindling glow from a flame. A draft of warm air touched her skin, yet there was no scent of smoke or a fire to produce it.

"Come on, let's go ahead and take the stairs so we can avoid meeting anyone."

Traveling up several flights of stairs, they were no challenge to Kindra, only an annoyance for their repetitive nature. However, as she watched, Anna's mobility degraded, becoming apparent that Anna was far from Kindra's physical capabilities.

"Okay, here we are on the sixth floor. Luckily, my apartment is right by the stairway access," Anna announced, trying to mask her winded breathing.

Through the door leading into the level, all Kindra could see was a long corridor with dark blue carpeting and dozens of doors on both grey walls. Through every doorway, beyond every wall, Kindra had zero expectations. Anna stopped at the door immediately to her left and began rummaging through her pockets for her keys. She nearly dropped them from being too anxious, having difficulty keeping her hand still enough to slide the room key into the keyhole. But as she successfully inserts the key, the door was unlocked and pushed open with haste. Once Kindra stepped inside, Anna shut the door, twisting every lock into place before finally taking a steady exhale.

"Are you all right?" Kindra asked with some minor concern in her voice.

"Yeah, I'm good," she replied with light enthusiasm and a shaky smile.

Kindra could quickly tell she was lying as she tried to hide her nervousness; it was an expression Kindra had held many times with Hildr.

This is probably what Hildr felt like long ago when she would sniff out my lies.

Without wishing to dig deeper into Anna's mind, the attention was redirected to the room's interior. From the point of entry, there was a room to the left and one to the right. The room on the right had a bed, while the left was filled with books, a thin desk, and a fluffy blue chair. Directly in front of Kindra was a wide cushion chair made of velvet in a summer yellow. There was an assortment of other things in Anna's residence that were unfamiliar to Kindra. She was sure she would soon find out the meaning of at least some of this stuff the longer she spends with Anna.

Anna dropped her backpack beside the front door and removed her beanie, tossing it on the tall dining table that appeared to be built for only two people.

"Welcome to my estate. Feel free to settle down and relax," she said. But Kindra remained in the middle of the apartment with her arms tucked close to her body. "Huh, let me see if I have anything for you to wear besides that old coat."

She disappeared into the bedroom while Kindra remained in place, willing not to disturb any of Anna's belongings. After a minute in the room, she returns with a bundle of clothing in her arms.

"Sorry, I don't really have anything your size. I grabbed the largest clothes I own." Anna held out the clothes in front of her for Kindra to take.

Before Kindra grabbed them, she sheds the coat, letting it plop on the ground with her bare form exposed in front of Anna. The young woman diverted her eyes out of embarrassment and respect for Kindra's privacy. It was a strange reaction since they were both women and were familiar with the female human anatomy.

"Wow, you're, uh, really quite jacked for someone wandering the street." Anna complimented her, but Kindra did not understand her meaning and did not know if she should take offense or be delighted.

"What do you mean by 'jacked'?"

"Oh, I'm sorry, it's a way to say fit or muscular. You, you're massive. Maybe even the leanest woman I've ever seen."

"It comes naturally from years of training and commitment. The best way to tackle the world is to be strong. Not just for myself, but for others," Kindra said.

"That's thoughtful. I don't think I have as much of a commitment as you to be physically active."

The people of Seattle, Washington, hold a more profound respect for personal privacy. Well, there is no need to make my generous host uncomfortable. I should hurry so we can get back to answering questions we have been meaning to ask each other.

The first article of clothing was a faded black short-sleeved shirt with a colorful picture of a snow-covered mountain on the front. It was surprisingly soft, possibly the most delicate thing Kindra had felt.

"Yeah, it was a souvenir shirt my parents got me when I moved here. It's too big for me, so I rarely wore it, and I got you some pajama bottoms that are too long."

Kindra slipped the shirt over her head, feeling the material compress around her body. It was tight, though not restrictive or uncomfortable. Kindra was sure it would tear the shirt if she flexed her muscles. Next, Kindra put on the soft black pajama bottoms that stop just above her ankles.

"Are these typical clothes of your culture?" Kindra asked.

"Uh, yeah, for sleeping. Not really something I recommend wearing outside in public, but nowadays, I guess you can. Um … are you hungry?"

"No, I am fine. Thank you for asking. I do not mean to be rude, especially after you displayed such kindness, but I request that we trade information."

"Ah, yes. That is probably for the best. Please take a seat at the table while I change really quick." Anna stepped back into the room, where she retrieved the clothes for Kindra and closed the door behind her.

Kindra went through the pockets of the old coat, retrieving her dagger and shield. She stared at the new blade, looking at herself in the reflection.

"I wish you were here, Hildr." She whispered softly before taking a seat at the small dining table and placing both weapons in front of her like silverware.

Where do I go from here in this strange land? There are many new things to learn before I am ready to progress in my journey. This will undoubtedly be a different task than the duties of a Valkyrie. But why me?

The door creaks open with Anna stepping out from the room in similar garb to Kindra's and carrying a thin rectangular object tucked under her right arm. In complete light, Anna's features were prominent. Her skin was pale and marvelously smooth, like it had never been tarnished by light or dirt. She took a seat in front of Kindra, her eyes staring at the dagger.

"Is everything all right?" Kindra asked.

"Yeah-yeah, I just never seen a knife like that before," she said, sounding nervous.

"It was a recent gift from a … dear friend," Kindra said, trying to keep her voice from trembling.

"Well, it's really nice." Anna placed the rectangular object in front of herself. "So, what—or I should say how—do you want to ask?"

Kindra's eyes grazed the wooden tabletop, drifting side-to-side as she tried to decide what to say. "I truly do not know how to start. I am confused about where I am and how I got here."

Anna rubbed her chin, then said to her, "How about you tell me more about yourself. Maybe we can start from there and see where that takes us."

"That will do," Kindra agreed. For what Kindra assumed would be a lengthy conversation, she clears her throat. Finally, she said, "I am Kindra, a newly inducted Valkyrie of Midgard. I was encased in the Valere Tree to be granted the abilities of a Valkyrie. It was supposed to be a month-long recovery. Yet, I ended up awakening inside a stranger's house after an unknown amount of time."

"Okay . . ." Anna quietly said with wide eyes but avoided connecting them with Kindra's.

"You are not convinced." Kindra bluntly stated.

"Oh no, it's just, I've never heard a story like that before. Valkyries? Like real Valkyries?!"

"You seem to have some familiarity with the Valkyries. Do you know about them?" Kindra asked, sounding more intrigued than critical of Anna's knowledge.

"Well, I'm not entirely familiar with their history or the individual members, but I remember hearing about them being skilled warriors."

"They are the best." Kindra immediately corrected.

"Oh, I'm sorry. Is that how you became so strong and learned how to fight?"

"Yes. I have been training to become a Valkyrie since I was nine. Every day was used for training where I had to push myself beyond my limits, learn a new skill, and earn the right to become a Valkyrie."

"That sounds like torture," Anna commented.

"It is surely not meant for everyone. I have known compatriots that died during their training, never even making it to the Court of the Valkyries to be judged."

"You seem pretty young to be a Valkyrie."

With a subtle smirk, Kindra said, "I am the oldest candidate to become a Valkyrie. My sisters before me were inducted when they were still teenagers.

My mentor … Hildr thought it would be beneficial that I wait and become mature in comparison to my sisters."

"Is Hildr your mother?" Anna asked.

"No, *she* was the Valkyrie who trained me," Kindra said in a firm tone and did not want to talk about Hildr any further for fear of showing weakness.

"Your family, then. What about your parents?"

Kindra turn her head leaning her back against the chair, her eyes scanning the walls of Anna's apartment for a few seconds.

"I have no family. Let us leave it at that." Kindra did not want to venture into the past before she met Hildr. At least not now to a stranger.

"Yeah, sure. You don't have to talk about it if you don't want to." Anna did her best to not offend Kindra; after all, she did see what she could do. "Right now, I'm just so enthralled by what you're saying. The tales of the Valkyries were thought to be just that, stories passed down from generation to generation until they eventually faded from memory by most of the world."

"Faded from memory? Have the gods never visited this realm to make their presence known? What if they are still in Asgard and never returned?"

"Yeah … that could be a possibility, but the world moved on from what you remember. The gods, the Valkyries, are no longer vital to our way of life. And in fact, it was not prominent in this part of the world."

"When did this happen? When did everyone forget about our existence?"

"I'm not entirely sure when, though I speculate that it was over a thousand years ago when the region that believed in your existence transitioned into an Abrahamic religion."

Kindra immediately stood up, wholly appalled to hear the news of her world disappearing.

"No! It cannot be! I was only supposed to be asleep for a month!" She backed up against the wall by the front door and slid down to the floor.

"Kindra, it is okay. Please calm down," Anna quietly said, trying to ease Kindra's escalated tension. "I'm here to help."

"Hildr was supposed to release me. It was not meant to be this way. My purpose—my destiny—was to be a Valkyrie." As her eyes grew watery, a battle was still being fought internally to prevent tears from falling. Even if the Valkyries were no more, Kindra must not disgrace them despite the overwhelming agony inside her. After a few seconds of slowly taking deep breaths to calm her rapid breathing, Kindra looked at Anna, who was carefully watching her. "Something went wrong when I was asleep. Something, a force of some kind, prevented the Valkyries from awakening me."

"A force? Do you mean something that has wiped out everyone from your time? Of course, it would make sense why you exist now and that we have not encountered any deities since then. But a force of that magnitude to rival the power of gods, wouldn't that have destroyed the world?"

"Yes, it would. But, for now, it is my only explanation for why they are all gone. I need to find out more."

"Look, let me see what I can find. I am really interested in what more you have to say about your time since there is truth to all the stories." Anna held out her hand in front of Kindra as an offering.

Gently accepting the young woman's hand, Anna tried to lift Kindra. However, she was straining to just budge Kindra's mass and ended up standing by her own power.

"Thank you, Anna." Kindra kindly said.

"Don't worry about it." Anna smiled. "I can use the company. It had been a while since I've had a visitor, and I could really use a break from college."

"Anna, tell me about yourself. What brings you here?" Kindra asked.

Anna guided Kindra back to the table, where they both returned to their seats. "Oh, I'm just here to receive an education and hopefully get a job afterward. It is a common goal in life for many people. I'm originally from California, which is six hours south of here. I've only lived in Seattle for a few years with one more year to go, hopefully."

"Then I pray that you receive much success and reach your goal. Anna, for your kindness, I offer you my services."

"What like a bodyguard?" Anna chuckled, but looking at Kindra's unwavering face, she quickly found that the Valkyrie was completely serious. "Oh, well, I'm honored."

The evening was spent reading about Norse mythology on Anna's rectangular device she called a laptop. Kindra was fascinated by what her computer could do. Although Anna had to explain to her multiple times how it worked, Kindra still had difficulty understanding and believed some form of magic was used.

From what Anna could find, most of the information was accurate by Kindra's account, at least when it came down to covering the essential details. However, some instances where people or events were wrongly cited, and the specifics changed depending on who told it.

When Anna asked Kindra if she wanted to hear Hildr's history, Kindra vehemently refused. She did not want to know what someone hundreds of years later had to say about her if they never knew her personally.

Anna produced a lengthy yawn amid reading on her laptop but said nothing about it. Kindra could see her eyes continuously narrowing along with her head swaying forward. "Anna, you are tired. You should get some rest."

"Nah, we can keep going—" Anna said before another yawn crept up after her in mid-sentence.

"Anna," Kindra softly said, placing a hand on Anna's shoulder, "you need to get some rest. You went through a lot today and deserve some time for yourself."

"Yeah, you're right. Gosh, you remind me of my mother, except nicer and with muscles." Anna stretches her body while sitting in the chair. "We can pick up where we left off tomorrow—err—later today since it's two in the morning. Thankfully, it's the weekend, so I have some free time. You can sleep on the couch if you'd like. I'll get you a blanket and a pillow."

Once again, Anna disappeared into her bedroom, reappearing shortly after carrying a neatly folded grey-colored blanket and a small white pillow covered with flowers. She placed them on the armrest of the yellow couch for Kindra.

"If you need anything, just let me know."

"Thank you, Anna." Kindra bowed her head. She smiled and then entered her bedroom, closing the door behind her.

Taking a deep, powerful inhale and slowly letting it out, Kindra stared at the couch in front of her. Inside her was a strange sensation developing in Kindra's heart as she now had some knowledge of her whereabouts in this world. There was no hiding that Kindra missed her home, the simplicity of her environment, her Valkyrie counterparts, and Hildr's words of wisdom and guidance. It was even more painful knowing she did not give a proper goodbye to everything she knew.

There was no resolution, and she would have to live with that.

Kindra sat on the couch to give it a feel before lying down. The cushions were softer than any chair of her time, and she felt like she was floating above the ground.

Drawing the blanket from the armrest and casting it over her body, Kindra lies her head on the pillow and did her best to empty her mind, at least for a small moment of peace.

Minutes passed while Kindra tried to find a comfortable position on the couch and put her mind at ease until dawn. Yet, thoughts were running through her head that refused to fade away. The softness from the couch was beginning to feel rather uncomfortable. Kindra never had a real bed since they would constantly be on the move, and they would set up camp wherever Hildr believed to end their day. A bed was to be a reward after years of hard work, where Kindra could finally settle down and start her own life.

Removing herself from the couch, she lay on the carpet floor, bringing the pillow and blanket along with her. The firm surface was more relaxing, with Kindra's body pressed against something sturdy. The carpet was an added cushion making it a preferable option to dirt. But as Kindra tried to get some rest in a new position, there was no reason to sleep. She had been asleep for thousands of years and needed to compensate for the lost time.

Kindra closed her eyes, wishing for the eventual collapse into the darkness, where she would instantly awaken when the sun came up.

CHAPTER EIGHT

"I heard it! Did you not?" whispered Verdandi, thrusting herself up on her bed. "You did not hear anything, Verdandi," Skuld grumbled, partially awakened after Verdandi disturbed their slumber. "Only ghosts of the past. Now go back to sleep."

Skuld turned on her wooden bed, facing away from Verdandi, to find a comfortable position to return to the dream world.

"I swear to you I heard lightning. And not just any lightning, but one that originated from the gods themselves."

"How can that be? The gods—their world—are gone. Now quiet."

Sitting on her bed, Urd, the eldest of the sisters, said, "No, nothing would have awakened Verdandi if it were of no concern. Something had surely caught her attention, and for good reason."

"What if it was simply a nightmare that Verdandi could not run from," Skuld tried to reason with Urd but knew it was futile to dissuade her.

"I think we have been away for long enough. Perhaps it is time we see what the world has been brought to in our absence. That means get up, Skuld," Urd said to which Skuld groaned in response. A small flame ignited in the palm of Urd's hand, illuminating their surroundings just enough for her to see Verdandi and Skuld on their wooden beds.

While it had been an untold amount of time since she had seen her sisters, neither appeared any different than when she saw them last. Verdandi still had her youthful heart-shaped face with her long straight brown hair straightened neatly over her body. Skuld, on the other hand, had sharper features and curly black hair covering her face in a mess.

Their beds were shaped in a triangular formation, with the corners nearly touching each other. All three of them sat on the beds facing the formation's center.

"I do not understand why you believe there is reason to be concerned. The gods have been gone for millennia; why would they be here? Why now?" Skuld continued to question.

"This is why we need to know what happened during our period of rest while the world of man continued to move on," Urd replied sternly. Then, she turn her attention to Verdandi, sitting to Urd's right, and asked her, "Verdandi, could you please give us a glimpse of the world we left behind?"

"Yes, sister," she replied, stretching her fingers and twisting her wrists that had gone stiff from being immobile. Verdandi held out her hands, making wide swirls as if she was paddling through a puddle of water. The floor in the center of the triangle glowed blue momentarily before a window opened into the outside world.

Since they last saw the world once ruled by gods and mystical beings, much had changed. Through the window, the three sisters instantly noticed how mankind had thrived over the years without interference from the gods or other beings of the nine realms. Next, Verdandi switched to a new location to observe. This one was a bird's eye view of a densely populated city filled with people none were familiar with. The city was constructed from man-made materials where grey towers reach past dark clouds.

"So, this is what man has become over the years," Urd whispered, fascinated by what was presented to them.

"This is man? Are you sure?" Skuld asked, wiping her tired eyes.

"Undoubtedly so. It appears they have evolved," Urd replied, then asked Verdandi to look at a new location.

The following location to appear was another vast city living in the desert that was more refined and glamorous than the last. The buildings were similar in size and construction but with one that was distinguishably taller than anything on the land. The people that inhabited this region were also different in complexion, wardrobes, and customs.

"They have certainly been keeping busy," Skuld commented. "I have never seen something like this before."

"*You* did not see this? Is this not what you saw in your visions, Skuld?" Verdandi questioned.

"Not like this. What we are seeing is something new that has spawned from their own fruition," Skuld told Verdandi.

"If this is not what mankind envisioned becoming, then why did we volunteer to go into hibernation?"

"Verdandi," Urd stepped in to settle the dispute. "Find us another view."

Flicking her wrist at the magical window, the image changed to a forest on fire in a foreign land unknown to them. Thick black smoke trails the sky as the flames on the ground devour everything in their path, creating a fine line between the burnt vegetation and the greenery in its path.

"So, this is what is happening to our fine world."

"Verdandi, do you know what or where you heard the disturbance?" Urd asked her.

Closing her eyes and motioning her hands, Verdandi concentrates on the event that sparked her awakening. "No, I cannot. It was a mere spark of their power and even then, whatever brought upon such power is only a faint signature of the residue."

"Then what shall we do now that we are awake?" Skuld asked.

"Let us not be too hasty in judging what lies before us. I believe we owe it to ourselves to see the new world in person and greet this new form of mankind. We must also find the source of what caused our awakening, as it could be detrimental to this realm. Verdandi, do you have any idea where it could be? The closest we can get to the point of origin?"

"I'm afraid not. What has transpired over time, these unknown territories, are completely new to me, so I am unfamiliar with where it came from. I suggest we try to learn of the location as we walk among the surface of the world."

"Very well. Let us split up, so we do not have to scour the entire world looking for what the gods left behind. This would also give us an insight into mankind's progression," Urd said to both her sisters.

Standing up from her bed, Urd touched the brick wall surrounding them, causing the roof to shudder and dirt and debris to fall. The crack of light peering down into their domain was powerfully blinding. Still, it was with great welcome to see something besides complete darkness. Fresh air flowed from outside, lightly padding against Urd's face.

"Oh, let us see what we have been missing," Verdandi said excitedly.

The three levitated from outside the well and touched down on the grassy field surrounding them. Nothing of man was close to where they resided. The well housing them was buried beneath a layer of dirt, either done on purpose or forgotten existence and consumed by nature.

"This is rather strange," Skuld said, taking a few steps to walk over the grass. "I imagined there would be something here. How is that humanity has cultivated, yet our domain is barren?"

"Yes, it is peculiar," Urd replied. "Verdandi, you go south. Skuld head west. I will take the east. Examine what you can of these people. We will reconvene here in two days to discuss our next move."

Chapter Nine

"Kindra . . ." whispered a soft, comforting voice that echoed in a void. "My dear Kindra … can you hear me?"

The voice was strangely familiar to Kindra, and she tried her best to piece together who it was coming from. Her mind moved sluggishly, feeling somewhat exhausted for unknown reasons. All Kindra could see was an empty black sky and barren violet land that extends indefinitely. Everything around her felt unnatural, but her senses could still pick up the surroundings.

"Where am I? What is going on?" Kindra said, feeling her words slurring from out of her mouth.

"Kindra, come closer," the voice said, echoing in the empty plane.

She spun around to find where the voice was coming from but could not be accurately pinpointed in this dark, desolate land.

"Who are you?" Kindra said aloud into the mysterious void she happened to be cast.

A swirl of black smoke appeared in front of Kindra. It took time to determine if what she saw was genuine and not an illusion of the environment.

"It has been far too long." The voice was feminine and strong. A faint reminder of the past.

Hildr.

"No! No tricks! Do not dare pose as the Great Hildr!" Kindra shouted to the dark essence.

"The Great Hildr, huh?" The billow of smoke condensed itself, creating a human silhouette. That same silhouette developed features resembling more of a woman, then it turned into a form of Hildr. "That is quite the compliment."

"Hildr? It cannot be … ." Kindra quivered, completely stunned to see a full image of her mentor. "How do I know it is really you and not some apparition?"

With a quick smile, the image of Hildr said, "I am glad your time in the Tree of the Dis has not made you soft. You look exactly the same the day you were sealed from me."

"By the Allfather, it really is you!" A smile widened on Kindra's face as she lunged forward, wishing to hug the Valkyrie in her arms, but suddenly stopped in her tracks to pay her respects and kneeled in front of Hildr.

"Kindra the Valkyrie, please," Hildr said, placing her hand on Kindra's shoulder where she could feel the woman's warm touch, "rise and greet me not as your mentor but as your friend."

Standing up, Kindra wrapped her arms around Hildr, holding her tighter than ever. "Where are we? Where are you?"

"Yes, I do miss you too, Kindra, beyond measure. But right, we do not have much time."

Kindra released Hildr, taking a step back to better communicate with her. "What do you mean?"

"We are in a different plane of existence, one outside the nine realms where we can only see each through your dreams."

"The dream world. Is this of Mare's doing? Are you trapped here because of him?" Kindra asked, with fear and anger in her voice.

"No. For what happened was the result of a greater threat."

"Hildr, what happened to our world? All the gods, the Valkyries, and the mysticism are all gone. Why have I not awakened thousands of years ago?" Kindra asked, sounding desperate for answers.

"I know you have hundreds of questions about what happened in the past, and believe me, I want to spend time elaborating on every detail with you. But for now, I need you to settle in this new world and continue to train for what may come."

"What is coming? What should I be preparing for?!" Kindra exclaimed, entirely confused, with more questions populating in her head.

A sudden yellow glowing star illuminated over Kindra's heart.

"You are starting to awaken. Kindra, do you remember the Valkyrie's Prayer?"

"Well, yes, of course, but what does that—" Kindra stammered but was immediately cut off by Hildr.

She firmly clutched Kindra's left wrist and said to her, "You will need to continue your duties as a Valkyrie and be an example for mankind, even if they have forgotten us."

The light from Kindra's heart intensified, blinding even herself. The warmth of Hildr's hand on Kindra's arm turned cold, and she could no longer sense her mentor's presence.

"Hildr!" Kindra gasped as her body sprang upward from the floor. Her heart beats rapidly as she tried to remember where she was, deciphering all the colors and strange objects around her.

Then Kindra recalled she was in Anna's apartment. She controlled her breathing to calm herself, bringing the blanket over her shoulders while thinking of what she saw in her sleep.

That was not real ... it could not be real ... It must have been an awful dream. But all of it was unlike any dream I had in the past. I could actually feel everything around me. And Hildr ... her touch ... that was real. It must have been!

Kindra rubbed her arm where Hildr last touched her, trying to remember how it felt before it all slipped away again. Looking down at her wrist, there was a new marking—a tattoo—that was not previously there. It was an illustration of Sigrdifumal's helm, the Valkyrie of Victory. Kindra never met her personally as she was slain many years before Kindra was born, but Hildr spoke of Sigrdifumal often as she was one of the original Valkyries. At times, when Kindra was young, she would catch Hildr speaking her name and even having full-blown conversations at night, though Kindra would see nothing but air.

From what Hildr had mentioned, Sigrdifumal would recite a prayer before every battle, which eventually became known as the Valkyries' Prayer.

Hildr gave this to me. It was real, and I will see her again. But I cannot go to sleep now. I need to be ready to fight.

Resting in the comfort of her own bed, Anna rested her head on a pillow, staring at the swirling ceiling fan. She had difficulty falling asleep since she had so many thoughts running through her mind about the events that occurred last night. As a result, sleep was pushed to the bottom of her list of priorities even though she was exhausted.

This woman that saved her was unique from the moment Anna saw her. It was not easy to believe or accept what Kindra had told her. Like other ancient religions, Norse mythology was phased out in favor of another religion that swept through the region. When people forgot about the stories, meaning, and magnificent characters, it was simply rubbed off as make-believe. Yet, to Kindra, it was real. There was no lie or belief based on deception in Kindra. To her, it was genuine.

Plus, someone may not be willing to diverge so profoundly into the mythos. Kindra, just by her name alone, was strange, though it could be just what she called herself, and her real name was kept secret. Her accent and features were fitting of a northern European. What truly caught Anna's attention was Kindra's impressive physique. Many athletes Anna had seen, even those on television on professional sports teams or the Olympics, did not compare to Kindra. If fully clothed, Kindra may not appear intimidating, which was a clever way to maintain one's anonymity. During their first encounter, Anna was quite amazed to see such striations and muscle groups that she did not expect a woman to have. Kindra was undoubtedly a specimen, more of an art piece than a living human being, with a physique uncommon for a homeless person.

Along with art were the distinct tattoos covering her arms and parts of her torso, or just what she could only see briefly. Nowadays, it was common for people to have tattoos with a desire to test their creativity. But Kindra's were something special, like they were done crudely instead of the usual tattoo machine. The designs and shapes were certainly based on old Norse scriptures, from what Anna could tell. However, the most impressive thing about her tattoos was the ink. Kindra was the first and possibly only person with ink that shined like pure silver, unlike the tiny sparkles from the glitter on temporary tattoos.

What can I really do for the woman besides make her comfortable? Maybe that is all I can do. Maybe she only needs someone to get her back on her feet and send her off alone. It could be days or weeks until Kindra can settle herself, but it's not like I have much of a busy schedule.

Anna was drawn from her thoughts once she heard movement over the hollow floors from the living room.

I guess she is up. Maybe that's my cue to get up too.

Anna pushed the covers off her, briskly stretching her tired body, then moved to the living room to check up on Kindra. As she opened the door, the first thing Anna saw was Kindra doing a handstand with only one arm. But as Anna blinked a couple of times to understand what she was seeing, Kindra began performing pushups using only the same arm while maintaining her entire body vertical.

"Wow. I, uh, guess you're a morning person," Anna said, hoping she was not interrupting her calisthenics.

"I apologize, Anna, if I disturbed your sleep," Kindra sincerely said, doing ten pushups before gracefully flipping over backward to greet Anna.

"Oh, no, you're fine. I was already awake. Since you're up, I guess you would like some breakfast then," Anna replied, moving towards the small kitchen.

"I cannot allow you to perform such a generous act, especially after all you have done already."

"Please, you're my guest. Besides, I like to cook. So, make yourself comfortable while I get something ready."

Tentatively Kindra watched Anna work the electric stove, pull out ingredients from the refrigerator, and start making a simple breakfast consisting of pancakes and eggs.

Savoring the sweet scent of the food Anna was cooking, Kindra sat at the table. While she waited patiently, the thoughts of what Hildr said in her dream roam around in her head. It was still challenging to understand what she meant by train for what may come.

Prepare for what exactly?

That could mean a variety of things, from combat to simple chores. It was best to know who or what she would be up against. That way, Kindra could tailor her training fully aware of what to expect. If Hildr believed Kindra was ready as she was, she would not have told her to keep training and continue her duties.

This is all just confusing. I would like to ask her what she meant tonight. But I should immediately start. It was also her idea to see this new world, be familiar with it, and understand it. And I am curious to see how different we are.

Anna set a plate on the table in front of Kindra. The contents were not entirely unfamiliar to her, and the scent was too good to turn away. Either way, Kindra would be a gratuitous guest and accept the offering.

"So, did they have pancakes where you're from?" Anna asked, taking a seat in front of Kindra with her own plate.

"If you mean we had bread, then yes, though not in a form like this." First, Kindra pokes at the stack of pancakes, finding a hint of amusement at how fluffy they were. Then, clenching two of the flat pieces of bread in one hand, Kindra began chomping down on the whole pancake.

Not until Kindra was more than midway through finishing her second handful of pancakes did she notice Anna staring at her. While consuming what was on her plate, Anna barely took two bites and used utensils.

"Is there something wrong?" Kindra asked as she was chewing her food.

"No, nothing. You must be really hungry."

"It is out of habit, I guess. I was raised to eat quickly so I could get back into the fight as fast as possible or avoid being ambushed by something else that was hungry. Hildr always told me, 'You do not have time to eat. You have time to train'. And if I took too long, we would skip the next meal to exercise instead."

"That sounds like a rough childhood."

"It was to prepare for a tough life. But, after some time, it felt more like a game than a punishment."

"Well, it looks like you can handle anything life throws at you."

"Being physically capable is only part of the solution. There is also the mental aspect that drives it all and even outweighs strength," Kindra said, slowly eating her food this time. "I am starting to sound like Hildr," she softly muttered to herself.

After their quick breakfast, Kindra waited for Anna to change into more suitable attire. Once she stepped out of her room wearing a red sweater and blue pants, Anna stopped to look at Kindra, who had her dagger in hand and shield attached to her wrist.

"Are you seriously bringing those?" Anna asked.

"These are my weapons. They go with me everywhere I go," Kindra simply replied.

"Yeah … but these days, those types of things are not entirely comfortable or common to see out in public. It can draw negative attention."

"Well, I'm not leaving them here," Kindra said, ending their debate.

"Hmm, let me see if I can find something for you." Anna entered the room opposite her bedroom and came out with a small sling backpack. "Here, why don't you just store them in here? So you can carry them with you while not keeping them out of sight."

"That is a fair compromise." Kindra took the bag and gently placed her weapons inside. The weapons would only be used as a final resort since she was more than capable of handling herself with just her hands. Slinging the bag across her body, Kindra said to Anna, "Thank you. Where do we go from here?"

"We're gonna get you some more fitted clothes, and then I'll show you around the city. So, stick close to me."

Anna lead Kindra out of her apartment building back to the street level, where the sleeping city was now active and alive. People of different races, shapes, and sizes roamed in all directions. There were more people here than in the villages of Kindra's time, and she rightfully expected so based on the scale of this city. Yet, Kindra was still captivated by seeing a crowd this large in person.

"C'mon, I know an athletic store not too far away that I think will be more of your thing," Anna said, guiding Kindra along the sidewalk.

Kindra noticed that people would instantly stare at her as she passed through the crowd. While she did not make eye contact with anyone, she could feel their eyes scan her body from top to bottom. Kindra was unsure if it was because of her exposed tattoos on her arms, her physique, the off-putting clothes Kindra was squeezed into, or her dubious curiosity.

Fitting in might be more complex.

CHAPTER TEN

Receiving an urgent call the night before in regards to a breaking-and-entering on Mercer Island, Detective Christopher Miles did a routine check of the scene to gather additional information the patrol responder may have missed. He saw a few workers from the electric company still trying to get the power back on for half of the island that went out abruptly last night. The only word he heard about the cause of the power outage was a freak storm that passed with no one forecasting its arrival. It was of little concern after living on the northwest coast of the United States since it was always wet and raining. Comes with the territory when the weather was controlled by the ocean.

The address brought Miles to a mansion near the western edge of the island, where the view of the front was blocked by tall, well-trimmed hedges. The only way through was a metal gate monitored by one security guard.

The man sure does like his privacy.

Miles pulled up to the guard post, flashing his badge to the man inside. The gate slid open, and he drove onto the wide driveway, where a small palm tree was planted in the center. Miles parked his car directly in front of the house, already noticing Eric McCullough standing outside on his stoop with an agitated look on his face. The expansive mansion was two stories tall and had a grey brick exterior. It was a rather lovely place and one of the better pieces of property on the island.

As he stepped out of the car and approached McCullough, the first thing said to Miles was, "Didn't I already speak to someone from the police department?"

Miles tried to maintain a smile, fully aware that it would take some effort on his end to get McCullough to cooperate.

"Good morning, Mr. McCullough. I'm Detective Miles. And yes, you are correct; you did provide a report regarding the incident on your property. I am here to clarify some information and make sure there was nothing misconstrued in the report," he said, doing his best to sound sincere and polite.

"What, do you not trust your own department on what is sent up?"

"I am just being thorough and checking to see if you remember any of the finer details from your encounter or if you noticed anything else since then."

McCullough crossed his arms across his chest. "Did you catch her yet?"

"Not at this moment, but we do have patrols out looking for the unidentified female. But could you provide me with the details of what you saw and what happened, just so I can get the facts straight from the source and ensure we got everything correct?"

Puffing a mouthful of air, McCullough said, "Fine. Last night when I was going to bed, I heard a loud bang go off in my house. I went to check out what it was, and that is when this random woman appeared and had me pinned against the wall with a fucking knife at my throat."

McCullough took out his notepad from the inner pocket of his coat, flipping through the pages to the notes he received about the case. "You said that woman was Caucasian, standing between five-foot, seven to five-foot, nine inches tall."

"Yeah, around there. She was strong, like freakishly strong."

Miles did some slight nods to show empathy and interest in what McCullough said, but it was not hard to believe someone could push him around. The man had to be a hundred-sixty pounds soaking wet, and it would not be much of an issue to pin him if caught off guard. Some of the female recruits could take him down.

"Did you get a good glance at what she looked like?"

McCullough shook his head. "No, it was too damn dark to get a clear view."

"And I guess there are no other distinguishing marks you could identify?"

Rubbing his chin as he recollected the events of last night, McCullough said, "Uh, well, she did have tattoos of some sort all over her body. I believe they were silver or grey."

"Okay." Miles jotted the description on his notepad. "Any idea what they looked like?"

"Again, it was dark. All I could see was the color."

"Where on the body did you see them? Arms, legs, neck?"

"All over. She was completely naked. She had tattoos on her arms, chest, back, maybe even more places."

Now that's an interesting detail. First time I heard of a naked woman breaking into a home.

"She also spoke in this weird accent. A little high-pitched. It sure as hell was not from around here."

"Did she say anything to you?"

"She sounded confused like she didn't know where she was. She only asked me who I was before she bolted off. She had to be on drugs or somethin'."

"Do you or your neighbors know anyone who fits this profile?" Again, McCullough shook his head. "What about the break-in? Any forced entry into your house?"

"None that I could find. I don't know how she got in. Perhaps through the glass ceiling in my atrium, but there is no easy way of getting up there, and it is at least a twenty-foot drop."

"Do you mind if I take a look inside to see what happened now that we have better lighting?" Miles asked.

Expelling a heavy sigh, McCullough gave Miles a nod and opened the door to his mansion. The initial impression garnered from entering his residence was that this man liked to spend a tremendous amount on priceless artifacts that could be bought. The front door immediately lead to the atrium, where the first thing Miles came across was a ruptured pillar on the ground. Debris was still scattered across the cracked tile floor. A couple of housemaids were busy sweeping the mess, building several piles that look like a field of anthills.

Miles looked up at the ceiling, noticing the large hole through the glass nearly ten feet wide. It was not one single pane of glass that was damaged, but rather multiple, like something blasted right through it. And Miles noticed it was a steep drop with nothing along the walls or close to the opening for someone to safely climb down. Moreover, the hole lay directly over the pillar, so whatever came through would have landed squarely on it.

"This is where it all took place," McCullough said, holding out his arms like presenting a giant art piece to an esteemed audience. The man really could not help himself.

Miles knelt in front of the pillar, touching the remainder of the base. It was hard as stone with different colored layers that run along the inside. "What is this? Petrified wood or something?"

"Yeah, in fact, I just bought it last night. It *was* about nine feet tall when I moved it in here."

His hand slid to the center of the trunk. There was slight moisture over the surface that may have been sprinkled by morning dew, as he never saw petrified wood contain any form of liquid. Some of the shards on the ground were black, appearing charred.

"Was this the only piece of property damage?"

"This and the window where she escaped." He pointed to the side of the atrium, where Miles saw one of the glass panels completely shattered.

Moving to check out the window, the only thing there was left were the hundreds of glass fragments on the lawn directly outside the mansion. McCullough told Miles the woman was completely naked and that she escaped through this window, but there was no blood on the ground or glass. Even an accidental step through a glass door while fully clothed would cause lacerations on the skin. And jumping through glass made to handle the weather in this region was no easy task. He had seen multiple people knocking themselves out from passing through one unintentionally. Looking from the broken window frame to the lawn, the fence line was about forty to fifty feet away from the mansion made of solid brick that must be at least eight feet tall. Nothing around the wall allowed for easy scaling, though it was not entirely impossible to crossover.

"Did she steal anything?" Miles asked.

"Not that I could tell. She just got up and ran when my security guard knocked on the door."

The information recited to Miles had stayed the same as the previous report he provided. He thanked McCullough for his time and returned to his car. Miles had come across many strange stories during his time on the force, some far more enticing than this one. Still, this one here was interesting to hear, nonetheless. Unfortunately, there was little he could go off on based on what he had. The island had been swept for someone fitting the profile for the last few hours, with the bridges passing through the island being monitored. As far as he could tell, the extent of this case would go no further than being a passive search for a suspicious woman with bright-colored tattoos.

Miles would mull over this case with a beer in hand if it were not so early in the day.

Chapter Eleven

"What is this place?" Kindra asked Anna, staring up at the large sign posted on top of the entrance to a store. The vibrant colors and calligraphy were alluring.

"It's where we're gonna modernize your style," she replied, sounding far more excited than Kindra. "Just try not to draw attention to yourself while we're inside."

"I will do my best to be discreet."

The store was quite spacious, containing many clothing, accessories, and equipment. These types of clothing do not appear to be anything Kindra would consider wearing. But it was about something other than what she would prefer. It was about her fitting in with today's society.

"I think you should wear something simple, so you can keep a low profile and still be active," Anna suggested.

She had Kindra try on a variety of styles and sizes of clothes to see what best fits her. Anna already understood that hiding Kindra's unique silver tattoos from sight was a good idea and picked long-sleeve tops. The materials were amazingly soft, a far cry from the thick leather, handmade fabrics, and natural fur of Kindra's day.

Stepping out of the changing room to showcase her new wardrobe, Kindra wore a grey T-shirt with an eagle print in the center. Along with the T-shirt was a white long-sleeve undershirt, and blue pants hug her legs but were not uncomfortably tight.

"What are these?" Kindra asked about the pants she was wearing.

"They're blue jeans. Nice ones, too, since they can stretch and are not as stiff as regular denim," Anna said, holding some clothes over her arm for herself.

Kindra dropped to the floor, performing wide-leg splits to test the tensile strength of the fabric. They surprisingly held well and did not bind anywhere between her legs. Next, she drew her legs together, lifting her body without using her upper body. Then, Kindra transitioned into a front split, feeling the pants stretch when pulled into a different position. Picking herself back up again, Kindra was delighted with the quality. They may pose nicely as adequate fighting garments.

"These will do nicely," Kindra said.

"Yeah … I could tell," Anna replied.

"Wow," said a young woman standing beside the changing room. "You sure do know how to sell a product. And I can see you definitely like to work out."

"Oh yeah, she is crazy about fitness," Anna spoke for Kindra. "You can't get her out of the gym."

Kindra was slightly confused in the conversation as they refer to her, but the woman simply smiled at Anna's joke.

"Then I should really look out for your fitness routine then," she said before entering one of the changing rooms.

Turning her attention towards Anna with a bewildered expression, she just said, "What? Don't worry. It is only a little fun when people ask, and they will ask since you look like a fitness model."

"I am not here to be a strength and conditioning model."

"Yeah, I know. But you can still be inspirational just from your image. If people see that you were able to reach this level of fitness, then they can too. You are pretty much an example of peak physical fitness."

"Example . . ." Kindra whispered, remembering the words of Hildr that were ringing through her ears. Anna may be onto something, as being an example did not have to be based solely on action. "I guess you do have a point."

Selecting a pair of light blue running shoes to complete her outfit, Kindra was now all set to walk among the people of today.

Anna offered to purchase Kindra a winter coat. However, Kindra politely declined the offer as she did not believe it was appropriate for Anna to spend such a luxury item on her. Aside from the expenditure, Elijuna was unbothered by the cold as she had spent time in harsher conditions. But Anna got her a black hoodie as a contingency if Kindra ever changed her mind, along with an extra shirt.

As a show of gratitude, Kindra freely opted to carry the bags as Anna directed her to the next place on their journey. There was a great sense of comfort now, thanks to the new set of clothes that disguises Kindra's presence. Though, she did still catch a few wandering eyes at her of both men and women. Not all battles can be won.

"Where are we going now?" Kindra asked Anna, who was walking a couple of feet in front of her.

"We're gonna check out the market," she replied with contained excitement in her voice.

"Market?" Kindra inquired.

"Yeah, it's pretty much a tourist destination, but once in a while, I'll come across something. Plus, it's a good place for you to kinda get a grasp of the people. We could also get lunch while we're out there."

"Well, food does sound good."

"Great! Now follow me."

Kindra followed her newly acquired friend down the streets. From where they started, the surface began to descend with the sea in the view from where they stood. The closer they got to the coast, the more people presented themselves in public.

"Here we are, the good ol' Pike Place Market," Anna said with her arms expanded towards the large, illuminated sign.

"This is unlike any market I have seen," Kindra said, examining the market's exterior from the corner of the street. She noticed several people standing outside the entrance, making poses and funny faces before moving inside the market.

"Then you should thoroughly enjoy how different it is. C'mon, let's go check it out."

Upon stepping beneath the awning, Kindra found herself in the middle of the elongated market, which was stuffed with people. There was barely enough room to keep people from brushing shoulders with each other. Yet, even as Kindra stood in the center of the hall, everyone walked around her like a stone in a river.

Anna grasped Kindra's hand and guided her through the mass of pedestrians.

The immediate sense that hit Kindra was the aroma of fresh fish and fish being cooked. One of the first partitions housed hundreds of fish, crustaceans, and oysters resting on ice for sale. It was quite a display that looked better than the fish markets Kindra had visited in the past. Many of the aquatic creatures were new to Kindra's eyes, with some quite bigger than the ones she caught as a child.

Further down the market, one seller had rows of bouquets containing such beautifully colored flowers. Kindra took a moment to gaze at the assortment of floral decorations and how neatly packaged they were.

"Wow, these are elegant," Kindra said, touching one of the long-stemmed flowers and feeling the softness of the pedals on her fingertips.

"For someone as big and strong as you, you surely do have a soft side," Anna commented.

"A warrior should always see the beauty in things and not solely focus on fighting," Kindra replied.

"Well, it is nice to see something underneath that hardened exterior."

A rushing pedestrian brushed hard against Anna which caused her to lose her balance and almost fall. Kindra quickly grabbed Anna's arm, stopping her from touching the ground, then carefully lifted her without any hint of effort on Kindra's part.

"Though a hardened exterior does have its benefits," Kindra said as Anna was brought back on her feet.

"Yeah. It sure does help. Thanks though. I should have warned you how busy it would be on the weekend."

"Then I'll be your mountain against the strong winds."

Anna smiled, then returned to strolling down the market.

As Anna said, the market opened Kindra to the various types of people funneling through this narrow hallway. They all seemed generally kind and pleasant to each other, simply viewing the items available for sale. Most held the same curious expression as Kindra, meaning this was a new environment to them as it was to her, however, they were obviously more adept at the setting.

Anna passed another fish partition and brought Kindra in front of a wide fruit stand. Like the flowers, Kindra was mesmerized by the numerous colors and strangely shaped food. Some of the fruit she recognizes. Some were similar to the ones she once had. Berries were berries, but the larger fruit, like the oddly shaped yellow-stranded ones, were new to her.

She picked up a round, purple-colored fruit with a soft outer layer that was quite firm. With the slightest twitch of her hand, Kindra knew she could make it explode. Giving it a quick whiff, she could smell the sweetness nestled inside. Then, without a second thought, Kindra bit a mouthful chunk of the fruit and felt the instant shock of sourness strik her tongue.

Alarmed, Anna quickly spoke to the fruit stand seller, who was keeping careful eyes on the powerful woman. "Don't worry, I'll cover for her." She then turned her attention to Kindra, whispering to her. "Kindra, you have to pay for the food first."

"This is good and juicy but really sour," she said with her mouth full.

"Well, I'm glad you're enjoying it, but please slow down. I don't want you to engorge yourself on fruit."

Kindra nodded and picked up a strange pear-shaped fruit with a bumpy texture on a black waxy surface.

"What is this?" she asked, but before Anna could respond, Kindra bit into the little sustenance.

"That's … an avocado . . ." Anna said, sounding defeated as she watched Kindra devour the avocado with the peel still covering it. The strange act caught the attention of not only the owner but the immediate surrounding individuals in direct view of Kindra. "Yeah … she's not from around here."

"This is really delicious," Kindra said enthusiastically.

"Okay … I'll get you half a dozen of them."

After Anna paid for a bag of avocados and the couple of fruits Kindra sampled, she quickly drove Kindra away from the partition to save herself from further unwanted attention. When they reached one end of the market, Kindra finished the entire avocado.

"Wait, did you just eat the whole thing?" Anna asked.

"Yes, it was quite delicious. Thank you," Kindra replied.

"There was a seed in the center. Did you eat that too?"

"I think so. There was something crunchy inside."

"Huh. I guess your strength lies in more than just your extremities. Normally, avocados are not eaten raw like that. Usually, it is scooped out, turned into a paste, and eaten as a sauce."

"Nonetheless, it was a rather tasty snack."

"Well then, do you still have an appetite?" Anna asked.

"I am open to enjoying more of your culture's food," Kindra replied to Anna's question.

"Good. I have a hankering for some fish, and I know a nice spot in the market."

At a separate area of the market, there was a small shop selling fish and cooked meals. Kindra thoroughly enjoyed the smell of grilled fish combined with the various ingredients and cooking methods.

"I thought I'd start you off with something simple. So I ordered you some fish and chips."

"I cannot wait," Kindra said.

There was a decent line to place an order and a relatively large number of people at the shop, thus fueling Kindra's curiosity about their attraction to this place. While waiting for their meals, they stay away from the crowd by huddling in the corner of the shop. Even if out of direct view, Kindra knew she was still drawing people's attention.

Why is everyone looking at me? Is there something that I am doing that singles me out as an outsider? I figured the clothes would hide my physique, yet I appear like a flame attracting fluttering moths.

"Order number fifty-eight!" yelled out one of the cooks.

"Oh, that's us!" Anna exclaimed, rushing to claim their food.

They sat at a little bar provided by the shop, which faced the part that sold fresh fish. Locked in the parlor was a slender young woman no older than Kindra, working behind the counter. She worked tirelessly to serve her customers, wearing only a worn blue sweatshirt, faded black pants, and an abrasion flat-billed hat. They might as well be battle armor. Her movements were strict and swift, displaying a tremendous amount of confidence, and the young woman reacted smoothly to the orders. Kindra was impressed by her work ethic and believed that if this woman was around in her time, she would be a talented warrior.

With the food finally presented to her inside a foam box, a pause was given before Kindra could eat. She saw six bread-like bricks with lengthy cut potatoes, or at least she thought they were potatoes.

"Um … where is the fish?" Kindra asked.

"It's right there. They're breaded and deep-fried," Anna said, pointing to the breaded patties.

"This is the fish?" Kindra cracked open one of the patties, noticing the layered meat steaming inside. Quickly stuffing the cooked fish in her mouth, the intense heat incinerated her tongue, but she kept her stone expression on her face.

"Kindra, wasn't that hot?" Anna asked, concerned but also curious.

"It was blazing," Kindra simply replied. "I like it."

"Oh … well, I'm glad you like it."

It took only a short time for Kindra to finish her entire meal, prompting Anna to quicken her pace to not leave Kindra stalling. Once they finished, Kindra wanted to gander at the fish on display now that the crowd had died down.

She always found sea life fascinating and mysterious for what lies beneath the waves. When Hildr made her swim in the sea, Kindra would dive as deep as she could to find seashells and colorful fish. For a time, it made her training a bit more enjoyable in her youth.

"I hope you're not planning on taking a bite of the fish," Anna teased, though Kindra was sure she was worried about her committing the act.

"No. I already had my fill for this afternoon. I prefer my fish either cooked or still fighting," Kindra replied.

"You're joking, right? Was that a joke?"

Kindra gave Anna a smirk at the corner of her mouth. Anna chuckled nervously, unsure how to accept Kindra's comment as truth.

"Well, I guess that is how a warrior like you entertains yourself."

"Amongst other things."

"Uh-huh. Well, how about a treat? I could go for a latte right about now," Anna replied, still holding her joyful attitude.

"Latte?" Kindra inquired, hoping she pronounced it right.

Anna spun around on her heels to face Kindra, saying as she walked backward, "It's a type of coffee which is like the staple drink of this city. So if you never had it before, you are gonna be in for a shock."

"What is it? Like some type of mead?"

"No … it's non-alcoholic, though that is an available option to add to your coffee if you'd like."

"Well, I will try it your way," Kindra said with a gentle grin and hopped around. As she made a complete turn, Anna unintentionally bumped into a middle-aged man walking in the opposite direction on the sidewalk, knocking a drink out of his hand. "Oh, sorry!"

"Watch where you're fuckin' going!" he shouted into her face.

Anna immediately showered the man with apologies, but he did not care for anything she had to say.

"Excuse me, but she has apologized. It was an accident—" Kindra stepped in but was quickly cut off from completing her statement.

"You shut the fuck up too!" he shouted, directing his frustration towards Kindra.

Tightening her jaw, Kindra dropped the shopping bags and took two steps forward in front of the man. She could see the anger in his eyes as they lock with hers, and despite being a grown man, Kindra sensed a child's attitude within him.

"It's okay, Kindra," Anna pleaded.

"What are you gonna do? Hit me?" he said, trying to provoke Kindra to make a move. "C'mon! I don't care if you are a girl. I'll fuckin' beat you down!"

Kindra's muscles tightened, and her fists clenched white as she stood her ground. Apparently, this person had no qualms about getting into a fight.

"Please, Kindra. He isn't worth it. Be an example, remember?" Anna said, trying to dissuade her from fighting, and picked up the bags off the floor.

An example … He should be treated as an example for his disrespectful tone.

Anna lightly tugged on Kindra's arm for her to move away from the situation before things escalated and caused a disturbance.

As Kindra allow Anna to guide her, the disgruntled man jumped right in front of her, unwilling to let this incident slip by.

"Where the fuck do think you're going?" He instigated, refusing to leave them be.

"Step. Aside." The words left Kindra's mouth with no inflection and sounded like a final warning.

He did not move and said, "What the fuck are you gonna do?"

Saliva spurts from his mouth, sprinkling over her face. Kindra had had enough of this stranger's pestering and disgrace.

"I said, move!" Then, using only the palm of her hand, she shoved the belligerent stranger away against the wall several feet from her. It was quick, powerful, and effortless on Kindra's part. The man said nothing more as he was astonished by the prod of her hand like she pushed a child. The air was quickly forced from his lungs.

"Let's go, Kindra, quickly." Anna tugged harder on the Valkyrie as if she was pulling on a boulder lodged in the earth.

The city was a deranged mess of loud noises, dense congregations, impure air, and crumpled earth. Urd tried to walk amongst the crowd of ordinary mortals. However, she quickly found that to be an impossible feat because of her golden hair and white complexion. The collection of people had brown skin and solid black hair, making Urd a more prominent figure.

She wanted to avoid unwarranted attention during her observation. Due to her appearance, everyone in the immediate view of Urd treated her with intrigue. She was familiar with the experience of admiration and praise, yet their stares were not the same. They hold any interest because she was a foreigner to these lands. None of them know of her, so they would have no reason to think of her beyond a normal human being.

Urd had forgotten what it felt like to be a nobody and to not have anyone, god or man, beseech her or her sisters to spare the life of a loved one. It grew tiring to hear the same pleas, cries, and attempts to bargain. Some of the stories that were told touched Urd's heart, and she averted their demise for the time being, but not everyone could divert fate and not all were immune to death. Even the Gods know this.

Moving through the city was beyond a simple task, partly due to the mass of people crammed on the narrow streets. Another troubling issue was that the locals continuously beg Urd for money or food. Being someone that obviously was not from here, their perception of her was she was someone of wealth. She could hear them speak to each other, thinking Urd could not understand them.

She did her best to ignore them, pushing their empty hands that were held out away from her. Yet, every age group, from children who barely learned to walk to the elderly who could hardly walk themselves, pressed Urd into giving something. What they were begging for was not her typical request and was rather odd to hear.

Not willing to say anything, Urd flicked her hand to shoo them away, yet they do not leave, at least not all of them. Those that understood her gesture were quickly replaced with someone else and continued to thwart her progress.

Enough stifling.

The sea of people following her every step was beginning to annoy Urd, and their persistence for a handout, despite her refusal, was unmannerly when in the grace of a Norn. She wanted to be left uninterrupted while she saw the world.

Reaching into the pocket of her tunic, the crowd smiled with their eyes growing wide in excitement as they had finally cracked Urd. Anxiously waiting to receive some form of offering she was carrying, the few standing in front of her push closer with their hands fully extended. From Urd's pocket was not what they were expecting: it was a small spool of red thread. Their short-lived eagerness quickly dissipated, with some retracting their hands in disgust. Urd wrapped the thread from the spool around her left thumb, then proceeded to wrap each finger without cutting the thread. Holding up her hand with her fingers spread, it tightened the thread. The crowd exchanged looks of confusion as to what Urd was doing. With her other hand, she pointed to four people in front of her: a middle-aged man, a young woman, an elderly man, and a little boy. Tracing her finger over the red thread, it glows a bright orange. Her audience became amazed at the spectacle, like Urd was performing a magic trick for them.

Using her fingernail, Urd cut one of the segments of the thread. The middle-aged man she previously pointed to suddenly dropped to the floor without even expelling a final breath. Everyone screamed after witnessing the phenomenon caused by Urd, pushing over themselves to get away from her. She continued to cut the thread, seeing the bodies she singled out collapse in mid-motion.

As the overly dense crowd quickly dispersed, leaving only Urd to remain on the street, she took a long-awaited deep breath.

"Finally," Urd grumbled.

In only a couple thousand years did she not expect mankind to grow so fast and to this extent. Also, within that time, mankind forgot about the Norns, the role they govern, and why the gods were no longer present. Therefore, she was quite surprised that her powers over fate could still be applied outside the world they once inhabited.

Hopefully, my sisters have come across something more appealing.

What Urd had seen on her first stop in the modern world had left her unimpressed.

Chapter Twelve

Moving several blocks from their previous encounter, Anna brought Kindra inside a small corner cafe. The powerful aroma contained inside such a small establishment was a blow to Kindra's senses. She could even taste the bitter scent on her tongue from every inhale.

Anna slowly returned to her normalcy once they entered the cafe. Kindra did not fully understand her concern to urgently evade the scene. It was evident by the man's silence and shock that she had won their little battle. The result was not as satisfying as she hoped but Kindra did get her point across.

"Are you doing well, dear Anna?" Kindra asked.

"Y-yeah, I'll be fine. Just give me a moment."

It was apparent that Anna did not favor confrontation, which was not something Kindra condemns. People react differently to various situations, especially stress-induced events. Even in her time, not everyone was a fighter nor supported the concept of war and battle.

"You know I could have handled that man back there," Kindra tried to assure Anna to calm her down.

"Yes, I know … it's just … let's just take it easy for a little bit. All right?"

Kindra nodded to Anna's request, letting the woman settle herself and take a breather.

After Anna went ahead and placed their orders, they moved to the patio to converse without anyone eavesdropping on their conversation. Since it was winter, only a few people were willing to sit outside.

"Hey, I wanna thank you again for sticking up for me. No one has really ever done that before," Anna said sincerely.

"It was my pleasure. Someone needed to show him the consequences of being rude. Thankfully, I was there and am quite a fair teacher." Kindra smiled, which shed its way onto Anna. Seeing such a shift in Kindra's assertive demeanor was instead a shock to Anna as she always imagined her to maintain a serious composure.

"Too bad I'm not as headstrong as you. Otherwise, I'd do the same."

"Oh, I am confident you are just as capable. You only need to unlock that inner part of yourself, that inner strength to confront others directly. You do not have to resolve issues with only your fists. That should be when communication has failed. Some people, like him, are unwilling to open up a dialogue."

"Yeah, I see your point. But if or when a fight does happen, I do not think I am prepared to throw down, even if it's against another woman."

"You only need practice. It is true that if you do get into a fight, always expect to get hit yourself. Even if you are winning, be ready to feel pain. You need to embrace it, understand the pain, and not fear it."

Anna brushed her bangs away from her eyes. "I feel like you've been in a lot of fights for you to be so wise on the subject."

"I have faced many battles, and there was a time when there were more losses than victories by the hundreds. Every battle won was a testament to my skill, proving what worked and the next level I need to achieve. Every failure was a lesson learned, showing me the areas I needed to improve upon and giving me insight on unsuccessful techniques in combat."

"You make it sound like a fond memory."

Kindra rubbed her right bicep, feeling the hardened muscle. She had forgotten how far she had come over the years. "Those were fond memories, and I surely do miss them."

"Well, we should probably go over some ground rules while we're here. A big one is to not get into a fistfight, not only because it will draw attention but because of legal issues. Here in the United States, we do not advocate violence. A person who strikes another is considered assault, and that is considered a crime."

Kindra gruffed at the idea that two people could not settle their differences with physical communication. Sometimes a lesson was adequately learned through pain in the same way it was known that fire burns if you touch it.

"Yeah, I know. The world has certainly changed. In some ways, good, and in others ... Well, they could use some work. For now, just know that you shouldn't hit someone if they say something that you disagree with or are vulgar. We have a thing called 'freedom of speech' in this country which grants us the right to say whatever we want—well, mostly. But if someone touches you, then the game changes. You still have the right to defend yourself and prevent any unwanted sexual assault."

"That seems reasonable but also very restraining," Kindra commented.

"We pride ourselves in thinking we have evolved into a well-mannered, civilized society. Overcoming years of settling scores through violence into a world built upon law and order where criminals are treated fairly, which is subjective. It's a complicated matter and becomes more complicated as time goes on. Even though laws are supposed to make us civil, we have reverted into our own form of barbarism where bureaucracy, fines, and legal disputes can ruin someone's livelihood."

"You do not sound overly supportive of your society."

"It's all right, I guess. There are still worse places out there. But honestly, things have greatly changed, not just from your time, but from when my parents' and even grandparents' time. I'm honestly grateful for living here. Believe it or not, there was a time when people were polite and considerate of one another."

A female cafe worker approached their table, carrying with her two large white cups in her hands. "All right, here are your two vanilla lattes."

"Ooh, yes!" Anna could hardly contain her own excitement. However, her eyes remained fixated on the hot beverage in front of her, and even as the server asked if there was anything else they would like, Anna quickly answered without shifting her eyes.

Kindra was curious why Anna was so exhilarated by a simple drink, especially one lacking the potent ingredient of alcohol. "I hope you're ready to have your senses knocked out."

"It does not seem like anything special," Kindra said, grasping the cup in front of her.

The warmth from the paper cup was the first thing she noticed, letting her gauge how hot it would be to ingest. Anna already brought the cup to her mouth, slowly tipping it just enough to take a sip. The moment the liquid touched her tongue, Anna drew back her cup.

"Oh, that's hot!" she said but remained positive.

Kindra brought the cup to her lips, feeling the immense heat coming through the tiny opening. A whiff of the mysterious concoction presented a sweet scent, smelling almost like cinnamon. She put her lips over the opening and tipped the cup, nearly leveling it with the ground and letting the latte flow like a spring into her mouth. The heat was intense, yet she did not let it overpower her ability to consume the drink. The mixture of bitter and sweet flavors was a unique sensation as she gulped down the latte. The warmth was soothing, especially against the brisk weather. Once the cup ran dry, she placed it down on the table, taking a moment to capture the full lingering taste clinging to her tongue.

"Didn't that burn?" Anna asked.

"It was excruciating but tasteful. I can see why this is a favorite of yours."

"Yes, well, normally, people would just sip it and relax. Though I must say, I do admire your pain tolerance. That is not something I will try myself. I bet you could eat burning coals and not wince."

With a slight grin, Kindra said, "I do not recommend it."

Anna nodded with a smile. Then, after taking a sip of her latte, she asked Kindra, "What do you plan on doing while you're here?"

"Honestly, I do not know. I can survive on my own, but not in a setting like this. Anyways, I need to fulfill my duties as a Valkyrie no matter where I am."

"And what are your duties? I mean, I heard the stories and read about them last night, but are they true, and are they still applicable today?"

The questions brought upon by Kindra were something she would need to think about since she was unsure how to proceed with her role. Was it something that she could still do alone?

"As with all Valkyries, we are to escort the spirits of the fallen in battle to glorious Valhalla or, if need be, to Hel."

"That seems like a lot of pressure and power for just one person. This might come from the values and beliefs of today, but it doesn't seem right for someone that does not know you to ultimately judge where you go in the afterlife," Anna said.

"They were our ways. To us, dying in battle, regardless of fighting for a noble cause or satisfying an insatiable acquisitive nature, was an honor and held in high esteem. Putting forth your life, the one life you are granted, is considered an act of bravery and should be rewarded, no matter the intention. Is that not what you believe?"

"Eh, it's a bit more complicated. I see where you are coming from, but for other religions, there is the belief in one God. One almighty and powerful God created the universe, and it is He who passes judgment on where a person's soul is to go. That'd be either heaven or hell, our version of hell."

"Is this what you believe?" Kindra asked, sounding curious rather than condescending.

"Yes … to an extent. I'm not a religious person by any means, but it is what I have been taught."

Kindra tapped her left thumb over the table. "And this god, does he have a name?"

"It's just God. Nothing else other than that."

"Have you seen your god?"

"Um, no … have you seen Odin?"

"No, I have not. But I have seen his son, Thor, once. He swung his mighty hammer, Mjolnir, into a glacier, splitting it in half like a log. I was supposed to meet Odin in Asgard and swear my oath to him when I awakened."

Anna took another sip of her latte, this time a longer one, while forgoing the burning content. "Well, we base our religion on belief, not sight. It is the invisible hand of fate from God where we come to witness His involvement."

"I see," Kindra said, but as she said that, she could see Anna appear disheartened. "I apologize, Anna. I meant no disrespect to your culture or your beliefs. I find it fascinating that there are different gods out there that I have never heard of. If you believe it is real, then it is."

"Thanks, Kindra. No offense taken."

"In order for me to truly be among you, I must know more about this world and carry an open mind."

"That is a good first step—" Before Anna could finish her sentence, a loud crash nearby interrupted their conversation.

"What was that?" Kindra asked, trying to pinpoint the origin.

"Sounded like a car crash. Pretty close from the sound of it," Anna replied, cupping her latte in both hands.

"We should check it out."

"What?! No way, it'll be crawling with police by the time we get there, plus they're the ones who will handle it."

Kindra stood up from the table and said with great enthusiasm. "I need to see what this is about firsthand. Now let's go." Kindra grabbed Anna by the wrist, pulling her from her seat and carrying Anna over the patio fence.

"There's a door, you know?!" Anna exclaimed, but the words were too late as Kindra hopped over the fence with Anna in her arms.

"Where's the crash?"

"Uh, I don't know, it sounded like a block away. Go that way." She pointed north, and Kindra ran while carrying Anna, who was still gingerly cradling the latte in her hands.

Chapter Thirteen

The weight of the small woman was of no consequence to Kindra. She might as well weigh no heavier than a rabbit in her arms. Rapidly traversing the city block, they come across a highway crammed with vehicular traffic. Beneath the highway was a large red truck and another white truck, flashing their lights as they cut off a lane on the street.

Kindra placed Anna on the sidewalk, where they have a direct view of the incident.

"Are these the police that you mentioned?" she asked Anna.

"No, those are firefighters and paramedics, but they are still first responders when it comes to emergencies." Anna squinted at the collision to get a better look at the details. It appeared to be two cars infused together with a red car that collided with the driver's side of a black car. It took Anna a moment to see through the crumpled metal to recognize the label on the side of the black car. "I think *that's* a police car."

The group of firefighters assessed the scene but did not appear confident of the condition of the people inside the collided vehicles. The number of spectators grew exponentially on the same street corner with Kindra and Anna. Everyone monitored the scene with their own devices, taking pictures or recording the incident.

"We should help," Kindra strongly suggested.

"Uh, no. That's not a good idea. Those guys are professionals. They can handle this type of situation," Anna quickly refuted.

There was a fair amount of dread in Kindra's heart as she could only observe from afar, feeling entirely useless. From Anna's voice, Kindra could understand her confidence in the first responders to fulfill their role. However, she would still like to offer her assistance in some way.

As Kindra watched the wreckage being pried open, she saw a figure stepping out of the black vehicle. There was something off about this person. The shape was that of a man, but an aura surrounded him, swaying in the air like thin smoke. He appeared to be disoriented from how his feet shuffle over the ground, and having trouble holding up his head as he sluggishly walked. None of the other first responders noticed him walk away from the incident. His clothing was dark blue for both the shirt and pants, with identical crests embroidered on the shoulders. It appeared to be a uniform similar to the firefighters and paramedics, but not entirely the same.

"Do police wear a blue uniform?" Kindra asked Anna as her eyes followed the man.

"Yeah, why do you ask?" Kindra pointed to the individual stumbling down the street, completely ignoring all the bystanders in front of him. "What are you pointing at? I don't see anything."

"The man in the blue uniform walking. Do you honestly not see him?"

"No, I don't. Are you sure you're not seeing something else?"

Kindra ignored Anna's comment and began following the policeman down the street. Anna immediately trailed behind, doing her best to keep up with Kindra's long stride. Breaking through the crowd, Kindra maintained a direct view of the policeman as he shuffles off the sidewalk onto the road while moving in the same direction. She crossed through the street, disregarding the moving traffic and the honking that ensued from her ignorance.

Kindra caught up with the policeman, who appeared lost.

"Are you well?" she asked him.

The policeman slowly turned around to face Kindra. He struggles to hold himself up and had to support his weight on one leg to remain still. "W-what happened? Can … Can you help me? I-I don't know where I am …" he said, sounding exhausted.

"What is your name?"

"It's … it's, uh … God, what is my name? Ugh, I'm so tired," he muttered, rubbing his head as he tried to remember his name.

Kindra looked at his uniform and noticed a golden nameplate over his right breast.

"Is it Wilkins?" she asked.

"Y-yes … Yes! Anthony Wilkins. I'm a police officer for … for the Seattle Police … Department."

"I am sorry to be the one to inform you, but I do believe you have perished," Kindra said, doing her best to display genuine empathy.

"You mean I'm dead? No-no, I can't be. I was just on patrol. I-I need to go home. I need to see my wife … my son … ."

Kindra took one step closer to the police officer and said to him, "You gave your life in the service of your duties. Valhalla calls for you, and you will meet your family in the afterlife."

Officer Wilkins examined his hands, taking a moment to finally realize that Kindra's words were true. He reached for the golden badge clipped onto his shirt, removing it from his person and holding it out in one hand. "I guess I will no longer need this. Thank you."

The badge was passed to Kindra, who graciously accepted it in her hand. Then, placing her other hand over his, Kindra softly said, "May you find everlasting peace."

The man blew away like ash in the wind, leaving only his badge behind in Kindra's possession.

"Kindra!" Anna called out, trying to desperately catch her attention. "Are you okay? You need to get off the street." She tugs Kindra back onto the sidewalk to let the cars continue unimpeded. "What's going on? You were talking to thin air."

"No, I was speaking to a police officer."

Anna cocked an eyebrow as she was not following what Kindra said. "You mean like a ghost or something?"

"He died during the car crash, and his spirit remained on this plane of existence, possibly to wander forever if not intervened." Kindra turned to face

Anna, then presents the badge handed to her. "His name was Anthony Wilkins, and he left me this."

Anna's jaw dropped with her eyes shifting from the badge in Kindra's hand to her eyes, then back to the badge. "This is a police officer's badge. D-did he really give you this?"

"Yes, he did. I am honored to receive it. He is the first person I ever granted a Passover to Valhalla." Kindra was engulfed with a sense of pride that she had never felt before. It was a humbling experience to be the one person to decide where a spirit was to go for all of eternity. She did not doubt that it was a wrong decision. Still, she knew she would eventually encounter more challenging situations that may change her morals.

Kindra placed the badge into her backpack for safekeeping. Then, looking back at the crash site, she could see the paramedics pushing a stretcher with a white tarp covering the body.

"I am fulfilling my duties as a Valkyrie, and that was only the first of many," Kindra said. "Anna, I know this is a strange thing to ask but is there a location away from the city where I can train without being seen?"

Anna took a deep sigh, giving herself a moment to think. "Well, there are plenty of places outside Seattle that are mostly wooded where you can conduct your training." She pulled out her cell phone and brought up a map of the city. "See, this is Seattle. We are here. Now, there are national parks to the west, east, and southeast. Around this time of year, there shouldn't be many people."

"I will venture southeast then," Kindra said, studying the ample greenery and snow-covered mountain.

"Okay … well, how about this? Why don't we get you settled with some camping supplies? Then I can drop you off in the woods so you can do your training."

A little smirk was shown on her face. "That would be greatly appreciated. Though, I am efficient enough to survive on my own in the wilderness."

"And I do not doubt that, but it could help you out a bit. You wouldn't have to spend additional time foraging for food or making a shelter."

"You do make a good argument. Only the bare necessities, then."

Chapter Fourteen

"This place is disgusting," Skuld murmured, doing her best to avoid the foul people roaming aimlessly on the street. Nothing but tents lined the street, covered in filth and pieces of trash being carried by the wind.

Skuld was in disbelief at how mankind "progressed" to this wretched existence. Even the hundreds of generations that have lived before them had better living conditions. At least the people that worshipped them took baths regularly. The inhabitants, in eye view, appear to enjoy the grime that lathers them, holding no regard for the thoughts of others.

"Hey, lady!" said one of the dwellers from the street, hobbling over to Skuld with an exaggerated limp. It was a middle-aged man wearing worn and damaged clothing that was just as dirty as his skin. "Do you got a dolla'?" he asked.

Skuld stared at him, cocking an eyebrow at his inquiry. Then, finally, she asked, "Why are you bothering me?"

"Bitch, I was just asking for a fuckin' dollar. Do you have any money?" he said.

Clenching her jaw, Skuld had never been disrespected by a mortal in person. Throughout the centuries, these inferior beings would beg and offer whatever they had to extend their pointless lives. Even if their end was not expected for decades at a ripe old age, they would try to gain favor.

Skuld grabbed this homeless man's wrist in one hand. "What the fuck are yo—"

Her hand glowed yellow from where she touched the man, cutting him off mid-sentence.

"Hmm, three years, two months, thirteen days. Even I am surprised at the outcome," Skuld said.

"W-what are you talkin' about?" he questioned, but Skuld ignored what he had to say.

"Such a waste of time and human potential," Skuld grumbled. "With no purpose to your existence, I see it is just to end it sooner than predicted."

Skuld drove her index finger into his chest, straight through the sternum, and into his heart. The breath inside him was pushed out, and any lingering air capacity drains from his body. The homeless man's eyes were gaping wide with his jaw slanted open. Skuld pressed her finger all the way through until her knuckles brush against his chest.

"My, how soft has your kind become?" Skuld whispered. Such a deadly maneuver was never much of a challenge for Skuld. Something like this would make her feel like she was pushing her finger through soft snow, but this man was easier than mortals before him. To Skuld, it was now like she dipped her finger through warm water since there was no resistance.

She drew back her hand and watched as the blood pumps from outside his body onto the asphalt. A choking sound was all the man could produce before he collapsed to the ground. Skuld felt nothing for the man except a sense of relief to be rid of his constant pestilence. To her, this man's life was no more significant than that of an insect where it had no meaning or good purpose and had become a hindrance to the rest of mankind.

As his body quickly succumbed to the immense damage to his heart, the other individuals on the street who were in similar circumstances stood shocked and in disbelief.

Urd will be disappointed in my actions, but I do not see any harm in it. All I am doing is cleaning up some of the mess left behind. It looks like this city could use it.

Skuld approached the next tent connected with trash and held up by rope against a chain-link fence. She drew a solid black dagger from her sleeve that fit perfectly in her hand. Cutting diagonally against the thin fabric, Skuld saw a woman lying on the floor in a fetal position wearing thick cold-weather clothing to protect herself from the brisk elements.

"What the fuck do you want?" the woman grumbled, not moving her head to see Skuld's intrusion, only feeling the cool air touching her skin to know her tent was open.

"I bid you farewell," Skuld said, holding no empathy or emotional inflection in her voice.

The unfamiliar voice startled the homeless woman, shifting herself upright to see Skuld standing through her self-made entryway.

"Who the fuck are y—" Skuld swiftly thrust the dagger into the woman's throat, silencing her before she could finish her sentence.

As Skuld stared into the woman's eyes full of fear that were shaking while trying to focus on Skuld, she wanted to desperately tell this woman she was one of the Norns. Though Skuld was very confident that no one knew of their existence, simply uttering her name would hold no bearing. It was pointless to enlighten a person, or people in general, of their role and the power they harness when they contain no respect for each other. A patient lecturer was also a characteristic absent from Skuld. She had a hard enough time tolerating Verdandi's immature antics. Skuld was unwilling to waste her time on a lifespan that ends in the blink of an eye.

The woman's life promptly slipped away from the excessive blood spilling from her neck. Only a gurgling cry slipped out of her mouth, and the blood bubbled from her throat as her last breath exited her body. Skuld removed the dagger and wiped the blood on the woman's sleeve.

Leaving the tent, Skuld immediately noticed the neighboring pedestrians watching her. There were dozens of them standing on both sides of the street in complete silence.

Skuld gingerly pointed her dagger towards an older man in his forties close to ten feet away, giving him a devious smile that could send shivers through a stone. "You are next."

The man spun around with his long grey hair swinging behind him and yelled, "Help! Help! This crazy bitch is gonna kill me!"

Skuld dropped her smile, trading it for an expression of pure displeasure, then launched the dagger with her arm fully extended. The small blade flew with such precision and velocity that it struck Skuld's next target in the back between the shoulder blades. She did not need to see exactly where it landed as Skuld was fully aware the knife severed his spine. After enough practice, she could deliver such a lethal kill blindfolded. Even coming from a thousand-year slumber, the muscle memory and familiarity of the sound itself have remained unaltered in her mind.

"It is such a delight that my skills have not degraded, unlike humanity," she said with a hint of glee ringing in her voice.

A large vehicle with bright flashing lights strolled down the street behind Skuld and made one blaring sound to notify everyone of its presence. Turning around to face the car, Skuld saw two men step out onto the street. They both wore identical black clothing as a uniform, each having a badge over their left breast on top of a thick black vest.

"All right, I need everyone to pack it up! You're movin'—" One of the men, a young fellow who was still in his mid-twenties with short blond hair and a thin frame, immediately freezes at the sight of the man Skuld killed.

"Is that a dead body?" His partner asked who appeared near the same age, give or take a couple of years, and stood shorter with a broader build and brunette hair.

The blond man reached for something on his belt that Skuld could not see from where she stood.

"You seem like you have some authority here," Skuld said to them with intrigue.

"Were you involved in this man's death?"

Skuld huffed a breath of air, replying to him, "*Man?* That was anything but. His life held no value or purpose, meaning it did not warrant to exist."

"Stay where you are. Get down on your knees and put your hands behind your head!" ordered the shorter man.

Skuld rebuked their demands. "You expect me to kneel to you?! A mortal?! How repulsive!"

She drew back her right hand while keeping her attention on the two men standing before her. The dagger dislodged itself from Skuld's recent victim, returning to its owner under her command, and directed the knife into the blond man's throat. He did not see the black-colored blade dart through the air as it blended with the dim evening sky. Clutching his neck near the point where the dagger protrudes from his flesh and blood dripping from the opening, he fell over on his back, overwhelmed in shock.

The second uniformed man drew out his weapon, holding it out with one hand and reaching for a device attached to his shoulder.

Skuld threw out her arm and launched another dagger hidden within her sleeve, striking the shorter man in the center of his forehead. He topples backward onto the street dead before his back hit the surface.

"Your life is accepted as payment for your disrespect," Skuld muttered. Screams were coming down the street, with people scurrying away from her. "I guess I can do a little cleansing before moving on."

Holding out her hands, the daggers were drawn from the shorter man's skull and the blond man's throat. Blood gushed from the narrow slit, and he desperately tried to apply pressure over the wound, yet Skuld already knew he was a dead man.

Chapter Fifteen

While Kindra would have been perfectly fine to venture towards the park alone, Anna insisted on delivering her there herself. The car ride was a more challenging undertaking than Kindra would have thought. Although she had to overcome the strange sense of motion sickness in the first half-hour, Kindra convinced herself it was like sitting in a carriage or onboard a ship. After that, it became tolerable, though the car was much faster and without constant rocking.

The city structures dwindled in scope and complexity the further they traveled. Yet, seeing the bundle of nature that continued to grow in the presence of modern man fills her heart with excitement. Almost like a return to her homeland. Almost.

Only driving around an hour and a half from Seattle, Anna found an adequate stop at a T-intersection to drop Kindra off.

"Are you sure you want to do this? Staying out here all on your own in the middle of winter?" Anna asked, making sure it was what Kindra wanted.

"I am sure. I experienced much harsher weather in my youth. To me, this is almost like a blooming spring. I will manage," Kindra unwaveringly replied.

"Well, I'll pick you up in three days at this exact spot around noon. That should give you two full days on your own. Now don't get yourself into trouble while you're out here," Anna said.

Kindra nodded as she stepped out of the car with a backpack carrying all her supplies slung over her shoulder. The air was much colder and free-roaming under the open wind than nestled in the city.

Before closing the door, she faces Anna and said, "You take care of yourself while I am away."

As she watched Anna's dark blue car turned around and drive down the road, disappearing around the bend of the tree line, Kindra stepped into the woods. The sweet scent of pine was a glamorous sensation combined with the growing frost surrounding her. Such silence was a neglected desire now that she was away from the clashing noises and various conversations that stressed her senses.

This patch of nature would do well for Kindra. It would help her settle herself more gradually than her initial entry into the present and focus her mind on training rather than other distractions.

Moving deeper into the dense woods, Kindra tried to forget what she had seen of the developed city and everything inside to better remind herself of the simple life she once had. While the technology was truly fascinating and simplified matters, hard work builds a person to be stronger and more resilient.

Kindra found a decent spot for her to make camp once nightfall arrives. For now, she placed the backpack beneath a layer of snow in the center of a bundle of trees. She carved her specific rune into the bark of one of the trees to help identify where she placed her belongings for later. However, it was unnecessary as Kindra had had a strong sense of direction since Hildr instilled it into her as a child.

As the sky was still bright and warm, Kindra started her training by sprinting through the woods, going as hard and fast as she could to test her speed and see how long she could maintain it. A fight for her life would push Kindra to her peak limits, and as a new Valkyrie, she must know the extent of her capabilities.

The ice-cold air entering Kindra's lungs was a powerful reminder of the many days she had spent running through the woods of her homeland. Kindra wanted nothing more than to return to those days, even if it meant she had to endure further pain and denounce her title as a Valkyrie.

The heat rose from the world's surface, with the sun producing a blinding light far greater than when Verdandi last stepped foot on Midgard. However, she did find pleasure in being free of the well's confinement for her and her sisters. Even though Verdandi was the Norn of the present with the ability to see the world in its current state, it was not equal to seeing it for herself. A beautiful painting did not fully capture the magnificence of the portrayed image.

Through the windows she created, Verdandi could not feel the passing breeze, the scent of the air, or the ubiquitous sounds stemming from life within a city. Verdandi had always favored experiencing a location firsthand rather than seeing it from afar. Urd had preferred Verdandi to use her abilities to occasionally glimpse at the world of man and the gods in Asgard to see what they were doing at that moment. Verdandi was not particularly fond of intruding on someone's personal life, yet she could not abandon her responsibilities. None of them could.

As she traveled along the coast, Verdandi enjoys the warm sprinkles of water splashing against the shore. Just from the mist touching her skin, she could feel the heavy salt content and how different the waters were from her homeland.

Further along the coastline in front of her was a dilapidated city that had expanded further inland. A black trail of smoke as thick as the night sky traverses into the air, far more significant than a simple forest fire.

Walking in the opposite direction of Verdandi were women and children who appear disheveled from their worn clothing and dirt-covered bodies. As she passed them, they would halt and stare at her with bewilderment, and Verdandi would do the same as she had never seen these types of people before. They were slim, almost malnourished, and have an incredibly dark complexion like coal.

Verdandi waved and smiled at each one of the locals that she walked past, but they remained perfectly still and fixed their eyes on her. Even though they were a curious bunch, the locals seemed rather timid and harmless.

A green-colored roaming object moved in her direction in the distance, where the radiating heat could be seen sizzling from the earth. Verdandi watched as it quickly traveled over the desert road. It did not take long for it to catch up to her and immediately stopped directly in front of her. Verdandi could almost smell the metal and the fumes from it. Four men hopped out of the vehicle, each wearing a different camouflage garment soaked with sweat.

"Who are you? What are you doing out here?" commanded one of the men wearing a faded green blouse with the sleeves cut off. In their hands was an unmistakable weapon of some sort made of wood and metal, though without a blade. Verdandi was curious about how it worked.

"Oh, I'm just a visitor from a distant land passing through," Verdandi said joyfully.

The small group quickly glanced at each other with confusing expressions on their faces. "How do you know our language?"

"I know many tongues," she replied with conviviality.

"Then you will come with us."

"Unfortunately, I will travel on my own," she politely declined.

The man pulled the lever on his weapon, making a loud mechanical click. From Verdandi's perspective, it may have the same symbolism as drawing out a sword in a threatening manner. The others of his party approach Verdandi without any regard for her. She noticed their scowling young faces, none appearing beyond twenty years old.

The oldest member, who looked to be eighteen or nineteen years of age, wearing a red scarf around his neck, firmly grabbed Verdandi by the right arm.

"I may not know of your customs, but I advise that you leave me be and you return home," Verdandi said, lowering her jovial tone. However, none of them responded to her warning and only followed the orders of their leader.

The teenager pulled on Verdandi's arm, but the Norn did not budge. Even as he tried to tug harder on her, visibly straining himself to do so, Verdandi remained right where she stood.

"Move!" he shouted, but Verdandi kept her eyes locked on the man in charge. The strange smirk on her face did nothing but instill a sense of fear and discomfort inside him.

Another boy stepped forward and grabbed Verdandi's other arm, trying to force the woman to move. But, unfortunately, even their combined effort was futile as they underestimated her strength.

"She is not moving," grunted the boy pulling on Verdandi with both hands.

"Ah, you see what it feels like to move an immovable object. It is similar to fate. No matter how hard you try or how many tears you shed, you can never truly divert your destiny. Unless, of course, you have made me an offer." Verdandi twisted her arms out from the grasp of the two boys, then quickly slapped her palms against their chests.

Neither of them expected Verdandi to move so swiftly, and they seized in motion the instant she placed her hands on them, unable to raise the weapons in their possession.

"I … can't move . . ." the eldest boy said through a stone-clenched jaw, unable to quiver his lips.

"Now *you* can be the immovable object. Stuck here in the present, baking in this fine desert heat until fate had finally caught up with you. Do not worry. It would not be long … or maybe it could last forever. I am not quite sure yet. I have not made up my mind," Verdandi chortled, skipping forward.

"Stop!" the leader shouted, raising his weapon to his shoulder and aiming it at Verdandi.

The instant he blinked, Verdandi vanished from her position in front of his weapon. She stepped out beside him with a small window hovering over her hand. She could see others worldwide operating the same weapon this group carries through her window.

"Oh, so that is how you use it," Verdandi said with keen interest, "And what destructive force it brings."

The leader pivoted towards Verdandi, but she quickly snagged the weapon's tip in her right hand before it could cross her face. Then she instantly jabbed her left hand's fingertips directly into his chest, directly over his heart.

He froze in place with an enormous shocked expression carved on his face. Verdandi yanked the weapon out of his hand, hearing a few fingers crack from being pried apart. A muffled scream was contained within his clenched jaw.

Reorienting the weapon into her shoulder like the others she had seen, Verdandi placed her index finger over the curved trigger. The weapon was aimed at the last man standing near the vehicle. He threw his rifle to the ground and raised his hands in surrender.

Verdandi held a grin on her face as she said, "Thank you for being so courteous."

With a jerk of the trigger, the rifle in her hands dances in her hands, creating loud deafening cracks like thunder. While she could not see the actual cause of its lethality, Verdandi saw the man's body violently wrenched like he was being pummeled by arrows. Blood and shredded flesh was torn off his fragile body. The amount of damage done to him was so devastating that he died before touching the ground.

"Oh my, this is surely a change from the simple bludgeoning weapons I have seen in my day. It is rather exciting. Far faster than an arrow, as well as more destructive. I am impressed by the ingenuity of mankind and their continued desire for destruction."

Verdandi dropped the rifle on the ground after expanding its usefulness. She moved towards the vehicle they rode on, examining every fine detail of the bulky machinery. The corroded state of the metal was still a far cry from the pieces she had seen forged by a hammer and heat source. Something like this and the powerful weapon she used would have certainly changed the outcome of the world the last time she was roaming Midgard. Of course, it would not have affected the gods, though amongst the mortals themselves, history would have most certainly changed.

Climbing into the cab behind the large steering wheel, Verdandi created another window in front of her. This time, she watched a random person in this world in the same spot she was seated operate the heavy machinery. Carefully following the movement patterns as the person in her window, the vehicle groans and rumbles.

"This is exciting," Verdandi said with childish glee.

Slowly, the large vehicle moved forward. Then, turning the steering wheel completely around, the vehicle followed her command and redirects Verdandi to face the city. It was a shaky start, but Verdandi was sure she would improve with more practice.

CHAPTER SIXTEEN

Once the glow from the moon peeked through the tall canopy, Kindra ended her run, where she performed a complete circle for several hundred leagues. While she could feel her heart pumping hard in her chest, it was not near the same stress level she had experienced before she became enhanced. If this were an activity during her time as Hildr's apprentice, Kindra would have vomited multiple times and felt her muscles cramp to the point they would cease.

Kindra was amazed and thankful to know her body could surpass the limits she once had. But sprints do not equate to conditions held during a fight, and it did not help her in the long run of her training, though it did present an idea of how far she believed she could go.

As Kindra heads back to her campsite, which was not too far, she lifted a fallen piece of timber nearly twice her size and carries it back on top of her shoulder. The weight was of little strain to Kindra's body, and even as she bears the timber, she could feel her body quickly recover from her day of running and adjust to the added mass.

On the return to her predetermined campsite, Kindra dropped the log right outside the collection of trees where her belongings reside. She drew out a green tarp from the pack and ties the corners to the surrounding trees, making herself a decent cover from the snow. The bark was stripped from the timber she brought to be used as makeshift walls to keep her warm. The remaining strips of wood were then used to build a small fire beside her settlement.

While the earth was damp, it was no real challenge for Kindra to spark a fire using her dagger and a rock.

The fire was slow to burn but grew into a nicely controlled flame. In the meantime, during the fire's build, Kindra got herself acquainted with her shelter.

Sitting beside the fire as the heat steadily increases, she opened a package of beef jerky that Anna provided. The taste was slightly bitter than what she expected but was far from bad.

Her day of full sprints helped to clear her mind so that she could return to the state she previously inhabited before her alteration. Kindra never had to develop her own training regimen, as Hildr was always in control of her life. She knew eventually that Hildr would not be around once she became a Valkyrie. Even though Kindra genuinely enjoyed the peacefulness of her evening run, it raised some concerning questions about her training. Due to her more resilient body and increased stamina, it could be more challenging to improve her current levels since Kindra would have to break those limits that seem too far to reach.

Instead of focusing on conditioning and strength, she should work towards improving her form and fighting technique to find the best way to combine her skills with this new body.

After an hour of warming up against the small fire, Kindra decided to end the day to rest for tomorrow. No reason to remain idle when she had little time to prepare herself. Taking out a thin, insulated blanket from the backpack, she wrapped it around herself and lies beneath the tarp. For such a light, thin material Kindra was quite impressed by how warm it was. Anna thought she was crazy for only taking a blanket to counter the freezing temperatures, but it was often more than what she got during some of her harshest winters.

The cold would not stop her, nor would Kindra allow it to hinder her training. This was all merely a challenge applied to test her resolve against the looming greater threat that awaits her.

Kindra did not expect to face such tribulations once she became a Valkyrie. Mostly she thought her issues would stem from decision-making concerns or having to attend several battles across the world at once. However, after what she had seen, the world was much bigger than she initially thought. Kindra's life never truly became simpler following her trial; only the duties have expanded with greater consequences.

The whistling wind moved through the woods, sounding like the rhythm of an elegant song. Kindra would not have heard such a serene chime in the city that only nature could produce unimpeded. She deeply missed the isolation and the comfort of being on her own, or rather without the dense population of mankind that Kindra was now responsible for protecting.

Drifting from the physical realm of Midgard to the dark void of the dream world where Kindra previously met Hildr, the young Valkyrie gazed into the vast emptiness that engulfs her. All she could feel was lonesomeness when standing in this open space where nothing else resided.

"You have returned, young Kindra," Hildr said softly, stepping out of the darkness in front of her.

"Hildr … What happened to you? Why are you here?" Kindra immediately asked, as it was a question that burdened her heart. She did not enjoy immediately hitting Hildr with pressing inquiries, but she needed to know. Kindra needed to understand what happened to their world while she was gone.

"Yes, I know you have many questions going through your mind about why we are here and, more specifically, how you came to be here in this new era." Hildr sat on the smooth black floor, crossing her legs into a comfortable position. "Please, Kindra, sit with me."

Doing as requested, Kindra sat on her knees over the ground directly in front of Hildr in the same manner she did as an apprentice. "Hildr, please, I want to know everything. All that has transpired while I have been away."

"Due to our limited time together, I will try to make this brief." From the controlled bearing presented by Hildr, Kindra could tell she was trying to hide something beneath her calm demeanor. "Only a couple of days after you were encased in the Tree of the Dis did the world we once shared come to an end. Unexpectedly, the Norns declared war on the nine realms that even the All-Father himself could not stop. The surviving Aesir Gods sealed themselves in Asgard, permanently closing the bridge from all realms. However, I doubt any of them are still alive at this point."

Kindra had heard of the legendary Norns, the deities of fate. As far as she knew, there were three of them who inhabited an old watering well near the Yggdrasil tree. However, she had never met or even seen any of them, only knowing of them by reputation.

"And you? Hildr, what happened to the Valkyries?" Kindra asked, afraid to know the answer.

"The Court of Valkyries was summoned too late to intervene and fell to the Norns. Kindra, it was no secret that I died in battle in our war against the Norns."

"What?!" Kindra's voice cracked. She extended her arms and grasped Hildr's shoulders. "But I see you. I can feel you here!" Kindra lunged forward tightly, hugging Hildr in her arms and immediately crying. "I should have been there! I should have died among my sisters!"

"Do not dwell on the past, dear Kindra, for your destiny lies elsewhere," Hildr calmly said, gently rubbing Kindra's back to soothe her. Hildr knew the tremendous amount of emotional pain harbored inside the young woman, and from the years they have known each other, she had hardly ever seen Kindra express emotions. She lowered Kindra's hands and held them in hers. "You survived for a greater purpose, one that none of us can follow."

"How is it that you are here? If you have fallen in battle, then why are you not in Valhalla, where you belong?" Kindra inquired, regaining her composure.

"Because our sisters were slain so quickly, not a single soul could enter Valhalla, causing us to drift aimlessly in the realm where we perished. Many of our younger sisters could not bear their presence as specters of their former selves. After centuries of unrest and ultimately decided to forgo their existence entirely as they lost hope of ever reaching the halls of Valhalla, where they would find peace. My only refuge was to wait in Mare's domain for your eventual return."

"How is it that I did not encounter you before? I was asleep in the Tree of the Dis for years."

"You were far too deep in a slumber within the Tree of the Dis, almost in a comatose state, that I could not interact with you until you were awakened."

"I cannot believe that all the Valkyries are dead … ." Kindra quivered, still processing Hildr's words.

"No, you are still alive," Hildr comforted her former apprentice. "Kindra, you carry our legacy and must instill a new sense of hope and strength in this current society where we are nothing but a myth."

"How? These people have no discipline or honor, or respect for each other. I cannot do this on my own. Not without your guidance."

"This is your journey. I know you can overcome any obstacle set in your path."

"The Norns. What happened to them?" Kindra asked, pulling back into her seated position and wiping away her tears.

"After completing their campaign against our world, the Norns returned to their hidden well and sealed themselves off from the rest of the world. No one knows what provoked them or their reason for wiping our existence from the world."

"That force you warned me about … was it the Norns?"

In a stern voice, Hildr said, "Yes, it was regarding them."

Kindra reeled back, staring into the dark void beside her. "Hildr … I … I cannot do this … ."

"Kindra—" Hildr began in a soft tone.

"No, I cannot battle the Norns on my own. If the gods and the Valkyries could not defeat them, what can I do besides fall as well? I do not have the same skill or power as our fallen sisters … or you."

Hildr placed a hand over Kindra's right hand to settle her anxiety, then spoke to her. "Which is why I want you to train. I have faith in you more than anyone I know."

The back of Kindra's hand beneath Hildr's glow yellow, along with a tender warmth resonating from her touch. After a couple of seconds, the light settles, and Hildr removed her hand. Over the back of Kindra's hand was another tattoo imprinted on her skin. This one was a rune of recovery, though it appeared slightly altered and inverted.

"What is this for?" Kindra asked, closely examining the silver ink that looked like it had been professionally done and was always there.

"This is to help you with your training and the challenges ahead." Hildr's voice switched to a sincere, almost maternal tone. "I saw you pass on your first soul today."

"You saw that? How?"

"I can still see a glimpse of your deeds from time to time." She smiled gingerly. "I am beyond proud to see you fulfill the duties of a Valkyrie and eager to see you progress into a fine warrior. The further you develop as a prestige Valkyrie, the greater your might will be in favor of our fallen sisters."

The glow over Kindra's heart illuminated once again. She firmly clasped Hildr's hand and begged her, "Please, there must be a way for me to bring you back to Midgard."

"Do not worry about me. Focus on being better—" Hildr's voice abruptly cut as Kindra was encapsulated in the blinding light, losing the warmth of her mentor's hand.

CHAPTER SEVENTEEN

"Hildr . . ." Kindra muttered as she rose from her sleep under the tarp. A cool sensation was layered over her cheeks as she took careful breaths to calm herself. As she touched her skin, Kindra quickly realizes they were streams of tears from her crying that have nearly frozen over.

When she was tearing up in her dream state, she must have done so in reality. From the new information gathered, only one thing was on her mind.

The Norns ...

Across her blanket was a thin layer of frost that softly broke apart from her movement. Although the temperature certainly dropped, with Kindra's breath visibly flowing in front of her face, she hardly felt it and was unbothered throughout the night.

Calming herself from the abrupt awakening with her final thought on Hildr, there was much for Kindra to process after her dream.

"AAHHHHH!"

A high-pitched scream traveled through the woods and instantly garnished Kindra's attention. She removed the blanket from her and gathers her dagger and shield. The screams were not too far, but she would have to hurry if someone was in danger.

She sprints through the woods towards the last sound uttered. As she grew closer, Kindra could hear the heavy breaths of a creature not of man and powerfully galloping over the soft ground. Whatever it seemed to be, it was quite large and must be five to six times her weight.

Once within distance, Kindra saw a young man and woman sprinting for their lives in front of her. Close behind them was an enormous brown beast, a ravenous bear in pursuit. There was no chance the couple could outrun the bear, and it did not look like it was willing to give up on its chase.

The young man tripped over the foliage, with the woman hesitating to turn back and help.

Kindra opened her shield and then leapt forward, colliding against the bear. The force was enough to divert the bear off its path and spare the man from being mauled. Taking a position in front of the bear, Kindra carefully watched the animal, observing its every movement to predict its intention. There was no question that the bear was angry, but there was no need to kill it, for it was only following its instincts.

The bear snarled at Kindra, standing on its hind legs to tower over her. It tried to invoke fear into Kindra for intervening and standing up to it, yet Kindra did not waver. Instead, both beefy paws were slammed against Kindra's shield. She shrugged off the bear's weight from her shield, which the animal did not expect.

Back on all four limbs, the bear lunged towards Kindra with its massive jaw wide open. Diving to the left, out of the bear's path, Kindra smacks the side of the bear's head with the shield. It was not a powerful blow to bring it down, though the loud *clunk* from hitting the skull made it sound much worse than it was. Kindra hoped it was enough to dissuade the bear from attacking and that they could both peacefully go their separate ways. But all it did was provoke the beast to increase its aggression.

"This is not a fight to the death," Kindra said to the bear.

A paw was swiped at Kindra, but she held up the shield to block the attack and then quickly maneuvers beneath the bear. Then, applying her strength as an answer to end this conflict, she lifted the wild animal off the ground. The solid mass of this creature was hardly a laborious task, and she easily tossed the bear far enough away from the couple that it rolled over the dirt.

In complete disbelief, the bear stood stunned at being thrown, perhaps never experienced the sensation.

Kindra took her stance in front of the bear with her shield at the ready. Smacking the face of the dagger against the shield, the loud ringing sound outmatched any roar the bear could produce, and knew it would be futile to fight. With a high-pitched whine, the bear turn around and trots through the woods, where it links up with a cub that appeared lost.

"Very wise, mother bear," Kindra whispered, then turned towards the couple to check on them.

"How … how did you do that?" the young man said, who had not moved from where he fell.

"From years of training," Kindra simply replied. "Are you injured?"

"I think I twisted my ankle. But I guess I should be thankful that's all I got."

"We've been hiking this trail for years and have never come across a grizzly bear in this area before. They've never come down this far south and should be hibernating around this time," the woman said.

"Can you stand?" Kindra asked.

"Yeah, I think so."

Kindra helps the man onto his feet, where most of the weight was carried on his left leg. While it appeared he could move his legs, the man would need assistance with walking out of the woods. The shield was thrown into the trees, clipping off a branch decent enough to support his weight walking.

"You two should hurry and leave before it gets colder."

"Yeah, we're not too far from the end of the trail. We can call the park rangers to pick us up. What about you?"

"I will be fine, do not worry. I will watch over the bear to ensure it does not attack you two again."

"Okay, sure. Thank you so much for coming to our rescue. I still don't know how you did that, but it doesn't matter. We're alive to ponder about it, which is good enough for me."

The two strangers followed the narrow path through the woods heading southeast, with the man using the tree branch as a walking stick.

Once they were out of view, Kindra leaped upward to retrieve her shield stuck in the tree trunk. For what it was worth, this was not a bad start for her morning. On the contrary, it was a pleasant way to limber up. Heading to her campsite, Kindra deconstructs her shelter and buries it like the day before, carrying only her dagger and shield. But, aside from the flurry of excitement in her, she must focus on training.

Moving a far enough distance from her resting area as well as from the roads and direct observation from wandering visitors, Kindra found a quiet spot nestled in the woods. At the base of a giant redwood tree, she pressed her hand against the moist bark. For something so massive and tall, it was interesting to know how long it took to reach this point.

Kindra balled her hand into a fist and then swung it into the trunk, breaching the solid layer like she was merely punching through a pile of snow. Not hurting one bit. As she removed her hand from the tree, she saw no break in the skin. There was a small amount of initial fear in Kindra as a strike like that would have broken her hand, yet she was perfectly fine. Retaking her stance, Kindra threw another punch, this time with more force and then again and again until she had found her perfect rhythm. Each hit was much harder than the last, tearing the bark right off the trunk with little effort on Kindra's part.

An explosion erupted along the trunk, expelling splinters in every direction. Finally, after enough blows against the tree, the tall evergreen began to lean towards the missing segment in the trunk, crackling the remaining wood that held it together. Then, swiftly moved out from under the path of the collapsing tree, watching it fall with an almost graceful movement. It slammed into the ground with a mighty thud and light tremor as a final message to its surrounding neighbors.

Even collapsed on its side, the tree was still taller than Kindra and should do fine for the next step in her training.

Drawing out her spear and shield, Kindra assumed her position. In the back of her mind was Hildr's calm voice, providing her the instructions Kindra had heard thousands of times in her youth. She slashed at the tree, performing her standard technique with the same precision of muscle control. However, because of her improved agility, Kindra completed strikes faster than before, requiring her to be more aware to follow up with another strike. Otherwise, she would be left open for an attack.

Kindra reset herself with the self-assessment of her first bout, then retried the same combination, improving where she noticed her flaws. If there was a hitch or slight hesitation in her motions, she would restart all over until everything became a smooth, fluid transition.

The words echoed in Kindra's head: "Do you want to be a Valkyrie? Then try harder!"

Although Kindra was alone in the woods, she could feel Hildr's presence behind her. It was as if she was watching her every movement. Critiquing the finest twitch of a muscle or breath taken out of place.

Kindra would do anything to hear Hildr yell out commands at her again.

Chapter Eighteen

While the first location was eye-opening regarding what they happened to have awakened to, there needed to be more to the world than Urd's first stop. So she traveled further west, strolling through a dense humid jungle that was all too uncomfortable.

"Why would anyone want to live in this miserable place?" Urd grumbled. She did not particularly favor hikes, even when strolling through a flat, sparsely populated forest, and preferred to remain near their well. Only on occasion would they venture beyond their territory. And, on far rare occasions, they travel to other realms, specifically Asgard, when the scrawny king invited them to a festival. She knew it was nothing more than to gain their favor passively. It would be humiliating and degrading for the god-king to beg for an extension of his fate or when he was due in person.

Odin would always say that he needed his reign to continue for the safety of all nine realms and that he was close to achieving universal peace. Urd never believed him. It was like trying to stop a plague from spreading or an infestation of vermin from multiplying out of control. In her mind, it was either letting the realms sort it on their own or eliminating the vermin altogether. Odin would not allow it, though it was certainly not a thought that had not crossed his mind. Despite his great power, he was too weak to enact such a charge. Which was hypocritical since his hands were soaked in blood along with his kin.

Urd smelled smoke passing through this humid air and could hear the low crackling of fire within the jungle. Moving towards the sound, treading over roots that stretch above the surface, Urd came across what appeared to be a small plantation built in a pocket of the jungle. It was unlike a farm she had seen, as the crops were mostly submerged in water. Goats and oxen were gathered in a pen near a simple wooden hut that was set on fire.

"You, white woman!" shouted a local at the edge of the small plantation. In his hand was a long, single-sided blade with a round tip covered in blood. At his feet were the remains of dismembered people. Urd surmised a woman and two children, though it required some piecing together for her to tell. "What are you doing? Why are you here?"

The immediate rudeness of Urd's presence did not settle well with her already tempered state.

This belligerent individual waved his weapon at Urd in a threatening manner.

Without dignifying him with a response, Urd wrapped the same twine she had used previously around both index fingers. Then, perplexed at her actions, he moved towards Urd with his bloodied blade raised.

Urd pulled on the line between her hands, and once the line was taught, the man freezes mid-step. The weapon fell out of his hand, his body cringing by an uncontrollable invisible force manipulating his muscles. She could see the grueling torment expressed on his face, only able to produce a tight squeal no louder than a mouse's voice. The life within this man was on the verge of slipping out of the thin husk that still stood. It was a fantastic method of torturing someone as their body began to die, yet their soul remained anchored to them. There was nothing for them to do except slowly wait for the thread to snap under tension which would finally release them. It could last as long as the thread remained intact. Urd had tested it multiple times by tying one end to a stone to strain it. Eventually, it was weathered enough that the weight of the stone finally tore all the fibers. The longest one held together was forty-eight days in the summer.

But Urd did not have time to wait and gawk at one person's fate.

"I bet you wish for me to stop," Urd spoke in a low voice. "Yet, once the pain ceases, it does not mean your suffering has ended. Your soul will have nowhere to go. Anyways, why keep such an end waiting?"

Urd quickly pulled the thread apart before the man's eyes and watched him plop into the moistened dirt.

CHAPTER NINETEEN

Kindra ended her night after thoroughly turning the entire collapsed tree into mulch, resting close to the fire she made with the spear hovering inside the flames to cleanse it. For the first time since her trial, Kindra truly felt tired. It was nowhere near the same level of physical exhaustion as that morning, but she did break a sweat which was a proud moment for Kindra. This meant there was a way she could improve herself.

She wondered what Hildr's thoughts were of Kindra's training. Throughout the day, Kindra applied the methods Hildr taught her to become a Valkyrie. But now that she was one was there something else she should do, or should Kindra stick with what she knew?

"I miss your counsel, Hildr," Kindra whispered to the fire. "No matter the predicament, you always had an answer."

Kindra strongly idolized Hildr not just as an incredible Valkyrie who was noble, strong, and brave but as the woman herself. The woman beneath all the armor; the woman in front of the lush, feathered wings; the woman who spent every day teaching Kindra something new, whether it be about the world or herself. Even if she failed to become a Valkyrie, Kindra strived to be just as wise, generous, and influential as her mentor.

Using the blade to stir the burning wood, she set the spear beside her in the snow to cool, watching the steam quickly rise off the ground. Not once did it change color from its exposure to the fire. After giving it a couple of minutes, she picked it back up and wiped the moisture off with a small cloth, feeling the warmth lingering within the metal.

As she slowly slid the cloth over the spear, she could not help but think about all the times she did the same thing with her old weapon and wooden shield. This led to Kindra thinking about the other apprentices who have yet to become Valkyries themselves. When she entered the Tree of the Dis, there were still a few Valkyries who were in the midst of training their legacies. She knew Hrund, Randgrid, and Göll were among the few Valkyries instructing young girls who still had years before stepping forth to address the council.

Although the Valkyries were no more, did those who were on their way to becoming a Valkyrie also perish? If there were apprentices who survived, they could have continued the lineage in their own way despite not receiving the gifts of a Valkyrie. Their history, training, purpose, and, more importantly, their downfall could have been shared across the world so everyone knew they once existed. That Hildr existed, a real person who was a legend in her own way.

Once this was all over, if she miraculously survived this confrontation against the Norns, Kindra would search for their council's and its members' remains.

After cleaning her weapon and wiping the shield, the fire was snuffed out. This leads Kindra to settle back beneath her tarp shelter, where she patiently waited to fall asleep and be greeted by Hildr again.

Before Kindra could open her eyes to the encapsulating darkness, she could hear a soft hum resonating like she was standing inside a cavern. However, when she looked upon the infinite barren land, no one was present to greet her. Looking around to find the source of the humming, checking several times due to the lack of orientation, Kindra saw nothing aside from herself standing in the void.

"Hildr . . ." she whispered, only to be answered by the continuous humming, this time louder when she called Hildr's name.

"Hildr!" Kindra called out again.

Without hearing a reply, a weight pulled on Kindra's heart to question Hildr's whereabouts. She was no longer a living physical being, so neither Kindra nor Hildr should be perturbed about death. However, there was the possibility Hildr's soul could have disappeared from this realm, just like some of their sisters.

Kindra carefully stepped forward into the mare, her hands held out in front of her in case she ran into something she could not see.

Hildr, where are you?

Throughout her life, Kindra was no stranger to fighting in the dark. She had spent far too many nights on her own, surviving in the wilderness and in battle, but this place was unlike anything she had experienced on Midgard. There was no moon, starlight, or shade of the horizon to help her eyes thoroughly adjust.

Every step she took was entirely silent, even when she did not intend to be stealthy.

"Long have I waited, trapped in this realm of isolation, reliving the nightmare that plagues us until our expiation," the mysterious voice sang in a light tone.

Kindra needed to find out where it was coming from, making her unsure if she was approaching the voice or moving away from whoever was singing. She balls her hands into tight fists as she felt an impending battle about to occur.

It was evident that Kindra was being stalked.

"Who are you?" Kindra asked into the vast darkness.

"Dear child, the one left behind, do not be afraid of the grim solitude after death."

Something inside Kindra gnawed at her to throw out her hands in front of her face, thus prompting her to act on her instincts. The head of a spear slipped between her hands which immediately provoked Kindra to grasp the spear, stopping the point from touching the bridge of her nose. On the opposite end of the weapon was a swirling silhouette still hiding within the shadows.

"Who are you?" Kindra repeated.

Leaning forward from the shadows was a hooded figure with grey-colored pauldrons. Beneath the hood, Kindra saw a woman with fair skin, untethered brown hair, and piercing green eyes glaring at her. Imprinted on the woman's face was a devious smile that was unnerving. It only took a moment for Kindra to recollect the person in front of her as Geirömul. She was another Valkyrie inhabiting the mare. Kindra stood shocked to see a fellow Valkyrie take up arms against her.

"You seem surprised, young one," Geirömul said, widening her smile, "Though I cannot say the same about you."

She yanked back her spear and returned to the enveloping darkness.

"Geirömul, why are you doing this? Where is Hildr?" Kindra asked.

The Valkyrie snickered, echoing in the realm. Geirömul was an experienced Valkyrie with many years of war under her name, standing on par with Hildr in skill and power. She was undoubtedly a figure Kindra did not want to challenge, especially one who was adept with a spear.

"Your Hildr is no longer here. No longer will she be around to pamper her ill-fitted student."

"What?"

"Ah, yes. Frightened are we now? I would not have expected any less of you." Geirömul's voice circled around her like a snake. "The cowardly sister who was too afraid to join her kin in battle and lay her life for a noble cause. The greatest battle the Valkyries ever fought!"

Geirömul's words stabbed into Kindra's heart as a dark truth she was trying to hide from, desperately fighting not to accept.

"I am not a coward!" Kindra exclaimed to the senior Valkyrie.

"Do not lie to your superior. I can sense your heart racing faster than the wings of a hummingbird. The soft quiver in the back of your throat as you try to hide behind your own words."

Geirömul's spear thrusted towards Kindra's chest, and instinctively, she held up her arm where her shield would be. After Kindra blinked, the shield given to her by Hildr appeared with her silver spear in hand. The tip of Geirömul's spear clunks loudly against Kindra's shield, sounding exactly like it would in the real world.

"So, those are the items Hildr gave you? It is truly a shame they did not go to someone more deserving. Someone who actually appeared at our finest hour where they could have been put to good use."

"That was not my fault!" Kindra thrusted her spear into the shadow where Geirömul's spear extended from.

Retracting herself away from Kindra, Geirömul continued to taunt her. "Your excuses do not dissuade me. I know what you are, and Hildr should have seen the sniveling little girl hiding under her wing."

Kindra let out a frustrated scream, swiping her spear wherever Geirömul's voice was heard.

"Is this the so-called warrior that challenged Rota and Kara? What a joke."

"Face me! Stop hiding in the darkness!"

Geirömul chuckled and said to Kindra, "There is no need to rush your death as you never did so before. I had waited a long time to share my thoughts and discipline you when Hildr did not."

The two Valkyries traded blows, with Kindra blocking every incoming attack but could not land a single hit against Geirömul. Kindra was furious, though, in her rage-induced reaction, she tried to control herself. She must avoid being drawn into throwing a wild flurry of attacks, exposing herself.

Geirömul was amazingly fast, Kindra would admit, nearly feeling the blade slice through her flesh. While she had never seen Geirömul in battle, there was no doubt that she was not holding back. Fortunately, Kindra's day of practice gave her some scope of her abilities to the point where she could fend for herself against Geirömul. It should be just enough to stray from her blade. She did not know the repercussions if a hit makes contact with her body, though she expects it to inflict as much damage as it would in the real world.

"You are eager to fight me but could not do the same when your sisters needed you the most."

"I loved my sisters. I would have given my life for them," Kindra replied.

"You should have given your life long ago and let someone better qualified carry our name through time."

Their battle grew in length, with both still standing untouched. This was the longest she had ever been in the dream world, leaving her to believe she would only awaken if she wins. The alternative was to be trapped in this empty void with Geirömul, where their fight would stretch for an immeasurable amount of time.

If Kindra was to at least make one blow against her opponent, she must be ready to take one herself. Ultimately, she would be satisfied to successfully complete a strike and see the pain on Geirömul's face before meeting her demise. All she had to do was choose the best hit to take that would not take too much out of her to deliver a counter. For Kindra, it would be ideal to be bludgeoned by her spear rather than thrust upon it.

The young Valkyrie tried to coax Geirömul into taking a swing, all while trying not to make it evident of her plan. She pressed harder toward Geirömul to reduce the reach of her spear, which would make it less effective in close combat.

As Geirömul noticed Kindra was too close, she quickly fanned her spear around to push Kindra back, but instead of retreating, Kindra stepped forward.

Although Kindra was expecting—hoping—for Geirömul to swing her spear at mid-level, the bronze head glided high on a path for Kindra's head. Every nerve told her to duck and abandon this idiotic maneuver. Despite adhering to her instincts, Kindra held true without flinching, for this was more than just getting a chance to attack. This shows Geirömul that she was not afraid and would not back down.

The wooden shaft bashed hard against Kindra's skull. Luckily for her, she was just close enough that the spearhead bypassed her entire head; otherwise, it would have brought her down to her knees. Embracing the pain without any additional thought, Kindra clutches the spear in one hand, gripping it as hard as she could so that Geirömul did not rip it away from her.

With Geirömul's spear locked in Kindra's grasp, she thrusted her spear into the shadow where Geirömul remained. Although Kindra could not see it, she felt resistance against her spear. Nevertheless, the hollowed scream from Geirömul gave Kindra the honest answer of piercing her target.

While it would have certainly brought down an average person, a Valkyrie, especially a veteran, would not falter so easily.

Just like Kindra, Geirömul was no stranger to pain.

Geirömul took a short step forward, then kicked Kindra in the stomach, throwing her backward and dislodging the silver spear. Kindra landed on her back with the wind knocked out of her. As she fights against her body to suck in the air surrounding this realm, Geirömul stood on top of Kindra with a foot pressed over her chest, fully revealing herself. Blood poured from the gaping hole in her side, yet she seemed unconcerned by it. She was dead, after all, so why bother.

Geirömul pressed hard on Kindra's chest, making sure she did not get the chance to catch her breath, then swipes the end of her spear against Kindra's jaw.

"You should have never returned and remained lost to time," Geirömul said bitterly.

The familiar taste of blood roamed within Kindra's mouth, and the desire to gulp air was powerful, nearly consuming her mind to panic just to take a sharp inhale.

Where she lay was a remembrance of the events of her trial, the pain she had to endure just to reach a verdict. The humiliation of laying down her arms was more painful than the hits and bruises. And Kindra was not going to let that happen again. She wanted a clear victory.

The shield was retracted to its compact setting. It was slammed into Geirömul's ankle with all the strength Kindra could muster. The bones snapped, causing Geirömul to produce a high-pitched scream with more emotion than when the spear pierced her body.

Geirömul withdrew her foot, allowing Kindra to finally breathe. However, she did not waste any time relishing in the glorious necessity. The spear was briefly downgraded into its dagger form as Geirömul stumbled backward, giving Kindra better maneuverability to direct the tip of the blade. Then, she transformed the dagger back into a spear, penetrating Geirömul through the heart while also giving Kindra a lift by pushing the end off the ground.

In a shrugged, inert stance, Kindra rams the edge of her shield into Geirömul's skull. The first hit stunned the elder Valkyrie, yet it was not enough to topple her. Kindra did not mind as she was yearning to hit her some more for what she said. Reeling back her arm, Kindra propelled the shield forward into Geirömul's cheekbone, forcing her off balance to plummet to the ground. Kindra plants her knee in the center of Geirömul's chest and immediately pounds the shield into her face, repeating every strike with more ferocity.

Every effort was used to not grant Geirömul the chance to breathe, fight back, or even speak. She did not want to hear the Valkyrie spew the words that haunt her, making her lament what happened.

After each hit, Kindra loudly gruff to hide her fatigue following every breath. Those rough, guttural sounds slowly turned into light whimpers, yet Kindra refused to alleviate her barrage.

Her arm grew numb from the physical stress.

There could not be any sign of weakness or mercy. Kindra never in her life expected to engage a Valkyrie in a fight to the death. They were to fight together, as sisters-in-arms, never against each other. But there was more at stake than Kindra's own ego or even her own life. For events beyond her control, Kindra must survive to stop the evil that annihilated them. Even if it means that Kindra had to kill her own sister.

"Kindra . . ." whispered a soft voice echoing in the realm.

She did not stop. In fact, Kindra was unable to hear it from the turmoil brewing inside her.

"Kindra!" Her name was called out again.

The subtle calmness of someone breathing behind Kindra caused her to twist around with her spear held out in front.

As the gleaming blade cut through the air, Kindra noticed it was Hildr who was standing behind her. The spear was halted right in front of Hildr's throat, who appeared unphased by the incoming attack.

"Hildr . . ." Kindra whispered.

The spear fell from Kindra's hand, clanging over the ground with the sound ringing for what felt like eons in this darkened world.

Sitting on her knees, exhausted and sore, there was not a word in Kindra's mind that she wanted to say. She would rather not say anything, only to drift into the shadows and not be seen.

Hildr knelt in front of her former protege, who had yet to move from where she fell. Lifting Kindra's head, Hildr saw the sweat on her face mixed with the tears pouring from her eyes and blood slipping through the corner of her mouth.

"Kindra, you did what you had to," Hildr said.

"It did not have to end this way. It was not my fault. She left me no choice—"

"Calm down, Kindra. Turn around and gaze upon the outcome of your battle."

Kindra was hesitant to look at the gruesome sight of Geirömul's body, but as she checked behind her, Geirömul was no longer there.

"What-where did she go?" Kindra inquired, searching for the Valkyrie.

"Kindra, that was nothing more than a test."

"What?! A test? That cannot be. Geirömul … what she did … what she said . . ."

Hildr placed her hands on Kindra's shoulders to ease her distressed state. "I saw you training in the woods, using the techniques I taught you. But, to be honest, this was all formulated by Geirömul. She proposed challenging your fighting prowess, examining how you have adjusted to your new abilities and where you may need improvement."

"No … Geirömul was determined. She was angry at me for not being there in your downfall. What she said—"

"What *she* said was not true." Geirömul appeared beside Hildr with the hood drawn back to unveil the Valkyrie in question. There was a drastic change in her demeanor as she presents herself in front of Kindra. The face that struck fear and doubts into Kindra was now one of sympathy and comfort as the scorn laced with animosity had been shed. For once, Kindra saw the tender expression of a wise Valkyrie, nearly identical to Hildr. Geirömul stood stoically, holding her spear upright in both hands. "Apologies for the crude statements. I know you are no coward. The unfortunate events that transpired were not of your doing and beyond you or any of our control."

Geirömul took one step forward, but from their previous altercation, Kindra subconsciously took a half step back. It was clear of Kindra's distrust of Geirömul, which the elder Valkyrie fully understood. Only when she placed a hand on Kindra's arm, feeling her warmth and gentle touch, did her presence soothe the young woman.

"You feel conflicted. Both Hildr and I can sense it. While I did try to antagonize you and tamper with your mindset through false claims, there was a small amount of acceptance of what I said." Kindra remained silent, unwilling to share her thoughts. "You should not blame yourself, not at the slightest measure. What happened in the past happened, and you, nor anyone, can change it. All you need to focus on is moving forward."

Kindra nodded but continued to keep her silence.

"When it comes to your combat capabilities, I can sincerely say that I am impressed. Not many of our sisters could land a hit, let alone put me on my back. Hildr here had come close, though it would usually end in a stalemate. I applaud your willingness to take a hit in exchange for attempting one yourself. It is a daring maneuver. With that said, you should work towards your speed and the power behind it. Although your pain tolerance is high, you should not have to rely on absorbing an attack in the hopes of seeking victory. Your skill with a spear and shield should ensure that."

"Thank you, Geirömul, for your input, and I am grateful for this experience. I am sorry for my brutality in our battle."

With a little smile on Geirömul's face that eased the tension between them, she said to Kindra, "There is absolutely nothing to be sorry about. In fact, I want you to be brutal. Be a fierce warrior in the face of the Norns and do to them what you did to me."

Kindra gave Geirömul a weary smile. "Yes, sister Geirömul. You can count on me."

"I have no doubt. I will leave the final remarks with Hildr," Geirömul said before vanishing into the darkness, leaving only Kindra and Hildr alone.

Hildr gazed at Kindra, who appeared to be perpetuating deep thoughts from the tightening of her lips. "Speak, Kindra."

"It … I was ready to kill her—Geirömul—a Valkyrie … ." Kindra quietly said.

"Yes, it is disheartening to have a sister battling sister. But you knew what needed to be done and acted upon it."

"It was hard, as I was not battling just her but myself as well. I should not have to fight the very sisters I am meant to avenge. I probably would have let her kill me if I did not have a purpose. Geirömul is a great Valkyrie like you. I only just started."

"Kindra, it is not about who is the greater Valkyrie or most experienced that deserves to reign. It is about what is right. A Valkyrie could sway from our code, and it is up to you to enforce that code. If I were stepping off that path, turning mad just as Geirömul displayed, I would expect you to overthrow me."

Kindra tightened her jaw. "Hildr, please do not say that. I would be reluctant to encounter you in such an affair."

"That was purely an example. From what I witnessed with your duel with Geirömul, you hold the inner strength to push through the tough choices. You need that devotion if you are to be a champion among the Valkyries."

"I do not want to go through something like that again."

"And I pray to Freya that you won't. But if it does happen, then you will be ready. I know it."

The return of the waking glow over Kindra's heart put an end to their conversation on the matter.

Hildr took a solemn gaze into Kindra's eyes, where it was returned in silence. A hand was placed on the young Valkyrie's cheek with Hildr's thumb wiping the blood from the corner of her mouth.

"I am proud of you, Kindra. I always will be," she said sincerely, "Never forget that. Continue to practice and train using the experience you received from Geirömul. I await your return as a better person than you were tonight."

The light shone brightly from Kindra, yet she did not look away or even wince as she watched the warm smile on Hildr's face until the world of shadows was consumed in white light.

The frigid air sharply entered Kindra's lungs. Opening her eyes to the natural light, she first saw the sun shining overhead through the thin blanket of clouds. Then, as she stretches her head around as her body awakens, Kindra noticed the trees surrounding her sleeping area shattered at the trunk with a few knocked to the ground.

Her actions during the dream must have transpired into the real world. Kindra surely had experienced her fair share of night terrors, but this one was powerful enough that it took control of her body, which resulted in her full strength being unleashed. At least she was away from the city where no one could get hurt. Sitting up from where she slept, the instant sting of sore muscles in her shoulders and abdomen shocks Kindra. She did not expect such strange discomfort to occur from a dream.

"How is this possible?" she groaned, standing up to examine herself.

No bruises were present on her body, and the spot on her cheek where Geirömul's spear made contact was unaffected. Nevertheless, Kindra could recall the intensity of the pain, the swath of disorientation after the hit, and the metallic taste of blood filling her mouth that followed. It was quite jarring to experience something so real with all the fine details to make that realm feel authentic.

Since she was not wounded from the aftermath of her dream sequence, Kindra collects her items through the wreckage she unintentionally made.

It was already late in the morning, meaning she needed to get moving so she could return to her training without wasting any more time.

CHAPTER TWENTY

Speed and power.

The honest feedback Kindra received from Geirömul floated in her head as she ran through the woods again, trying to think of a way to improve her training regimen. The sessions she performed yesterday did help her in finding a new understanding of her abilities, but the same practice of maneuvers would only develop Kindra's speed, not her power.

Moving further into the woods, Kindra came across a clearing in the brush where a decent-sized lake lies beside the base of a small mountain. The beautiful dark blue water was also clear enough to see the bedrock that lines the shore. Kindra approached the calm water, dipping her hands and cupping the cool liquid to drink. The lake, mountains, trees, and rock formations give Kindra a faint memory of her home. As much as she would love to bask in the fluttering sensation, Kindra could not lose herself to such emotions, which could spark grief and envy. She must remain focused to fulfill her duties.

She looked upon her reflection in the water, seeing the young Valkyrie staring directly back with confusion and uncertainty harbored in her eyes, masked by the stone wall of confidence.

If Hildr were here, what would she do? What would any of the Valkyries do if they were in my place? Had they received a second chance in life, what would their choices be against the foes that robbed them of their existence?

With a hand swathing beneath the surface of the water, feeling the light resistance pressed against her open palm and fingers, a thought swirled into her mind. Rather than practice her fighting technique on land, which was nothing but air to oppose her body, the resistance from the water would offer more. It would strengthen her form and build upon her explosive power to meet the same speed as on land.

No one seemed to have visited the lake for quite some time. Kindra did not expect anyone to venture to this spot at this time of the year.

Kindra disrobed, placing her clothing inside the backpack to keep them dry. The frigid air touching her bare body did not bother Kindra. It was nothing more than a childhood memory that she had become accustomed to feeling. As her feet touch the ice-cold water, Kindra took a moment, not in preparation to dunk herself but to steady her breathing, for she knew this would not be an easy task.

Hildr would want it to be challenging.

Drawing out her shield and spear, she walked along the bedrock, moving toward the heart of the lake. The weight of her armaments, as well as her own muscularly dense composition, allowed Eluna to remain fully submerged.

The silence within the water offers a fantastic sense of tranquility where Kindra felt secluded from the world. For now, it was just her.

She slashed the spear in the same manner as instructed by Hildr, noticeably sensing her body was moving slower than on the surface. Following up with her shield, the expansive disk caught all the surrounding water, requiring Kindra to push against the force that fights her in all directions just to complete her attack.

Although the strain was heavy and put Kindra in an uncomfortable position, the stimulation in the effort she had to expend was satisfying and exciting. She wanted a challenge. One that her mentor would deem adequate for a newly inducted Valkyrie.

Scouring through the dry, deserted earth in search of the hidden power that called them, Skuld knew she was growing closer, though she did not know the direction to take to meet its origin. The magical energy resonating from this mysterious entity could be sensed only, meaning it could not easily be tracked. It was like a whiff of smoke blown by the wind that once it reached Skuld, she could recognize the scent but could not see the black plume or feel the heat of the burning fire. All Skuld knew was that the being resided somewhere in this foreign land. How close was yet to be determined.

As her feet kicked up the dirt in front of her, Skuld cursed at whatever force that awakened them to where she now had to walk this realm of mankind in a desert and even left this dreaded place alone.

Forming before Skuld out of a violet cloud was a window with Verdandi smiling on the other side.

"Hello, dear sister!" she said enthusiastically.

With a deep sigh expelled from her mouth, Skuld said with disdain, "Hello, Verdandi. What do I owe the pleasure of seeing you presently?"

"Oh, I am simply checking on my sisters. Seeing where they are at and if they are staying out of trouble," Verdandi replied, ending her sentence with a subtle laugh.

"One seeking the wrongings in others is often the one most guilty of said persecution," Skuld calmly said.

Verdandi laughed as if Skuld told a mild-mannered joke, shaking her head, "Dear sister, you have such a vivid imagination and have clearly spent too much time with your own thoughts."

"I think I prefer sticking with my own thoughts."

Through the window, Skuld could see a dense forest with rolling hills in the background.

"I am sure you do. Anyways, have you caught wind of our reason for being here?" Verdandi asked.

"Maybe," Skuld plainly said.

"Maybe?! Ooh, can I join? It is so boring over here."

"No. Again, it may be only a hint. And you know how angry Urd would be if you disobeyed her order."

"Fine then," Verdandi pouted. "I will continue with my 'survey of the land' for judgment by my lonesome."

Skuld ignored Verdandi's whining and fights to hide a smile from appearing on her face as she savors her sister's envy.

"Good. If anything comes about my search, I will inform you of what I found."

"Oh, please hurry! I do not know how much longer I can wait."

"Well, developing patience will be good for you. Now, do not say anything to Urd. I would not want to bother her any further with what could be a false lead."

"As you wish, Skuld. I hope to hear from you soon."

Skuld nodded, then swipe her hand across the portal, disrupting the cloud that connects them from different parts of the world. The anxiousness that will build in Verdandi as she waited for an answer enticed Skuld to delay her search, but her own curiosity sparked a strong desire to know as well.

The faster she could find this entity, the faster they could return to rest and end Verdandi's meddling.

Chapter Twenty-One

Kindra breached the surface of the water to nothing but the beautiful moon shining overhead with the light reflecting off the calm water. She was astonished that she only needed to come up for air a dozen times after spending most of her day underwater. An expanded lung capacity was not an enhancement Kindra expected to receive. However, she was grateful as it allowed her to improve herself.

Swimming towards the shore, Kindra felt the strain on her shoulders and the fatigue in her core. The soreness was light, yet the subtle twinge in her muscles made Kindra smile, almost like a slight tickle coursing through her body. In comparison to where she was yesterday, Kindra wanted to know how much she had improved over the course of a day. Hopefully, enough to make a difference in her battle against the Norns.

As she walked along the lakebed, stepping out of the cool water to instantly be greeted by the air that breezes past her, Kindra found herself in such an elated mood that everything that had happened was almost wiped out of her mind.

Quickly starting a fire by the lake, Kindra let herself dry off before putting her clothes back on. This break from training allow Kindra's heart to slow its rapid pace. One of the greatest enjoyments in Kindra's life was the burning sensation in her chest from undergoing intense training. Through Hildr's guidance, Kindra developed the mindset to embrace the harsh life of a Valkyrie and find the positives to all the drops of sweat and spilled blood. For Kindra, it was for the betterment of her warrior skills and efficiency in battle. If she were to fall, it would be at the height of her power where she would earn a glorious death fitted for a Valkyrie.

Even if Kindra did not live life as a traditional Valkyrie, she would die as one.

Soaking the warmth from her small fire, Kindra watched the flame dance in front of her as her body slowly dries.

She hoped it would be more pleasant for tonight's encounter than the night before. A quiet conversation with Hildr would suit Kindra just fine, as she thoroughly enjoyed her lectures. Her voice was like a serene sound unmatched by any instrument. If Kindra knew the last moment of seeing Hildr alive was when she was sealed in the Tree of the Dis, she would have asked many more questions relating to being a Valkyrie, about life throughout the years, and about Hildr in general.

On the off chance that Kindra must duel against another Valkyrie, she was confident enough that her skills have improved from her day of training to come out victorious again. If Geirömul was seeking another bout, Kindra would surely oblige.

Once dry enough for clothes again and treating her empty stomach with an assortment of dried meats, the new campsite was prepared for Kindra. This time she spaced herself from the surrounding trees in case she became violent, just as she was the night before.

"My dear Kindra, although it has only been one night amongst a few, I can already see how much you have grown," Hildr said, stepping out from behind the black curtain of the dream realm.

"Well, I am filled with glee that at least *you* sense a difference," Kindra replied, trying to make light of the situation. "I hope I am not here to undergo another test."

"No. No, test tonight. It is not my intent to traumatize you each time we meet." Hildr smiled, then said, "Come. Walk with me."

Moving beside her mentor, Hildr set the way and the pace into the void. At every step, Kindra expected to walk straight into a wall, but if Hildr was unafraid to voyage in such darkness, then she would mirror the same.

"Hildr, from your encounter with the Norns, I want to know if there is any way I can defeat them. Any weakness I can exploit where I can gain the upper hand."

Giving a soft chuckle, Hildr said, "I am glad you are still thinking methodically instead of going blindly into battle."

"I would rather not battle if there is a way to avoid it."

"And there is the maturity I have been cultivating. But to answer your question, I am afraid not. None of us knew how to adequately take down the Norns before we met our end. What I can tell you is that while they are immortal beings, they are not invulnerable. The only one who could deliver an effective blow was Kara by using her speed to strike while we distracted them. Only a mere flesh wound on the one named Skuld. That was Kara's final act before her life was taken."

"So, am I just supposed to hit them as hard and fast as I can? Not really much of a strategy."

"True. Though it should be something to consider."

Kindra shook her head, hoping there would be more to help her prepare herself for a battle that now seemed like an attempt that would be made in vain.

"Since you are here, I thought I should reunite you with an old friend."

Cocking an eyebrow, Hildr halted as if they reached a certain point, a destination, in this false world. Then, from a swirling cloud of darkness hovering in front of them, the first thing to appear was a pair of golden braids that stand out perfectly from the pitch-black surroundings.

"Hlokk!" Kindra screamed as she quickly realized it to be her fellow Valkyrie apprentice—a friend.

"It is none other than I, dear sister," Hlokk said with an endearing smile on her youthful face.

They both rushed towards each other and tightly embrace. Hlokk rested her head against Kindra's chest while Kindra pressed her cheek on the top of

Hlokk's head. Even under the unassuming physique, Kindra sensed the mystical strength in the petite Valkyrie.

"I thought I would never see you again, you big dumb oaf," Hlokk said, trying to hide her cries with laughter.

"Not even a skinny twig like you can hide from me," Kindra replied with the same playful energy.

Pulling themselves apart with their watery eyes staring back at one another. They each took a moment to collect their thoughts after spending so much time asunder. There was no change in Hlokk's appearance as she still resembled a young adolescent who had withheld her jovial nature.

"I am elated that you became a Valkyrie! Apologies for my absence during your trial. But I heard you took a beating by going up against Rota and Kara. Very impressive."

"It would have been more impressive if I won the battle," Kindra said.

"You should not downplay such an achievement. If it were me on trial against two Valkyries, I would have certainly been pulverized before judgment could be called. But, after what we have been through, survival is a victory of its own."

"Hlokk … how did you end up here?"

While maintaining her positive attitude, Hlokk said, "Those of us who were away in other realms were called upon to return to Midgard. By the time I arrived across the Bifrost, nearly half of our sisters were slain. The Court of the Valkyries was utterly destroyed. When I and a handful of Valkyries who answered the call from other realms confronted the Norns, they tore right through us as quickly as those who fell before them. For me, well … I took a blade across the throat from Verdandi's bronze sword." Hlokk slid her index finger over her neck right where it happened, with her keeping a cheery demeanor. "She nearly took my head clean off in one swing. I can still hear the witch's godawful cackle."

Hearing Hlokk describe her own death with such glee was disturbing, but after years of contemplating the event, Kindra could surmise Hlokk must have gotten over her death and accepted what happened. After all, what else was there to do when residing in perpetual darkness.

"It is disheartening to hear of your passing, and it should be me to apologize for not being there to join you in battle."

In an expression of dismissal, Hlokk taps Kindra's shoulders and presents a wide smile that reveals the dimples on her pale cheeks. "As much as I would love to be with you again in the real world, it would break my heart to see you here as well, trapped for all eternity. Now, I am not going to bombard you with a bunch of motivational words to inspire you to take on the challenges that lie ahead. As much to sister Hildr's displeasure." She glanced at the elder Valkyrie, who had a look of disdain on her face but remained hushed. "You already know what you have to do, and I am confident in your ability to maintain direction. So you do not need me to repeat the same song heard from our sisters. Since we trained so close to each other, I have no real advice or extensive battle experience I can provide for you on your journey. But I want you to do one thing for me."

"Sure thing, Hlokk. Anything," Kindra quickly said, holding onto Hlokk's hands.

"When you wake up and return to the real world, I want you to enjoy your time there. Bask in the freedom, luxuriousness, and grandeur of the new world we, unfortunately, left behind. I want you to live the life that I never had. As we all found out as I found out none of us are impervious to death. You never know when your final moment would be, so it is best to enjoy it while you can."

The lightheartedness began to crack on Hlokk's young face. Even after all this time of collecting the right words to say to Kindra, they were still difficult to speak once the time finally came.

Kindra clutched her petite friend close to her body as she did not want to see Hlokk cry.

"For you, I will," Kindra whispered.

"Good. Because I have been craving a warm glogg for years."

"Hlokk," Hildr quietly called out.

"Right." Taking a step back, Hlokk untied her right shoulder pauldron. She gazed at the gold and silver plates laced over a layer of red suede one last time before handing it over to Kindra. "Here, please take this and my gauntlets. I no longer have a need for them. Not in this place."

Kindra took the pauldron as well as the two gauntlets. The gauntlets were unique in that they were crafted in Vanaheimr by the Vanir from stone with mystical crystals embedded over the knuckles and the back of the hand, making them not only indestructible but the ability to absorb raw energy to boost the wearer's strength. They were a gift from Mist when Hlokk earned the right to be a Valkyrie. Mist thought it would make up for Hlokk's petite frame.

"Hlokk … I " Kindra began.

"You need not say anything, sister Kindra. I know we will meet again and under better circumstances. Do not worry. I will be keeping Hildr company. I am quite surprised she has yet to grow tired of my antics." Hlokk smiled, and they both looked at Hildr.

Breaking her silence, Hildr said, "Yes, I am astonished as well. Patience is one of the great attributes you would develop while inhabiting the mare. Though, Hlokk here does remind me of a young version of you, Kindra. So, I am thankful for her company."

"Aw, see how sweet she is? I still do not know how you ended up as her pupil," Hlokk said to Kindra.

With a smirk, Kindra replied, "It was pure fate."

The awakening glow over her heart appeared once again. She hoped she could disregard the sensation and remain in this realm with her mentor and best friend.

Hlokk hugged Kindra, squeezing her tightly in her arms. "I wish you did not have to leave, sister, but know that I have never been happier to see you and cherished every moment of it."

"It was great to see you again as well, Hlokk."

Chapter Twenty-Two

Kindra awaited behind the tree line at the intersection, patiently waiting for Anna to arrive. Not long after posting herself in the woods overlooking the vacant road, she saw her friend's car slowly approach.

"Hey, Kindra. How were your nights in the wilderness?" Anna asked through her window as she stopped along the side of the road.

"It was enlightening. Very enlightening," Kindra replied as she walked in front of the car to the passenger door.

She sat in the cushioned seat with her belongings settled on her lap. There was not a word spoken from Kindra's mouth when she entered the car. She barely even made a sound when she breathed.

"Is everything all right?" Anna asked with a blend of concern and curiosity in her voice.

"I am fine, Anna. Do not worry. I just had a lot to think about while I was out here," Kindra replied.

"Okay," Anna plainly said, turning the car around to head back to the city.

Aside from the heat flowing through the vents, there was a long period of awkward silence between them. It was easy to tell that Anna did not want to prod into anything that may be too personal or uncomfortable for Kindra to talk about. There was so much for her to discuss and relay what she went through, especially in her dream, but Kindra did not know how to explain it, and even if she fully describes the events over the past two days, would Anna believe her. This was already a test of her imagination. Either way, Kindra needed to say something.

"Thank you, Anna, for retrieving me. I know it is a lengthy trip for you, but thank you." Kindra said to break the silence.

Anna grinned, replying with, "It was nothing really. I don't mind the drive. It's rather relaxing and nice to get out of the city."

The nearly two-hour drive back to Seattle was filled with thoughts of Kindra's time in the woods: the moment she was dropped off and ran until the moon rose, her discussion with Hildr on the first night where she learned about the Norns, the encounter with the bear, the tree she cut down with her bare fists, and the recent battle with Geirömul in her dream.

Just as Kindra envisioned, Anna had difficulty comprehending some of the incidents she was describing, but after the young woman's close contact with a Valkyrie, she seemed more open-minded to a range of possibilities. Anna asked as many questions as she could, which Kindra did not mind. They would help Anna grasp what she said and become accustomed to the words that were unfamiliar to her.

Even as they entered Anna's apartment, she continued to ask questions, reminding Kindra of a curious child. In a way, almost like when Kindra was a child and kept bombarding Hildr with questions. Thankfully, Hildr had extraordinary patience and seemed unbothered by Kindra's curiosity.

"Does this mean you'll need another camping trip in the woods?" Anna asked after Kindra was going over the input Geirömul provided.

"Maybe, but I must find the best method to train myself. She told me to focus on speed and power."

"Yeah, I can see that being a bit of a problem when you're already fast, strong, and a powerhouse. I'm honestly surprised you need improvement."

"There is always something to improve, which does not have to be only physical." Kindra set her backpack beside the doorway and said to Anna, "Please, let me show you something."

"Huh? What do you want to show me?" Anna shyly asked.

Kindra waved for Anna to come closer. "You have shown me a tremendous amount of your world, helping me by sacrificing your time and fortune. So, I want to teach you a couple of things from when I was growing up."

"Okay . . ."

Retrieving her shield from the backpack and extending it to its full size, Kindra held it in front of Anna. She had never seen it fully expanded outside of its compact form, standing baffled to see her reflection in the pristine polished metal.

"Go ahead and take it," Kindra softly said.

Grasping the rim of the shield on both sides, nervous her palms would smudge the surface, Anna gently took it from Kindra's grasp. The full weight was an aspect Anna did not prepare for, and she nearly dropped the shield once it was transferred to her possession.

"Wow, this is heavier than it looks. And you carry this around like nothing," Anna commented.

"It takes time to develop the strength and skill to wield such an item where it can be used both defensively or offensive. You should have seen my previous shield, the one I trained with in my youth. It was much heavier and bulkier than this one."

"Well, I can see how you got those muscles."

Kindra smiled, then motions her hand in a figure-eight for Anna to follow. It was an apparent struggle for Anna to lift the shield with one arm, having to use her entire body to complete the motion. After a couple of tries of moving the shield into a sloppy figure-eight, Kindra clutched the rim, alleviating some of the weight off Anna to help her complete another few cycles.

Breathing heavily, Anna asked Kindra, "Okay? What now?"

"That was merely a warmup to get your arm primed."

"Warmup? And what do you mean primed?"

"Now, I want you to strike me."

Anna quickly shook her head in bewilderment at Kindra's request. "You want me to hit you?"

"Do not worry, Anna. I have taken many beatings in my life. Anything you throw at me would hardly produce a tickle. So, if you may, strike me with the shield as if I was a foe."

Kindra stood in front of Anna just beyond arm's distance.

Appearing nervous to even consider such an act of hitting her friend, Anna adjusted her stance, not for the best fighting form but to prepare herself for the weight distribution. Anna let out a high-pitched grunt before attempting to thrust the shield. Due to the lack of sufficient strength, the shield was only partially raised, carrying her body under the momentum. Kindra caught the shield effortlessly before Anna could stumble from the momentum dragging her to the ground.

"Good, but we want better," Kindra said, resetting Anna into her beginning stance. "Plan each step in your attack. Do not improvise the small movements. Thrust the shield forward, push off with your leg opposite the shield, and make sure it lands in a firm stance. The power appeared to stem from your upper body, but it actually comes from your legs."

"Okay." Anna took a deep breath, then lunged towards Kindra.

Once again, she caught the shield with one hand. This time Anna brought it just below Kindra's chest.

"I see how you are towards a friend. Now show me how you deal with an enemy."

Returning to her starting point for another try, Anna charged forward, using her full body to propel the shield as hard as possible. Upon seeing the exertion given by Anna, Kindra allow the shield to hit her directly in the sternum.

The blow was barely a tap against the Valkyrie's hardened body. Anna quickly reeled back, afraid that she may have inflicted harm upon Kindra, but as a smirk rose across her face, the fear dissipated, with Anna even chuckling.

"That was much better. Now, let us work on the other arm."

"Other arm?!"

After a brief strength and conditioning session, Anna fell to the floor on her back, drenched in sweat and laughing from the small amount of delirium caused by her fatigue state. Kindra proudly stood to see her friend exhausted, knowing that a person became stronger and better through hard work, stress, and weariness.

Holding out her hand, Kindra gently lifted Anna back onto her trembling legs and took hold of the shield.

"You did well for your first lesson, Anna," Kindra said.

"Is this what you did as a child?" Anna asked.

"In a way, yes. Though not as forgiving nor so brief. Imagine doing this at a much younger age when it could go on for hours until it is done right." Kindra rubbed the palm of her right hand as the memory of those long, painful days resurfaces. She remembered the sting of the leather strap grinding against her hand, rubbing it raw until she started bleeding, and the flesh was stripped off her palms.

Fond memories.

"Well, I appreciate the workout," Anna graciously said, using a small towel from the kitchen to wipe the sweat off her face.

"Under any other Valkyrie's supervision, this would only be the start of a day full of activities. You must also be ready to receive punishment as much as deliver it."

"Yeesh, you really did have a lovely childhood," Anna said sarcastically.

Despite her sarcasm, Kindra firmly said to her, "It was the best childhood I could ever ask for."

"In that case, I'm glad you could experience it. Say, let's go get ourselves a drink. I could surely go for one after all this," Anna suggested to Kindra.

"That does sound like a treat."

"Cool. Let me just take a quick shower and change. Do you need to wash?"

"I am fine, thank you. I had a thorough wash last night."

"Um … okay. Well, just give me like fifteen minutes," Anna said, quickly moving into her bedroom.

Kindra followed Anna through the streets a few blocks from her apartment building to a favorite local bar. The sun pressed on the edge of the horizon, with the light fading faster from the towers built by man. The city life seemed less active when the evening unfolded, acting more like a calm river than a flood from a ravenous downpour.

There was hardly a distinction at the bar's entrance from the surrounding buildings and businesses of similar purpose. Once inside the bar, they each sat on the round stools at the bar counter. Only a half dozen people were inside the open room scattered throughout the interior, with one other person sitting at the edge of the counter.

Approaching them from the other side of the counter was a man with a medium build, round features with a face mostly hidden beneath a red beard. He was youthful and friendly, asking the two women what they would like.

The various types of bottles were intriguing. If Kindra did have to choose, her time would be spent examining each bottle before narrowing down her choice of drink. Instead, Kindra remained quiet, referring to Anna's judgment on what to order. "We'll just take two lagers on special," Anna said.

After making her order, the bartender slid two glass bottles in front of them on a couple of thin paper coasters. Anna picked up her bottle, and Kindra mimicked her movement in grabbing her own. The unbelievable touch of the ice-cold glass bit her fingertips as she raised the tip of the bottle to her lips. The cool liquid rushed into Kindra's mouth, with the alcohol immediately hitting her tongue. A sweet and light taste it was, it surely was more refined than the handcrafted mead or self-fermented wine, which did not always turn out as great as she hoped.

Kindra held the bottle in front of her after taking her first sip. Then, studying the label on the side and rolling her thumbs over the grooves on the glass, she gave off a light chuckle.

"What was that?" Anna asked.

"This is a fine drink. I think Hlokk would have enjoyed it," Kindra said, smiling at the thought of her dear friend.

"Who is Hlokk? Is it another one of your fellow Valkyries?"

"Yes, she was a Valkyrie, but she was also my friend. We both met as young apprentices training to join alongside our mentors on the court. Hlokk was a few years younger than I was. She was instructed by Mist, and from time to time, we would come across each other during our days of instruction. We had a friendly rivalry between us. Sometimes Hildr and Mist would pin us against each other into a match, where we not only tested our capabilities but the level of instruction from our mentors. It was much their game as it was ours. Hlokk was a nimble little thing and always loved a good laugh. Even when she was tired, bruised, and bleeding, Hlokk would often produce a smile and laugh, which would make me do the same."

"You laugh? So, not all of you were serious all the time?"

"Hlokk was special. I think Mist chose her because she was the exact opposite of her in that Mist was quiet, reserved, and a mysterious character—and I do have my own fun—I like to laugh too."

Anna took another sip of her beer before asking Kindra, "When was the last time you saw her?"

"The last time I truly saw her alive, it was almost a year before I attended the trial. She was already declared a Valkyrie by then and was off doing an assignment in Vanaheim, or at least that is what I heard."

"So, what makes you think she would like the beer?" Anna asked.

With a smirk on Kindra's face, she said, "Hlokk always enjoyed an ale no matter the occasion. I always found her with her own horn tankard in hand, drinking as if it were her last and water was nonexistent." Kindra raised her bottle. "I drink this in your honor, Hlokk. You would have loved it here."

Kindra poured the beer into her mouth. The alcohol was only slowed down by the exchange of air within the bottle and was entirely consumed after a few seconds. Once the bottle ran dry, Kindra slammed it on the countertop, nearly crushing the glass from the amount of force applied in her gesture.

"May I have another?" Kindra politely asked Anna.

"Uh, yeah, sure. You finished that one pretty fast," Anna quietly commented, then directed her attention to the bartender. "Yeah, can I get another for my friend here? I didn't think she'd be this thirsty."

"Sure thing." The bartender generously replied and quickly fetched another bottle of beer for Kindra.

"Is this something you normally partake in?" Kindra asked. "This does not seem like your type of setting if I may speak freely."

"Eh, not really. Only on weekends or days when I'm trying to destress after a test or week-long study session. I'm pretty much a social drinker. I don't like simply drinking alone, except for maybe a glass of wine."

"Only a glass?"

"Well yeah, I don't suggest drinking a whole bottle just by yourself." She paused for a moment, then backtracks her words. "But you could probably do fine with a bottle just for you. You may have way too much muscle mass that a bottle wouldn't give you a decent buzz."

"This serving is just fine. I do not intend on revealing my true self until I become more acquainted with your society."

"Yeah, that would be a good idea."

After Anna moved onto her second round, Kindra was already enjoying her fourth without showing the slightest inebriation. The alcohol, even at minimal levels, did help soothe Kindra's mind. Such lithium allowed her to pick apart her recent experiences and figure out what she needed to do to face the masters of fate.

I have seen a small portion of the world thus far, yet I still need to figure out how to assimilate into their society. Everything is so complex that it could take me years to understand half of it. Not to mention the history I was not a part of. Thankfully, the longevity of a Valkyrie will grant me adequate time to study this new environment— if I make it long enough.

A flat-screen television similar to the one in Anna's apartment hung over the bar. The screen displayed a news channel with a male reporter casually saying, "The unexpected deaths that occurred two days ago in downtown Los Angeles were still under investigation. Several homeless civilians were murdered on the street, as well as police officers responding to the incident. Eyewitness reports state the culprit was a single unidentified woman dressed all in black who used only knives to inflict fatal wounds. The Los Angeles Police

Department has been searching for the unidentified woman and using all available surveillance equipment to determine her identity and motive. As of now, the woman is still at large."

Anna shook her head from the news report and said, "This world is really turning into a big dumpster fire. One person doing all that?"

"Yes, that is rather strange … ." Kindra agreed, taking a sip of her beer.

Yanking open the front door, a group of young men stumbled inside the bar. There was a total of six of them who all appear in the same age bracket as Kindra and Anna. Neither of the two women gave the group any attention. Instead, they kept their heads forward. The men were loud, boisterous, and overly obnoxious the minute they stepped inside. They were begging to be noticed as if they were glamorous champions or skilled warriors returning from a victorious battle.

Kindra had come across many of equal standing who, for a moment, feel invincible. From her experience, it was best to avoid confrontation. Otherwise, they would quickly be reminded of their mortality.

The two women attended to their beers in silence. Kindra could sense the nervous tension rising inside Anna as she tried to sit still on her stool, acting like she was oblivious to the commotion behind her. In contrast, Kindra was calm and relaxed, partially from the stack of beers she consumed, but even if she was completely sober, Kindra held no trepidation. Their constant barrage of loudly prattling over a game that Kindra was unfamiliar with only annoys her.

"Hey," one of the men pointed towards them, "check out the brunette at the bar."

The group, in unison, turned their attention like a flock of pigeons to the bar counter. Once their eyes settled on the Valkyrie, they all childishly snickered, failing to contain their excitement. As they chattered amongst themselves, unable to be discrete due to their level of intoxication, Kindra could hear the men talk about them. There were many words Kindra was unsure of their context, with some that were entirely new, but she could infer the group's conversation.

A member of the small group was heard making his way toward the two women, his shoes squeaking as they slide over the tile. Kindra could hear him breathing heavily as he stood behind her. The scent of alcohol was heavier on him than the bar itself.

"Hey there, gorgeous," he slurred, leaning over the edge of the bar on Kindra's left side. "What brings you here?"

Kindra ignored him and took another sip of her beer, keeping her eyes focused on the shelves of liquor bottles aligned against the wall.

"How about another drink?" he asked. Kindra held up her glass bottle to signify that she still had more than enough left to consume. "C'mon, you can hang out with the guys and me. We would love to meet you, and you know, have some fun."

Kindra flexes the muscles on her jaw, which Anna quickly noticed.

"Remain calm, Kindra. Remember, they are only words," Anna whispered to Kindra. When she spoke, there was a subtle accent that Kindra could pick up, and she surmised she must have spoken in her native language.

"Yes. I know." Kindra replied through her clenched jaw.

"Damn girl, what is that? Chinese? Japanese?" The young man drew in closer, where his head hovered over Kindra's shoulder, close enough where she could smell his putrid breath covered in alcohol. He placed his hand on her thigh, gently rubbing closer between her legs, and whispers into her ear, "You sure do fit nicely into a pair of blue jeans."

"Ah, shit . . ." Anna muttered in Korean, ducking her head over the bar.

Heated, Kindra was filled with an immediate explosion of rage while maintaining a stone composure that had waited far too long to be unleashed.

Kindra set her bottle on the countertop and faced the intrusive stranger. The displeasure contained within Kindra was thoroughly displayed on her face, but the young man was too drunk to notice. She quickly grasped his wrist before he could venture any further, applying tremendous pressure so fast that Kindra felt the bones snap in her hand. Releasing a hollow scream for only a second, he was yanked forward with his face slamming into the wooden bar counter.

After seeing their friend collapse on the floor unconscious and bleeding through his broken nose, the rest rapidly form around Kindra and Anna at the bar.

"What the fuck did you do to Michael?" one of them asked aggressively.

"Take your friend and leave. Now!" Kindra replied, keeping her back facing toward the group.

"What'd you say, bitch?" said another member.

As she ignored his vulgar response, a glass bottle was smashed into the back of Kindra's head, shattering perfectly in half. Kindra remained fixed on her stool, not moving an inch from being struck by the bottle. To her, it only felt like a tap by an insect against her head that could have easily been ignored if she was not paying attention. Cupping one of the empty beer bottles on the counter in one hand, she swung it around so fast that none of them saw her bring it forward. The closest person standing behind Kindra took the glass bottle directly to the face, where it shattered into a hundred pieces. Completely disoriented, the individual stumbled backward, falling over on a table.

"Oh, shit! Trey!" One of them shouted.

Kindra stood up from the stool, and as soon as her feet were planted on the floor, the remaining four members start throwing punches simultaneously. Raising her arms to her face, every punch was blocked, and their combined strength could not cause Kindra to waver from her stance. In their brief pause, the men process through their diluted minds how none of them landed a significant hit against Kindra. She kicked the bottom of Anna's stool, pushing her away from their altercation and giving Kindra some breathing room.

This was not her first time fighting more than two people at once. Kindra had fought bigger, stronger men who had years of training and a sober mind when she was a little girl barely able to hold up her shield.

Using only her forearms, Kindra shoved the group back to break them up. She struck the man to her right, who wore a thick puffy coat with an open palm into his stomach, causing him to instantly spurt out a breath of air as he rolled on his back to the floor. Kindra then swung an uppercut beneath the chin of the tall man beside him, listening to the loud crack as his teeth instantly collide. The punch was not delivered at full strength as Kindra figured that if she went all out, it would have surely snapped his skull back, killing him. Instead, she wanted to savor this fight—if this could even be considered a fight—and would like to release the pent-up stress inside.

The next opponent threw a wobbly straight punch at Kindra, lacking the confidence to use his full strength. He was either afraid of Kindra or was reluctant to hit a woman. She caught his fist firmly in her hand, which had hardly any power behind it. Then before he could withdraw his arm, Kindra pulled him closer, which caused him to lose his balance, and he was shoved into the last man in line.

The first person she dealt with, Michael, as his friends called him, stood back up and charged towards Kindra, tackling her midsection with high hopes of bringing her down. The maneuver only slid her less than a foot over the tile and did nothing against her stance. It was pretty laughable since the attempt was weak and not something she expected from a larger foe. Kindra gave him a slight bump of her elbow in between his shoulder blades, loosening his hold around her waist. She could even hear him forcefully exhale the air back out of him.

Grasping him from beneath his waist, Kindra lifted him and swung him around into one of the other two men.

"I had my expectations low, but even then, I am still greatly disappointed," Kindra grumbled.

Her comment, along with her condescending tone, did not settle well with the angry bunch, only fueling their aggression. Hopefully, it would be enough to provoke them to continue fighting and not whimper away. At least not so quickly.

"You fuckin' bitch!" muttered the man who dodged one of their friends being flung towards him. As he rushed towards Kindra, barely holding himself up, Anna hopped off her stool and threw a weary fist into the man's face. The sudden interjection caught him off guard. Once he took a hit to the head without mentally preparing for it, it stirred his drunken mind and made him collapse into a table.

Anna quickly held her hand, which must be writhing in pain.

As she stood, shocked for Anna to join the fight, a punch was struck against Kindra's cheek while she was momentarily distracted. The hit failed to harm

Kindra or even push the flesh on her cheek. Instead, it did more damage to the man who threw the punch. He screamed as he fell to his knees, cradling his hand, which Kindra could tell was broken. Rather than return the favor or kick him while he was down, Kindra slapped the man with an open palm hand against the face. The amount of force was light compared to a solid punch by Kindra, though it was hard enough to knock him unconscious.

"No man should ever lay a hand on me!" Kindra growled, turning her gaze toward the others who were still considering continuing the fight.

Stepping towards the man named Trey, as he tried to scurry over the ground, he reached into his coat and drew out a small device that Kindra had only seen once before.

"Kindra, watch out! He has a gun!" Anna screamed.

Entirely confused, Kindra spurts out, "A what—"

BANG!

The thunderous sound from the object in the man's possession was deafening, and Kindra felt something slam into her right temple. It was a sharp, burning sensation unlike any other. She reached up to touch where the pain was coming from, feeling the warm trickle of her own blood sliding over her brow. It was with astonishment that something so small could have any effect on her to the point it could draw blood.

He drew blood … ? A normal, drunken human was able to make a Valkyrie bleed!

With an enraged growl, her eyes gleamed like an animal provoked too hard and ready to lash out.

"Wha-what the fuck are you?" Trey stammered, holding out the gun in his hand for another shot.

Kindra gripped the seat of one of the stools at the bar, quickly swinging it around and knocking the weapon out of his hand. Then, with an enigmatic scream containing a flurry of slurs discharged into the air, Trey rolled backward, holding his crooked hand out. It was quite a glorious feeling to hear his screams, even if painfully released through a broken jaw. He probably had the highest-pitched scream Kindra had ever heard, especially for a grown man.

The weapon he used against her slid far enough away from his grasp beneath a table, leaving him utterly defenseless on the floor. Although the man had one fully functional hand, he would not continue to fight, not even for his own life.

"I'm sorry! I'm sorry!" he cried.

Grabbing him by the collar of his shirt, Kindra pulled him upward to get a clear look at his trembling face. His eyes rapidly dart across Kindra's face, bypassing the angelic features now cascading a devilish appearance. Her hand balls into a tight fist in front of Trey's face, and Kindra slammed her hand through the tile floor, punching deep enough that only her wrist was above the surface.

She slowly drew back her fist and held it right in front of him, saying to the petrified man, "That should have been for you. You should not seek a fight if you do not know your enemy." Kindra pulled the man closer. "I should kill you for shedding the blood of a Valkyrie, but I will let you live so that you and your ilk are aware of the consequences of dealing in matters beyond your station."

And instead of a punch, Kindra gave him an open-palm slap. Just as before, the amount of strength applied was minimal, but it sent a powerful wave of pain to throb through his fractured jaw that Kindra might as well have punched him. He cried in agony before losing consciousness from the cumulation of agony sprouting throughout his body.

Michael painstakingly stood up, but instead of looking back at Kindra or his friends spread across the bar floor, he dashed for the front door. Kindra took wide strides towards him to prevent his escape. Once she got within a few paces of reaching him, he pulled out a gun from his jacket, shooting indiscriminately inside the bar.

She jumped in front of Anna, taking two bullets in her upper torso near the left collarbone. If Kindra were not there to take the hits, they would have certainly continued their course toward Anna.

Kindra shrugged off the light taps against her body, quickly spinning on her heels to check on her friend.

"Anna, are you all right?!" Kindra rushed to ask, examining Anna from head to toe in case a bullet slipped past her. Immediately, Kindra noticed Anna holding her right hand close to her chest as it began to swell after she punched one of the men.

"Y-yeah, I'm fine," she stuttered, nervously shaking in the seat.

"Bless Freya for your good fortune."

The screeching sound of tires burning over the street right outside the bar, squealing like frightened pigs, immediately diverted Kindra's attention from Anna to the one who managed to flee. Kindra sprints past the entrance, unintentionally breaking the glass door off the frame as she stepped outside. She caught a glimpse of the culprit speeding down the street, then took a sharp left at the intersection.

"Kindra! What do you think you're doing?" Anna frantically asked as she could sense the eagerness inside her to pursue the man like a lioness watching her wounded prey get away.

"He needs to be stopped before someone else gets hurt."

"Are you sure you need to be the one to do this? This seems like a job for the police," Anna tried to persuade Kindra to let him go, yet she could see Kindra had already made up her mind.

"It is my fault he got away. I am going after him. Anna, head back home and tend to your hand. I will meet you there when I stop him."

Knowing that Anna could not change Kindra's mind, she simply said, "Just please don't kill anyone. I don't want to see your face on the news."

Kindra grunted disapprovingly but agreed with Anna's request. "I will not kill him."

Leaping up to the building where she saw the car whip around, she sprinted towards the other end to catch a view of the car while it remained at a reasonable distance. Through the use of her ears, the sound of the screeching tires directed Kindra to move west of her position. A glimpse of the car weaving between the traffic told her it was Michael.

She followed after the car, jumping between rooftops, pushing off walls, and doing whatever she could to reach Michael. In a straight shot, Kindra could have easily caught up to him, but as obstacles line her path, including Michael's erratic driving, this proved to be a decent challenge.

I wish the gods granted me wings so I can make quick work of this drunken fool.

Michael banged his car against others as he tried to flee from the bar. She did not believe he noticed her pursuing him, but after witnessing her abilities firsthand, Michael must be terrified and without a clear mind to think. All he wanted to do was get as far away as he could.

This might be it!

Kindra pounced from the edge of a rooftop towards Michael's car. Landing perfectly on the roof, her body slid over the smooth metal until she jams her fingers through the surface to keep her held in place. The car swerves, nearly driving off the road into the sidewalk packed with pedestrians. She punched through the driver's window and yells to Michael, "Stop—whatever this is—now!"

"What the fuck?!" he shouted, having difficulty keeping his eyes on the road.

Taking a hard left turn in an attempt to throw Kindra off, she instead used the momentum to swing around the car and perch herself on the hood. With Kindra in clear sight of Michael, he pulled out his gun again and immediately began firing. At the same time, Kindra drew out her shield, blocking every bullet meant for her.

Growing more aggravated, the shield was slammed into the hood straight through the engine block. The car sputtered, quickly losing speed.

"No-no-no!" Michael stammered.

As Kindra broke through the bullet-riddled windshield for Michael, he jerked the steering wheel to the right. The car jumped over a curb and plunged into a hardened structure, bringing the vehicle to a sudden stop.

Strangely, at the moment of the abrupt stop, Kindra could see everything occur in a much slower fashion as if time was delayed just for her. It could be her heightened senses that allowed her to see it all unfold. Or perhaps the adrenaline spike had fine-tuned her already enhanced body, which she could take full advantage of temporarily. The metal crinkled from the front to the cabin. Glass was thrown toward Kindra as she fell backward. Remarkably, Michael was jettisoned from his seat through the windshield. While she would prefer to let him fall in fate's direction, Kindra promised Anna she wouldn't kill him.

Catching Michael in midair, she pulled herself downward, rolling over the ground with the car flipping over them into a construction crane. With the two of them tumbling over the dirt to a complete stop, Kindra landed on top of Michael, holding up her fist, ready to punch him. However, she noticed him completely still on the ground upon closer inspection. He was not dead, just unconscious, giving Kindra some slight relief, though she would have been fine if he did perish from the collision.

The creaking of metal demanded her attention as the crane suffers severe damage from Michael's car and began to lean towards a hollow, skeletonized building.

"Run! It's coming down!" shouted a construction worker.

"What?!" Kindra muttered.

Ugh, I should crush him for what he has done! But the blame should not solely fall upon him. I need to stop this.

Charging towards the falling crane, the steel cables that tether the mechanical beast snap like thin cloth twine, whipping against the structure. Amid one cable parting from the base, Kindra quickly grasped it in both hands and instantly tugs as hard as she could to hold it at bay, just long enough for others to flee. Though it was a struggle to uphold, not due to lack of strength as Kindra was capable of holding the weight, but due to her needing to have the same mass to counterbalance the crane. Her feet tread through the dirt as she fights against the forces pulling on the other end of the cable.

She took out her spear in one hand, then jams it into the ground, hoping to work as a stake to keep her anchored. Every muscle in her torso and arms flexes for her to remain stationary. Gritting her teeth, she maintained her hold.

More people ran away from the building while they still had the chance to escape. But a few of them, passing Kindra, halt to witness this one woman displaying inhuman levels of strength.

"Go!" she shouted, startling them to revert to running away.

Her one-handed grip on the cable weakens, but it was not as feeble as the dirt which kept her in place. Soon the earth cracked with the spear loosened and unable to anchor Kindra, yanking her from the surface to swiftly follow the collapsing crane into the partially constructed building. She shut her eyes, preparing for the eventual collision.

Kindra blasted through a concrete wall on one of the upper floors but fell once the crane broke the levels beneath her. Only after a handful of seconds did everything settle, with just the lingering flecks of dust to disrupt the silence.

This is what you wanted, Kindra. Unfortunately, a Valkyrie's life is not always glamorous ... Kindra's thoughts grumbled in her head as she recovers from her multi-staged landing.

No part of her body was in pain or aching in any manner, but Kindra did not feel entirely at her best right now. She was glad to be holding onto her weapons, their loss would be detrimental, and she would peel the earth apart to find them. As she stood up, brushing all loose debris, there was a slight pause for her eyes to quickly adjust to the darkness. Although all seemed perfectly still, some delicate vibrations pass through the building.

"Help . . ." cried a hoarse voice from within the darkness.

Kindra followed the voice to a fissure through the floor with the long body of the crane pressed inside. Then, carefully, she dropped to the bottom of the fissure, doing her best to not disturb the wreckage.

"Please help me! I-I can't move!" an older man said from under the rubble.

"Steady your heart. I will help," Kindra calmly said.

First, she cleared some of the debris off the man for him to catch his breath. Then, as some of the building material was removed, Kindra got a clearer view of what was pinning him. The crane sat on top of a concrete slab, preventing it from crushing the man.

"I am going to lift the debris. Are you able to crawl out?" Kindra asked.

"Y-yeah, I think so."

Grasping the corner of a metal rung and the length of the crane, Kindra pushed the hunk of steel upward with all her strength. At first, it did not feel like it was moving at all, but after a couple of seconds, the object was dislodged from where it rested. The amount of energy applied was not as much as Kindra expected for something quite large. Yet, it was also unlike pressing up freshly cut timber. Once the crane was lifted, the man crawled on his forearms from under the pile as fast as possible.

"Thank you! Thank you!" he exclaimed once fully liberated.

Kindra gently set the crane down, hoping the shift in angle would not disrupt the already weakened foundation. Although the average human could not see his surroundings or himself, Kindra could see his condition in the dark. She noticed blood spots over his lower body, but nothing appeared to be broken.

"Come. I will get you out of here." Grasping him by the waist, Kindra extends her shield in front of her. Then charges straight through the rubble, easily breaking through the several tons of concrete and metal as if it were soft snow.

Outside the confinement of the wrecked building, they could both breathe the air free of the fine dust. Kindra releases the man, who fell to the ground due to his legs buckling from the rise of fear that overtook him.

Despite escaping death thanks to Kindra, the man crawls away from her, fearing what he did not understand.

"Go, seek aid," Kindra stated, which eventually broke through to the man.

As he quickly moved to safety, only going a dozen paces, he turn back to say to her, "Th-there are still more men inside."

"Then I will seek their liberation."

She jumped back into the crumpled building, hoping she did not find any wandering souls to pass over.

Walking amongst this new crowd of people in a new city, Skuld found this setting more pleasing than the desert or the last piece of civilization she visited. The air was much crisper and more refined, mixing perfectly with the cold, wet environment. Skuld enjoyed seeing her breath rising from her mouth in front of her eyes. While she did hold subtle amusement of the weather, Skuld knew all too well that if her sister, Verdandi, was here, she would constantly be blowing air to see her breath.

For all these centuries, Skuld never understood why Verdandi chose to maintain her preppy, almost immature nature. When they were children, it was expected they act like children, which in ways they did. But like any child, they eventually mature as they get older. Verdandi never truly broke out of that phase as the centuries stacked upon themselves. Or she preferred to keep a happy persona to find light and enjoyment because they were immortal and have a dark responsibility bestowed upon them. Skuld saw herself as quite the opposite of Verdandi, accepting their gloomy role of ending the lives of others. Often too soon for many. Although Skuld bore her life as an ongoing burden, she was unlike Urd, who saw it as a position of management and rule like a kingdom.

The evening moon shone brightly through the cascade of light from this city encapsulated by the sea. She could feel the mystic power much greater this time, almost calling her. With such a more precise trail for Skuld to follow, she would need to play nice to these "people" to not draw unwanted attention and cause her prey to flee. From the power lingering in the city, Skuld refused to believe the entity to be a God or an Aesir. She found it hard to believe one would hide amongst mankind and not outright reveal themselves to the world. However, Skuld was not worried, only curious to know who this person was since it was why Skuld and her sisters were awakened to this new world of mankind.

She approached what appeared to be a construction site for a new building about eight stories tall and still intended to go further. Clutching the wire fence surrounding the area, Skuld observed the intricate movement of the workers and the machines they built to assist them. It was like watching a colony of ants making their mound, equally knowing their place in the process.

CHAPTER TWENTY-THREE

Kindra rummaged through the concrete, clearing as much as she could of the rubble to see someone, anyone, who may have been buried. But instead, she came across a collapsed floor, largely intact, blocking her path. Even though Kindra could easily shatter this slab with just her fists, doing so would create more of a mess and possibly do more damage to the structure.

Grasping the edges of the concrete, Kindra had to squat down and drive herself upward with most of the weight born by Kindra's lower body. This was the challenge she had been seeking when it came to testing her physical strength. Using nothing but her grit, the slab rose to her shoulders. From there, Kindra quickly moved beneath the concrete and began pushing with both her legs and arms until she could stand upright with the slab held over her head.

Unearthed from the rubble, Kindra saw a bright orange vest poking out of the grey floating dust. She stood in an awkward position as she could not draw this person out of the wreckage without letting go of the slab.

"Get up. Move!" Kindra grunted, hoping her words would stir the individual to act while she still had strength.

After a quick gust of wind brushed against the half-buried individual, the body shifted as if life sparked back into it again. Then, amidst the realization that death had yet to claim their soul, the body rose from the debris. It was another man, this one more of heavier build, who was confused about where he was and the events that led to his current predicament.

"W-what happened?" he muttered, fixing his yellow helmet squarely over his head.

"It … is pleasing to know … you are alive … truly," Kindra grunted as she held up the concrete, "but please … hurry … ."

The man was astonished to see the tremendous strength of this one woman alone bearing such tremendous weight no human could equally embrace.

"Please!" she pleaded again, snapping the man from his dumbstruck mind.

He scurried around Kindra as she stood as the pillar which separated him from his doom.

The seconds dragged with Kindra holding the concrete over her head. She maintained a clear mind with steady breaths to remain focused on the task at hand and not be swarmed with discomforting thoughts.

With the man far enough away, Kindra lunged forward beneath the slab, escaping the plummeting mass by moving further inside the building. The entire structure quaked, with fresh dust blown throughout the wreckage.

Surely, that was enjoyable.

Kindra hoped he was the last one beneath this crumpled pile of stone and metal, but she needed to make sure rather than rely on hope. Lives outweigh the inconvenience.

The building shows less damage the further she moved inside as the destructive hand of the crane fails to reach this far.

"Oh God," cried a voice in the darkness. "Pl-please help! Anyone!"

Quickly moving towards the sound, she came across a woman near her age, wearing the same brightly colored vest as the man before. A fallen pillar pins her left leg. The woman quickly took notice of Kindra's presence.

"Please! Please help me! My leg is stuck!" she cried.

Kindra kneeled beside the woman. "Take careful breaths and brace for the pain."

"What?!" she quivered, but before Kindra could respond, both hands pierced through the pillar and began hoisting it up.

The instant the hefty pressure was relieved, the tender nerves sent a surge of pain once the circulation resumed. Yet, the woman knew not to dawdle and immediately crawled from under the pillar.

"Thank you," she repeatedly stammered, crying as the sudden pain overcame her senses. It did not take Kindra's enhanced vision to know the woman's leg was broken. She could hear the bones grinding and the squelching of blood and flesh from where she stood.

"So, *you* are the entity that brought us to this wretched world," said an unfamiliar voice that sounded gruff but feminine. It certainly was not someone in distress. Kindra searched through the dimly lit floor for the origin of this mysterious voice.

"Show yourself," Kindra commanded.

Stepping from behind a thin pillar, Kindra vaguely saw the silhouette of a slender woman appearing in front of her. As her eyes begin to settle, she noticed the woman was clad in a thin black dress, but one that did not have modern fabrication or designs she had recently seen. This was a gown reminiscent of one worn by someone wealthy and of great importance in her time. Runes embroidered on the trimming mean further, as in further into one's life.

"It is unbelievable that you would waste your time on these commoners," she said to Kindra with pure distant ringing off her tongue.

"Who are you?" Kindra asked, watching the woman stroll over the undamaged section of the building.

"I should be asking you the same thing. You are obviously not a normal, mortal person, and you are not an Aesir god," she said intriguingly.

A sudden abnormal chill ran throughout Kindra's body, and she was fully aware of this woman's unique presence that radiates magic. Magic from her world. And far beyond the power of the Valkyries themselves.

"You are one of the Norns."

A smirk rose on her face feeling like a dagger glaring at Kindra. "Yes, child. I am. My name is Skuld. I can see the future of every being to discover their fate. Yet, strangely, I cannot see yours. Like us, you seem out of place. Something that does not belong. An anomaly."

Kindra clenched her jaw and balled her fists as she stood in the presence of a Norn. A fire burns deep inside her with every muscle waiting to be unleashed.

"You … You are the reason I am here. You killed my family!" Kindra shouted.

"Your family? Child, my sisters and I have ended the lives of hundreds of thousands of families, including those of royal blood and gods. What makes yours any different?"

The lack of empathy and humorous tone from Skuld's tongue instantly caused Kindra's blood to boil. She lunged forward, wanting to rip the smirk off Skuld's face and beat her until all was left was a crimson puddle of blood. But, as Kindra grew closer, Skuld vanished away from in front of her. "You will pay for what you have done to the Valkyries!"

"The Valkyries?" Skuld chortled, reappearing from behind another pillar to Kindra's left. "The tribe of warrior women who were too arrogant to acknowledge their own end were punished by picking up after us. Odin, the fool. You should thank us for sparing you from such servitude."

"How dare you speak of them with such disrespect!" Kindra roared, leaping toward Skuld again and swinging her fist. Skuld quickly changed places, causing Kindra to punch through a pillar where she once stood.

"Do you honestly think of yourself as one of the prestigious Valkyries? I see you have the temper and raw strength but lack the skill or intellect. And yet, how is it I do not know who you are? You seem too old to be a Valkyrie. During our campaign, we have ended the fates of many Valkyries who appeared far younger than you. I will have to inform my sisters of your existence. That a woman posing as a Valkyrie walks these lands."

"All of you will fall!"

"By your hand? Unlikely."

Skuld threw two daggers out of her sleeves, not towards Kindra but directed at the pillars behind her. The ceiling above Kindra began to shake from the loss of its support, and cracks erupt along the surface.

"I am confident we will meet again," Skuld said calmly before fading into the darkness.

Kindra rushed towards the injured woman, lifting her in her arms, and sprinted towards the exit. The floor above them came crashing down, and Kindra knew she would not be fast enough to escape. Not for the both of them. Expanding her shield and placing it against the woman's back, Kindra told her, "Hold on."

She threw the woman forward on top of the shield, who screamed throughout her time in the air.

The collapsing floor finally caught up to Kindra and slammed hard against her body.

Consumed in the endless darkness, Kindra could feel her body connected to the supernatural world. However, unlike the previous two times when she entered the dream state standing, Kindra found herself lying flat on the floor in the same position as she fell in the real world. There was even a brief ache in her neck after she realized she was transmitted to this otherworldly plane.

"Why are you on the ground?" Hildr quizzically said, appearing in front of Kindra. The elder Valkyrie's warm smile instantly filled Kindra's heart with joy.

As she rose from the ground to greet Hildr, Kindra said, "How could I be here? I have yet to fall asleep."

"You do not need to cross into this plane from fatigue or slipping into a slumber, though I do not recommend using this particular method. Now, what have you learned since our last meeting?"

"The Norns. They are here. I have met one of them," Kindra said with a slight tremor in her voice. She shook her head and said to Hildr, "I do not know what to do. If they are here now, that means there is no time for me to train to fight them."

"I knew time was not in your favor, limiting your growth as a Valkyrie. But I already know you are a strong, capable warrior. With our help, we can make you stronger."

"Our?" Kindra curiously whispered.

A pair of muscular arms wrapped around Kindra's waist, lifting her in a powerful grip.

"I am so glad to see you, little sister!" Kindra figured it was Rota.

"I am glad to see you again as well," Kindra said as the air was painfully squeezed out of her. Rota set Kindra back down and faces her. "It is astonishing you still have your tremendous strength."

A wide grin on Rota's face was a contrasting image to the brawny demeanor that Kindra had witnessed before in her life. For once, the large Valkyrie appeared overjoyed with a newly adopted exuberant character.

"I prayed to one day see you again. The last Valkyrie in all the realms, traversing on Midgard," Rota rejoiced, making Kindra slightly uncomfortable as it felt like she was speaking with an entirely different Valkyrie. "You have become a figure of strength yourself, little one. I am sure you would fare much better in a second bout if given the opportunity."

"I believe my head is still ringing after that last fight," Kindra said, rubbing her temple.

Rota unleashed a hearty laugh that echoed in the realm and slapped a hand on Kindra's shoulder with enough power to rattle her body despite having the Valkyrie enhancements. "You hit pretty hard yourself; keep that in mind."

"Rota." Hildr softly spoke to drive the conversation forward.

Switching to a calmer persona, Rota said to Kindra, "I understand you face a difficult path, one that the combined might of the Valkyries themselves could not thwart. We hope that *you* are the second chance we never had, and the might and power of Valkyries will be passed onto you." Rota's hand brightly glows yellow over Kindra's shoulder like Hildr once did when a rune was inscribed on her body. "Dear Kindra, I grant you, my strength. May it aid you in your journey. I know from Hildr's wisdom and guidance that you are mature enough to use my gift properly."

Kindra was clueless of what to immediately say and only responds by telling Rota, "I am truly honored to receive your gift and hope to make you proud."

"You already have by being a surviving Valkyrie. Now before you go … ." Rota quickly grasped Kindra with her large arms and immediately squeezes her. "Give me a hug!"

The air was forced out of Kindra, and though this was the dream realm, she could feel every bit of strength tightening around her body. Kindra was unable to breathe in Rota's grasp. But she could not succumb to defeat, not here in front of Rota and especially in Hildr's presence. Using the strength she had, Kindra pushed against Rota's powerful arms.

The world grew darker, and the large Valkyrie fades from Kindra's eyes. However, even in the darkness, she did not stop and kept pushing for liberation.

Kindra awakened in a darkened mass of crumpled concrete and steel pressing on her body. She vaguely remembered how she ended up in this situation, but it did not matter. For now, she needed to find a way to get out of it.

Placing her hands on the surface in front of her, Kindra pushed with all her might to lift not only her body, but the debris stacked over her as well. It was a slow process to move a hair upward each second, though that was all Kindra needed to know she was making progress.

Once enough room was garnished beneath Kindra, both feet were planted firmly on the floor, and she began pressing herself up. The colossal weight bearing over her was a struggle to move, yet it was also a simple task. All she needed to do was keep pushing. Finally, the pile shifted off her, giving Kindra an opening to escape this mound. She stared into the violet-colored sky and took a deep breath of the fresh, cool air.

The clothes on Kindra's body were shredded, barely clinging to her body. Thankfully, her flesh was left far better, with only a few minor abrasion marks and bruises. She walked out of the collapsed building, moving towards a darkened part of the street devoid of bystanders.

A soft whimper whispered in the darkness, too low that it could be misheard and disregarded amongst the sirens. Kindra should leave before the police arrive, but as she continued to hear the whimpers, it drew her attention that she could not ignore. It was a cry for help.

Following the cries to a degraded corner of the construction site, Kindra removed the debris, searching for the origin of the sound. Kindra lifted a wooden panel, where she saw a fully grown canine on its side, motionless, with blood pouring from its mouth. The sight was disheartening; no matter if it was a human or not, it was a life unnecessarily lost. Although Kindra found the canine's body, it seemed to have died minutes before her search and was not the cause of the crying. Directly below the deceased canine was a small pup, all in black fur, shivering on the ground.

Kindra gently scooped the pup in one hand, hoisting it up to her face, and took quick note that it was a boy. Upon closer inspection, the puppy had yet to fully open his eyes and had a minor laceration across his short snout. A swipe over the cut on his soft hide with her thumb caused the pup to yelp as she clears the blood. Kindra gently rubbed the top of his head while softly blowing warm air through her mouth to calm him down.

"You're coming with me, little one," she whispered, carrying the pup close to her stomach as she ran away.

Chapter Twenty-Four

Stepping through the broken doorway to a seemingly small bar, Detective Miles entered the establishment, watching a few paramedics attend to a group of males in their mid-twenties. Shattered glass from beer bottles and mugs lay scattered across the floor. Yet, despite the collection of broken items such as furniture, drinkware, and injured people on the floor, there was little bloodshed.

He got a call to investigate the incident involving a physical altercation and eventual discharge of a firearm in a public setting. Bar fights were frequently reported, though they were often not too serious. The only reason he was called in was for the firearm being discharged inside the bar.

Aside from the injured individuals, the only non-first responder in the bar was a Caucasian male in his early thirties wearing casual clothes fitting the bar's aesthetics. He must be an employee who witnessed the event take place. All other witnesses seemed to have fled when the situation started to turn violent. Miles had visited this bar a few times in his tenure to grasp the area he would be serving. He never had any issues with the place.

Approaching the young man with a calm swagger, not paying attention to the injured group. Miles flashed his badge as he introduces himself. "Evening, I'm Detective Miles with the Seattle Police Department. Are you Mister Donahue who reported the incident?"

"Yes, I am," he replied with a manageable amount of anxiety in his voice. Possibly not his first rodeo to an event like this before.

"And you witnessed everything that occurred?" Donahue nodded. Miles drew out his notepad and pen. "Can you explain to me, in detail, what happened and those involved?"

"Uh, yeah," Donahue began, taking a moment to formulate his thoughts, "The gist of it: two women got into a fight with a bunch of guys here in the bar."

"The two women. Can you please describe them for me?"

"Well, one of them was Asian and pretty short, roughly five foot four at the most. The other woman was something else entirely. She was white—or Caucasian—from what I could tell, standing at around my height with a much larger build, almost like a bodybuilder or crossfitter," Donahue said with astonishment.

"All right. Can you please continue?" Miles said to keep him on track.

"Uh, well, when they arrived, they pretty much ordered a few drinks and didn't bother anyone. I gotta tell you, that tall one can really down some drinks." Donahue could see the displeasure on Miles' face of adding unnecessary comments and quickly redirected his posture, though Miles wrote down his statement. "They were sitting at the bar the entire time, just conversing with each other. Maybe half an hour after they arrived, this small group of guys came in."

Donahue pointed to the injured men on the ground.

"And what happened to them?" Miles asked.

"When they showed up, they appeared to already be intoxicated, talking loudly and laughing. It wasn't until one of them approached the two women that was when it pretty much started. The women did their best to ignore the catcalling until that one guy placed a hand on the tall girl's leg. That's when it all went down. She yanked him into the counter and then fought the rest of the group."

Miles glanced at the men littered on the floor, noticing the damage inflicted upon them.

"One woman fought four men?" Miles inquired.

"I think it was five, actually. One of them got away—" Donahue's eyes widened in surprise. "—She was fast, like a trained fighter. She fought all of them without breaking a sweat."

"I see. And who fired the gun?"

"I believe it was the guy with the broken hand, he pulled out a gun from his jacket, and at that point, I ducked beneath the counter. I heard the gun go off, but I'm pretty sure he missed it. The one person who ran out of the bar fired a gun a few times as he made his getaway. As the last man escaped, the tall woman chased after him along with her friend. For a second, I thought she was an off-duty police officer since she went after the guy despite having a gun."

"At what time did they leave?"

"Uh, I'd say eight forty-five or so."

"During this whole fight, did either of the women say anything during their altercation?"

Donahue scratched the back of his head for a moment before speaking. "They didn't say anything when the fight was going on. The Asian woman shouted out her friend's name a couple of times; it was K-something. I couldn't make it out clearly, though it wasn't a common name, that's for sure. She did say something to the last man who had his hand broken before they left, but I'm not sure what it was."

"Well, it is still something to note. Do you know which way they went?"

"I think they took a right outside the door. The guy who ran sped off in his car."

Then this must be related to the incident at the construction site.

Miles closed his notepad and took a gander around the bar for further evidence. He quickly noticed the bulbous black camera coverings attached to the ceiling. "Do you have an interior surveillance system?"

"Uh, yes, we do," Donahue quickly replied.

"Do you mind if I get a copy of the time frame of when the event happened for further investigation?"

"Sure, let me just go download it real quick." Donahue headed towards the back of the bar, pushing through a pair of swing doors.

While he was getting the surveillance data, Miles turned around to see what else he could find. He knew he would have to interview the injured bunch, though it would most likely be a hospital trip since only one was barely conscious.

A small forensic investigation team arrived at the scene, automatically following their routine procedures. Miles walked along the side of the bar to get an overview of the events that took place. It was impressive that one person, let alone a female, could do this much damage. If these men were drunk, it retracts some of the story's stellar qualities. However, coming out of a drunken brawl unmarked was still a questionable feat on its own.

This would be another mystery woman who had done unimaginable things for him to investigate.

Unlike the glass fragments, a small, hard object rolled beneath Miles' shoe. Moving his foot aside, he saw a partially crushed metal object no larger than his pinky with a dark copper-colored surface. Right away, Miles knew it was a spent bullet, possibly the one discharged during the incident. Looking up at the ceiling, there were no bullet holes or any impacts on the surfaces near where the bullet lies. It was simply lying there.

"Can I get an evidence bag over here?" Miles said to the forensics team, pointing down where the bullet remained.

Chapter Twenty-Five

Returning to Anna's apartment with the newly acquired pup in hand, she quietly knocked on the door to not alarm her neighbors.

Frantically undoing all the locks, Anna swung the door open, producing a gust from her swift movement that blasted her short hair all over her face.

"Kindra, thank God you're back. Finally … and with a dog?" Anna said, with a sense of relief in her voice.

"Yes, I found him alone, so I could not leave him behind," Kindra replied as she entered the apartment.

"God, Kindra, you're a mess," Anna commented, referring to her tattered clothes and a thick layer of dust plastered over her, "What happened out there?"

"There were complications in my pursuit. How is your hand feeling?" Kindra asked Anna.

"It's fine. The swelling is starting to go down after I put ice on it." Anna replied.

"If it is any consolation to the pain, I am proud that you finally took your stance," Kindra said with admiration.

"I appreciate it. Didn't think it would hurt so much."

"Once you develop a stronger form, eventually your hands will be toughened enough for you to be able to hit harder and ignore such minor discomforts."

With a smirk on her face, Anna said to Kindra, "Well, I'll give myself a break from fighting, though I would like to get better."

She set the small pup on the table under the yellow light of the hanging lamp. His little head wandered inquisitively, his body nervously shaking like it was shivering in the cold.

"I heard of a serious incident that occurred once you left the bar. There is a developing story on the news about an incident at a construction site. I'm assuming you were involved," Anna said, taking a seat on her couch and placing a bag of ice over her hand while watching the television.

"I did not mean for events to go in that direction. I followed the man who fled the bar and tried to stop him before he could harm someone else."

"Ah, I see. Hey, I don't blame you for what happened. You did what you thought was right and managed to save a few people."

Kindra remained quiet, instead attending to the puppy rather than thoughts of the recent events.

Anna stood back up from the couch and moved towards Kindra.

"Do you have a name for him?" Anna asked, standing beside Kindra to see the pup.

"I will name him Bjorn," Kindra said, gently rubbing her hand over his head to calm him.

"Bjorn?" Anna inquired, nearly having trouble pronouncing the name.

With her eyes kept on the pup, Kindra replies to Anna's curiosity, "In my tongue, it means bear."

"Oh, that's cute." Anna fetched a small hand towel and soaked it in warm water before handing it to Kindra. "He's your little bear."

Kindra gave a friendly smirk as she wiped the crusted blood off his snout, muttering, "Yes. My little bear."

A growing sense of comfort warms Kindra's heart as she succored the fragile being—a child—in her care. Kindra halted her movement of wiping Bjorn with the towel, standing frozen next to the table. Her gaze remained fixed on the pup, almost in a stonelike trance.

"Kindra, are you okay?" Anna asked concerningly.

"Yes, Anna, I am fine. Just embracing a … relapse of memories," Kindra said through as much understanding as she could of the feelings she was nursing.

Not wanting to divulge any personal thoughts, Anna asked Kindra, "Say, do you want to wash and get yourself cleaned up? I'll watch over Bjorn for you and see if I have anything he can eat."

"That sounds splendid, Anna. Thank you." Kindra said, gently moving Bjorn onto the couch cushion, who was too afraid to move.

Removing what was left of her clothing, Anna quickly turned her head away from Kindra's half-naked body, though Kindra was not at all bothered. "You could just undress in the bathroom. C'mon, I'll show you how to use the shower."

After Anna's brief introduction on how to work the shower, Kindra thoroughly enjoyed the warm water sprouting from the overhead faucet on top of her skin. Although hardly a sweat was dropped amongst her nightly activities, it was a great refreshment to cleanse herself of what happened. This was no dip in the Jotun Hot Springs, but it was still soothing.

Water had always brought a sense of comfort and ease to Kindra, even in the worst of times, no matter the form. Perhaps it was a trait she picked up from Hildr since a swim was considered a reward to wash away the day or days of training. At the end of it, she emerges as a brand-new person with improvements to her previous self. Hildr also never shied away from training in the rain. She believed rain was the perfect gift from the Gods as it allowed them to train while also rinsing themselves. The way Hildr embraced the power of a storm was incredible to Kindra and beyond admirable. She did not fear anything the God of Thunder could throw at her. While Kindra would wince from the crackle from the tail of lightning, Hildr would proudly laugh at the circumstance, sounding louder than the fiercest tempest on Midgard.

She missed hearing such joyous resonation.

Hildr's laughter could still be heard, and her lips quivered when that fond memory resurfaced. She lets the water pour over her head and run down her face. That way, she could not feel any untethered tears moving across her cheeks as a Valkyrie did not weep for their fallen sisters.

With the steam rising past Kindra's stature, it became clear she had spent enough time in the shower and needed to continue her day. As she ended the downpour of warm water passing through the faucet, a moment was taken with Kindra standing motionless in the shower. The lingering water rolled off her body, and she watched as it all traveled down the drain at her feet.

There were many troubles ahead for Kindra that she was sure of, but if Hildr did not waiver for an instant, fully aware of facing her last battle, then Kindra would mirror that unshakeable mentality of her mentor.

Exiting the bedroom, Kindra wore pajama pants and a blue bathrobe, a few sizes too small for her.

The shirt Kindra wore was no longer suitable for wear. However, the pants, although ripped along the legs, could still be mended. Besides, Kindra liked the rugged appearance as it fit her personality better. Luckily, Anna bought her a spare shirt.

Anna fixed a bed out of a cake pan with folded towels on the bottom as a cushion. Bjorn was placed in the middle, where he was busy nibbling on a slice of bread.

"I made him a bed for the night, gave him some water, and let him eat some bread in case he was hungry. Tomorrow, we can pick him up some real dog food." Anna said.

"Thank you, Anna. I am certain that I speak for the both of us in respect to your hospitality."

"It's nothing. Bjorn here is a good boy, and it has been a long time since I took care of a puppy before," she said with resonating excitement. Bjorn's presence may have brought back fond memories as a child. Kindra, on the other hand, has never cared for an animal as there was no time in her training.

"Well, I'm going to bed, so I'll see you two in the morning."

Anna left for her bedroom, leaving Bjorn with Kindra in the living room. Taking the pan bed to the floor with her, Kindra set him beside her next to the pillow, where she could keep a watchful eye over him. Without even finishing the piece of bread, Bjorn was curled into a ball, fast asleep. Extending a towel over his tiny body to keep him warm, she stared at him peacefully, breathing until she, too, drifts away in her slumber.

Chapter Twenty-Six

Materializing in front of their buried well, which rested in the full sun, Skuld found Verdandi and Urd waiting upon her discovery. As usual, Verdandi displayed a difficult time containing her jittering excitement. Urd was the complete opposite, appearing stifled with only an expression of mild curiosity about the urgent news Skuld had to present to them.

"Sisters," Skuld began, "I hope your travels have favored good fortune."

"Not as much as yours, apparently," Urd said, crossing her arms.

"Please, Skuld, I cannot wait any longer," Verdandi exclaimed like a child. "I want to know now."

Skuld glared at her immature sister for her impatience. "In my travels, I came across the entity which caused our awakening. There is a girl on lands far away from our own who claims to be a Valkyrie."

Urd shifted her expression, growing more attentive to Skuld's findings. "A Valkyrie?"

"A real Valkyrie? Did we not kill them all?" Verdandi asked.

"As it may seem, one has survived, though, through unknown means," Skuld replied.

Urd stepped forth. "Are you sure it was a Valkyrie?"

"She displayed great strength, speed, and visibility in the darkness beyond any normal human and even recognized me, despite the rest of the world forgetting our existence."

"Is that truly the reason why we were brought here?" Verdandi said, expressing disappointment in her voice and on her face. "She does not sound like any of the reputable ones either."

"Shall we dispatch the last of the Valkyries?" Skuld asked, "She is alone and seems inexperienced. Nothing but quick work to eliminate her."

Urd took a moment to consider their options. "No. Let us see what we can learn from this child. Maybe we can persuade her to join our cause."

"That may prove difficult as she is adamant about our destruction."

"Any stubborn child can be disciplined with the right amount of force."

"Try doing that to Verdandi," Skuld muttered under her breath.

Verdandi heard Skuld's comment but kept her mouth shut, spewing only a deathly glare toward her sister.

"A Valkyrie, no matter how young, can still be a powerful asset. If she joins us with or without her own accord, then we will have a strong enforcer that can move on our behalf."

"An enforcer for what?" Verdandi asked.

Slowly pacing around the hole, Urd calmly said in a stern voice, "Sisters, during your survey of mankind, what did you see?"

Skuld and Verdandi exchanged looks with each other, equally confused by Urd's sudden query.

First, Skuld said, "Plenty of undisciplined, disrespectful mortals."

"Oh, yes, a bunch of them. But they did have neat little toys with them … that were mostly used on each other," Verdandi added to the conversation.

"Yes, even without Tyr around, man continues to wage war amongst themselves," Urd said with her thoughts on the modern world. Then, shaking her head, she said, "And we thought the Gods were cruel towards man."

"Then what would you have us do?" Skuld asked.

"We will undo our mistake. Mankind must be removed, quickly, for the world to survive."

"But sister, Urd, who will dominate this world if mankind is gone? It cannot be us, and it certainly cannot be the Gods." Verdandi inquired.

"The void must be filled," Urd agreed, "It is not in our role to assume such responsibilities, but perhaps we ought to let the beings who were wronged in life exist once again. Maybe without man, they can prosper and do better for this world."

"Well, I do miss seeing some of the mystical creatures. At least they never bothered us," Verdandi said with enthusiasm ringing in her voice.

"That would be a benefit to mankind's eradication; no more constant crying and begging."

Urd stepped closer to her sisters and then gently clutches their hands. "Then we have an accord. Mankind will fall, and the beasts of Midgard will once again reign unimpeded in their place." She turn her head towards Skuld. "Take us to the Valkyrie, where we may attempt to persuade her."

CHAPTER TWENTY-SEVEN

"**M**y sweet Kindra, are you rested?" Hildr's voice asked softly.

Opening her eyes, Kindra immediately noticed the realm appearing a shade brighter than the last, almost a smokey grey. She found herself lying on her side on the ground in the form she fell asleep. Looking behind her, there was a large oak tree towering over Kindra. This was the first natural object she had ever seen in the mare.

"How—why is there a tree here?" Kindra asked, touching the rough bark to see if it was real, or at least real enough to this realm. To Kindra, there was a strange feeling of Deja vu, like she had seen this tree before, but it lacks any distinguishing markings or color and simply looked like a regular tree.

"You tell me. This tree was brought here by your doing." Hildr replied, who also placed her hand on the trunk.

"*I* brought this tree? Why would I bring an oak tree into the mare?"

"You do not remember, do you?" Hildr said as her hand slid down the bark. Kindra stood lost in Hildr's words. "This was the tree where I found you."

"Oh . . ." Kindra muttered, embarrassed for forgetting such a crucial moment in their history. This was a tree that used to be planted close to her home. "I am surprised you remember that day so clearly."

"Well, of course. It was not only a life-changing moment for you but for me as well. I still remember seeing the little girl lying beside this tree in the dark, full of fear and sorrow. Heh, seeing you grow up into the woman that stands before me, seems like two different individuals."

"Yes, if it were not for your counsel, I would not be the person I am today."

Hildr gently smiled, moving away from the tree. "Come."

Before Kindra parted, she gave one last look at the oak tree, gazing at its brown-colored leaves and tall stature, then pushed off the trunk to catch up with Hildr.

"What lesson do you have for me today?" Kindra asked as she approached her mentor.

"Tonight, I only want to observe your—" Hildr swung her elbow towards Kindra's face. But she immediately caught it before it could collide against the tip of her nose. "—fighting prowess."

Although Kindra would detest a fight with Hildr, now that they were both Valkyries, she was curious and excited to undergo a sparring match. Drawing her weapons out of thin air, Kindra took her stance in front of Hildr.

"Are you afraid to face me without your arms?" Hildr taunted, keeping her hands absent from her favored ax.

"I have no fear. I only imagined you would like to finally strike me down," Kindra replied, letting her shield and spear vanish into smoke.

"Oh, I have overcome such thoughts years ago." Hildr smiled. "Now come, I wonder if you have what it takes to defeat me."

With a wide smile on her face, Kindra lunged towards Hildr, throwing a right-handed fist. Hildr dodged her attack, but Kindra knew she was never going to land the hit; instead, it was to force Hildr to make a move and get closer.

"I hope you do better than that," Hildr said.

"I am only giving you a fighting chance." Kindra shot back.

The two Valkyries exchanged blows, though neither could land a perfect strike against the other. It had either been a fist missing by a sudden last-second turn of the head or a kick just out of reach, hitting nothing but air. Kindra was surprised at how fast Hildr was—to finally witness her true speed—even after all this time in the mare, and the high level of skill she displays had not dwindled.

Kindra was proud to witness the grace and ferocity of the woman who trained her, still fighting like the great warrior she always was in Kindra's eyes. And based on the swift drew of Hildr's attack that were blocked by Kindra, she was earning more tremendous respect from her idol.

In time, their breaths become deep and labored, with sweat running down their faces. Eventually, only their forearms and outer thighs became sore from blocking the other's attack. Meaning it would come down to whoever could endure the most pain without letting it affect their performance. If there was one thing Kindra could do, it was taking a great deal of punishment.

At the block of one of Kindra's punches, there was a minor twinge in Hildr's jaw as she grits her teeth to endure the sting in her arms. It could almost have passed unnoticed, but Kindra had spent so much time with her that she could decipher the subtle discomfort on her face. She had to hide the joy inside; otherwise, to not warn Hildr of her discovery.

Throwing a powerful straight punch toward Hildr's chest, she made a quick block with both arms crossed over her heart. While her legs and upper body absorbed the blow, her arms were weary, and a quiet grunt escaped her lips. Following her attack, Kindra kicked at Hildr's side, throwing the elder Valkyrie off-balance and granting Kindra the opportunity to strike.

Blow upon blow, Kindra finally broke Hildr's stone guard and landed several punches into her abdomen. Once she began to bow from the amount of power and agony inflicted, Kindra swiped a swift uppercut into Hildr's jaw. The collision of bones made a loud clack like two rocks were smacked together.

Hildr stumbled backward with one hand covering her mouth. Her shoulders shutter and a chuckle expel from her mouth, with Hildr proudly stating, "That was a beautiful strike."

As she drew down her hand, there was a wide smile on Hildr's face, with a small trail of blood dripping from the corner of her mouth. At the first sign of blood, Hildr eases her muscles as a passive sign of forfeiture, which caused Kindra to do the same.

"Your skills have indeed improved. I never expected the day to come so soon for you to deliver a hit like that." Hildr said.

"The outcome is equally surprising," Kindra commented.

They closely approached each other with their foreheads gently touching.

"It was you who gave me strength, courage, and my title. I would give it all up just to have you back." Kindra whispered.

"Yes … and I would stand down as a Valkyrie to be with you." Their time together was interrupted by the signal of Kindra about to awaken. "Do not think you have bested me. A proper match is still essential to determine who is deemed the better Valkyrie."

"Then I shall prepare for such a contest."

The morning sunlight passing through the windows touched Kindra's eyes, and she could hear the soft whimpers of Bjorn in his makeshift bed.

"It is okay," Kindra whispered to the pup, sliding her finger around the base of one of his ears. The single touch from her instantly soothes the infant and drew him closer to seek comfort.

"Ah, you're awake," Anna said as she stepped out of her bedroom. "And so is Bjorn. So how was the little guy on his first night?"

"He was fine. We both slept peacefully." Kindra replied, pulling the blanket off of her.

"Well, you better take him outside on the grass before he wets himself. I'll go ahead and make us some breakfast."

In agreement, Kindra scooped Bjorn in one hand and escorted him to the ground floor. She watched him hop over the dew-covered grass as he situated himself. As she waited for Bjorn to finish, Kindra observed the city inhabitants walking the street, paying no attention to her. However, some did shed admiration for Bjorn walking around in circles.

For once, the city seemed peaceful. No one appeared aggressive or hostile towards one another. People were either pleased or indifferent to those around them and only carried on with their day. A young man walked by Kindra, and when they unintentionally made eye contact, he flashed her a smile and said good morning. Caught off guard by such courtesy, Kindra hesitated with her reply, giving as much a generous tone as she received.

After what she went through, it was easy for her to distrust anyone from this time, yet right now, the simple interactions were quite pleasing. She wondered if any of them know about the events that happened last night at the construction site or if they even care. What did not directly affect them may not be a concern in their daily lives.

Bjorn made high-pitched barks, catching Kindra's attention.

Picking him in her hand with his belly wet from the dew, she held him up to her face. Bjorn sniffed the air and wags his stubby tail, entirely oblivious to Kindra standing in front of him. She felt a tenderness for this little creature, probably from its vulnerability and youthful character.

"Come. Let us get something to eat, for I know you hunger," Kindra said, tucking Bjorn under her arm and entering the apartment building.

Once she reached the appropriate floor, Kindra came across an older man walking towards her from the other end of the hallway. He seemed more organized, wearing a grey-colored suit with a black suitcase in his right hand. Kindra paid no attention to the man moving in her direction, immediately turning towards Anna's door. As she knocked on the door, the man gave a curious expression to see a stranger present this early at Anna's apartment.

"Hello," he said, sounding tired, like he had a long night staying up. "Did Anna get a roommate?"

"Excuse me?" Kindra said, facing him with Bjorn at her side.

"Anna. She still lives here, right?"

The locks were rushed apart as Anna jumped straight into the conversation. "Oh, hi, Chris! I see you've met my new roommate—slash—personal fitness coach, Ki-Kim."

"Fitness seems right," Chris said, taking a quick moment to study the woman before him. "And you got a dog too?"

"Y-yeah, we just adopted him yesterday actually," Anna quickly said before Kindra could open her mouth to say anything.

"Well, it's nice of you to have company. I know school can get hectic at times."

"Don't worry about me. Kim here has been keeping me pretty busy,"—Anna softly chuckled—"It sounds like you need some rest. Long night at the department?"

"Like you wouldn't believe. You and, uh, Kim, stay safe out there. Things have been picking up recently."

"Thanks for the heads up, Chris."

"Anyways, I'll let you two get on with your day, and I'll finally get some sleep. It's nice to meet you, Kim." Chris held out his hand in front of Kindra.

With only a slight moment of hesitation, Kindra grasped Chris's forearm in a traditional greeting.

"Heh, that's a new one. You have a helluva firm grip there." He looked at her hand, noticing the uniquely colored tattoo. "That's an interesting tattoo."

Kindra quickly drew her arm back and said, "They are a family design."

Chris tilted his head from her statement. It was either out of curiosity about her selection of words or the voice that spoke to them.

"Well, you two take care," Chris said as he entered through the door opposite Anna's apartment.

Once Kindra stepped inside the room, Anna immediately threw questions at her. "Did he say anything or ask you about what is happening?"

"No. He seemed rather polite. Only spoke a few words before you entered the conversation. Who is he?" Kindra asked as she put Bjorn back in his bed.

"Aside from being my neighbor, Chris is a detective for the police department. I hope he doesn't find out your heroic deeds in the city, or trouble could ensue."

"He seems like an honest man. If anything does come from my involvement with your city, then I will accept the consequences." Kindra calmly said.

"How're you, the mature one here?"

Kindra rubbed Bjorn's head and replied, "I had a great instructor who preferred to defeat fear with maturity and thoughtfulness."

"Well, I could use someone like that in my life right now. Anyways, breakfast is ready for you and little Bjorn there."

Following their morning meal, the two young women, accompanied by Bjorn in their care, ventured out into the city again. From the brisk sight of early city life, Kindra wanted to see more of the lighter side before running into another inevitable fight.

"My phone says the vet is about a couple of blocks from here," Anna said with her eyes fixed on her cell phone screen.

"What will this—vet—individual do for Bjorn?" Kindra asked as she carried Bjorn in her hand.

"The vet will give Bjorn his needed immunizations and make sure he is a healthy boy. They'll take good care of him, don't worry."

The quiet walk through the city was pleasant. She did not realize that after the small amount of time she had in this modern world, Kindra became accustomed to the infrastructure and crowds of people. Eventually, Kindra would assimilate herself as a person of this time and not only a dissident of her own.

"After we take Bjorn to get his shots, what else do you plan on doing? Are you gonna go back to training?" Anna asked.

"I must, for I need to better myself for my upcoming battle."

"And have you figured out how you are gonna do that?"

Kindra shook her head, saying, "I have yet to discover an adequate means of improvement. Till then, I have a lot to think about."

They passed multiple shops along the way to the veterinarian, coming across various signs and displays of items for sale. The methods to draw people to purchase something seemed complex to Kindra's eyes, bypassing the things of necessity for personal image and entertainment. This would undoubtedly be a place for Hlokk to enjoy, who would have frolicked at every glamorous new sight.

Anna halted in front of the door to the veterinarian's office, saying to Kindra, "All right. How about I take Bjorn inside for the check-up, and you can wander around the block? Is that good with you?"

"Yes. But what is a block?" Kindra inquired.

"Oh. It's just following the sidewalk all the way around."

"Are you trusting me to survive on my own in this city?" Kindra asked.

"Oh, I trust you to take care of yourself. It would be a pleasant reprieve for you to see what's out there."

"Yes, I can manage."

Anna smiled. "Good. Now don't go too far. And please, don't hurt anyone."

Producing a smirk, Kindra nodded. "I will refrain from causing any harm. You have my word."

"We'll meet you in a bit," Anna said before entering the veterinarian's office with Bjorn.

Kindra watched through the transparent pane of glass Anna and Bjorn sitting on a row of plastic chairs.

Turning around to face the vast city, Kindra pondered what to do now. Kindra finally had some liberty to herself, though she did not know where to begin.

Anna did tell her to simply follow the sidewalk.

Pivoting to her right, she walked along the concrete path on her own. Numerous people traveled along the same route. This time, it felt like more people were around since Kindra was alone.

There were many sights on this short journey that Kindra had yet to see. Her eyes peered at every sign, picture, and building in view.

The first turn around the corner brought Kindra to a confined courtyard with a small patch of lush grass. Vendors lined the yard, many selling paintings and various artwork.

While still walking along the sidewalk, Kindra glanced at the paintings, admiring how detailed and stylized each one was compared to the art Kindra had seen by the artists of her time. In addition, the various colors were captivating, making Kindra wonder how long it took to just do one of those paintings. It was an impressive talent to create something so immaculate.

Kindra continued her walk to see what else the city had to offer.

Standing outside a shop was a young man wearing faded, worn-out clothes that did not fit this setting and were more like workstyle attire. On his head was a burnt straw hat with an upward-curved brim. An unkempt beard covered the young man's face, though it seemed to be by choice. Strapped across his body was a wooden stringed instrument that he strums his fingers across. The sound was unique to Kindra, though it was not at all unpleasant. She watched him play the instrument eloquently, knowing exactly where to place his fingers without looking.

Kindra joined a small audience to witness the spectacle. The young man began to sing with a baritone voice, slowly speaking lyrics with a simple rhythmic pattern. In spite of the chill, he played with passion.

Kindra stood amongst the crowd with her hands clasped in front of her lap, listening to the music. The performance was nothing out of the ordinary but offers a sense of tranquility.

Beside Kindra was a mother holding onto the hand of a little girl caught in the same hypnotic spell as Kindra. She peered down at the girl stomping her feet and dancing to the rhythm while holding her mother's hand. The image brought a sense of warmth to Kindra's heart as it reminds her of a time before her training when she acted the same way.

At the rapid strum of his musical performance, the young man swiftly removed his straw hat and bows to the audience. Everyone clapped and offered the man praise. Those who were generous enough dropped currency into a tin can directly in front of his feet.

That was rather pleasing. Far better than the loud noises I have heard from this city.

As the crowd dispersed, Kindra followed along and returns to walking the sidewalk. Moving a casual pace, the song kept playing in her head. It was an addictive tune, with Kindra humming the rhythm as she walked.

Turning around the block corner, Kindra came across a small shop, unlike the others surrounding it. This one contained various trinkets and memorabilia not commonly found in the other stores Kindra had seen. Walking inside the shop, Kindra viewed the collection of items for sale. Pictures of the city, puzzle pieces, glass lenses, colorful rocks, and clothing patches were on display along with a bunch of things seem random to be together. The more peculiar items consisted of large art pieces, mannequins, and stuffed animals.

Many objects in the shop were unknown to Kindra, though they captured her curiosity. It was fascinating how ordinary people came up with such ideas. She leaned forward to view a rotating crystal ball on a miniscule water fountain.

How is it doing that?

Running through the store was a toddler who escaped the clutches of his parents. With uncontrollable excitement to see the shop, the child slipped behind Kindra, accidentally bumping into the corner of a shelf. The shelf shook, causing a ceramic vase to tilt and fall.

Quickly extending her right arm, Kindra captured the vase as it fell with an open palm before it could crash over the child.

"Thank God!" the mother said to Kindra. "Thank you for saving my son." The mother then redirects her attention to the little boy, not knowing how close he was to being injured. "Daniel, come here!"

The stern voice coming from his mother quickly changed the boy's face. He slowly walked to his mother, defeated, and took her hand.

Hildr would not have been so forgiving if I was his age.

Kindra set the vase back on the shelf where it originally was placed.

Although Kindra did not expect to run into a situation like this, she was delighted to have been present in this shop to prevent what could have been a fatality.

The mere thought of encountering the spirit of a child brought a grizzly chill over her skin. A dreadful memory slipped into her mind, one she thought buried long ago. Kindra quickly shook her head to rid such a thought before it could pollute her mind any further.

I should head back to Anna.

Chapter Twenty-Eight

After a long night that alerted the entire department, Miles finally had a decent moment to settle down for himself. Before he could clock out of work, additional reports were collected from eyewitnesses at the construction site incident and officers who responded to the scene. The survivors who were extracted from the building all spoke of being removed by a female with ridiculous levels of strength. None of them could provide a solid description of their rescuer, only that she felt lean, strong, and spoke with a strange accent.

Strange accent … strong …

Miles took a seat at his desk with his work laptop open. Scrummaging through his laptop bag, he took out a CD of the surveillance footage from the bar and inserted it into his computer. The captured footage covered the events occurring approximately four hours before Miles requested a copy of the surveillance material.

The camera was positioned directly over the bar counter with a broad view of the establishment's interior. At the start of the video, there was nothing significant, as the bar was relatively empty at this time. He skimmed through the footage for images of the suspected females or the group of males beaten. So far, the first hour was uneventful, with most occupants walking in for a few minutes and then leaving.

Just over halfway through the surveillance footage, Miles saw the two women matching the description from Mister Donahue enter the bar and was shocked at the image.

"Anna?! Is it really her?" Miles said aloud. The quality of the footage was not great, and the frame rate was rather slow, but after years of observing various types of footage, Miles could break it down into a reasonable image. Also, knowing Anna fairly well, he could notice her physical features and quirks. Besides Anna was her new roommate, Kim, who was very distinguishable from her size, confident posture, and unique facial features. From some angles, the silver tattoos on her hand could be seen.

Miles watched the moments of Anna and Kim having a few drinks and simply conversing at the counter. Roughly twenty minutes later, the group of drunken gentlemen stumbled into the bar. The two women kept their composure, ignoring them even when invading their personal space. It was not until one man placed a hand on Anna's friend, did things rapidly change. Kim's movement was so quick that the camera barely caught them with the man who touched her instantly put to the ground.

The agility of this woman, combined with her physical strength, was purely incredible. Miles could not believe it and would have thought the footage would be edited with special effects for the internet. Yet, the damage was accurate, and the pain was not scripted. She knew exactly what she was doing, moving like an expert fighter. Even Anna joined in punching one of the men. Miles never knew she had it in her.

When one of the men pulled a gun out, Kim showed no sign of fear or any hint of concern towards the weapon, almost like she was unsure what it was. The flash from the pistol was noticeable in the camera, yet the bullet impact could not be seen. Kim's only reaction to the gunshot was touching her forehead as if she got hit herself. But she was still standing.

Could she have really taken a round to the head? No, it can't be. It must have been faulty ammunition or some weird angle.

He continued to watch the footage, which showed another moment where Kim voluntarily stood in front of Anna and took a few more gunshots to the body. The first time may have been a fluke, but multiple failings would be near impossible, and it did not seem like Kim was wearing any type of body armor. Shortly afterward, Kim rushed out of the bar in pursuit of the one man who was unaccounted for by the time Miles arrived. This also led to the crane incident at the construction site.

Who or what is Kim? She does not appear to be like anyone I have ever come across.

Miles would have to request surveillance footage from the intersections and local businesses along the route for more information on what happened up to the collision. But for now, he had finally found his mystery woman, and the witnesses were not exaggerating in their statements.

Chapter Twenty-Nine

Kindra reunited with Anna at the veterinary clinic with little Bjorn in her hands. "How is he?" Kindra asked.

"Your little boy is doing fine and is in perfect health."

A sigh of relief escaped Kindra. "That is great."

Kindra took Bjorn in hands and raised him to see his happy little self. She noticed a light blue collar around his neck with a silver pendant. "What is this?"

"Oh, I also got him a couple things like dog bed and some food to get him started. I hope I spelled his name right on the dog collar."

"I trust your judgment for I only know the rune for Bjorn."

Rather than heading straight to her apartment, Anna guided Kindra and their new companion to a quiet spot along the coast. Sitting on a bench facing the indigo water, they watched the calmness of the waves pass by and enjoyed the reduced noise from the cluttered city. Bjorn rested on Kindra's lap, tired from the concoctions given to him.

As she slid her hand over his body, Kindra said to Anna, "Thank you, Anna, for the expenses you provided in taking care of Bjorn. Finding someone willing to shed such generosity for a stranger is difficult. However, I *will* find a way to repay you for all you have done."

"It's all right, Kindra. After all, you did take several bullets for me. But, honestly, since you're facing some pretty powerful forces, money doesn't seem like a concern right now. I feel like there are bigger things at stake."

"Ah, the confrontation of one's mortality does present a different view towards their life and how they managed it with others. Still, not many, at least in my lifetime, have offered a level of kindness and comfort except for one."

"I'm assuming you mean Hildr. You know, after witnessing someone like you, who can be quite dangerous if pissed off, I can't imagine a nice Valkyrie like Hildr to have ever existed."

"Hildr was truly a gift among the Valkyries," Kindra said, feeling a strange tug around her heart as she spoke kindly of her mentor. However, she could no longer withhold her thoughts as she knew they would fester. Eventually, ripping her soul, which would undo all of Hildr's work. Kindra exhaled a deep breath before saying to Anna, "When I was young before I conducted my training to become a Valkyrie, I had a family of my own. A mother. A father. Two older brothers."

"Oh . . ." Anna quietly whispered, not expecting Kindra to talk about her previous life. "What happened to them?"

"I was nine years old at the time during the midst of a heavy winter. It was in the middle of the day when I was searching for food. A few days prior, I found a fresh rabbit burrow along one of our hunting trails and thought I should check if it was still occupied. I found the burrow, collected my hunt, and headed back home. That was when I heard my mother scream." There was a slight shudder in Kindra from her last sentence. "I ran as fast as I could, still hearing her screaming and my father yelling. There were loud horse whines along with the clanking of metal. By the time I was halfway home, a growing plume of smoke had risen above the trees where we had lived. When I saw the smoke, I sprinted through the woods as fast as I could, leaving behind my rabbit in the snow. I have never been so afraid in my life, and when I got there … I could not believe what I was seeing. Our home was raided and set ablaze in their wake. My family was slaughtered … ."

Kindra paused for a moment to collect her thoughts on the subject, with Anna patiently waiting beside her. Her hand gently slid across the length of Bjorn's small body to keep a part of her mind still busy.

"My father was beheaded, still clutching his blunt-bladed sword. My mother … She tried to flee with my two brothers. I found her with a hole in her back fitted for an ax. And my brothers, Brant and Erling, were struck by arrows. They were killed right before touching the tree line. They were only children, just a couple years older than I."

"Oh my god, Kindra, I'm sorry. That's such a terrible thing to happen to anyone. Do you know who did it?"

"No. And I never will. I buried the remains of my family on our land … beside a great oak tree behind our home … All I had to dig up the dirt were my own hands which were scraped and bleeding by the end of it. At that point, I was too exhausted to cry and rested over their graves, lying with my family for one last time. Nightfall came, and yet I did not move from that spot. It was a harsh, cold night, from what I remember, surrounded by nothing but darkness and the piling snow that seemed to fall with no end. At that moment, I was hoping—pleading—to meet my death so I could reunite with my family. Before the break of dawn, that is when I saw *her* floating in the sky beneath the crescent moon. At first, I thought it was a twinkling star, but the longer I gazed, I noticed her large flapping wings that kept her in the air."

"Do you mean Hildr?" Anna quietly asked.

"Yes. She was the most gorgeous woman I had ever seen. So strong and brave, yet gentle and forgiving. I can truly say that I was mesmerized the moment I saw her."

The more Kindra thought of the Hildr, the further she traveled back into that moment she stood with her mentor.

The Valkyrie gracefully approached the young Kindra sitting on the frost-covered earth, paralyzed as to what she was seeing. As she touched down on the ground in front of Kindra, the little girl clutched her tunic over her heart, too afraid to speak, letting only the billow of white fog escape her mouth.

The armor worn by the woman was unlike any other. It was finely crafted with smooth metal plating and incredibly polished that it shone like a star in such low light that an ordinary blacksmith could not have made it.

"Do you know what I am, child?" the woman asked in a light yet stern voice.

"Y-you are a-a Valkyrie." Kindra stuttered.

"That is correct." She kneeled in front of Kindra, doffing her brass helm that covered most of her head. Kindra could then fully see the Valkyrie's dark green eyes, coupled with her long ginger-colored hair and fair skin. Yet, even as she rested in the same cold forest as Kindra, her body did not shiver. "I am Hildr. What is your name?"

"I-I am K-Kindra, d-d-daughter of H-Harald."

Hildr smiled at her. "It is a pleasure to meet you, Kindra, daughter of Harald. Please, come with me. I will help you."

The Valkyrie held out her ungloved hand. Kindra stared at her open palm, hesitant to accept her offer. She did not know this woman; worst of all, Kindra would be separated from her family, but Kindra knew she could not stay here, not by herself. Another thought that crossed her mind was that maybe Kindra did pass from the cold, and the Valkyrie was here to shepherd her soul to the afterlife. If the latter was true, she would be reunited with her family. Kindra placed her hand over Hildr's, who gently wrapped her fingers, drawing Kindra closer.

Lifting the little girl off the ground, Kindra could feel the Valkyrie's incredible strength, even far greater than her father's, beneath the layers of armor. Flushed with a sense of security, she rested her head on Hildr's broad shoulder, feeling her entire body relax.

Hildr expanded her feathered wings and lifted off the earth effortlessly, moving as naturally as a bird with Kindra holding her tightly.

"So, is that when you started your training?" Anna asked Kindra.

"Not immediately. Hildr brought me to her camp, where she gave me a choice," Kindra replied.

Sitting at the edge of a small campfire, suckling the gentle warmth from the flame as well as from the morning sun, Kindra tried to keep her eyes off the Valkyrie, who sat on a log in front of her. The crackling of the wood subsisting the fire was the only sound trickling in the silent woods. The little girl could sense Hildr's eyes gazing at her through the fire. It was unsettling, but Kindra was too afraid to say anything, nor did she want to act rudely, especially towards a prestigious Valkyrie.

Clutched in her tiny hands was a roasted piece of cooked venison yet to be consumed, thus losing its warmth. Out of all the sensations bubbling inside Kindra, hunger was not one of them. Vomiting was more of an occurrence than eating.

"You should eat, child," Hildr said, disturbing the silence between them. "You need to uphold your strength."

Kindra slowly brought the piece of meat to her lips but did not part them to taste the food in her hands.

"Speak freely, dear Kindra," Hildr said. "Do not hold your thoughts inside."

Kindra's eyes scattered in every direction except at Hildr. She wanted to say many things but did not know how to tell them or where to begin. It was like her life suddenly ended, yet she still lives, only with no one important in her life to share it with. For starters, Kindra thought she would state the obvious. "I, um … never met a Valkyrie before."

"Not many meet us in their lifetime. Are you familiar with our duties?"

Kindra lowered the venison to the fire to reheat the now cool meat. "My mother used to tell me stories of the Valkyries. They are to bring all the souls fallen in battle to Valhalla."

Hildr grinned at Kindra, which loosened the evident tension inside her. "Yes, Valhalla is a glorious resting place that awaits those deserving."

"Is … that where my family was sent?" Kindra whispered, sounding afraid to present such an inquiry to her.

A steady breath was exhaled through Hildr's nose, and the muscles flex in her jaw as the grin fades. The change in the Valkyrie's expression immediately instills Kindra with a slight sense of fear for asking such a thing, causing her to quickly divert her eyes down to her feet.

As Hildr took a moment to think about what to say to the girl, she noticed her body trembling.

"Kindra." Hildr softly spoke. Looking up at her, tears slid down Kindra's face as she quietly sobbed for her lost family. "I know the tremendous amount of pain nestled in your heart at the loss of loved ones. Do not think too deeply about where they might be or how you wish you met their same fate. You must remain strong, not only for yourself but in their memory."

"I do not think I can be strong. I am not like you," Kindra said, her cries becoming more distressful.

"I can make you strong," Hildr said.

Kindra stopped her sobbing, muttering from her mouth, "What?"

"It will not be easy. There will be many days of grueling hard work that will test your body and your mind. But in time, you will become hardened to face anything without fear. A true warrior. And through my guidance, you can become one of the greatest warriors in all the nine realms. You can earn the right to be crowned a Valkyrie. Would you want that?"

"I … can be a Valkyrie?" Kindra whispered.

"You can be anything you want to be as long as you are ready to face the challenges that lie ahead. I can show you how if you are willing."

The glorious thought of joining the highly esteemed Valkyries filled Kindra's heart with glee. Such an opportunity—an honor—could not be passed. As rare as it was to see a Valkyrie right before being consumed by the shadow of death, it was even rarer to be given a chance to train with one.

"Yes … yes!" Kindra said excitedly.

"Then eat and get some rest. You will need your strength if you are to undergo all the rigorous training to turn yourself into a Valkyrie. Your family would be proud to see their daughter be one of us."

"My life changed that morning. Every single day after, I became stronger, more independently capable, and educated by Hildr's teachings. If it were not for her, I would not have made it past that night."

"I know you said she was a great mentor to you, but you speak of her as if she were your loving mother."

Kindra sat in silence, her eyes fixed on the sea, and her hand halted in motion. As much as Kindra always cherished Hildr's presence, she had never declared or even admitted the great Valkyrie as a mother figure. Such a thought seemed inappropriate as their relationship was meant to strictly be master and apprentice, but as she got older, the strict care turned into pure affection. No other was treated the same way as Kindra. It was common for a Valkyrie to separate themselves from their apprentice as they may wind up dead during training or killed during their trial. Yet fully aware of the possibilities, Hildr held Kindra close to her and vice versa.

"I ... I did love Hildr in the same manner I once shared with my own family," Kindra said with a subtle crack in her voice but was immediately corrected. "Hildr ... she was all I had left."

"Did you ever tell her that?"

With a faint shake of her head, Kindra replied to Anna's question. "Our bond was so strong that words need not be said. Though, I wish I did."

Anna gently placed a hand on Kindra's shoulder. "If you are as close as you say you are, then surely she knows."

"Thank you, Anna."

"When it comes to family ... Do you ever plan on starting one yourself?" Anna nervously asked.

"I never thought about starting a family, and even if I did cherish the thought, a Valkyrie could never bear children."

"Why? Is that some sort of rule you have to abide by?"

"No ... It is because once a Valkyrie enters the Tree of the Dis, they become barren. This is the reason why Valkyries seek an apprentice to train."

"Huh," Anna said with intrigue, "Then maybe you were the daughter Hildr never had."

"While I do appreciate your kindhearted words, I do not believe Hildr would think of me as so."

Anna shrugged and said unconvincingly, "Eh, if you say so."

CHAPTER THIRTY

Making a high-pitched yawn, Bjorn picked up his head to smell the stale air inside the apartment complex hallway. Kindra admired his quirkiness.

"So, now you wake up," she gently said to him.

He makes a trembling howl in response which caused Kindra to crack a smile.

"You really are warming up to little Bjorn. Careful, you might lose your tough girl image," said playfully.

"It will only add to my opponents underestimating my potential," Kindra replied. "Besides, as you said, I would like to explore this softer side with Bjorn. He may help me assimilate with your world. Do you not agree?" —Kindra spoke to Bjorn, scratching the back of his ear—

Upon standing in front of the apartment door, Kindra paused before stepping through the doorway. She could feel the sense of being watched and even hear controlled breathing coming from behind the door to Anna's neighbor, Chris. Looking back at the door opposite Anna's room, she waited for something to happen. For an attack to ensue as if being stalked by a predator.

"Kindra, is everything all right?" Anna asked from inside the apartment.

"Yes. Everything is fine," Kindra slowly replied, stepping inside the apartment and closing the door behind her.

Anna set Bjorn's new bed near the couch, with Kindra gently placing the puppy on the cushion. Then, quickly rubbing his head on the soft, fluffy material, Bjorn put himself to sleep after his long day of being poked and prodded by helpful strangers.

"Are you hungry?" Anna asked as she started pulling pans from beneath the stove.

"I can surely eat."

"I thought so. I'll try to pack something with enough protein for you."

"Is that something that I need?" Kindra asked, slightly bewildered.

"If you want to keep your muscles, then yeah. We have come a long way since your time when it comes to building muscle."

"If it keeps me strong and makes me stronger, I advocate it."

"Good!" Anna said happily and took out the ingredients from the refrigerator.

Kindra was amused and somewhat envious of Anna's cooking skills. She never had adequate time to perfect the craft, solely relying on overcooking meat or eating it raw with the blood still dripping warm. Though when given a chance, Kindra did like to bake. Mostly simple loaves with ordinary ingredients that even Hildr enjoyed. Since the process took time to grind the wheat, it was usually on days of rest when Kindra would have the opportunity. They would sit by the fire waiting for the dough to eventually rise, with Hildr offering a story of her youth. Making bread was not even a lesson taught by Hildr. Kindra learned it from her mother.

How Anna knew what to pull and the exact measurements to make seemed almost like it was second nature to her. She required no references or double-takes on what was needed. Perhaps it was a family tradition, or she spent a hefty amount of time on her own that she picked up the hobby.

Where can she be?

Urd could sense the girl in question, feeling the mystic energy hovering within this new city. Compared to the places she had visited, this one was far more sophisticated and refined, with the people appearing more civil to an extent.

Walking the streets in her gown, she caught the eyes of the locals, yet it was more out of fascination than taboo. Even Urd found apparel that was not commonly worn by others and seemed out of place for this environment to be catching the attention of the locals.

She could confidently tell the girl had passed through this area as the hard ground was saturated with her essence and seemed rather fresh despite Skuld's encounter. Furthermore, the girl did not flee once confronted and did not try to avoid them.

The sidewalk became so crowded with pedestrians that it requires Urd to make an effort to go forward. Growing tired of diverting her steps and battling for dominance just to move one foot forward, Urd stepped onto the street where the mechanical carriages stroll in order. People were yelling at her. Telling her to get off the road and honking their horns for her to move. Words would not settle their nerves, and Urd did not hold the inclination to respond.

Walking in the direction of traffic, one individual shouted while sitting in his vehicle. "Get the fuck off the road, bitch!"

Urd tightened her lips, stepping towards the rude individual. Then, with her index and middle finger out, Urd thrust them into his forehead, penetrating the skull with ease like a knife through a grape. The angry, smug individual fell flat, half his body hanging over the door.

Bystanders screamed as they witnessed Urd execute this man effortlessly in public view.

I guess I shall draw the woman out. If she is a Valkyrie, then there will be plenty of death which she cannot ignore.

Sirens could be heard rushing by Anna's apartment complex, an endless symphony as one faded away, another followed right behind the last.

"What is going on out there?" Anna said, intrigued by the commotion. She got up from the dinner table, moving towards the screen door to view the activity outside. Kindra followed after Anna since if it sparked her attention, then it must be something worthwhile to see.

"Is this normal?" Kindra asked, watching emergency vehicles speed through the street.

"No. This must be something pretty big." They could hear a door slam shut from outside the room in the hallway with footsteps running towards the elevators. "Huh, I guess it must be really big if they have to call Chris back on duty."

Kindra slid the screen door open and stepped onto the patio to get a better view of what was happening. The cool air brushed against her cheeks, carrying with the winds a faint scent that did not belong. It was the aroma of something of a mystical nature. Perhaps Kindra's mind was falsifying the air redolent of magic, but a gut feeling told her it was genuine and needed to be investigated.

"I need to see what they are after," Kindra said.

"I knew you were gonna say that." Anna quietly said. But instead of trying to dissuade Kindra or speak out of fear, Anna said, "Let's go check it out then."

Kindra cocked an eyebrow at her.

"What?" Anna questioned. "It's not like I can stop you from doing anything. I have a better chance of convincing people that water is not wet than keeping you from getting into trouble. Plus, you're born to help people in a crisis. If a bunch of cops are rushing to an incident, then it might be something worth getting involved with."

"I am surprised by your tenacity to face possible danger."

"Maybe you're just rubbing off on me, but I'm sure there is nothing you can't handle. And the police may have questions if things get out of hand, so it is best if I explain things."

"Then I am glad to have your assistance," Kindra said contentedly, then lifted Anna into her arms.

"Wait! What are you doing?" Anna quickly said with panic, returning to her voice.

"We are taking the fastest route," Kindra said, trying to hide the playful tone. "Remember, Anna, no fear."

The young woman shut her eyes as Kindra hopped over the railing. Anna clutched onto Kindra tightly like a child. While Kindra enjoyed the exhilaration of the descent, it was more pleasing to have someone in her care. Kindra softly lowered her legs on impact with the ground to avoid injuring Anna from the sudden stop.

"Kindra . . ." Anna whispered, "Can … Can you put me down?"

Lowering her as requested, Anna stumbled over the sidewalk, taking a moment to collect herself after going through what she believed to be a near-death experience.

"Will you be all right, Anna?" Kindra softly said, carefully watching her friend stand on her trembling legs.

"I think so. A little warning next time."

"Where is the fun in that?" Kindra cheekily said, which only sparked a scowl from Anna.

"Now you want to joke around?" Anna said.

"Come now. We must investigate what may be troubling the city." Kindra held out her hand for Anna, who took it without question, then let Anna climb onto her back.

Kindra followed the sirens and found a police roadblock not too far from Anna's apartment.

"Where is she?!" commanded a woman whose voice growled louder than the surrounding sirens.

"Ma'am, stand down!" a police officer said over a loudspeaker attached to his car.

"How dare you speak to me like some common mortal!" she said. Aggressively pacing over the street lathered with blood.

It did not take a genius for Kindra to know this woman was someone from her time, and she could guess it was one of the Norns. But which one did she have the pleasure of seeing this time?

The woman swiftly approached the police officer with uncanny agility, proving her mystical nature which even surprised Kindra. Then, grabbing the police officer by the throat, she lifted him off his feet and scrunched her fingers together on her free hand, ready to pierce this man's body with just her might.

"Kindra—"

Before Anna could finish calling her name, Kindra sprang into action, wrapping her fingers around an iron grating on the sidewalk and ripping it out of the concrete. Rapidly spinning around, she releases the grate like a disc. The woman caught the iron grate mid-air as it makes its way toward her head.

"Hmph, I knew you would eventually show yourself," the woman said, dropping the policeman from her grasp to face the Valkyrie.

Kindra stepped forward to confront one of the deities of fate and keep her attention to leave the others unharmed. Though Kindra was doubtful.

"Who are you?" Kindra asked.

"I should be the one asking who, or more importantly, what are *you*?" she said in response to Kindra's initial question. The woman glanced at the grate in her hand, saying to Kindra, "It is undeniable that you have skill and strength far superior to a normal human."

"I already explained to your sister, Skuld, who I am."

Shedding the enraged expression off her face, the woman said, "Yes, my sister has informed me of you, but I am here to ensure she was not mistaken. A Valkyrie?"

The Norn shook her head.

"I am a Valkyrie. My name is Kindra, the last of my great sisters and their avenger for your treachery," Kindra said with pride.

"Ha, you expect me to believe you? Do not make me laugh. The Valkyries are nothing more than ash scattered over Midgard."

Kindra balled her fists and tightened her jaw.

"Do. Not. Disrespect. My sisters." Kindra growled.

"Oh, is that a threat?" The woman snickered, pacing side-to-side along the width of the street, obviously not taking Kindra seriously.

"Take it as you want. You will not harm these people," Kindra demanded.

"You call these cretins people? They are nothing but overpopulated vermin that pretend like they are orderly."

"They certainly do not need you, Norn!"

"You will speak to me with respect, child! I am Urd, Leader of the Norns and the ruler of every living being's fate."

"I do not care who you are. All I want is to seek vengeance for my fallen sisters."

"Your aspirations will only lead to your demise. Just like the other, real Valkyries did," Urd said without humor or derision and threw the grate in her hand back at Kindra.

The iron grate flew at an insane speed with just as much applied strength in her throw as Kindra's, slightly catching her off guard. However, instead of snatching the grate out of the air, Kindra deflected it with Hlokk's gauntlet. While it did not inflict any harm against Kindra, she felt the power inside Urd.

Let this be a good fight.

CHAPTER THIRTY-ONE

Rising into the air above the street, the Norn swiftly removed herself from dueling Kindra directly, traveling just out of jumping distance for Kindra. "Mankind is unfit to rule this world. Their constant bombardment of each other is doing more damage than the Gods ever could have imagined. Now, let me introduce this form of mankind to the monsters forgotten by time." Urd raised her hands towards the heavens.

The street tremored before shifting into a complete earthquake, with cars bouncing around and light poles toppling over. Materials that coated the exterior of the nearby buildings broke off, falling like hail onto the layer of concrete. People who stood to observe the Norn were also collapsing from the powerful vibrations. Kindra maintained her stance over the moving earth, unbothered by the quakes. Anna clung onto Kindra's arm as she was the only thing stable around her.

The asphalt beneath Urd erupted like a volcano. Street fragments fly into the air, some larger than Kindra herself, and crash onto the cars halted on the road. A beefy hand of four fingers and greyish skin rose from the fissure, digging into the hardened ground as it pulled itself up to the surface. Another hand punched from beneath the street, widening the hole where it now stretches across all four lanes.

Drawing its head from out of the opening, a massive beast climbed from out of the ground. It lets out a heavy roar like a marine animal breaching the calm surface of the sea.

"Oh god, what is that thing?" Anna asked, holding the Valkyrie's arm tightly like a scared child holding her mother.

"It's a troll," Kindra grumbled.

"A what—" The weight and power of the mighty behemoth, as it stood up in the city, delivered a tremor that caused Anna to cut her sentence short and regain ahold of Kindra for balance.

"Anna, stay back and seek refuge while I deal with this beast." Kindra opened up the bag and wields both her dagger and shield.

"Do you think you can tackle something that big?" she trembled.

"I had slain many before I was Valkyrie. So this shall be no challenge for me," Kindra replied, whipping the dagger to its full length. The sun glimmered off the polished surface, nearly as bright as the burning star itself, instantly catching the eyes of the troll.

The beast snarled at the woman opposing him, the white vapor of his breath rising like smoke from a raging flame. Yet as this imposing creature stood before Kindra, she did not back down or waiver a single muscle in its presence. In retaliation to Kindra's defiance, the troll picked up an empty car beside him, lifting it with ease in both hands, then threw it at her. Kindra carefully observed the trajectory of the flying vehicle, quickly making its way toward her. Her legs were locked, and she firmly gripped the handle over the spear as she waited for it to come closer.

As the vehicle eclipsed the sun, casting Kindra and Anna under darkness, she expanded her shield and swung the spear upward simultaneously. The layers of steel and composite materials were sliced perfectly in half without apparent effort from Kindra or the blade of the spear. The shield was thrust forward, colliding with the two halves of the car, where they divert away from her position. The immense force impacting against her shield did not stir any tremor in Kindra's body, not even a twitch in her placement over the ground.

"Anna, go!" Kindra commanded and quickly heard her friend's footsteps blend with the fleeting spectators.

The troll was displeased to see Kindra still standing and untouched. Rather than throw another car or confront her directly, he diverts his attention toward the city. Charging down the street heading east, the troll thrashes at the city structures and people trapped within his path.

Kindra jumped on the roof of the car beside her and immediately gave chase to the troll, leaping from vehicle to vehicle to avoid the stream of frightened people. A sliver of excitement rose within her, yet it was overburdened with anger and rage. Kindra moved as fast as she could in pursuit of her prey. The lumbering beast flung any object it could get its hands on toward Kindra. Cars, mailboxes, street signs, light poles. Anything within reach to avert her path. Every object was dodged or split apart with her spear.

As much as she wanted to face the Norn who summoned the bumbling creature, she was wrecking less havoc than the troll.

BANG! BANG! BANG!

A volley of gunfire was sent from the few police officers occupying the street. The bullets penetrate the surface of his flesh, dealing no significant damage rather than only becoming an inconvenience like bug bites. He halted his charge from the minor stings and loud noises from the police. Disgruntled that a small group of humans opposed his presence, he snarled at the puny beings for their feeble bombardment.

Both fists slammed onto the street, behaving like a frustrated child, causing a quake to rumble on this small corner of the city. He grabbed a policeman who lost his balance in one hand and raised him close to his face for closer inspection. Squirming in his grasp, helplessly outmatched by the troll's superior strength, there was nothing for the policeman to do but watch as his end grew near. Then, with a flash of his large tusks, the troll opened its maw, ready to devour the human. But before he could draw the policeman into his mouth, Kindra's spear drove deep into his shoulder, forcing him to release the man to fall to the ground.

The height from which the policeman fell injured him enough to be incapable of moving away from the troll's path. Raising a foot over the policeman with the intent to stomp him, Kindra rushed forward, sliding over the street to the vulnerable man. The shield was held over her head, and the impact was blocked. The full weight and power of the troll were born with one arm, barely a struggle for Kindra. The street cracked under tremendous pressure, unlike Kindra, who was thrilled to put her strength on trial against a more formidable opponent.

The troll pressed harder on Kindra's shield, yet she remained fixed like a mountain.

"You will not bring me down." Kindra gritted her teeth, then, using both hands, pushed as hard as she could against the shield.

The troll underestimated Kindra's might and tumbles backward into a tall building. With a brief window between them, Kindra swiftly pulled the policeman up by the collar on his vest and shouts to his compatriots nearby, "Hurry, take him!"

Two other officers take him from Kindra's hold, quickly dragging him away from the battle.

Kindra adjusted her stance to face the troll, who had regained his composure. Releasing a thunderous roar at the immovable Valkyrie, his giant fists were hammered where she was just standing. Every subsequent attack Kindra dodged with great speed and finesse, almost like a lightly choreographed dance. The troll was uncoordinated, a common trait she had seen amongst others of its kind. However, he had an impressive amount of strength that Kindra should not underestimate. Even as a Valkyrie.

She needed her spear back to bring it down for good before more people get hurt.

As the troll's large, opposite the arm with Kindra's spear punched through the city's foundation, it gave Kindra the perfect opportunity to scale up the troll's appendage to get closer. Her agility far outmatched his reaction time, so by the time he was aware of her movement, Kindra was already on top of his shoulder. The edge of the silver shield was thrust directly into his mouth. The protruding tusk was splintered like ice, and several teeth fell loosely from their placement. In agony, the troll produced a deep wail and tried to swat Kindra off his body.

She flips over his head to the other shoulder, then withdraws the spear in one yank from his flesh. The crimson blood dripped off the blade as if it were nothing but pure water, though it was not enough to bring down the beast.

He shuddered Kindra off his shoulder, who gracefully landed on the street, instantly taking a defensive stance based on pure instinct. However, seeing his blood made the troll more aggressive as he rapidly slammed his fists into the ground. Kindra dives under every swinging arm, using the dagger to slice through the rough flesh.

The sharp pain expressed on the troll's face fills Kindra with glee that she could not hide the glorious smile on her face.

As the troll continued to fight, doing a poor job of hiding his anguish, it was apparent he was worn down physically. His sluggish movements, heavy breaths, and lack of strength in his attacks force him to thrust his weight at Kindra. Rolling to her left out of the path of an incoming open hand, she threw her spear into the troll's right leg above the knee. The sudden impalement drained his strength for him to stand. As he fell, Kindra carefully positioned herself in his shadow. Following the same tactic she tried on Rota, except with the combined enhancements of a Valkyrie and Rota's gift of strength, Kindra swung her shield into the troll's face as hard as she could. A loud crunch resonated within the street with his head snapped backward at the neck.

While powerful, the rapid beating in her chest was nowhere near strained. *That was far too enjoyable.*

"I have come to face the Norns!" Kindra shouted, knowing they watched her fight in its entirety. "Answer my challenge!"

"Who are you to make such demands?!" Urd said beside Kindra.

The sudden appearance surprised her, yet Kindra did not let such minor trickery thwart her and swung her spear at Urd. The Norn caught the blade in her hand effortlessly before it could scratch her throat.

—What!—

No one besides another Valkyrie had the same speed and strength to hold her attack. She quickly parried with her shield, but Urd took one exaggerated step back, letting the metal swipe in front of her. Urd was quick to react and hardly looked like she was rushing into position.

No, she is not faster than me!

Kindra realigned herself to attack. Slashing furiously, though in a controlled manner, at the Norn. Each attempt was dodged without any counterattack. Urd only displays a stern expression as she weeds through every charge thrown by Kindra.

How is she this fast?

"Do you honestly believe one little girl can defeat us? We wiped out your entire clan, yet you wish to oppose fate," Urd said.

"I will avenge them!" Kindra shouted.

"Yes, I have heard that same statement many times before, and none have yet to claim victory."

She tried to not let her frustration consume her, but it was difficult for Kindra to ignore her inability to land a decent hit. It was not like engaging Hildr or Geirömul. Urd was not responding as one would in a fight, preferring to not deliver a blow herself. Instead, it was more focused on dodging Kindra's every movement. She was not a warrior, at least not on the same level as a Valkyrie.

Stay calm. Do not lose yourself. You trained too hard to fall from fighting like an amateur. Urd could be testing me as much as I am testing her. All she is doing … is causing a distraction …

Kindra swung her shield behind her, instantly blocking the surprise attack from another Norm wielding a bronze sword. This one was different, with a round, jovial face and delicate features. She was even smiling as she stood in front of Kindra. In a way, she reminded Kindra of Kara. This one must be Verdandi, the last of the sisters, to show herself.

"Wow, you have such beautiful eyes," she said to Kindra with a devious smile.

For someone who appeared dainty and playful, Verdandi was powerful even for Kindra to bear. Kindra brushed her off the shield without a word, adjusting herself for the unexpected inclusion of a second opponent. Thrusting her spear toward Verdandi, she simply swipes the pole with her sword with the same mannerism as if Kindra were nothing but a child.

With the same tenacity she had shown Urd, Kindra continued to fight, taking this moment seriously and refusing them to take advantage of her.

As Kindra pushed Urd with her shield while swinging her spear toward Verdandi, a sharp pain stabbed Kindra in the leg. It was such an intense sensation that it weakened Kindra enough to fall to her knees despite her best desires.

No … No, this cannot happen …

Looking down at her right leg, Kindra saw two black daggers pierced through her thigh and could even feel the fine point grinding against the bone. This was the first time since her Valkyrie enhancement for Kindra to have any object pierce her flesh.

A bullet could break the skin, but the weapons from deities could surely harm or even kill her. Grasping one blade by the handle in her hand, ignoring the searing pain in her leg from the slightest touch, she drew the blade out of her flesh.

Halfway out, Verdandi slammed the pommel of her sword against the side of Kindra's skull, jerking her head to be carried by the blow. Then Urd kicked Kindra in the back along the spinal column, thrusting the Valkyrie to the ground.

"Are you done acting like a spoiled child?" Urd asked condescendingly.

"I will never yield," Kindra grumbled, pushing off the ground with her spear.

"Certainly, no surprise there," said Skuld, stepping from the shadows to stand beside her sisters. "Only a fool would press onward against an opponent who outmatches them. Which says a lot about the Valkyries."

"Silence your tongue!" Kindra screamed, slashing her spear at the disrespectful Skuld.

The Norn draped in black stood unafraid of Kindra's scream or the glimmering blade of her spear slicing through the air toward her. Then, in a remarkable flash of speed, far quicker than Kindra's, the bronze sword from Verdandi easily halts the spear, producing a deafening clank as they meet.

"This one sure does have a temper. Are you sure she is a Valkyrie?" Verdandi said, still holding her smile.

Gritting her teeth, Kindra lunged at Verdandi, managing to tackle the woman to the ground.

Yes! I have her. Do not waste this!

She quickly raised her shield and brought it down, but before she could deliver the strike, a dagger stabbed Kindra in the back, throwing her off balance which had her slam the shield into the street, missing Verdandi entirely. Verdandi disappeared from Kindra's grasp, reemerging further in front of her.

"Oh, so close," Verdandi teased.

Kindra grunted as she stood back up, bypassing every sharp scream in her body.

This is not how it was supposed to go. I-I trained for this very moment, yet this is not the outcome I hoped for.

While Kindra was willing to die for her cause, she could not ignore the grave disappointment tugging at her heart. Kindra even wished to be struck down in battle like a true Valkyrie. Her sisters had an enormous amount of faith in her to avenge them. She thought her training and Valkyrie capabilities would give her the edge against the Norns. Yet, they were greater than what she expected.

She must not—could not—give up.

Kindra removed the daggers embedded in her thigh and the one in her back by swinging her spear around to dislodge it.

Think, Kindra. There has to be something you can exploit.

"Do not ridicule the girl, Verdandi," Urd said, "She is just too slow to figure out she has already lost. Even the dead have difficulty accepting their demise."

"I am not dead, so I have yet to lose," Kindra replied. She retracted her spear into its dagger form, considering that it was too long for her to move swiftly and that if she could get closer, she may have a better chance.

The Norns spaced themselves apart, surrounding Kindra in a triangular formation.

"You have already lost because we control the fate of all beings," Urd said. Urd held up a spool of red thread from a pocket in her gown. Then, curious, she tilted her head and said, "Ah, Now I see. When we destroyed the world, you—your soul—were still a part of it. Now that the old Midgard no longer exists, our ability to manipulate your fate has ceased. That is why we could not instantly find you."

"That means we have to end your life through traditional means," Skuld said in a monotone voice, holding out her daggers in both hands.

Kindra raised her shield to cover herself, and rather than rush to attack, she waited for one of them to make the first move. Then, behind her protective shield, Kindra whispers, "Sisters, give me the strength to vanquish our foes."

As the Norns circled Kindra like hungry vultures, the first to lunge forward was Verdandi with her sword drawn back, ready to be driven forward. Kindra could see her draw near, and once close enough, she side-stepped to let the blade slide past her head. In that instance, Kindra hooks around Verdandi's arm and yanks her down. Verdandi crashes on the ground hard on her back, fracturing the street with her embedded in the asphalt. Even a puff of air was extracted from her mouth.

Good, but I need to be better.

Next to charge was Skuld, pouncing in the air and throwing her daggers at Kindra. The shield blocked their advance, though as they ricochet, Urd snagged one in the air and swiftly threw it at Kindra, where it pierces the back of her shoulder blade. The strength to hold up her shield vanishes in a flash, leaving her arm to slump at her side.

What?! NO-NO, MOVE!

Occupied with her screaming thoughts, Skuld landed in front of Kindra, then threw an elbow into her face. It had enough force to knock Kindra on her back and drive the dagger further inside.

Kindra screamed towards the heavens, sounding more frustrated than in pain.

"Ha, I was waiting for her to scream, and she does it so eloquently," Verdandi snickered.

"This pitiful excuse of a fight does not have to continue. You can still walk away from this with your life," Urd told Kindra.

"I ... am ... Kindra ... a Valkyrie ... and I will fight ... to the end ..." Kindra said in a tired voice as she rose again to face the Norns.

Urd shook her head to see the defiance in the young Valkyrie. "So stubborn."

Kindra lunged at Urd with her silver dagger out, hoping to silence her mouth, which had done nothing but spew obscenities about Kindra and her fallen sisters.

Urd did not move as Kindra drew closer, only locking eyes with the young woman. The blade waited for the moment to be plunged into Urd's heart, with Kindra desperately wanting to see the blood drain from her body, but before she even got close enough, Urd vanished, and not only her but the entire city.

Kindra's dagger cracked into a stone, spraying sparks in all directions. The streets were replaced with a rocky desert, the horizon devoid of any man-made structures or even people, leaving only Kindra to stand by herself. Although the world appeared different, it was nowhere near as hot or humid as a desert should be, feeling just as cool as Seattle.

"What is this?" Kindra muttered softly to herself.

The cracking of rocks caught her attention, yet they were not from the collision of the small pebbles and sand found in the desert; these were loose rocks rolling over a flat surface.

I was not teleported to a new location. This is only an illusion.

She listened closely to the peculiar sound of grinding rocks, gauging where her opponent stood. Then, pinpointing where one of the three sisters was located, Kindra threw her dagger, which lengthened into the spear.

Urd instantly appeared, snatching the spear out of the air effortlessly.

"So, you figured out what many of your sisters could not. Very Impressive," Urd said, even producing a smirk.

A dagger flew from the shadows, and Kindra's instincts told her to bring forth her shield, but she could only partially move it since her arm was completely numb. The dagger stabbed Kindra just above her left knee, bringing the Valkyrie to kneel in front of the Norns.

"But they, too, could not prevent their own demise," Skuld said with a low chuckle resonating from her throat.

Before she could stand, Verdandi slashed her sword along Kindra's back, effortlessly slicing through the toughened flesh as if it were that of a mortal being.

"The blood of a Valkyrie is a glorious sight!" Verdandi said excitedly.

Urd could sense the drive inside Kindra to stand despite her wounds. "The Valkyries have certainly taught you many things, but humility is not one of them."

The elder Norn threw the spear back at Kindra, penetrating Kindra's abdomen on her right side. It was then that she collapsed, stifled by the immense pain, that she could not make any sound from her mouth.

"No . . ." Verdandi said disappointingly, "it was over too soon."

"Not soon enough. The girl still squirms like a fish separated from the sea," Skuld commented, slowly approaching Kindra with a dagger in her hand.

"Sister Skuld," Urd calmly said, holding up her hand to stop her sibling. Then, with a frustrated grunt, Skuld backed away for Urd to step forward.

—*Come on, get up! You can still fight! You have to*—

Grabbing a handful of Kindra's hair on the back of her head, Urd jerks Kindra's head upward to meet eye-to-eye. "You brought this upon yourself. I want you to know that."

Kindra glared at Urd in silence, doing everything she could to control the agony raging inside her.

"Only my sisters know how much I would love to kill the last of the Valkyries." Urd rips Skuld's dagger from Kindra's leg, causing her to yelp from the sudden infliction that sparked up her appendage. She placed the blade on Kindra's cheek just below her eye. "It would surely be satisfying to watch your line end here. I could watch as your lineage slowly fades from memory, but for once, I am willing to offer asylum. I would like to see you join us if you survive this ordeal. You can help reign a new world where humanity no longer exists."

"G-go to Hel . . ." Kindra muttered, spurting blood from her mouth.

"I admire your spirit. I truly do. It is one of the finer qualities of the Valkyries that is respectable and such a characteristic that would be cherished in our duties," Urd tightened her grip on the back of Kindra's head, "But now is not a time to test me. Take heed of the options I grant you. The first option is that you forgo this childish pursuit for vengeance and pair yourself with us.

The second option is simple: if you face us again, then we will kill you. I can assure you it will be far faster than this little skirmish. Finally, there is a hidden third option. Depending on my mood and how much resistance you put up against us. If the fire in your heart still burns when we meet again, we may imprison you in our well, tortured for years until obedience finally gets through your skull. For such a headstrong person as yourself, a thousand years may be adequate time for you to gain a new perspective. I will give you three days to come up with your decision. In the meantime, welcome the new flock from your world entering this one. And to help with your transition—" Urd drove the dagger into Kindra's face, carving a rune into her flesh.

Kindra screamed as Urd drags the blade down her cheek and tried to stop her, but Kindra lacked the strength to fight, and her efforts were easily pushed aside. Once Urd was done, Kindra could feel the blood rushing from the sliced flesh, and although she could not see it, she knew Urd carved a hagalaz rune from the long straight lines.

"Remember, three days," Urd said before yanking Kindra by the hair back into the street.

It was a minor discomfort compared to everything else that cried out in agony. The spear lodged in Kindra's abdomen was the most excruciating sensation, with her not daring to even touch the weapon.

Urd stepped away from Kindra with Skuld behind her, carrying a scowl, followed by Verdandi, who smiled and gave Kindra a playful wave of her hand before they all disappeared. Leaving Kindra writhing alone in pain.

H-how did this happen? I ... I failed ... I am sorry, Hildr ... I failed you ...

Chapter Thirty-Two

Kindra's hands pressed over the searing pain in her side, feeling the warm blood freely pool in her palms. Her eyes were slammed shut as she desperately tried to fight against the agony that consumes her entire body.

"Kindra!" Hildr screamed.

Thrusting her eyes open, the nerves on fire instantly ceased, and the thought of all the pain coursing through her body vanished from her mind. Her rapidly beating heart dampened like awakening from a nightmare. Kindra fell to her knees in front of Hildr, breathing heavily as she settled into the dream realm, heaving for air that was not there.

The surface was different. No longer was it a solid, dry mass. Instead, covering the ground was a level of water at finger length deep that was just as black as the rest of the realm.

She did not question the sudden change.

"I-I failed … I failed you, Hildr," Kindra cried, refusing to face or even stand in front of her.

"Stand up, Kindra," Hildr softly said.

She did not move a muscle, only letting her tears fall into the water.

"Kindra. Valkyrie of Champions. Stand." Hildr said sternly, more as a command than a request, with her posture straightened.

Her legs shook as she brought herself up in front of Hildr, but Kindra kept her head down even as she stood. The confidence that she once held was gone, feeling nothing but a shadow of her former glory. How could she present herself after a failed attempt to stop the Norns?

Hildr placed a finger beneath Kindra's chin, tilting her head to look into her eyes. Kindra's face trembled as she did the best she could to keep any more tears from pouring.

"You have not failed me." Kindra turn her head, but Hildr quickly diverted the young woman's face back toward her. "Do you understand? You have not failed. You are still alive."

Hildr's eyes grazed over the rune freshly carved on Kindra's face, with the elder Valkyrie tightening her jaw out of anger at the sight of her student being marked by the Norns.

Kindra shook her head. "I could not stop them. Not one. And I was impaled by my own weapon. A Valkyrie should never be defeated by her own arms. It is shameful and such a dishonor to the Valkyries and you."

Hildr firmly gripped Kindra's shoulders to comfort her young former student. "Kindra, I know the humiliation and thoroughly understand your embarrassment of what happened. Believe me."

"How can I? You are a great Valkyrie who has fought numerous battles. I am nothing but an unskilled amateur. Even if I escaped death, I have to live with the mortification that I was unable to defeat the Norns and that they used my own spear against me. I should have never been declared a Valkyrie. You chose the wrong person—"

Hildr slapped Kindra on her left cheek, which completely stunned her. It had been too long since Hildr struck her protege in such a manner. The powerful sting burning along her skin resurfaced as a memory of what happened. The slap left Kindra completely frozen, where not a single muscle on her face moved. Not even to breathe.

"Do not *ever* say that again." Hildr's voice was strong and serious. "Kindra. Every Valkyrie has known defeat and humiliation, no matter how great they are. And that lesson is not learned merely through the means of death. Some of us encountered such predicaments decades after our trial, which, if not confronted, affected the performance of our duties. Because of that hit against their pride and the degradation of their confidence, many could not recover and perished as a result. I do not want that to ever happen to you. I wish you did not have to face the same mistake we left behind, but this is the passage that you must venture through." Hildr cradles Kindra's face in her hands as she nervously nodded to her words. "Trust me when I say that I know how you feel. How else do you think I ended up here, and why could I not hand you my ax?"

"Hildr … what are you saying?" Kindra quivered.

Releasing a deep sigh, Hildr quietly said, "On the night we assaulted the Norns, the sister who can see the future, Skuld, knew our exact intent. She knew every step of each Valkyrie in our battle before we knew ourselves. With this knowledge in hand, the Norns were able to systematically eliminate us. I was caught in an illusion brought upon Verdandi, same as you, where I thought I was atop a tundra mountain for a moment. At the precise moment I dropped my guard, Skuld threw her daggers into my arms, where I lost my grip on the ax. Urd retrieved my ax from the ground, then turned the blade against me, chopping right over the collarbone until it sliced through my heart. To this day, Urd carries my ax. My ax!" While upholding a stern expression, tears were sliding down Hildr's cheeks. Kindra had never seen her mentor, her teacher, cry before in her life, which was beyond dispiriting. "Do not let that moment crumble you. Learn from it! Return stronger!"

The heartfelt pain burrowed within Kindra grew more intense. But the cold sinking feeling she had reshuffled into a burning sensation of rage the longer she stared into Hildr's eyes. She hid all this pain from Kindra, but it also seemed like she hid it from herself centuries after the horrible incident. Kindra hated the Norns before when they slaughtered her sisters, but now she was seething for the suffering they put Hildr through.

"I have and will never give up on you, Kindra. You should not give up on yourself."

"I … I will do my best … ." Kindra whispered.

The hardened instructor exterior on Hildr's face was switched into the caring mentor with a gentle smile. Her hand rubbed over Kindra's cheek, where she was slapped, and said to the young Valkyrie, "That is all I ask for from you. What I learned about you is that your best is more than enough to conquer the toughest of challenges. Even if you fail, know that you will once again be amongst your sisters. That we will be united."

"Urd will pay. I promise you she will fall."

With a subtle nod, Hildr releases Kindra and took a step back. "Then you best collect yourself as there is more for you to do in the real world."

"The old world our world has returned, and the creatures that once roamed Midgard are wreaking havoc on mankind which completely forgot about their existence. What should I do?"

"You should ask yourself, 'what *can* you do?'" Hildr replied.

"I ... can fight?"

With a nod, Hildr said, "Then you fight. Fight for humanity."

"What ... What about the Norns?" Kindra shook her head, "They were far beyond my skill level. I could not even touch them. I thought I was ready."

"Kindra, you are ready. Far more ready than any other Valkyrie I know, and you are blessed to face the Norns and live. Use that painful experience to figure out a plan. Even if the world is in chaos, you still have time."

"Thank you, Hildr ... for everything," Kindra whispered, "If there are one person's words that I trust, they are yours."

Placing her hand on Kindra's cheek over the rune, there was a gentle warmth from Hildr as the scar healed. With a smile, Hildr said to her pupil, "Just know I am with you every step of the way, and you can never disappoint me. Now, I need you to embrace the pain."

Hildr jabbed her fingers into Kindra's side in the same spot she was impaled, igniting the torment.

Waking up on a medical gurney, the surging pain reemerged in Kindra's abdomen. She saw the spear still within her body with bandages around the broken flesh.

"Kindra, you're awake!" Anna jumped up from her seat in the corner of the room but could not move very far as she was restrained to the seat via a metal cufflink.

"A-Anna … where am I?" Kindra asked as she did her best to disregard the pain after each passing breath.

"You're, uh, in the hospital. You were picked up off the street after your battle, and, well, the doctors did what they could. They were able to remove the knives but couldn't do anything about the spear or the open wounds on your body. Your skin is just too tough for their instruments. They could not even get an IV to numb the pain."

Kindra tried to reach for the spear, but without even lifting either of her arms, she noticed restraints strapping her body to the bed.

"What? Why am I like this?"

"Um … the world saw what you and those other women could do, so everyone is terrified. The only reason they let me stay by your side is because the police thought I could calm you down in case something bad happened when you woke up," Anna replied. "I actually had to beg them to let me stay."

"Bjorn? Where's Bjorn?" she tried to exclaim, but the tenderness in her abdomen prevented her from raising her voice.

"Don't worry, he's here." Anna picked up Bjorn with one hand out of his bed, which was beside her chair.

Stepping into the room in a hurry, Chris briskly walked up to Kindra at the foot of the bed. "Kim, or Kindra, whatever name you go by. I need to know exactly what the hell is going on with you, those three women, and these goddamn monsters appearing out of nowhere?" he questioned.

"Where are they? Where are the Norns now?" Kindra asked, ignoring Chris' curiosity.

"The Norns? Who are the Norns? Were they the women you were fighting?"

"I have to go … I have to stop them … stop all of this…" Kindra bursts the nylon straps that keep her body in place and gripped the exposed handle of her spear with both hands.

"What?! No, you're not leaving!" Chris shouted, grasping Kindra's arm. "Help!" I need help in here!"

A group of medical staff and police officers rushed inside the small room, instantly seeing Chris wrestle with Kindra for the spear.

"No, you should stay here and get medical help," Anna pleaded, desperately trying to persuade Kindra to not fight.

"You do not know what you are up against!" shouted Kindra as she pushed Chris and the others away from her. Even in a weakened state, they were no match for her power.

Under Kindra's touch, the spear slowly reduced in size, and as it did, she could feel the smooth surface pushing around her innards. Kindra screamed as she pulled on the metal but did not stop. Even when her own body was telling her to halt and leave it be, Kindra used all her strength to keep going.

"Kindra, stop! You can't take it out!" Anna said from beside the gurney.

The words *stop* and *can't* only fuel Kindra to not give in. The rise in Kindra's heart caused the machines to furiously beep, alerting the hospital staff of her rapid change in vitals.

The polished metal gradually slid upward though there was still a lengthy amount to draw out. Kindra could feel every single twinge of the blade as it cut through the layers of soft tissue and muscles. The pain was tremendous and even worse when it was self-inflicted, halting Kindra's need to breathe.

Half of the gleaming blade had risen. With one last burst of energy and a loud, defiant scream, the dagger was dislodged from Kindra's abdomen. Once the tip cleared from the opening it made, she finally took a breath of air as a reward. It was not a deep inhale due to the tenderness of her wound, but it was gratifying to feel the sharp intake of the sterile air brushing against the back of her throat.

Kindra tightly clutches the dagger's handle in her hand, not willing to be parted from her weapon despite the damage it had done. It was Hildr's gift nonetheless, and Kindra wanted to drive it straight into Urd's heart.

The beeping slows down, matching Kindra's internal rhythm.

"Kindra, are you all right?" Anna asked timidly.

"I feel ... much ... much better," Kindra replied exhaustedly.

The hospital staff steadily approached her as the abrupt escalation Kindra displayed dwindled from the removal of the dagger. One nurse gently wiped the beads of sweat accumulated on Kindra's forehead while the other examined the gaping wound in her stomach. In wide-eyed disbelief, the nurse near her wound exchanged looks with her affiliate.

"The wound is, uh, healing," the nurse said, sparking the other member to see.

They both witness the tissue beneath the serrated skin slowly mend together. No blood was rushing out, and all fibers cut by the dagger had reconnected with the superficial layer as the final piece. It took less than two minutes for the entire wound to be healed, leaving only a hairline scar behind as a faint reminder of what happened.

Thank you, Hildr.

Kindra crunches herself up from the gurney into a seated position, taking a slow deep breath as she was no longer restricted by the dagger in her body. There was still a lingering soreness, but eventually, it would fade away. If that was all she had to feel after being stabbed, then she could handle a little discomfort, even if it was indefinite. Kindra was glad to be alive and get the second chance her sisters did not receive, though she could not waste it.

"Do not move," Chris instructed with his gun pointed at Kindra.

"Where is my shield?" Kindra asked, again ignoring any of Chris' questions.

Throwing her legs over the edge and giving herself a decent push off the gurney, Kindra stood on both wobbly limbs in the middle of the room.

"I said don't move!"

She stared into the man's eyes which appear confident and angry but hides the fear behind them. All except for Anna have never encountered someone like Kindra, and they are right to fear her. She was afraid when she met a Valkyrie for the first time as a child.

"Miss, you should lie back down," the nurse said, following Kindra.

She ignores the woman's pleas and instead swung her dagger, moving faster than Chris could blink, and slices the front of his gun. He flinches backward, dropping the remaining half of his gun and raising his empty hands. When Chris's gun's rear half hit the floor, the other police officers draw their weapons.

"I am not your enemy," Kindra sneered. "My duties include the protection of mankind, and I will do that with or without your help. I am the only one who can stop the Norns. If I fail, then mankind will be erased forever."

Chris, along with everyone else in the room, stood in silence. Even with guns pointed at her, Kindra showed no sliver of fear and only displayed a substantial yield of her aggression.

"Lower your weapons," Chris ordered the other police officers standing beside him. Then, after taking a deep breath, he asked Kindra, "What do you plan on doing then?"

"Stop this merging of our worlds and hunt down the Norns. But, for me to do that, I need my armor."

Chris shook his head, conflicted about what to do, but after a moment, he hesitated to say, "Fine. Right now, we all have bigger issues to worry about. Our city is in chaos along with the rest of the world. If you're here to help us, then prove it. I'll … make a call, see if I can let the police department know you are not a threat." He turn to one of the police officers and said, "Damien, get her belongings."

Kindra stepped forward, which startled Chris, but as she placed a hand on his shoulder, she felt him somewhat relaxed. "Thank you, Chris. You are a good man. I know this is difficult for you as a protector as well. But, nevertheless, I will do everything in my power to ensure the safety of your people."

The sincerity and respect from Kindra's voice carried a lot of weight, solidifying her conviction. If there was one thing she wanted Chris to know, it was that she was devoted to keeping her word.

The police officer who retrieved Kindra's armor handed her a clothed bag seemingly struggling to hold it in both hands. Finally, he set the bag on the floor in front of Kindra and backed away with the rest of the other police officers. Rummaging through the bag, Kindra quickly put on Hlokk's gauntlets and her pauldron, then slipped her hand through the straps on her silver shield.

She did not realize how much her armor and weapons complete her. Without them, she almost felt naked.

"Anna," she softly said, "I am taking you and Bjorn home."

Kindra ripped off the chair arm, leading Anna by the arm to Chris.

"Can you please release my friend?"

CHAPTER THIRTY-THREE

The streets were riddled with hundreds upon hundreds of frantic people screaming and crying as well as gunshots erupting at every corner of the city. Kindra and Anna stand at the hospital entrance, soaking all that lies before them. Strangely, even though Kindra had seen such creatures in her old life, it still made her in awe. Trolls, a brunnmigi here and there, dozens of draugrs, and even creatures that exist in other realms, such as elves and wolves of Hel. Like Kindra, they seemed lost, confused in this new land with modern architecture and technology.

"Oh my god … Kindra, there are so many of them," Anna quivered, standing close to Kindra.

"I cannot believe they did this," Kindra muttered angrily.

Patients were being rushed inside the hospital with lacerations and bite marks over their bodies. Some were even being admitted with missing limbs that create a stream of blood over the floor. Soon there won't be enough room to tend to all of them. Also, the place would be vulnerable along with all occupants.

"Hold onto Bjorn tightly," Kindra instructed as she carried her friend in her shield-wielding arm.

She sprinted head-on into the chaotic city, dodging the frightened citizens and speeding cars. Hundreds of muscles sting and burn as they have yet to fully heal. The mystic creatures quickly noticed Kindra's presence, diverting from their current task to focus on the one being who did not belong.

A wolf with dark black fur and glowing emerald-green eyes charges towards them, leaving behind a trail of black smoke on the ground from the touch of each paw. Kindra could sense its hunger as it growls. It pounced at Kindra with its body straightened like an arrow, keeping its mouth shut until it was close enough to sink its fangs into the flesh of whoever was nearer.

Kindra swung her spear into the beast's head, smacking it out of the air.

One down out of an unknown amount. She could only hope a finite number of creatures had been resurrected.

By the time they reached the base of Anna's apartment complex, Kindra had struck down over two dozen feral, mystical entities, drenching her spear in a mixture of different types of blood. Then, leaping to Anna's balcony, she set the young woman down with Bjorn in her grasp.

"Anna, secure yourself here in your home. Do not go out, and do not let anyone or anything inside," Kindra lightly instructed. Her composure was contained to not escalate Anna's already panicked state.

"Okay, Kindra. Are you going to be all right all by yourself?" she said. "You're pretty much facing an army."

"Armies can fall as well. I will do what I can to keep you and Bjorn safe. You two are the only things I have left in this world."

Anna smiled and said, "Well, I think someone would like to say goodbye."

She held Bjorn in her arms, presenting him to Kindra. Gently clutching the pup in both hands, Kindra gazes into his beady black eyes that have finally opened to witness the world around him. Her fingers rub the soft fur on his belly, causing him to kick his leg back and forth. Kindra kisses Bjorn's forehead, whispering to him, "Now you be a good boy while I am gone," then hands him over to Anna.

"I'll watch over him," Anna said, "You just take care of yourself out there."

Kindra bowed her head and then jumped off the balcony to deal with the chaos stirring below.

"Do you honestly think she will come to her senses and become subservient to our cause?" Skuld asked Urd as they lingered around their buried well.

"Honestly, I would not be surprised if she fled," Verdandi interjected before Urd could comment on her thoughts toward the subject. "You put the fear of death in that little girl's eyes. She probably would have traveled the Bifrost into Hel to escape your wrath if she could. I know I would."

"I would say that I have my hopes she would take the smart route, but the Valkyries are not known for their pristine intelligence and wisdom, especially the young ones. They are like ravenous beasts, craving for battle and will only calm themselves once they have satisfied their thirst for blood. If she sticks to her Valkyrie ways, she will be overwhelmed in transporting spirits of the fallen until her very soul gets caught in the same flood," Urd said to her sisters. "Her cooperation is not necessary to our plot, though it would be beneficial to have a new set of capable hands to do all the heavy lifting."

"Yes, I would hate to get my hands bloodier than they need to be," Verdandi said, examining her nails.

Skuld ignored Verdandi's input and asked Urd, "You gave the girl three days. What do we do till then? Start a fire and tell stories until three moons pass?"

"Ooh, that does sound rather lovely," Verdandi elated. However, her voice dwindled as she took notice of Urd's stone expression that did not bend to her playful humor.

"Our efforts will not be halted despite the pending decision of one girl who calls herself a Valkyrie. One way or another, mankind must pay for its irresponsible and destructive nature. Spread yourselves out in the world and bring new life to those far-off lands. It would be impossible for one Valkyrie to protect all of mankind when the world is falling apart. Also, feel free to carry out mankind's eradication by your own hands in case you are looking for some excitement."

Skuld grinned from Urd's previous sentence and grimly said, "As you wish, sister."

"I assume neither of you could contain yourselves during your survey."

"Oh, whatever gave you that impression, dear sister?" Verdandi said coyly with a bright smile on her face.

Urd rolled her eyes, flicking her wrists for Skuld and Verdandi to do as commanded.

Anna placed her dining table against the screen door with several bed sheets covering the glass, stacked chairs, and numerous textbooks against the front door. She hunkered down in her bed with Bjorn beside her. Anything that lit up or made a noise was turned off so that it could not attract the monsters. It was unknown if they could reach her this far off the ground level, but Anna would not want to risk it when it could be avoided.

She could hear people screaming throughout the building, running through the hallways, banging on doors, and the occasional gunshot. If she were not afraid of what was lurking outside, the frightened people would have certainly done the job.

She held her cell phone close with her headphones on, looking up the news of what was happening in the city and everyone else was experiencing. All over social media, people were posting pictures of various creatures they encountered, many that Anna had not previously seen.

Society was certainly not prepared to combat such a mysterious force. But, honestly, who knew these creatures existed. Anna only came to accept the plausibility that they could be real once she came across Kindra. She also questions what else that was once a myth could be lying out there. Now that there were beings of Norse myths on the loose along with the powerful Norns, Anna was unsure whether to pray to God, Odin, or give it up altogether.

Anna only hoped Kindra came back in one piece.

"Bless Freya . . ." Kindra whispered as she gazed at all the creatures clamoring over every city's surface. Even as a child, she did not witness as many mystical creatures in one location simultaneously.

I must maintain order. It is what my sisters would have done.

Slamming her spear against her shield made a loud hollow bell-like sound, drawing everyone and everything's attention toward her.

Kindra kneeled over the street with her spear staked before her and the shield resting at her side. Lowering her head to recite a prayer, a prayer taught to Kindra on her first day of training by Hildr.

"Hail day, hail the sons of day. Hail night, and the daughter of night . . ."—a stone troll pounded the road with its fists at the sight of Kindra— "Gaze on us with gracious eyes . . ."—the stone troll stampeded towards her, leading an army of draugr— "Award us victory, we who wait. Hail the Gods, Hail the Goddesses . . ."—crawling down from the buildings were a pack of wulvers eager to join the fight— "Hail Earth who gives to all. Wisdom and fair speech give to us, and healing hands while we live."

The city quaked from this horde of beasts that wanted to tear Kindra and the rest of humanity into oblivion. If Hildr told her as a child this would be her life, the challenges she would face, Kindra wondered what she would have said then.

"I hope you are watching, Hildr," Kindra whispered.

As the stone troll towered over her like a man above an insect, ready to slam his giant, jagged fist where she kneeled, Kindra quickly stood with her shield raised over her head. The stone fist blasted into a flurry of shards and rubble, posing no equal to the magical steel or might of a Valkyrie.

Hildr never promised Kindra an easy life and had made it very evident to the contrary, though she did often speak of having one worthwhile. Even if she said Kindra would get the chance to die as a Valkyrie, she would have volunteered to seek such a glorious end. From what Kindra knew of their lineage, she would be the only Valkyrie to have faced an army by herself and hopefully live to tell the tale.

Chapter Thirty-Four

The darkness descended upon Seattle hours after Kindra left Anna and Bjorn in her apartment. Most of the vocal sounds had died down from her neighbors. Hopefully, everyone either escaped while they could or hunkered down in their room, just like Anna. Every once in a while, she hears a car speeding by her apartment with a subsequent loud crash. Bjorn would emit a high-pitched bark at every disturbance from outside or significant jostling of the building. Luckily, his voice was still fairly quiet and was contained within the confines of her bedroom.

Anna had avoided looking outside to see the damage or any of the mythical beasts. She had seen far too many horror movies to know that something would instantly notice her once she took a peek. Besides, Anna was sure of herself to be unable to stomach the destruction and gore that litters the streets outside her window. She had already seen enough on social media to last her a lifetime. Her cell phone constantly receives emergency text messages, telling people to seek shelter, not to go outside, and not to confront unknown animals.

More of these strange, unnatural creatures have been spotted in different states as well as internationally, spreading like a plague. Those brave enough to battle against the monsters quickly realized how inferior their weapons were, with only a few managing to escape with their lives. So far, it was unclear if only magical items like Kindra's weapons could kill them or if they were just resilient to the weapons of modern-day man.

Throughout the day, Anna did come across footage of Kindra uploaded on the internet. People captured her, leaping from fight to fight, slaying all the monsters in her path, and saving people caught during this invasion. Although Anna had seen her move in person, it was still amazing to witness this one woman in action, displaying the courage to face these things alone. No one knew who she was and could barely capture a clear shot of her face with their cell phone cameras. Some dubbed her the Seattle Angel, with others giving her the title of Warrior Woman, Seattle Savior. Only recently were a couple of people with high-definition cameras able to see the runes etched into her shield. And by carefully examining her armor, they renamed her the Valkyrie in the West, or simply The Valkyrie.

The darkness had not changed Kindra's ability to fight, and neither for her enemies. On the contrary, she felt quite comfortable in the dark. After each creature that fell by her spear, Kindra reminisces on the times she was in the mare and how the realm was absent of light.

Did Hildr know I would be fighting in such darkness? And the training she put me through up to the point of my trial ... was she aware I would be up against so many beasts, too many for one Valkyrie to handle? In my last week with Hildr, all she had me do was test my endurance, stamina, and capacity to overcome great discomfort. And that was while I was still mortal.

Despite the tremendous pressure of having the fate of the world—this entire realm—on her shoulders, Kindra found some enjoyment in her task. Now she could unleash her full strength and speed, applying all her training correctly.

A screeching wail was produced near the shore, sounding nothing like what an average human could emit. But none have made such a terrible screech from the beasts she had encountered today. It truly sparked her interest to figure out what else had entered this world.

Moving towards the origin of the sound, slaying a few wulvers along the way, she quickly reached the edge of Seattle. However, there was nothing here.

The shore was vacant of life, either mystical or natural, with even the water calmly rolling by.

"What was it?" Kindra grumbled.

A low growl burst from a grouping of bushes near the road, obviously of a wulver and not the strange screech she heard earlier. Wulvers. The human-wolf hybrid always creeped her out with its man-shaped build and erect posture, moving in the same manner as a wild animal. Wolves were terrible enough, but coupled with the qualities of a human makes them worse.

His eyes glow a bright yellow as they reflect the light from the moon lingering in the sky. Like their bipedal cousins, these creatures were adept at hunting in the dark, preferring to stalk humans than deer or elk, which were a better offering. It was almost like they were preying on fear rather than the quality of sustenance. Rising from the bushes with its eyes fixated on her, it showed no remorse towards Kindra. The blood of its kin dripping off her spear or splattered on her shield did not sway its conviction.

Kindra did not even have to get herself into a proper fighting stance as she could come up with over fifty ways to kill this being without taking a step.

There was a disturbance in the water. A large creature bursts through the surface and immediately snags the wulver from the ground. It plunged into the sea so fast that the wulver could not let out a yelp. The water-based creature struck with such speed and precision that Kindra barely caught a glimpse of it before it submerged itself with its captured prize. She rushed to the point where the water met the concrete, looking over the handrail only to see the population of rising bubbles that quickly settled once noticed.

—thrusting out of the water in front of Kindra was the head of the serpent—

Kindra backflipped away from the edge into a crouch with her shield raised in front of her. The serpent held its head high above Kindra, carefully studying her. The body was smooth with a dark green hide that appeared almost black, completely absent of scales like a typical snake. It had a long snout, forming its head into a diamond shape, which also conceals the majority of the row of teeth in its snout.

"Woah . . ." Kindra whispered in awe. "It is a sjöorm."

Kindra had never seen a sjöorm, or sea serpent, in person. Most of her knowledge came from stories of others who they learned of from another party's observations. She thought they all died out except for a few who partook in being a spirit warden, a *rå*, for lakes and rivers. The Norns truly dived deep into the past to reach for entities that were even a myth to the people of Kindra's time.

The sea serpent struck like a land-dwelling snake, missing Kindra as she rolled out of its path. She lashes with her spear, creating a small slash along its neck. It drew itself back from Kindra's quick counterattack, which only gave it a sharp sting and nothing fatal.

Taking a careful position over the grass by the shore, Kindra held back her spear in preparation to strike at the best opportunity. No matter how large this creature was, she would not move or show the slightest sign of fear in its presence. The serpent launched towards Kindra with its mouth gaping open, capable of devouring her whole if only she allow it. Once within the distance of its maw, the spear was thrust forward, stabbing it through the roof of its mouth, but it did not travel far enough into its skull.

Damn …

The serpent snapped backward, whipping its head with Kindra still clutching her spear by the end. She endured the wild thrashing, trying to maintain her grip on the spear. It cried that same high-pitched screech that attracted her, nearly deafening Kindra now that she hung at the funnel projecting this awful sound.

The tail wrapped around her waist, yanking Kindra from its mouth along with the dislodgement of her spear. She was drawn into the water, swiftly pulled deep under the surface. While submerged in the cold darkness, Kindra could partially see the long body of the serpent hidden under the depths. It traveled further than she could see, where the rest of the body resided in the abyss, with the tail poking out from the black mass.

Even with the spear removed and Kindra pulled into the water, the serpent refused to release her. Instead, it tightens its hold over her waist. Kindra's core fights the serpent's immense strength to keep herself from being crushed as well as not having the bit of air she had forced out of her.

From the spear to the dagger, Kindra stabbed into the tail wrapped around her body. She could feel it jerk from the instant her blade pierced its hide, yet it did not undo its hold. Repeatedly stabbing the hefty mass of muscle, an oily cloud of blood envelopes her.

Let me go, damn you!

Plunging the dagger deep into the serpent's tail, she pulled it aside, slicing along the length of its body and making a tremendous gash. The pain-induced roar from the serpent could be heard underwater, eventually releasing Kindra to swim rapidly toward the surface. She had no idea or reference on how deep she was dragged, though Kindra believed she was not near the shallows.

There was a mighty splash followed by a rush of water brushing against Kindra. She paused to face the presence of two eyes glowing orange like the evening sun staring directly at her. The serpent let out its distinctive scream while submerged now that it had Kindra in its sights. The eyes quickly grow more prominent as the serpent darts towards her.

The spear was formed in front of Kindra, held horizontally, preventing the serpent from crushing her in its jaws. With the serpent's mouth pried open, she used her shield to bang against the jaw, shattering several teeth from their placement. Kindra broke off one of the fangs with her hand, then stakes it into the serpent's tongue. She collapsed the spear, letting the sea monster close its jaw around her. The fang kept Kindra from slithering down the serpent's throat, despite its constant attempts to force her into its stomach.

Kindra held out the dagger further down its mouth, and once in position, she formed the spear into its full length, piercing the serpent through his skull. From its powerful thrashing and the gurgling scream underwater, it seemed she hit her mark.

Come on, just die already!

Her thoughts screamed for this watery beast to succumb to its fate before she, too, sank along with it.

The violent thrashing softened with the body swaying under the gentle ocean current. She quickly dislodged the spear and pried open the jaws to see the flickering moonlight point upward.

Kindra swam toward the moonlight but halts to look back at the serpent. The eyes were no longer glowing, with the lengthy body of the sea serpent drifting to the murky depths where the rest of it remained.

She returned to swimming toward the surface. Upon the breach, welcoming the air back into her lungs was a fine reward for her victory against the sjöorm. She had never battled a sea monster before, and if she was not a Valkyrie, the turnout would have ended differently.

Resting on the bank to the city, the sirens, screaming, and roars from mystic beasts were still ongoing.

Kindra used her upper body to push herself up from the bank, but before she could escape the water, a set of hands grabbed her ankles and swiftly yank her back into the sea. While submerged, Kindra twisted around, wrestling the entity that had her in its clutches. A bundle of long black hair drifts in the water, appearing human-like. Sprouting from the hair were two clawed hands with webbing between the fingers like a duck's paddle feet. Kindra quickly grabbed them by the wrist, keeping them just far enough from clawing her face. A face appeared from the swirling plume of hair, carrying an almost human woman's features, albeit altered for the aquatic environment, with smooth, pale skin. This woman had solid white eyes absent of pupils and an array of pike-shaped teeth.

A Nixie?

Water spirits like this one were typically gentle creatures who sang lovely hymns and were a joy to interact with. Neither Kindra nor Hildr had never had any qualms with these beings. However, this could be from a separate clan or one that was corrupted by the Norns' magic during her resurrection.

Several high-pitched whistles were coming from behind the nixie, and Kindra could see the presence of numerous others swimming toward her.

Oh no …

Chapter Thirty-Five

By the time dawn arrived, Anna was already awake. Sleep did not come easy for her, and it was worse for Bjorn due to his heightened senses that could pick everything which frightened him. For now, he was asleep after tiring himself out from his interrupted sleep cycle.

Anna rechecked her cellphone for news of what occurred overnight and if there was anything about Kindra. From what she found, there were multiple articles of attacks. Hospitals were overflowing with first responders unable to respond to calls. During the invasion, people were trapped in work offices, and groups were trying to fight back to no avail.

She continued to scroll for anything referencing her Valkyrie friend. Finally, coming across a video titled *Superhero Girl*, captured on the west side of Seattle in Elliot Bay sometime after midnight. The footage was grainy and not focused as the person was recording the event far away and from multiple floors off the ground. But what could be seen was the water raging from a battle occurring beneath the surface. Strange creatures were seen being knocked out of the water. Even the limbs of these beings were tossed into the air.

The clash lasted almost ten minutes with nothing but these underwater creatures in the video. The waters eventually calmed, reverting to their regular steady waves. Soon after, a lone figure crawled out of the water, hunched over the shore. Anna instantly knew it was Kindra from the polished chrome shield and spear in her hands. Through the limited zoom of the recording, Anna could see the exhaustion expressed in Kindra's stance and subtle movements.

With only a brief catch of her breath, Kindra stood back on her feet and started running along the shore, heading north.

"My god, please be safe, Kindra," Anna whispered from under the linen covers.

The sun returned to its normal position in the sky, nearly touching midday. Kindra's body was covered in blood, a gory rendition of a grotesque rainbow from the various creatures she had come across, including humans. Amongst her obligation to rid these beasts from Midgard, she also had to fulfill her Valkyrie duties of transferring souls to the afterlife. Some spirits wandered near their corpse, or what was left of it, while others died in Kindra's arms and were put to peace after their final breath.

Kindra prepared herself to handle the grief and alienate her emotions from her responsibilities, but not for this many people. Inside her was a complex combination of rage and sorrow. Although she would hate to admit it, Kindra hoped to become numb to this task.

She did everything she could to slay the beasts wreaking havoc in her realm and aid the mortals in trouble. There were even times when Kindra had to assist the police and firefighters in rescuing people who were trapped or unable to fend for themselves. But, no matter how inconvenient or the extra effort put into saving these people, Kindra would give them her all and keep her word to Chris.

From monster to monster, Kindra ventures, saving as many unfortunate souls as she could, resulting in her traveling beyond the limits of Seattle to the neighboring towns. But it was a thread Kindra had the misfortune to pull, and it was up to her to say when to stop.

I ... cannot go any further. I have to get back to check on Anna and Bjorn. I need to know if they are all right.

These inhuman beasts were testing her abilities, not to the same extent as the Norns. Still, they were more challenging to kill than any average person.

Kindra turned around on her heels and sprints towards Anna's apartment. If she found more monsters lurking within the city, they would face the same fate as the ones who once stood in their place.

Anna quietly cooks a pot of soup on the stove. She was afraid to even make the smallest of noises, like the jostling of silverware or clinking of glass which could attract unwanted attention from outside.

WHAM-WHAM!

A pounding on the screen door startled Anna enough she almost dragged off her pot of soup from the stove.

"Jesus!" she screamed while trying to keep her voice down.

"Anna! Are you still here?" From the sound of her name being called, Anna intuitively knew it was Kindra. She could easily recognize her voice without moving the table or pulling off the sheets covering the glass. Who else would be on her patio?

She rushed to open the screen door. Once the glass door was pushed aside, Kindra stumbled inside the apartment, nearly tripping over the carpet. The Valkyrie's body was saturated in multi-colored blood, with barely a square inch of her skin untouched. Even her face was covered as if it were warpaint. Kindra's arms were swollen, showcasing all the striated muscles and veins filled with blood. The blue jeans, which were no longer blue, were ready to rip under the tension of her legs that have been getting her from battle to battle.

"I am glad you are safe," Kindra said, sounding exhausted and doing her best to produce a smile. "I must return to the war outside."

Her legs almost gave as she turned around, about to leave, but quickly regained her composure to stand.

"Kindra, no. You need to rest," Anna said, holding up her arms to stop Kindra from leaving.

"Anna, please, there is much at stake, and the world needs me—"

"—the world needs you in a condition to keep fighting. You're no good to us dead. And as much as a warrior you are, willing to die for your cause, this world needs you alive."

Kindra did not want to argue and, deep down, enjoyed a moment to rest. It was only in her battle against these mystical beings, did Kindra realize that their claws and teeth did more damage than any blade or bullet from man. Despite having a robust and enhanced body, it was not impervious to magic.

Anna guided Kindra to the couch, letting her gently lie down on her side. The cushions felt remarkable against her skin and tensed muscles, allowing them to relax with the pressure taken off her body. The mere touch of the pillow against her face almost put Kindra into a slumber.

"Just stay here for a second and gather your strength," Anna said, quickly moving to the bathroom and coming back with a wet towel.

"Where is Bjorn?" Kindra whispered hoarsely.

"Don't worry, he is lying on my bed. I think he knows you're here. Bjorn seems to be searching for you," Anna replied, which brought a weary smile to Kindra's face.

Holding out Kindra's arm, Anna slid the wet towel over her, following the curvature of Kindra's muscles to wipe away the blood. The warmth was gentle and soothing. As the gore was cleansed off Kindra, Anna noticed several cuts and deep, red abrasions along her arm. She knew her wounds would eventually heal rapidly, but seeing them on Kindra—a Valkyrie of all people—was unsettling and very concerning about what she was up against.

"I kept up with you on your journey. From the moment you were in Elliot Bay to the south of Yelm. I thought you were gonna keep going to California."

"You saw?" Kindra muttered.

"Of course. The world knows of you now. Everyone with a camera tried to take a video of you at the moment kicking ass. You're amazing out there."

"It is not amazing when I have yet to win the war."

Anna gently rubbed the towel on Kindra's face, clearing her cheek of blood and dirt to see her pristine skin underneath.

"Baby steps. You're doing great out there, knocking them down one by one."

"It is not enough … there are so many of them … I cannot defeat them all … ." Kindra said, her words slurring as she began to drift from consciousness.

"Hey, don't worry about the numbers. No matter what, you're making a difference." Anna moved the towel over to Kindra's neck. "Your drive and courage are really impressive and quite inspiring. Makes me wish I was someone like you, you know?"

As Anna looked over at Kindra's face, she saw that the Valkyrie had fallen fast asleep on the couch. She seemed at peace, possibly the most tranquil Anna had ever seen Kindra. Even with her face partially bloodied, Kindra looked like a sleeping beauty.

Anna continued to clean Kindra in silence, happy to help her friend in these troubling times.

Chapter Thirty-Six

Returning to the dream realm, there was a drastic change to its otherworldly appearance. No longer was it a vast void of nothing but darkness. Now Kindra stood within a colorful meadow filled with spring flowers and knee-high grass. An overcast sky was present over the sun, which brought a small amount of light to this reimagined realm. She also found herself wearing the blue tunic she once wore instead of the modern clothing bought by Anna.

Not too far from where she stood, Hildr patiently waited with her hands crossed over each other in front of her lap. Kindra heads towards her, and with every step, she could feel the grass brushing against her legs and her feet rolling over the soft soil.

"Hildr, is this real?" Kindra asked once she became in range to talk.

"It is as real as you perceive it to be," Hildr replied.

"What happened here?"

"This is drawn from your imagination. Remember, this is *your* dream."

Kindra gazed at the meadowlands that appear to go on forever with nothing else in sight. "I dreamt this?" Kindra whispered.

"From what I see, it looks like you miss your homeland."

Turning her attention back towards Hildr, Kindra said, "I miss more than just the land."

A slight grin slid across Hildr's face, showcasing the fine wrinkles over her cheeks.

"We have watched you tackle the great army ahead of you without fear. Kindra, because of your upkeep of the Valkyries' values and going beyond your duties by being a protector of man, someone special has requested to see you."

Someone special?

Forming on the right side of Hildr, a swirl of smoke emerged from thin air, growing exponentially like a living entity until it became larger than Hildr. Out of the top of the smoke sprout, two golden wings made from the polished metal itself. The billow of smoke drifts away like a gentle breeze passed through the meadow, and a strong figure emerges out of the dark cloud in rose gold armor. There was only one person among all the Valkyries to wear such glamorous armor.

It was Freya, Goddess and Queen of the Valkyries.

Kindra stood frozen at the sight of the majestic warrior clad in golden armor. She was the mother to all the Valkyries before their creation. She even trained the Goddess, Herja, who built upon the skills she learned to form the Valkyries at Odin's command. However, no one, not even Hildr, had ever met Freya in person, as she never left Asgard once Herja took control of their outfit.

Freya's face was covered behind a full-casted helm that was expressionless yet daunting to see in person from the lack of emotion.

Immediately, Kindra fell to her knees with her head lowered to respect the great Valkyrie queen.

"Y-your grace . . ." Kindra stuttered. It had been too long since nervous anxiety had encompassed Kindra with such power when in the presence of an individual who demands respect. "I ... I am humbled in your presence but do not deserve to meet you under these circumstances."

Freya removed her helm, unveiling an older woman who, despite holding several wrinkles on her eyes and cheeks, was quite a beautiful and physically fit individual. She had long blonde braided hair with only a few silver strands. Aside from the elegant appearance, Freya's light blue eyes foretold the years had endured by her. While Freya was their elder and in a position that refrains her from battle, she maintained a muscular build with a broad figure that the armor could not hide.

"Kindra, the Valkyrie of Champions and the last of my beloved sisters. If there is anyone more deserving to meet me, then they surely do not exist in any realm," Freya said with a deep but gentle voice. "Please, do not kneel, for we owe our lineage to you."

Freya offered her hand out for Kindra, who hesitantly grabbed it and is raised to her feet.

"You have certainly grown since the day Hildr declared you to be her apprentice and trained so hard through many winters to reach this point."

"You were watching?" Kindra asked.

Freya smiled and said, "I have watched over every Valkyrie from the day their mentors selected them to their final living moment." But then, the smile on the great Valkyrie's face fades. "Seeing those I deemed as my sisters perish in one night was the most dreadful time in all my years, and my heart grieves for all we have lost. It should not have ended that way. But Hildr never gave up hope, and I relished her faith in you."

"I am humbled to hear the words coming from you."

Kindra never expected Freya to have such a light, caring personality as she imagined the great Valkyrie to be a gruff and hardened veteran. But the stories passed on by the council have spoken of the kindness and love given by Freya.

"Each passing day, I have seen you become more powerful by fulfilling the wishes of your fellow sisters and your desire to improve yourself. It is quite admirable for any warrior. With that, I offer you my power. Something that no other Valkyrie possesses. Kindra, hold out your hand."

While Kindra was slightly confused, she did not hesitate to do as commanded and extends her arm with her hand open. Reaching for the scabbard clung to her hip, Freya swiftly drew out her sword. The blade was narrow and almost as tall as Kindra, entirely made of polished silver with a triangular pommel. Wrapped around the handle was a brown leather strap that stretches from the pommel to the golden curved guard. Although the weapon appeared ceremonious, there was no doubt it was used in battle.

"I present to you the Midgard Stjarna. Her gift allows you to wield the power of the gods. May she serve you well in battle as she once did for me."

Freya skillfully flipped the long sword in one hand and held it out for Kindra to take. Carefully with as much respect to Freya, Kindra wrapped her fingers around the leather-bound handle, feeling the weight and crafted metal in her possession. She could see mystical runes aligned along the blade at the perfect tilted angle. The Midgard Stjarna, or simply Stjarna, which meant *star*, was a legendary weapon among the Valkyries that no other could compare in its sheer power. Odin commissioned Stjarna only for Freya as he believed it would help secure her role as the Valkyrie queen, but from what Kindra had heard, she rarely used it as Freya advocated for skill or any weapon. This philosophy was passed down to her council, which developed them into the finest warriors the world had ever seen.

"Can you feel it? The power resonating within her?" Freya asked.

"Yes. Yes, I can feel it," Kindra replied.

"Good," Freya smiled like a proud parent. "With this now in your charge, I relinquish my status as Goddess of the Valkyries. I pass that responsibility onto you."

"What?!" Kindra exclaimed, flabbergasted by Freya's declaration, but before she could say any questions or even refute, Freya immediately interjected.

"You are the inheritor of everything we left behind: the knowledge, the training, and virtue of the Valkyries."

"But I have only been a Valkyrie for a week at the most. I am not ready for such an undertaking far beyond my station," Kindra said.

Freya gently placed a hand on Kindra's shoulder, but even as delicate as she tried to be, Kindra could feel the immense strength pressed on her.

"Then we share something in common. When Odin directed me to lead a clan of superior warriors to escort the souls of the fallen to Valhalla, did you believe I was prepared to carry out such an order?"

Kindra paused for a second as she thought about Freya's words.

"From what I have seen, Hildr did not only craft a fine warrior worthy of being amongst us, she developed an upcoming leader. Even if she did not realize it herself then."

The awakening illumination in Kindra's heart glowed as bright as the new sun in this rendition of her dream.

"Your grace … I have no words that describe how grateful I am to meet you tonight and the great honor you have bestowed upon me," Kindra quietly said.

"Even if our council still stood, you would be the ideal candidate to take my place. Do us all proud, young Kindra. Be the balance of all realms. Hildr and I, and all the spirits of our sisters, will cheer for you."

"Take care, Kindra," Hildr said with a smile and watery eyes as the blinding light spread across the realm.

She woke up, not from the natural conclusion of her rest but from the sirens breaking her slumber, hitting Kindra like water poured over her. Kindra thrusted herself up from the couch, startling Anna, who was standing in the kitchen.

She glanced at her hands and saw herself cleared from the copious amount of blood once lathered over her skin. Kindra also noticed her hands were empty. Unlike her previous returns from a dream, Kindra lacked any material that may have transferred the planes. Freya's treasured Stjarna was nowhere near her.

Could it have been real? It had to be. I felt the Midgard Stjarna in my hands, felt Freya's presence.

"Kindra, are you all right?" Anna asked.

"Yes … I must leave. I am needed in the world," Kindra said, sounding just as tired as she was before her nap.

Despite not wielding the famed weapon of Freya, Kindra must engage the foes outside with her battle-proven armaments. She would use her hands if it came down to it.

"Kindra, you have only been asleep for less than a couple of hours. You should rest some more."

"If I needed rest, then the Gods would have granted it," Kindra said as she picked up her dagger and shield. Sitting in his bed, Bjorn made short, squeaky barks at the growing noises outside the apartment. Kindra approached the pup, sliding her fingers over the soft fur on his head. "And you, do not overburden yourself by protecting this home."

As she opened the screen door, she felt the gust of wind brush against her, carrying the sound of screams of both man and beast and the heavy scent of smoke. Vaulting over the patio's edge, Kindra quickly descended from the erected structure towards the battlegrounds that await her. Both feet pound the earth, unable to match her power.

"It's her! It's the Valkyrie!" shouted a frantic woman on the street.

At a younger age, in a different life, Kindra would have flourished in recognition of her presence as a Valkyrie, but now, such a title bore a heavy responsibility that Kindra presently understood.

Roaming the same streets was a Draugr, carrying a beaten mace engorged in fresh blood. Tightly gripping her dagger, Kindra lunged forward, swiping at the undead warrior. Entirely outmatched by her speed, she sliced the head clean from its body like the removal of a button pom flower.

While the dealings of one enemy were swift, there still lay days of work ahead of Kindra. An endless quantity that seemed too great for just one Valkyrie.

Upon touching the ground again, Kindra saw scores of other draugrs wandering the city. Far more than when she entered her slumber. She questions where they were coming from, where all these beasts of a forgotten world were spawning. A few of these drones were soggy, dragging with them kelp, thus meaning these sprouted from the sea.

She cut through them with ease, barely letting them land a strike against her shield. In a heartbeat, Kindra could kill a total of three. Ten on a single breath.

If she had the help of someone of equal skill to join her in battle, such a feat would hastily be put to an end. Under the gravest of circumstances, Kindra would even take her adolescent self.

A section of the street was clear of draugrs, for now. Yet there were more monsters she must face.

Her efforts equate to scooping water out of a sinking ship with only her hands during a rainstorm. Kindra needed to find a permanent solution.

The Norns.

They brought upon this madness, and it should be their downfall to resolve it. But from Kindra's previous encounter, it would not be so simple, and with such a challenge as this where the whole world was in jeopardy, neither should it be. To face them now could mean death. However, the longer she waited to confront her demons, the more powerful they become. In turn, the weaker Kindra would be to oppose them.

Even if Kindra sought the Norns, they could be anywhere in the world, evading the whim of her presence. Moreover, no amount of speed, including Kara's, could match their ability to teleport.

The ground trembled, disturbing the city where the building sway like trees in the wind.

"Has Hel blessed me with another troll?" Kindra muttered, staying her legs over the tremoring lands.

She could hear the sloshing of water from the shore on the west side of Seattle. There was no reason to dwindle in times of need. Kindra charged towards the disturbance to restore the balance.

Before touching the edge of the city, the culprit to why the earth tremors reveal itself, crawling from the waters onto the solid man-made foundation. Covered in pine trees and moss, a powerful beast presents itself, much larger than any she had previously encountered. It was indeed a troll, though this was one constructed of moistened vegetation of these lands, appearing to have been born from the forest of the neighboring island.

This forest troll stood hundreds of feet tall, captivating the grey sky with its foliage coat.

"In the name of Odin ... ." Kindra whispered.

The troll quickly took notice of the woman standing before him with a rebellious nature. His yellow eyes pass through the layer of trees over his face, glaring at the woman with a clear expression of resentment.

"Return to your slumber and do not intervene or face the repercussions." Kindra gave the troll a final warning.

"The world should not be made of stone and metal." The troll replied.

Balling his hands into fists, the towering creature presented his decision. As it approached, Kindra stood in awe at the incredible size of this being, casting her into the shade like a mountain. She fashioned her spear for battle, but in comparison, her weapon was a mere sewing needle. Yet, there was no fear within the young woman as she was willing to tackle this beast on her own. The only thing plaguing her mind was the amount of effort and time wasted to bring just one opponent down. It would be like a mouse trying to defeat a horse with nothing but tiny bites against its hide.

In the time the troll took its first step towards her, Kindra jettisoned up the building beside her to quickly meet a more suitable level to attack. There were many ways for her to attack, though less at making an effective blow. Pouncing on his arm, she drove through the dense trees that pose as armor over its flesh. The spear pikes into the rough, bark-like surface where Kindra could maintain her stance. There was hardly a sign of discomfort from the enormous beast as she staked her position, and as she struck with her shield, it only made minor cracks.

Emitting a growl of annoyance, the forest troll reached for the Valkyrie burrowed beneath the green canopy like a tick. The gust passing through the trees prompts Kindra to dart from its hand, which grew closer, ascending higher on his arm near the rounded shoulder.

A spear was not the best weapon for a creature this size. An ax would be the preferable choice, and Kindra truly wished she had Hildr's signature weapon for this job.

Wedging her shield into a narrow fissure on his skin to hold herself in place, Kindra tried the spear, this time to slash at the hardened surface. Only a few fragments chipped away from Kindra's strikes. In time, she could breach through and sever his limb, though Kindra did not have the time or patience to hack away at one foe.

The troll's hand slid up his arm towards Kindra. Once again, she had to abandon her efforts to avoid being crushed. Atop his shoulder, which was nearly free of standing trees, the face of the troll stared back at her with a menacing brow.

"Do not sway my hand any further!" Kindra said, hoping the behemoth would yield in its advances.

"The Norns grant us life and purpose to rule this world once again," he replied, "And no Valkyrie will stand in our way."

Kindra drove the edge of her shield into his shoulder, then swiftly swung the spear on the exposed end like a hammer over a felling wedge. A deafening ring erupted from the collision of metal, sending a powerful vibration to course through his extremity.

A heavy howl was blared from the troll, proving her attack was far more effective than simply thrusting the spear.

He flinched from the sharp spike of agony thrust into him, losing strength in his left arm, where it dangles freely. Rather than swiping at Kindra again, the mighty beast threw his shoulder against the closest tower to rid Kindra off his body. Tremors caused Kindra to lose her footing and tumble over the troll's shoulder without her shield. She collided against several trees in her rapid descent, feeling only the little brushing of branches against her body that no cloth could protect her from. A trunk strong enough to bear Kindra's mass stopped her from traveling further. Adjusting her orientation on the troll, she traveled up his torso towards the reclamation of her shield.

Hovering over Kindra's position was the troll's hand that moved closer. The lack of a quick means of evasion leads Kindra to hold out her spear and brace the end against his body. As he pressed over Kindra, the spearhead pierces his open palm, sending only a dreadful sting. With the blade lodged firmly in his flesh, Kindra was plucked from where she stood and brought upward for the troll to take a closer examination of the Valkyrie.

At a greater vantage point with the troll's face in sight, Kindra jumped from his hand, soaring towards his glare. The silver spear was extended forward with a solid straight arm as she plummets the blade into his right eye, passing more than half of her weapon into the soft gelatin tissue.

The troll's voice soared higher than before, jerking his head back from the pain. Green blood gushes from his eye while the blade remained in place. Drawing the spear, blood pours on Kindra, drenching her in the green viscous fluid. As she tried to withdraw herself, the troll swipes at her in midair before she could escape his brow. He shoved Kindra to the streets, where her body fractures the ground on impact.

Groaning from failing to dodge such a natural movement, she pressed onward with her battle against the forest troll. Kindra could beat herself up later for such a misstep.

"Is that all you can muster?!" Kindra shouted.

Removing his cupped hand from his bleeding eye, he scolds Kindra. Both hands were raised into the air with an obvious intent to bring them down over Kindra to crush her.

The Valkyrie stood ready and steadfast by the impending attack.

When he lowers himself, that will give me the window to retrieve my shield and make another attack at his head. I should work around his blindside—

—"Reach for her"—

—"What?!" Kindra muttered, hearing the faint familiar voice of Freya behind her. She rushed to look back but found no other Valkyrie present. Only an empty street. Was her mind making it up, or was it truly Freya speaking to her?

The troll's fists collided on top of Kindra as she stood distracted by the voice of a ghost, forcing her through the asphalt. Her body ached tremendously from not being ready to brace the power. Another worthy punishment for Kindra dropping her guard in the middle of a battle. But as she recovered, the voice she just heard repeated itself in her head.

Reach for her.

Reach for her.

Kindra tried to decipher the message if it was indeed from Freya. Yet, her mind struggled to overcome the pain and growing fatigue that abuses her body. Even with the recovery rune given to her by Hildr, it barely gave her enough energy to continue.

Who do I need to reach for? Why is Freya telling me to reach ... for her?

The thoughts of what she went through last night in her dream reminded Kindra of the gift Freya presented her. The Midgard Stjarna. Although Kindra woke up without the legendary weapon in her hands, she felt the power in her palm.

The troll drew back his hands, letting Kindra have the chance to breathe, and her body decompress. She could feel a sharp burn over her right cheekbone, with blood slowly trickling down her face, where Kindra could tell it was an abrasion burn. Of course, it was nothing compared to other wounds she had received throughout her lifetime, but the audacity of such an attack to draw blood filled Kindra with anger for both the troll and herself for letting it happen.

Pushing herself off the ground, Kindra leapt out of the small crater just as the troll brought down another fist to finish the job. As she rolled over the street into a crouch, the thought of Stjarna entered her mind.

Kindra held out her hand to the sky.

"Come to me, Stjarna . . ." Kindra whispered.

There was nothing but complete silence while she waited for a response. Even the forest troll stood bewildered by Kindra's stance and her pause from fighting.

Aid me in battle, please!

The troll balled a fist, holding it up in the air, perfectly blocking the morning sun. Kindra did not move a muscle. She would bear the pain and stand again if the beast brought her down.

The giant fist was swung down as Kindra remained still, only watching as the troll followed through with its attack.

A flash of light glimmered in the sky, penetrating through the troll's shoulder and immediately stopping his strike. Darting straight into Kindra's hand was the hilt of Stjarna, which fits perfectly as if it had always been a part of her. The weight and fine details were the same as in her dream. A blue bolt of lightning spiraled over the long blade, containing the power borrowed from Thor, then wrapped around Kindra's body.

"It is real!" Kindra said, shocked to wield such a weapon.

Within that same flash of light, her entire outfit changed. No longer wearing the shredded blue jeans, ripped T-shirt, and sneakers, her wardrobe was now a tan suede tunic dress with golden metal plates laced over the leather. It even intertwined the gauntlets and pauldron belonging to Hlokk into one connected piece. Kindra's messy, blood-stained hair was now wiped clean and neatly braided in a traditional fashion for a Valkyrie ready to engage in battle.

She donned her helm, which perfectly fit her head, and unlike the helm of her sisters, this one wrapped around her face instead of covering it. The most significant addition to this new armor gifted to her was the inclusion of large wings of polished silver metal feathers which moved just as elegantly as a bird's own.

Although Kindra had awoken from the Tree of the Dis as a Valkyrie, it was the moment when she had her wings and glorious armor that she genuinely felt like one.

The troll hunched over the earth, gasping for air as blood pours through the clean opening in his shoulder.

Kindra stood tall in her new armor and said to the troll, "You can still walk away from this."

After a few hefty heaves, the troll angled his head toward Kindra. "My kin will tear this world and finish where I left off. You will be dead with the rest of your kind."

Giving his final answer, which suited Kindra just fine, she lunged forward with Stjarna thrust out. A hand was raised in a futile attempt to block her advance. The blade quickly penetrates the monster's flesh like any ordinary being, sending the bolt of electricity coursing through his arm to the rest of his body.

The sheer power was too great for even a troll of this size to embrace, thus causing him to withdraw his arm with Kindra still attached and fling her straight into the air. With her reaching the height of the surrounding towers, Kindra took advantage of the added distance and time by coming up with another attack. Grasping the blade in one hand, the power streams from the weapon into Hlokk's gauntlet, with the gemstones glowing the same blue color as the lightning. She could feel the absorbed energy harnessed in the gauntlet waiting to be released.

With her body descending, Kindra reels back her fist containing the power, waiting to deliver the devastating payload. Watching as the Valkyrie drew near with its one good eye, she slammed her fist directly into the troll's forehead, unleashing the stored power of the gods. The troll's head exploded into oblivion, tossing the fragments that once made its skull across the edge of the city, with the body collapsing into the bay.

Kindra used her newly acquired wings to glide back onto the earth's surface. It was a shaky landing as she had never used such apparatuses. But in time, they would become a natural part of her like she was born with them.

Gazing at the powerful sword in her hand, it was indeed a blessing from Freya since it made quick work of the forest troll. This could give her an edge over the Norns.

She held the Midgard Stjarna to the sky where a bundle of clouds immediately formed under her order.

"Take me where I am needed," Kindra commanded, with the clouds shooting a stream of lightning that touched the point of the sword and then carrying Kindra to the clouds.

CHAPTER THIRTY-SEVEN

The bolt of lightning transports Kindra across the lands faster than any living being or even modern human technology. Hundreds of leagues passed beneath her in the seconds she soared through the air.

The lightning struck the asphalt road of another densely populated city, one beyond the view of her previous location. A glance at her surroundings, Kindra noticed the skies were brighter than the gloomy overcast of Seattle and were too encompassed by the sea. She appeared to stand in a suburban neighborhood built over rolling hills. Monsters freely roamed the landscape, unleashing destruction and chaos on these helpless citizens. While they need assistance to combat these creatures, there appeared to be no significant difference in the environment that requires Kindra's immediate attention—

—GRAAHH!

A loud, deep roar bellowed throughout the city, sounding nothing like anything she had previously heard in Seattle. The wind instantly changed direction, brushing against Kindra's face in a powerful gust.

Soaring directly over Kindra was a mighty winged beast twice the length of a city bus with thick red-orange scales, almost like a soaring flame in the skies. The head was sharp and had a snout that looked like it was carved out of obsidian. The back, as well as the whipping tail, were layered with spikes.

Oh no, not a dragon.

Kindra had seen a few dragons in her time, ranging in various shapes, sizes, and abilities. However, Hildr warned her to keep her distance when she was a child, as she was not prepared to battle such a creature until she reached her Valkyrie status.

Time for me to give these wings a try.

With the spear in her left hand and Stjarna held in her right, Kindra pushed off the ground using her legs. While in the air, she tried to think of the concept of flight as a natural part of her, or at least as natural as she could formulate since Kindra had never received formal training on how to fly.

Hildr made it seem so easy.

The wings flapped slowly under Kindra's control, feeling rather strange, like a tickle along her back. Although cast from several metals, they move with sheer grace, flexibility, and the lightness of real feathers on a bird. She remained afloat, moving at a decent velocity for a beginner, but she must quickly master the ability of flight to efficiently battle the dragon, who had known the skies all of its life.

Kindra rose above the city, seeing the vast landscape of skyscrapers, homes, and even a large, orange-colored bridge. If this were any other time, Kindra would surely have enjoyed the view and the sensation of being above the surface.

The dragon swept low to the surface, spewing a heavy concentration of red fire like a beam of light over the homes built on the hills.

Using Stjarna to call upon the lightning, it produced a deafening crackle of thunder to echo once it touched the blade, quickly garnering the dragon's attention. It shifted in flight, giving a wide berth around the tall structures and getting a direct view of Kindra hovering in the air.

"Yes, come here," Kindra whispered, trying to keep her nerves in check as she watched the dragon soar towards her.

Once it recognized Kindra as a threat, the dragon let out another deep roar and flapped its enormous wings faster, creating a powerful gust to blow against the ground. As it grew closer, she flew toward the dragon head-on. Figuring when she was in proximity, it would not be able to react as quickly due to being committed to its attack. Swiftly, Kindra passed underneath the dragon's neck, slashing through the scales with the fine blade of the sword.

The dragon screeched, instinctively jerking its body upward in mid-flight, hitting Kindra with the hurricane winds from its wings when she was under his belly. The great force overpowered Kindra's ability to fly, shoving her from her path. In an instant, her stomach twirls inside her body.

No-no-no!

She tumbled in the sky, trying to regain her balance. Both her wings flapped wildly under her alarmed mental state as all she could think was for them to move, but it only made things worse since it continued to disorient her fall.

Stop!

Kindra's entire body stiffened, letting her collect herself during the rapid descent. With a slow roll in the air, Kindra oriented herself upright, then rapidly flaps her wings like a hummingbird, stabilizing her into a hover. Exhaling a breath of air that was unconsciously held as she plummeted, Kindra searched for the dragon. She looked up to see it diving straight towards her like a falcon with its mouth wide open.

A quick thrust of her wings pushed Kindra backward, just in time for the dragon to rush past her. She flew higher to gain some distance from the dragon while also formulating a decent plan. Resting under the sun, she could see its reflection in her polished wings at every moment they move within her peripheral vision.

Kindra deviously smirked as an idea sparks in her head.

The dragon swung around for another direct attack from an ascending angle. It drew near with haste, its burning eyes scolding at the tiny Valkyrie floating in place.

Although this giant fire-breathing lizard was hellbent on tearing Kindra to shreds, it was still mesmerizing to witness its power and prowess that made them feared for generations. Dragons were unique in their own way, and she had yet to see something comparable in this current time.

The beast readied itself to deliver its final strike, fuming smoke from the slash in its neck.

Just beyond its reach, Kindra encapsulated herself with her wings reflecting the light from the sun until she was as bright as the blazing star itself. It was too bright for the dragon to handle, causing it to close its eyes and pick its head up. With its attack spoiled and neck thoroughly exposed for Kindra to exploit, she unshielded herself. Spinning the wings with such velocity that the feathers became fine blades and sliced clean through its throat.

The final roar from the dragon came out as a high-pitched gurgling squeal with burning embers escaping through the opening. The life force swiftly faded, and its body dropped from the sky, falling with a near gracefulness in its form as a final act before clashing with the bright blue water.

"That was quite exhilarating," Kindra said to herself as she hovered above the earth, basking in her hasty victory.

Static sparks along the blade on Stjarna, gathering the minuscule amount of electricity on its own accord.

Does she have a mind of her own? Can it work independently?

—the storm clouds return over Kindra's position—

Well, Freya did tell me to trust Stjarna...

Holding up the powerful weapon to the heavens, another lightning bolt touched the point of the sword, taking Kindra for another trip through the skies.

CHAPTER THIRTY-EIGHT

Returning to the land she once visited, Skuld sat atop one of the many buildings that tower over the city, observing the chaos that consumes the region. Usually, she would hate all the screams and crying, but for just this once, she enjoyed the songs of the tormented. It was a vocalization that would not last long. Skuld did not need her ability to foresee the future to know that; all she could do was cherish it while she could.

Once it finally did grow silent along with the rest of the world, she may take some time to dismantle the remnants of mankind. The makings of a ghost race should not have to clutter the domain of the beings who would soon flourish in the realm. Their memory would be gone, and Midgard would start anew.

A rapid formation of clouds appeared over Skuld, blocking the afternoon sun with a dark grey mass that instantly turn the city into night.

"What is the meaning of this?" Skuld aggressively muttered. She could tell the difference between magic conjured by her sisters and those of the gods.

An explosion of lightning appeared before her, creating such a powerful flash of light that even she must shut her eyes from the illumination. Once the light settled, Skuld opened her eyes to see a glamorous figure clad in golden armor sporting silver wings gracefully flapping to keep the figure afloat. At a glance, Skuld knew it was neither Verdandi nor Urd hovering in her presence.

The glowing silhouette stared angrily at Skuld so much that she could sense the fuming passion behind those eyes. Skuld recognized the image of a

Valkyrie. Her first thought upon seeing the distinctive armor was that it must be Freya, the Queen of the Valkyries herself, returning from the dead. It was a foolish thought as she witnessed the Queen fall in battle when she joined the remaining warriors on Midgard. Upon closer inspection, Skuld saw the Valkyrie as the one who opposed them.

Ugh, not you again...

"So, you returned and with wings this time. Now you look like a real Valkyrie, if only momentarily," Skuld said, not moving her seat on the edge of the skyscraper. "I hope you came here to pledge your servitude willingly."

"I am here to stop you. All of you, and put an end to this madness," Kindra said.

A smirk appeared on Skuld's face as she shook her head after listening to Kindra's statement. "I lied. I was hoping for that defiant, arrogant response to come from you so I could put an end to you myself. But do you think you can stand a chance against me? You are no match for a Norn, even with your shiny armor." Skuld casually stood, reacting as if Kindra's presence inconveniences her moment of relaxation.

"I do not fear death, for I know what follows if I die. But for you, there is nothing. Your soul will never poison the company of those in Valhalla."

"Such bold words from someone who was clinging to life mere moments ago."

"My actions will be far bolder," Kindra stated.

Skuld rubbed her hands together, producing a thick black smoke to ball up in her grasp. Releasing the smoke, it encircled Kindra inside a giant ring. Out of the black swirling cloud were sharp grey wings. Creatures of a diabolic nature, scores of them, no larger than a man, surround Kindra, waiting to be unleashed. They were humanoid with the same wings and leathery features of a bat.

"I do not believe you have ever come across these beasts in your meager lifetime, for they were far before your time in lands not your own. They were one of our first trial runs of removing an entire race years before taking on the gods and your Valkyrie kin."

The bat-like creatures snapped their jaws at Kindra, eyeing her as the only form of sustenance to satisfy their hunger. Like the wulvers, Kindra developed a creepy vibe from their stares, fueling her desire to quickly rid them.

"My sister, Urd, would disapprove of me killing you, but I refuse to be pestered by the likes of you. Rip her out of that armor and feast on her flesh. I do not want anything left of her as a symbol of her existence."

The freshly bred monsters made a terrible screech once allowed to binge on the Valkyrie. They stormed towards her as a collective. Kindra slashed her spear to keep their distance, quickly cutting them in two or dismembering their limbs, separating them from their wings. Those who made it past her guard received the sharp blade of the Midgard Stjarna.

The combination of both weapons swiftly allowed Kindra to dice through these feral creatures, but their numbers were great and continued to be summoned due to Skuld's magic as she stood in her place, watching it all unfold.

They clung to her wings, doing everything they could to stall her flight and move closer.

There are too many … I cannot take them all out at once through conventional means and try to get close to Skuld …

As the grey clouds blanketing the sky lingered, there was a rumbling of thunder that shook the air.

That's it!

Shielding herself beneath her wings, these flying monsters clamored over Kindra, fruitlessly clawing on the mystical metal to reach her. And with a powerful thrust, she shoved them away, creating just enough space for her to move unimpeded. Stjarna was held up to the clouds, and in the instant of her outstretched arm, a volley of lightning extending their bright blue roots simultaneously struck the hundreds of beasts surrounding her. Every single one was incinerated the moment the raw power of the gods touched their flesh.

All that was struck by lightning plummeted towards the earth with only their wings flapping from the rushing wind.

Kindra swept toward Skuld on her perch, snatching the Norn as if Kindra was a bird of prey. She slammed Skuld's face against the neighboring skyscraper, dragging her skull along the concrete exterior deep enough to break through layers of glass and metal. Skuld did not scream, only producing a surprised yelp for being snatched by Kindra.

A battle in the air was not the most ideal way to fight, at least not for Kindra when she had hardly any experience or had developed a proper fighting style. So, for now, ferocity and improvisation would have to do.

Kindra slammed her shield directly into Skuld's face as hard as she could, yet it was not enough to express the rage boiling inside her. Only a thin draw of blood poured from Skuld's nose. Kindra wanted broken bones, shattered teeth, and a geyser of blood to flow; however, she was pleased to see the Norn bleed. She just needed more of it.

In an attempt to break away from Kindra's grasp, Skuld threw out a dagger, but Kindra caught her wrist in an instant before thrusting it beyond Skuld's reach. Then, firmly seized by Kindra, she gave Skuld a solid headbutt, using the indestructible metal crown to her full advantage. The blow was so powerful that they burst through the concrete wall into the building itself.

They rolled over the floor somewhere above the middle of the skyscraper. Kindra could land on her feet, while Skuld did not have the luxury and slid on the floor to a sudden stop. A wad of blood was hacked from Skuld's mouth, and she struggled to catch her lost breath.

"I would have advised you to surrender, offering you mercy to change your ways for the betterment of this world, but all I seek is you and your sisters dead. It is a fair trade for what you did to mine," Kindra said, stepping towards Skuld.

The Norn wiped the blood from her mouth, flabbergasted to see the red fluids once again. It must have been long ago when she was a child since she saw her own blood.

"You bitch . . ." Skuld muttered, "I knew Urd should have killed you. We should have dismembered you when the chance arose."

"This is blood for blood."

Kindra threw her dagger into Skuld's back, making a hoarse scream as she tested her vocals, which had never reached past her normal octave. As Kindra approached Skuld, thrashing from the sharp pain on the floor, black daggers were tossed from her sleeves at the Valkyrie. They were nothing but a temporary distraction that was quickly blocked by Kindra's shield. The seconds for Kindra to protect herself from the daggers gave Skuld the time to get back on her feet.

While still shaking off the discomfort and unexpected confrontation that led Skuld here, Kindra rushed forward and slammed her shield against Skuld's torso, pinning her against the wall. Stjarna was brought up, ready to be delivered into Skuld's head. At the thrust of the sword, Skuld tilted her head just enough to pierce the wall behind her.

"My sisters will hear of this! There will be no mercy for you!" Skuld sneered as she stared into Kindra's eyes.

"Then tell them I am coming for all of you."

Kindra slashed the sword across Skuld's face, creating a deep serration through the flesh on her left cheek. She squealed from the sting but was immediately hushed when Kindra's dagger extended into the spear, penetrating completely through Skuld's back and exiting her chest.

Skuld toppled under the momentum and, as she fell, vanished before touching the ground, leaving only a tiny plume of smoke in her wake. Wherever Skuld went, Kindra knew she would be with her sisters to deliver the message.

Gazing at the spear held in her hand, the blood of a Norn dripping off its reflective surface was a triumph she had desired for quite some time. Finally, returning the favor of the blood drawn from her and her sisters.

CHAPTER THIRTY-NINE

There was a loud, urgent call like a high-pitched whistle that only the Norns could hear originating from Skuld. For every one of these calls, they all know to meet at their well. Urd waited with Verdandi for news from Skuld. She kept herself together while Verdandi nervously wrings her hands in anticipation.

"Calm yourself, Verdandi," Urd instructed.

"But Skuld has never sent a call. What if she is in trouble or needs our help?" Verdandi rapidly said. It had been years since Urd had heard Verdandi quiver, and it was quite unnerving, but Urd always knew Verdandi had a difficult time controlling her emotions.

"I am sure she is fine," Urd said without any elevation in her voice.

"But-but-" Verdandi stammered.

"Verdandi, quiet."

The young sister bit her bottom lip like a child with only her jittering body to express herself.

Slipping through a smokey portal, Skuld landed face-first into the long grass, barely moving after she fell in front of them.

"Skuld!" Verdandi shouted.

Urd rushed to Skuld's aid with Verdandi right behind her. Cradling her in Urd's arms, she gazes at their sister, who was riddled with cuts along her back and left side of her body. Her face was covered in blood. Her own blood.

A single horizontal laceration ran along her right cheek, deep enough that Urd could almost see into her mouth. If Skuld tried hard enough, she could split the tissue in half.

"My dear sister, what happened to you?" Urd soothingly asked.

"She returned. The Valkyrie. She sought me out … ." Skuld said with her blood clinging over her teeth.

"The Valkyrie? How?" Verdandi asked. "She is nothing but a girl with a bad temper."

"That girl … did this to my face!" Skuld shouted with a finger pointing to the gash on her cheek.

"Ease yourself," Urd said to Skuld, "Let your body heal."

"We need to stop her."

"We will." Urd set Skuld on her bed inside the well to rest. Such wounds should not take too long to fully heal, though none of them have received the same level of damage as Skuld in their lifetime. Even the great war they fought did not invoke a drop of their blood.

Urd stood outside the opening of their well with Verdandi.

"I cannot believe this girl was able to do this to Skuld—to a Norn—of all people," Urd said with frustration in her voice, trying to mask her rage.

"How is this possible? Not even the greatest among the Valkyries could do such a thing," Verdandi commented.

"I would say we may have underestimated the girl, but there seems to be something else besides her own nerve that has granted her power. She was not this strong when we confronted her."

"Should we hunt her down now that we have her answer?" Verdandi asked. "I vote for evisceration."

Urd genuinely smiled like a happy mother, then pats Verdandi on the shoulder. "While I enjoy seeing you develop resentment towards the Valkyrie, we should not be too hasty, or else we may fall into the same predicament as Skuld."

"We need to avenge our sister, Urd!" Verdandi insisted.

"And we will. But first, show us where this Valkyrie is located."

Verdandi created a window for them to see, capturing the Valkyrie in the performance of her duties as she slays the beasts they just resurrected and saves the commoners.

"So, now she has her armor," Urd grumbled.

"Is that her? That looks like—"

"—Freya's armor, I know. But that is impossible. Freya was slain before this girl received wings of her own. And what is this? She possesses the Midgard Stjarna."

"How could she ever have found her? The Midgard Stjarna was lost to the winds when Freya fell!"

"The Valkyries … they must have found their own ways of communicating with Kindra from the grave." Urd spat for speaking the name of the young Valkyrie.

"Then we must kill her before she gets more powerful," Verdandi said.

"No matter how powerful she becomes, a Valkyrie will never be strong enough to defeat us at our combined might." Urd gently rubbed her chin as she watched Kindra take on all beasts in her path. "We will confront this lone Valkyrie and properly respond to her ongoing defiance."

"Does that mean we will kill her?" Verdandi asked with a jolt of excitement.

"Not quite yet. The girl will be beaten to the brink of death, and once Skuld has recovered from her wounds, she should also partake in the amusement. Out of all of us, she deserves the most retribution."

Verdandi smiled, then said, "Where do we begin?"

Chapter Forty

Traveling from one city to the next across the oceans and over mountains, Kindra was doing her best to eradicate the evil spreading throughout this realm.

The endless number of beasts did not burden her as she grew accustomed to her duties as a savior and protector. Being a Valkyrie required her to always be ready and to respond to every incident around the world, it was a life she knew would be taxing and consume her own wants and needed, but she was more than glad to have accepted Hildr's offer. After every soul she came across was saved either from death or sent to Valhalla, Kindra only hoped she was making Hildr proud.

Kindra resided in a densely populated city, possibly with the most people she had ever seen at once, and almost had similar features to Anna. However, their native tongue was accented differently when they spoke, or rather when they screamed.

She stabbed into the heart of a lingering Alp with her spear. For some strange reason, this city was riddled with Alps, mystical vampiric elf-like creatures capable of shapeshifting. The first one she encountered, Kindra thought it was a variant of a wulver with its small stature and akin to wolf-like features instead of a man. Thankfully, they could be eliminated just as quickly without any specific method.

The unique sensation of magic flowing through the air drew Kindra's attention. Before, she was barely conscious enough to detect magic, but now that she had grown into her enhanced Valkyrie senses, magic could be picked up like heat from a fire.

So far, only a small amount of warmth had yet to bloom, but Kindra knew it was *them*.

"Why are you wasting your time saving the lives of insects?" Urd asked as she appeared on the same street in front of Kindra.

"Yes. Please enlighten us?" Verdandi added, following behind Urd.

Kindra held out her shield with Stjarna at the ready.

"My duty is the protection of mankind. There is nothing that can dissuade me from my charge. Otherwise, I would betray my sisters and the lives they all sacrificed," Kindra replied, taking a firm stance to give the Norns their answer.

"Just because you wield the armor and arms of a Valkyrie does not mean you are capable of defeating us."

"These are merely tools. It is with heart and devotion that will bring you down. Just like I did your sister."

Verdandi bit her tongue hard enough that a stream of blood poured from the corner of her mouth, then screamed at Kindra, lunging towards her with her bronze sword appearing in her hands.

"Verdandi!" Urd shouted, but her sister ignored the frustrated call of her name.

Yes. Get angry. Act like a feral beast. It will only make you all the more predictable.

The bronze sword was thrust forward but was immediately blocked by Kindra's shield. Since Verdandi was too close for Kindra to stab her with Stjarna, she punched Verdandi in the face with her hand wrapped around Stjarna's handle. The Norn did not anticipate the rapid counterattack and took the punch at full force, pushing her back a few steps. Completely stunned to take a hit like that, Verdandi cradled her face as blood dripped from her nose, leaking between her fingers.

"Ah, I hate the Valkyries!" Verdandi shouted.

Kindra swiftly darted towards Verdandi, swinging Stjarna at her legs that stand unprotected—

—Clank—

—Urd stepped forward, blocking the sword with a weapon of her own, a finely crafted bronze ax. An ax Kindra could recognize anywhere in the flash of a second. Hildr's ax. Swinging Stjarna upward, where the sword and ax were locked, Urd pushed Kindra back a few paces with amazing strength.

"That ax ... it does not belong to you!" Kindra grunted.

"Then come and pry it from my cold dead hands, just like how I did it to its original owner," Urd replied.

Kindra made a rageful roar and gave a powerful shove to throw off Urd. She knew Urd was only trying to get under her skin and dilute her performance with angry thoughts, but she must control herself and think logically.

Urd swung the ax without skill or finesse, using only raw strength to lob the great weapon. It was a mockery to Hildr and her ax.

The large blade on the ax was allowed to swing right in front of Kindra, missing quite significantly for her to attack. Stjarna was thrust towards Urd, but even within her proximity, Verdandi threw in her sword to parry Kindra. She slammed her fist into the center of Kindra's chest, pushing her back and causing her to cough a breath of air.

"Do not think I will let you off so easily," Verdandi said.

The hit in her chest was discomforting at best, but it was not the punch that affected her.

There was a strange stiffening in Kindra's body, starting from where she was struck to her extremities.

What is happening?

She could feel her fingers loosen over the Midgard Stjarna.

NO!

Kindra flexed her muscles, regaining control of all her body parts and tightening her grip over her weapons.

"What?" Verdandi gasped, "How ... it's the armor!"

Kindra was confused about what Verdandi was trying to do if her body was meant to seize entirely from that one hit. However, she was glad for the armor given to her by Freya. Otherwise, this fight may have ended much quicker than the last.

Verdandi slashed with her sword while Kindra still unraveled herself from Verdandi's last punch. Kindra threw up her shield, slapping the bronze sword away, which allow her to drive Stjarna into the ground and summon a bolt of lightning to strike the hilt.

The powerful surge of energy from the sky blasted the street, blowing Verdandi and Urd away from Kindra.

I do love this sword.

In the aftermath of the lightning smiting the earth, Kindra rushed towards Verdandi since she was the closest and weakest of the two. Clearing the dust and lingering smoke, she eyes the Norn on the ground. Her light pink dress was streaked with dirt and oil from the street, and a few droplets of blood from her nose.

Ready to deliver the tip of Stjarna into Verdandi's body, she vanished from her position on the ground, leaving Kindra only to stab into the crater she was last seen.

"Stop running away like a coward!" Kindra screamed in frustration, but as she said, she unconsciously spoke in her native tongue.

Approaching Kindra from behind, Urd bore the ax over her, ready to strike her down.

A wing emerged from Kindra's back, immediately blocking the ax on its own.

Was that from me, or did the armor move on my behalf? Either way, it did a fine job of stopping Urd.

Kindra whipped herself around and kicked Urd in the stomach, pushing her a dozen feet away.

"How dare you make a mockery of the Norns!" Screamed Verdandi from above, holding out her sword over her head.

Kindra's wings extended upward, snatching the blade out of the air before it could touch the tip of Kindra's helm.

"Need I say more?" Kindra taunted Verdandi, hoping the immaturity of her characters bleeds into her ability to control her anger.

"I will rip your soul out of your body!" she screamed, slashing wildly at the Valkyrie.

Kindra was able to block most of the slashes on her own but had the good fortune of having her wings handle the remaining volleys she was not quick enough to thwart.

Upon a clumsy thrust, Kindra grabbed onto and brought Stjarna over Verdandi's dominant hand, slicing the flesh behind her knuckles which caused her to release the bronze sword. Under massive duress from the sting in her hand, this granted Kindra the prime moment to deliver an uppercut with her shield.

Kindra heard Verdandi's jaw crack loudly from the collision of teeth. Since Verdandi was never a true warrior, she did not consider keeping her tongue tucked behind her teeth. Such a thoughtless move resulted in her biting a piece of the delicate muscle off and filling her mouth with blood. Hopefully, this would put an end to her constant laughter. This was more of a favor for her dear friend, Hlokk than herself.

"Verdandi!" Urd screamed in terror.

The final blow to Verdandi was again put on hold as Urd stepped forward, swinging the ax upward. The blade passed right in front of Kindra's face, almost slicing through her cheek if she were a finger length closer. Kindra was quite glad Urd had no familiarity with using the ax in her possession, as she would have known the proper measurement and dexterity of the weapon.

Urd assisted in bringing Verdandi back onto her feet. Tears ran down Verdandi's face as she had difficulty bearing her pain and simply lets the blood rush out of her mouth. It even made Kindra wince a bit as she recalled the harsh lesson growing up. Yet, Kindra held no sympathy for the woman and wanted her to suffer more than just a bite of the tongue.

Kindra twirled towards them with her wings acting like razors soaring above the ground. The Norns vanished from the path of Kindra's wings. While they might not admit it, they were afraid of confronting Kindra. She could sense it.

CHAPTER FORTY-ONE

Kindra searched for the Norns in the city, knowing they would not venture far and give up so easily. It was their pride that Kindra was sure would bind them to this fight.

C'mon, where are you?

"Help! Please help!" screamed a man nearby.

Although Kindra was focused on killing the Norns, she could not divert from her duties. So she quickly followed the pleas, moving around several buildings until she came across Urd. In her left hand, she held an elderly man by the back of his head.

"You are protecting *these* people?" Urd said distastefully,

"Urd put him down!" Kindra demanded.

"Such fragile beings, more so than when the gods were around. I pity their existence."

"I will not say it again."

"Hmph, what is one less life to worry about, eh, Kindra?" She crushed the man's head as simply as a chicken's egg and held just as much remorse for the life lost.

"No!" Kindra screamed, lunging towards Urd.

Upon taking one step forward, Verdandi emerged right past Kindra's peripheral and swung her bronze sword into Kindra's shin. The blunt impact against the bone erupted the dormant nerves in her leg. The gold-plated guards protected Kindra from the blade severing her flesh. Yet, the amount of force was so substantial that she felt the bones underwent a stress fracture and causing her to topple to the ground.

You have been through worse. Now get up!

By the time Kindra took a knee to stand on her good leg, Verdandi had swiped at her head, hitting the bottom of Kindra's helm. She knew Verdandi intended to slice through Kindra's neck in the same manner as she once did to Hlokk but consumed by rage, Verdandi could not hone on her target. Her leg did far better in absorbing the impact of the sword, putting Kindra through a spell as her head rang from the metals colliding, and she felt a strain in her neck.

"Just die like the rest!" Verdandi shouted, swinging her sword again.

As she aimed once more at the soft spot between her helm and armor, which was unprotected, Kindra raised her shoulder, bouncing the bronze sword off her—Hlokk's—pauldron.

I owe you a toast for saving my life, Hlokk.

Once Verdandi's sword cleared over Kindra's head, she struck Stjarna straight through the right side of Verdandi's abdomen near the kidneys. The sudden impalement left the Norn in shock, incapable of screaming. Only a squeak burst out of her open mouth a couple of seconds afterward.

"Get away from her!" Urd ordered.

Kindra used her wings to propel herself backward, dodging the mighty ax before it could chop her in half. A line of warm blood trails down the side of Kindra's head, touching her right ear. To Kindra, it was better to spill blood than to lose her life.

There was no doubt in Kindra's mind that Verdandi had never felt such agony before in her many years in Midgard. If Kindra was the first to have introduced glorious pain to the Norns, she would accept it as a great honor.

"Verdandi, can you still fight?" Urd asked as she held her sister in her arms.

"Y-yes … I am not dead yet," Verdandi replied, cupping the wound in her abdomen with both hands. It was a futile attempt to hold back the blood as it seeped through her palms, staining her once elegant gown.

"The blood of a Norn is a glorious sight," Kindra calmly said.

Verdandi and Urd glared at Kindra, with the former on the verge of breaking down in tears.

Raising Stjarna towards the sky, the clouds collected themselves in preparation to offer their hidden power. Electricity sparked within the formation, yet before it could be drawn, a black dagger flew from out of the shadows in an alleyway. It struck Kindra perfectly in the area where the shoulder meets the back, which was only protected by leather. The leather was thick enough to prevent the blade from piercing all the way through, though the dagger had ample depth that caused Kindra to drop not only her hand but also Stjarna.

Caught in the moment of enduring the sharp pain and shock of disbelief, Kindra quietly curses at herself for letting a sliver of discomfort afford her control of Freya's sword.

"Your fate belongs to me!" Skuld shouted.

Kindra reached for Stjarna on the ground, nearly touching the leather-bound handle before Urd swung Hildr's ax straight into Kindra's chest. The armor absorbed the impact, and Urd knew it would protect her, but internally, Kindra felt the collision pass through her sternum and into her heart. She was knocked back, flying for a full city block until she suddenly stopped by crashing into the engine of a cargo truck.

While she did not want to cough, Kindra had to let out the blood from her mouth before she could choke on it. Splotches of blood and saliva sprinkle over the front of her armor. Looking down at where the ax made contact, she noticed a small hairline dent across the center of her chest. The ax and the armor must have been made of the same material and required a solid hit to do any damage.

Kindra pulled herself out of the wreckage, landing back on her trembling legs. She could not let them deliver a hit like that again.

Skuld leapt for Stjarna on the ground. Holding out her hand, Kindra silently calls for the Midgard Stjarna to return to her. The sword slid out from under Skuld, darting straight towards Kindra, where it perfectly fits into her hand.

With all three of them now in the fight, this would be the ultimate test of her resolve. A rematch after their previous encounter, which to them was only a game. Now it was not only for Kindra's life but the fate of all the nine realms: Jotunheim, Vanaheim, Alfheim, and even Asgard would be vulnerable to unrestricted manipulation. Kindra was the only one who stood outside their control and could make a difference.

"Sisters, let us finish this Valkyrie together," Urd said with no objection. The Norns charged towards Kindra, bearing their arms.

I cannot die. I have to live for the memories of my sisters, for Hildr. And I have to win so Anna and Bjorn can live.

Through the use of her shield, the Midgard Stjarna, and both armored wings, Kindra was able to ward off every attack from the Norns. There was no exchanging of words, only the deafening sound of metal on metal that spoke for them and expressed the rage within each of their hearts.

Despite the wounds they suffered, none of them degraded in speed, giving their all in the hopes that one party would eventually fall. Kindra wanted to focus on one Norn to eliminate while they kept their eyes out for her to slip up on a thrust, swing, or foot placement. The years of Hildr's discipline for Kindra to execute a precise, well-executed maneuver were put forth.

She could sense the surprise hiding behind their scolding faces at how long she was lasting against the three of them under their combined efforts. It was a spectacle for even Kindra to admit, as she still remembered the beating she received when she met the Norns. But that slate had to be wiped clean to not plague her performance.

Through the expense of fighting to their maximum level, the sound of labored breathing expels from their mouths. Verdandi breathes the hardest due to her wound. Kindra wanted to laugh and would have done so in the same way as Hlokk or Kara, but such a distraction was not appropriate under these circumstances, and she had to do it internally.

This is nothing. I was bred for this!

In their growing exhaustion, Kindra increased the amount of power on her end, which would siphon more of their energy. Although they may be blessed with superhuman strength and agility and witnessed centuries of war, none of them were as conditioned or practiced in combat. As a result, they were not skilled warriors. They were only the ones who decide when a warrior meets their end.

Moving too fast for them to keep up, this was the best moment for Kindra to make her move before they became self-aware of their fatigue. A swift swing of her shield pummels into Skuld's hand, cracking the small bones. The Norn sisters flashed their attention at Skuld as she screamed, and in their occupied thoughts, Kindra punched Verdandi with the use of her wings as she stood as the weakest link.

With Urd the least affected of the Norns, there would need to be particular emphasis on her. If she was slain without Hildr's ax in her possession, it would be lost forever.

The glistening blade on the Midgard Stjarna gave Kindra a quick idea or more of an inquiry. Freya told her Stjarna could borrow the power of the gods. So far, she had only tested it by imitating the God of Thunder, but what about other gods? There could be many valuable abilities that could give her an advantage.

The Magnificent Baldr, grant me your power!

Stjarna instantly glowed white, a pure white far greater than the burning sun itself. First, there was not a speck of a shadow or reflection on the blade, then it grew immensely brighter, emitting a blinding flash that cascaded the land in white. Both Skuld and Urd grunted from the powerful illumination.

While stunned by the intense light, Kindra bolted toward Verdandi, hastily scooping her from the street by the bosom of her gown. Kindra slammed Verdandi against the wall of a tall concrete structure, causing her to squeak on impact. Rapid punches landed on Verdandi's body, hitting her at several spots on her torso as hard and fast as Kindra could deliver before she could escape. Each hit delivered a mighty blow that cracked the concrete, driving Verdandi into the surface of the building. Blood spurted out of her mouth after every punch forced the air out of her.

Even as Kindra's arms were starting to fatigue, she did not let up, only gritting her teeth and hitting harder.

She breached through the structure with one final punch into Verdandi's chest. Before Kindra could pursue Verdandi from out of the shadows, Skuld latched onto Kindra's waist, then dragged her into the shadows.

The sensation was irregular, feeling like tumbling underwater, then in a flash, greeted by the morning sun.

They plummeted into the sky far above the city.

Throwing out her wings, Kindra broke herself from Skuld's grasp and hovers in the air.

What is the point of bringing me up here when they know I can fly?

"If only your dead sisters put up a fraction of a fight as you are, then maybe they would still be alive," Urd said, appearing in the sky in front of Kindra.

"Yes, those wretched beings would have put up a worthy fight if that were the case," Verdandi added, appearing on Kindra's left as she wiped the blood from her mouth with her sleeve.

"By controlling their fate, none of them had a fair contest against any of you," Kindra replied.

"It was by our hand that humanity even made it this far," Skuld commented, soaring to Kindra's right. "Who do you think would have filled the void if not us? Your precious Valkyrie sisters? Ha, they would have cost more lives than save."

"Fate should be left to the people to decide!"

"You live in a fantasy. I should have guessed when coming from an entitled Valkyrie who has yet to grow up," Urd said.

"And she never will." Skuld charges with her daggers laced between her fingers.

Holding out her shield in preparation for the Norn to get closer, Verdandi moved once Kindra turned her back. Instinctively, her left wing was directed to block the incoming attack. But as it moved to absorb the thrust of Verdandi's bronze sword, Kindra felt her body instantly plummet.

That is why I was brought up here ... I will fall out of the sky if I use my wings other than to fly.

Kindra pushed herself upward, hastily moving towards the gloomy clouds. As the floating moisture lightly patted against her face, sliding off her cheeks like tears, a glimmering light twinkles in front of Kindra.

Just from the flash that was near impossible to see, Kindra knew it was Hildr's ax by the shine and unique blade coming towards her. She ducked beneath the large blade that swung over her head, and while caught in the motion, Kindra drove her shield into Urd's stomach. There was hope in Kindra that it was enough to break Urd's hold on the ax, but she kept a firm grip as if out of spite.

Though it was not going to stop Kindra from trying.

Ascending higher, breaching the white blanket hovering over the earth only to be greeted by the yellow sun, the Norns did not follow. Although Kindra could not directly see the Norns, she could sense them stalking in the clouds.

"Show yourselves!" Kindra demanded.

"I will never follow the commands of a fucking child!" Verdandi screamed, launching through the misty clouds. The Norn's eyes no longer wield the same rage and ferocity as they once did when this battle commenced. All Kindra saw was a frustrated child in a grown woman's body.

As she sprang forward with her sword out, tethering the clouds behind her, Kindra quickly directed Stjarna toward Verdandi. The moisture froze in an instant, solidifying around her waist and over her shoulders.

"What?! No!" Verdandi screamed as she plummeted from the sky.

A searing pain struck Kindra in the back, right between the wings, knocking the wind out of the young Valkyrie. Skuld hooked her arm around Kindra's throat to hold herself close, then repeatedly stabbed Kindra with her dagger.

"Die! Die like your sisters!" Skuld shouted into Kindra's ear as she drove the dagger through her flesh.

Caught in her anguish from Skuld's interjection, Urd stormed through the clouds with the ax dragging at her waist. Kindra tried to draw her wings to protect her, but with Skuld secured on her back, the Norn held her left wing in place, which kept her left flank exposed.

No …

The fine, heavy blade of Hildr's ax slammed into Kindra's abdomen, where the plating was thinner. She had yet to recover from Skuld's barrage of stabbings and was again deprived of air. Finally, with Skuld vanishing off Kindra's back, she let the Valkyrie fall from the sky, plummeting back to the earth. Kindra tried to breathe, yet as her mouth rested open, she could not draw a single breath despite the vast amount of air whooshing past her.

Please breathe.

She plowed into a building, but it was not enough to stop her from moving. First, passing through the structure, then through another until she smacked into the black asphalt like a fallen star did it all finally end.

Upon impact with the earth, creating a crater within the foundation, she let her chest finally expand to draw in air into her screaming lungs. A part of Kindra's body was numb, only feeling warm blood sliding down her back.

Somehow Skuld found the chink in her armor to deliver a significant wound. The wing on her fight flopped on the ground beside her, no longer holding the strength to lift itself.

Then let us fight on the ground.

Kindra retracted her wings, holding up her shield in its full form along with the Midgard Stjarna in hand.

"Only with that armor of yours and that damned sword are you able to be a match for us," Urd's voice echoed, yet she did not reveal herself.

"I am tired of your excuses! A true warrior does not hide behind lies!" Kindra shouted.

"And like all true warriors … ." Verdandi sprang through the window of an untouched building with her sword held steadily outward. Kindra blocked the point of the sword with her shield, yet as she held against the Norn, her strength was dwindling, and Verdandi took notice. "… they all die."

Kindra thrusted Stjarna to counter Verdandi's attack, but she did not intend to remain in place to block and instead vanishes from in front of Kindra. Amidst Verdandi's disappearing act, the solid black blade streaming through the air was noticed by Kindra. Aimed for her skull, Kindra tilted to dodge

Skuld's dagger. However, she barely moved fast enough and caught the blade gliding across her cheekbone. The fine cut along her flesh was scarcely enough to cause a wince in Kindra or a flutter of the brow.

As she regained her stance, another dagger pierced Kindra's hand, causing her to release Stjarna.

"No!" She hoarsely screamed. Letting it fall out of her grasp from a minuscule wound was an insult to Freya.

Reaching for the powerful weapon with her other hand, Urd instantly appeared and swung the mighty ax. The blade collided with her shield and knocked Kindra backward into a small restaurant beneath a housing complex.

"Quick, take the sword to the well!" Urd ordered. Skuld picked up Stjarna and vanished from the street.

"No!" Kindra screamed, rushing towards Urd.

Verdandi slashed the supports for the structure, causing it to violently shutter. Along with the crackling sound of concrete were numerous screams and whimpers from inside the structure of people who were unable to vacate the area. Kindra moved to a pillar cut in half by Verdandi, posting herself between the two ends, and used all her strength to keep it stable.

"Get out!" she shouted, hoping everyone would take this time to run away. The weight of it all was too great for Kindra to manage, even with Rota's strength, but she gritted her teeth and kept her focus.

"Look at you. Trying to stop the inevitable. Either way, these people will die, but all you are doing is postponing the process," Urd said.

Kindra ignored her, focusing solely on the building.

"I wish you could have joined us and seen the world evolve for the better." Urd gazed at the head of the ax in her hand. "But I will not delay your death either."

Urd lunged forward, ready to swipe the ax at Kindra while she held up the fractured pillar. If she removed one hand, even the strong one, to defend herself, the structure would collapse on top of her and those still inside. Kindra did not know how long or how many would escape, though all she needed to do was give them as much time as possible.

When Urd came within reach of the ax, Kindra's left wing emerged to take the brunt of the swing before it could touch her midsection. Urd struck again with the silver wing shielding against her attack.

Just a little longer. I can bear this weight …

Kindra quickly tried to move the wing to prevent the blade from chopping her like a tree.

Standing behind Kindra while she was defending herself against Urd, Skuld jams her dagger through the slit in her armor at her side beneath the ribs. Kindra's mouth gapes open from the instant shock of pain, leaving her unable to only let out a dry scream. In an instant, Kindra's strength instantly diminishes, and she was brought down to a knee, struggling to hold the floor above her in place.

I … I can no longer … keep it up …

Kindra could see the three sisters watching her fail to uphold her position, eager for the moment to witness when it all came crashing down on top of her. Their stares give her a quick energy boost, but it was only briefly. Just like her declining strength, Kindra could feel her blood drifting from the stab wound in her side.

With the structure breaking apart, it finally collapsed on Kindra in a flash. Only her left wing partially protected her from the falling debris. The tremendous amount of pressure piling on top of Kindra was crushing her. While she remained on the ground, the dagger pushed itself further into her body. She could not pull it out at this time, only able to embrace the searing pain until everything settled. The pounding against her wing slowed as well as the tremors that rattled the earth. The accumulation of rubble layered over Kindra not only impeded her from standing, but it also restricted her breathing.

—*Just relax*—

Kindra desperately coached herself to fray from panicking, which would exacerbate her situation. Placing both hands against the wing, she pushed with all her strength. But nothing moved.

I can do this! This will not be my grave!

There was a subtle shake in the environment.

Do not give up!

The rubble shifted, though, remain in place.

Grunting loudly to draw more power towards her cause, the debris was pushed off, allowing Kindra to crawl out of the pile. Along the way, she uncovered bodies that were unfortunate to make it out in time. Completely pulverized into a bloody mess, Kindra could barely tell the age or sex of the victims.

"Go … and find peace . . ." Kindra whispered, hoping their souls would make it to a restful afterlife, far enough away from this chaos.

As she reached the crumbled housing complex's peak to breathe fresh air, Kindra was grasped by the back of her helm. Aggressively, she was shoved face-first into the concrete, sliding down the jagged mound into the street. Once at the street level, her head was lifted and immediately shoved back into the asphalt.

A powerful migraine stirred inside Kindra's skull, making her nauseous with a growing internal battle to not vomit. Blood pours from her mouth, with some debris cutting her gums.

In a complete daze, all she knew was that she must still fight, but the how was no longer functioning in her brain.

Kindra's left arm crawled forward over the street with her hand open, trying to call for Stjarna to return to her.

Skuld appeared above Kindra and dropped her dagger into the back of her hand, pinning it to the ground. Kindra screamed though it came out as a wet gurgle with blood spurting out her mouth.

"Your sword is not coming," Skuld sneered.

Stepping forth to the weakened Valkyrie, Urd held up Hildr's ax and then brought it crashing down on Kindra's arm.

—*CRACK!*—

The armor protected her from the limb being severed, but the blunt force trauma was enough to break the bones underneath. The snap was almost as loud as thunder, making it all the more daunting for Kindra to hear.

"Damn you!" Kindra screamed, fighting to hold back the tears in her eyes.

"Ah, now she shows fear," Urd chuckled while short-winded.

While hunkered on the ground, trying to catch her breath, Kindra watched as the sweat drips from the tip of her nose onto the grey concrete. Then coincided with droplets of blood.

"You ... will not ... win ..." Kindra said, through heavy breaths and exhaustion hindering her voice, no longer holding the threatening tone she once had at the start of their battle.

"We have already won. And we will always win, for you cannot defeat fate," Verdandi coldly said.

Urd tightened her jaw and made a low growl in response to Kindra's continuing defiance that had not dwindled an ounce, even in her disrepair. Gripping the handle of Hildr's ax so firmly her hand turned pearly white, Urd stepped forward, then swung the ax upward to the sky. The blade collided with Kindra's head with such appalling force that it knocked her helm clean off.

Kindra fell on her back, coughing up blood while the world swirls through her eyes, and every sense was numb, as if she had been disconnected from this realm.

"I will admit that I—we—have underestimated the strength of the Valkyries. Yet, their time has come to an end with your death," Urd said exhaustedly.

"I ... prayed ... for a ... glorious death ... thank you . . ." Kindra said.

Her statement did not settle well with Urd as it was apparent that she wanted Kindra to beg and cry for her life. Like the numerous desperate souls who kneeled before them at their well. Although weary from battle, as evident in her lethargic movement and sweat-drenched face, Kindra's appreciation for meeting her demise gave Urd the energy to raise the ax once more.

There were no more words from the head of the Norns or her siblings. It was just one final act to end it all.

Kindra watched as the blade was lifted over Urd's head, ready to deliver the final blow.

"Hildr ... know that I ... I did my best ... and I am ready ... to be reunited ... with my sisters," Kindra whispered.

The ax was brought down with as much power Urd could muster.

Kindra never imagined herself being struck down by her mentor's ax. Yet, strangely, she was rather glad to die by such an honorable weapon.

Closing her eyes, Kindra waited for the moment when everything ceases. She was not expecting the bludgeoning force or the searing pain which would end her life. Instead, all that Kindra felt was a warmth nestled in her heart. Almost the same feeling of excitement now that Kindra would see Hildr and they would never be departed again.

Before the blade could touch Kindra, a hand reached out from a ghostly portal, gripping the ax's handle just beneath the bronze head. Opening her eyes, Kindra saw the hand that prevented her demise.

"That ax belongs to me."

Stepping through the portal, Hildr emerges from the mare to stand as a white apparition.

"What?" Urd whispered, and before she could react, the spirit of the once-great Valkyrie punched Urd in the stomach and then kicked her away, parting the Norn from the bronze ax.

"H-Hildr?" Kindra muttered under her breath, caught in the same disbelief as the Norn. She was unsure if she imagined her great mentor here with her or if she was hallucinating this moment born from meeting her end.

"Aye, dear Kindra. We have returned thanks to you," Hildr replied, offering her hand.

Kindra removed the dagger that had her pinned and reached for Hildr's hand, feeling the warmth of her skin under Kindra's touch. She was truly here.

"*We?*" Kindra inquired as Hildr lifted her onto her feet.

The portal widened, and the entire council of fallen Valkyries who remained in the mare stepped onto Midgard for the first time since their last battle. Rota, Kara, and Hlokk carried their signature weapons along with the traditional Valkyrie spear for those who handed their arms to Kindra. The fallen Valkyries form a barrier that separates Kindra from the Norns. Her sisters came to her rescue.

"Hildr, why … how are you here?" Kindra asked.

"Your hand. When the rune broke, and your blood touched the scripture, it granted you the moment to use my gift," Hildr said.

"The gift of resurrection … ."

All this time, Kindra thought it was the rune for recovery, but when it was given to her by Hildr, the depiction was altered to encompass Hildr's ability of resurrection. Then that means every moment Kindra recovered from a wound or fatigue, it was all her own doing.

Kindra steadily made her way toward the formation to join her sisters.

Hlokk slammed her spear on the ground, creating a thunderous quake to travel through the streets. "Make way for the queen!"

The Valkyries, in unison, parted with a generous amount of space for Kindra to step through the middle. Kindra glanced at Hlokk, standing to her right, and held a wide smile on her young face while maintaining a stiff posture. She never in a million years envisioned Hlokk addressing Kindra as queen and was even choked by the words coming out of her mouth along with the presence of her family thought lost.

On the ground in front of Kindra was her helm, which was knocked off by Urd's swing. She collects the battered helm, dripping with her blood on the inside, then slipped it over her head.

"You … all of you are dead!" Urd shouted in horror.

"Death was only a part of our story," Herja said as she stood not as a leader of their congregation but as one of the warriors ready to fight once again.

"Our brave sister will not go to war alone," Rota said.

Bang!

They all slammed their arms on the ground.

"The Norns no longer have control of our fate," Mist followed after Rota.

Bang!

"And the queen will not fall this day," Kara stated as she clanged her swords together.

Bang!

"No, she will not," Hildr sternly said.

Drawing out her spear, Kindra said to the line of Valkyries, "Sisters, Midgard needs you once more. Become the saviors of mankind and help me vanquish the enemies who robbed you of life."

They all shouted with their battle cry, roaring as loud as they could that even the gods residing in Asgard could hear. Kindra pushed off with her right foot, leading the charge of the Valkyries. Joining her against the Norns were none other than her mentor, Hildr, and her best friend, Hlokk. The remaining Valkyries took to the sky to wipe the city and the rest of Midgard clean of the mystical monsters plaguing mankind.

The Norns stood frozen, for once captivated by fear as they stood against forces out of their control. Now they face the Valkyries untethered. They face true warriors.

CHAPTER FORTY-TWO

Kindra lunged at Urd with her spear, who was now left defenseless. Vanishing from her position in front of Kindra, the head of the spear pierces into the concrete. Although she missed her target, it was gratifying to know the fear harbored in their breasts. They now understood every living being's fear, and they, too, were not impervious to death.

"C'mon, I thought you were braver than that," Hlokk taunted Verdandi with a bright smile on her face. Seeing her high spirit in this fight raised Kindra's own.

Urd reappeared further down the street, and when fully materialized, Hildr emerged directly behind her, delivering a punch to Urd's face, which brought the Norn down. Without wasting time to stab Urd as she may disappear again, Kindra instead performed a downward swipe of her spear, slicing the right side of Urd's face.

Hildr swiftly swung her ax, only for Urd to vanish as Kindra predicted.

"Ugh! For beings who adhere to fate, they surely do not accept their own," Kindra commented.

"They are being challenged for once, and I am glad it is you who stood against them," Hildr replied.

"Heh, I hope you two can abbreviate this bonding moment. The Norns are not defeated yet," Hlokk said, using her spear to bash away Verdandi's frantic slashes of her sword.

Kindra smiled at Hildr, then they both rushed to aid Hlokk.

Throwing her spear at Verdandi, the Norn arched backward, narrowly dodging the silver weapon as it soars across her eyes. As much as Kindra would have loved to have landed the hit, it was not intended to be the fatal blow and was only a distraction for Hlokk to make her move.

A quick thrust of the traditional spear pierced Verdandi in her upper left thigh, causing her to shriek loudly in a high pitch.

Deviously grinning, Hlokk said to Verdandi, "Not laughing now, are you?"

Verdandi did not reply, only staring back at the young Valkyrie with tears rolling down her cheeks.

"Verdandi!" Skuld cried to her wounded sister. She launched a volley of daggers from her sleeves. The spear was viciously removed from Verdandi's leg, prompting her to fall on her back, and cry in agony.

Hildr flapped her wings, creating a strong gust of wind to blow the daggers out of the air.

Wow …

Although Kindra had witnessed Hildr fight, giving her all against the deities who took her life was remarkable. Encountering her in a sparring match was challenging enough, but battling Hildr in her fury was something Kindra would never want to be on the receiving end of.

"No-no! This cannot be!" Verdandi cried as she pressed the gaping hole in her leg that was bleeding profusely.

"This is for the lives you took," Hlokk said with an eerie glee.

"Please, I am sor—"

Hlokk slashed her spear before Verdandi could finish her sentence, slicing clean through her neck, which separates Verdandi into two pieces.

"Now that is how you decapitate a foe," Hlokk said as she watched the light fade from the Norn's eyes. Once the very life force evaporated from Verdandi, her entire body turned an ash-colored grey and solidified into a marble statue.

"V...Verdandi . . ." Skuld softly mumbled. "No … No!"

She released a dreadful scream, expressing the anguish in her heart at the death of her sister. It was enough to draw a sliver of sympathy from Kindra as she also knew the feeling of losing a loved one, but their actions caused Kindra's loss.

"You will suffer for your insolence!" Skuld cried, ready to pounce at Hlokk, but was thwarted by Urd.

"No, Skuld," she said to her sister, trying to control the tremble in her voice. "If they want death, then let us oblige them."

"As you wish … ." Skuld replied through her clenched jaw.

Urd drew out her spool of twine, unwinding the red line to the length of her wingspan.

"Your twine of fate no longer affects us," Hildr said.

"It is not meant for you," Urd replied.

Skuld cuts the end of the twine, continuing to move down the length of the line.

What are they doing?

A body fell from one of the surrounding buildings, plopping onto the concrete surface without any remorse or prevention of the descent. Then another person fell along with people on the street, dropping in a snap of the fingers.

"No … stop her! They are killing people!" Hildr shouted.

Kindra sprinted towards the two Norns. Withdrawing Kindra's spear pinned in the side of one of the structures, Hlokk threw it back, and Kindra snagged it out of the air. As she leapt into the air, ready to bring the weapon down on Urd, they disappeared from their position, and she clashed with the ground.

"Damn!" Kindra loudly grunted.

"Remain calm and keep your wits with you, Kindra. I do not want you to end up like us," Hildr said. It was pleasing to hear her guidance once again.

They are fast, though it is only because they can relocate themselves on a whim. I wonder why they would need to be anywhere and everywhere so quickly. All they do is sit in their well. They are not tasked with our job to be at every battle, every conflict, in the world. But if my battle is with them, then I can follow them to their location. The only problem is I was never taught how to do it.

"Hildr, how do I track a battle's location?" Kindra asked.

Hildr tilted her head with a curious expression on her face which then produced a warm grin.

"My dear, Kindra, all you need to do is open a portal by using your wings, and you can find your desired battle," Hildr replied, using her wings to demonstrate how to make a portal. Her feathered wings perform a circular motion directly in front of her.

Kindra drew out her wings with the right wing still having trouble moving, but it was her will to make it move. Duplicating the same maneuver as Hildr, the air morphed into a silver haze, swirling an opening where Kindra could see them. The two Norns were still frantically cutting the twine.

"There you are," Kindra growled and charged through the portal with her spear.

Appearing above the Norns, who were completely stupefied by Kindra's sudden presence, Kindra thrusted her spear into Skuld's shoulder, tearing her away from Urd.

"WHAT! HOW!" Urd yelled.

With Skuld pinned to the ground, unable to flee or given a chance to escape Kindra's wrath, the shield was slammed into her face. The first strike landed directly on her nose, cracking loudly in the air. Then, she quickly delivered another blow into Skuld's head before Urd could attempt to intervene, feeling Skuld's jaw snap at the hinges.

Right as another hit was about to be made, possibly one that would obliterate Skuld's head, Urd tackled Kindra from behind, causing the both of them to roll over the roof. Skuld spurted blood out of her gaping mouth along with broken teeth that were shattered into tiny fragments.

Urd wrestled Kindra on the ground, doing her best to gain the advantage, but she was not a fighter in the same way as Kindra, relying on brute strength rather than skill. An arm tried to hook around Kindra's throat to gain control. Instead, she caught the arm snaking around her neck, holding it away just far enough to keep her breathing.

Twisting underneath Urd's grasp, Kindra uppercuts her in the jaw with her shield, then quickly kicked her in the stomach to part from her.

While still pinned to the floor, Skuld fruitlessly tried to pull on the spear, but she lacks the strength to dislodge it, and because the spear was embedded in her body, Skuld was unable to teleport herself to a new location.

As Kindra was separated from Urd, she quickly directed her attention back towards Skuld as, the weakest and most vulnerable opponent. Leaping up with her shield raised, Kindra glanced at the Norn lying on her back. Past the blood and torn flesh, there was nothing but absolute terror in the woman's eyes as she could only watch as Kindra drew near. The image created a slightly conflicting emotion in her gut. Under different circumstances with another enemy, Kindra may have offered mercy since she detested killing someone defenseless and unwilling to fight. However, Kindra subdued the conflict, remembering the powerful entity that lay before her and the travesties she had done. If anything, this would be a peaceful release.

Skuld held out her hand for Kindra to stop, yet it did not sway the Valkyrie, and she slammed the shield with all the power in her body into Skuld's head. The impact produced a devastating bang like an explosion absent the fire. The floor cracked the instant Kindra made contact, and all three of them fell through the roof. As they fall, the spear was plucked from Skuld's body right before the debris toppled over her.

Settling onto the floor beneath the roof, Kindra propelled herself out of the wreckage to gain space and avoid being trapped again.

"Where are you?" Kindra muttered quietly to herself.

After a dozen seconds of not seeing movement, Kindra became increasingly concerned and skeptical of the Norns. A single floor collapse was not enough to kill them, though she could not speak for Skuld.

Creating another portal with her wings, Kindra traveled to Urd's destination, coming across the eldest Norn hunkered on her knees in the middle of a grassy field. Beside her was a vast depression that seemed to run deep beneath the surface.

Urd twiddled the black necklace belonging to Skuld in her hands, now laced in a fine grey powder. "She is dead. Both of them. All because you could not let go of your damn fidelity!"

"I may have been the instrument, but it was your hand that shed their blood," Kindra replied.

"Do not speak to me like I am an ignorant child!" Urd said, enraged. She stood up to face Kindra. "We did what needed to be done for the better of this world. Something a Valkyrie will never understand."

"Yes, I know your motives are just as mysterious as mine is to you, but genocide is not the answer."

"And I am supposed to take the word of the one who was on a solo campaign to eradicate the creatures that once shared the world with you?"

"The world is big enough to hold man and beast. Those who attack mankind will reap the consequences, but the creatures that can live peacefully with the modern world will also receive my protection."

Urd scoffed at Kindra's declaration. "Everyone seated in power has made such claims in the past. Believing they are the pinnacle of maintaining harmony in the universe. Even Odin himself carried such foolish thoughts. We were the ones who then toppled such great abuse of power. Without us, you will be corrupted by your own beliefs. Just because you are a Valkyrie does not make you a pure and lawful entity."

"I am what I choose to be, and my promise to my sisters will steady my virtue."

Kindra removed her helm and gently dropped it on the grass next to her feet, letting the cool air blow through her braided hair. Her spear was drawn from its small dagger form, and she held it by her side for her final confrontation with the last deity of fate.

"Dear child, there are many things you do not know about your sisters," Urd said, holding up Verdandi's sword in her right hand and one of Skuld's darkened blades in a reverse grip in her left.

Kindra did not want to seek further into their conversation, only willing to end this fight once and for all.

Holding up her shield and spear, Kindra edged toward the Norn. As she made her move, Urd ran in Kindra's direction, roaring in her charge. The sword clashed with Kindra's shield, bringing them to push against each other for dominance. Kindra maintained her footing, driving as hard as she could with the use of her entire body. The injuries she sustained in these last few days were certainly not forgotten and kept resurfacing from the flex of her muscles that were working to the limit.

Kindra thrusted her spear, but Urd spun away from the blade and, in doing so, tried to slash at Kindra's head. She ducked beneath the bronze blade and swipes at Urd, hitting her midsection with the shaft of her spear. It was not enough to bring her down, though it did inflict enough harm to produce a seething grunt through her teeth.

"Spoiled child!" Urd said, swinging both weapons in her hands.

"For how am I spoiled if you took everything from me?" Kindra taunted Urd, trying to provoke her to act wildly and sporadic.

Urd furiously slashed the dagger and sword at Kindra, meaning her plan worked to draw Urd into a blind rage. Although Kindra had difficulty blocking every attack, she made a point to grin at Urd, which added fuel to Urd's burning fire inside her.

A thrust of the sword, this allowed Kindra to clasp Urd's arm and keep her close. Now locked under Kindra's grasp, a headbutt was delivered straight into Urd's face, reopening the fresh wound and igniting her senses. Too exhausted and angry to scream, Urd only stepped back to cradle her bleeding face.

"You have lived for many years but know nothing of pain," Kindra said as Urd stepped away to recover herself.

"Silence yourself!" Urd tossed the dagger as a distraction.

Kindra quickly swiped it away with her shield and noticed Urd instantly appear in front of her with Verdandi's sword ready to be driven forward. It was like an angry beast charging toward its helpless prey. Kindra split her legs, dropping her beneath the angle of the sword, and then propelled the spear into Urd's unprotected stomach.

There was an immediate halt to Urd's charge as the spear passed completely through her body. Blood slid down the silver pole toward Kindra's hand. Urd dropped her sister's sword from her hand.

"I ... cannot be slain ... by a Valkyrie child . . ." Urd muttered.

Standing up, Kindra said to Urd, "It is time for the Norns to adhere to their fate."

Urd fell to her knees. Kindra quickly moved to cradle the Norn in her arms as she collapsed to the ground.

"By killing us ... you ... have doomed ... the realms . . ." she said, causing blood to spill out of her mouth.

"Perhaps. But it is not for me to decide."

Urd scolds Kindra yet kept her mouth shut.

Kindra released a deep sigh, then said to Urd. "You and your sisters have fought valiantly, becoming the greatest battle I have ever encountered. Because each of you has fought to the death, you and your sisters will be granted passage into Valhalla, where you will find peace."

"Do not indulge me ... with your pity . . ." Urd's face turn grey in the same manner as Verdandi's when she died.

"I do not pity you. It is our way to reward a glorious death. But you will stay away from the Valkyries."

"We ... shall await ... your arrival . . ." Urd warned, with her strength quickly fading.

"Then I will be prepared." Kindra collapsed the spear into the dagger, removing the blade from Urd's torso.

The blood expelled from the opening just enough before Urd's entire body completely ceases into a solid marble mass. Then, at the touch of the subtle breeze against Urd's final form, the statue of the last Norn crumbled, passing through Kindra's fingers and arms like soft ash into a pile on the grass.

The Norns were finally no more.

Chapter Forty-Three

"You did it, Kindra," Hildr said, floating above Kindra along with the other Valkyries. Kindra stood up to meet Hildr as she glided back down to earth in front of her. "The Norns are finished."

"Indeed they are." Hildr placed her hands on Kindra's shoulders. "Kindra, you have done the unthinkable. You have saved the realms and avenged your sisters. I am so proud of you."

"Yes!" Hlokk rushed to hug Kindra, squeezing her tightly in her arms. "Thank you!"

The powerful constriction ignited the tender senses scattered throughout Kindra's body, causing her to emit a low grunt through her teeth.

"Oh, sorry, your highness," Hlokk retracted, smiling sheepishly.

"Please, Hlokk, we have known each other since we were children. Therefore, you do not have to refer to your queen in such regards," Kindra smiled, which made Hlokk snicker.

"Who would have thought that the last to join our ranks would be the one to do better than the rest of us?" Rota said in a jovial tone.

The Valkyrie spirits surrounded Kindra, shouting praise, patting her fatigued shoulders, and congratulating her efforts. Their cheer was far more grandeur than when she was declared a Valkyrie at her trial. This whole event felt more like a true testament to earning the title. Kindra wanted to cry as she watched the remnants of her sisters shed their admiration.

"Kindra, you have surpassed my expectations, revealing yourself to be the greatest of us. When I . . ." Hildr's voice trembled as she stood in front of Kindra. "I began your training … ."

"Hildr . . ." Kindra softly interjected, "you did not raise me to become a sister—"

Placing a hand on Kindra's cheek and smiling, Hildr said to her, "I raised you as my daughter."

Kindra embraced Hildr in her arms, no longer caring if her sisters witnessed the tears running down her face, for she had earned this moment of happiness.

"Thank you so much, Hildr. For Everything," Kindra cried.

Hildr held her beloved student—her daughter—firmly in her arms.

"You know what comes next?" Hildr whispered.

"Yes," Kindra replied. "But I do not want you to go. None of you." Kindra released Hildr and then took one look around to see the faces of her sisters. "Thank you. All of you. If it were not for your assistance, training, and guidance, I would have fallen in my attempts. You gave me a second chance to fight for you. To achieve victory."

Kara bowed in front of Kindra, saying, "You took something from all of us to give to the world."

"Our memory lives in you," Geirömul said, tilting her head out of respect for Kindra's position.

"And none of you will be forgotten," Kindra replied. "For your service, I will deliver your spirits personally to Valhalla. Hildr, will you be my guide for one last time?"

Hildr took Kindra's hand. "Of course, my queen."

The world disappeared into a flash of pure white light, and she could feel the cool air rushing past her.

The light dimmed as they were brought to the entrance of a large stone citadel, one of impossible size, colored with ivory-white walls and gold trimmings. A chimney in the center releases a plume of white smoke into the bright blue sky.

"We made it, Kara," Rota said, hugging one arm around her smaller sister. "We are truly here."

The Valkyries shuffled toward the tall oak doors laced with various scriptures and artwork in pure disbelief that the great hall lies before them. Kindra could not imagine the emotions harbored in every one of them after spending centuries trapped in Mare's domain, wondering if they would ever set foot into this divine place where warriors finally rest. They all touched the doors except for Hildr, who stood by Kindra's side. Before any of the Valkyries could push open the doors into Valhalla, every single one of Kindra's sisters turned their heads to look back at her.

"We owe everything to you, Kindra," Freya said, "We shall fill this very hall with songs of your name and build a special place for you when you arrive."

Kindra bowed her head in appreciation before turning her attention to Hildr. The woman who taught her—raised her—developed Kindra into the warrior she was today and appeared different to her now. Kindra could see the maternal affection in her eyes.

"Kindra, you have and will always be my greatest creation," Hildr said with sincerity. Appearing in Hildr's hands was her bronze ax. "Please, take my ax. I have wanted to give her to you for many years, and I trust no one else to wield her."

Grasping the ax in her hands, Kindra became familiar with the weight and texture of Hildr's favored weapon. Although she had used the ax numerous times in her childhood, it was not the same when it was gifted to Kindra for her to keep.

"I will take care of her," Kindra said.

Hildr gave a warm smile, then said to her, "Know that you can travel between Midgard and Valhalla, meaning you can visit us at any time."

"Then I will regularly visit to make up for the lost time."

Placing an arm on Kindra's shoulder, Hildr calmly said, "Your journey does not stop here, nor does it end with you being the last living Valkyrie in all the realms. Renew the Council of Valkyries. Train new warriors to take our stead."

"I, uh—Yes! I will revitalize the glory of the Valkyries. And I may have an idea on where to start."

Hildr nodded, accepting Nila's words. Then she brought herself closer to Kindra, whispering into her ear, "Return to the council where you partook in your trial. Our treasure remains for you."

Kindra was unsure of what she means yet agreed to Hildr's request. "May you find everlasting peace and joy in Valhalla."

"I will find peace with my sisters and joy when my daughter visits us." Hildr's hand slid down Kindra's arm into her hand, then parted as Hildr walked towards the doors.

As the Valkyries all set a hand against the entrance, the doors slowly opened, revealing a flash of light through the crack as well as a bellow of laughter from inside, followed by the exuberant playing of music. It was inviting and something far deserving for all of them.

The Valkyries passed through the entrance, enamored by the glorious festivities they had been patiently waiting to meet in the hall. All but Hildr walked inside, taking a final look at Kindra standing outside the doorway. Hlokk gently grasped Hildr's hand as she stood idle, escorting Hildr inside with the doors closing behind them.

Epilogue

Climbing up a frost-covered hill, feeling the cool breeze nibbling at the skin on her neck, Kindra enjoys the frigid air entering her lungs.

Whipping behind Kindra beneath her backpack was a maroon cape made of silk connected to Hlokk's pauldron that she made herself. It was a mixture of formal and casual wear for a Valkyrie, with each Valkyrie wearing a unique colored cape. Hildr's was scarlet red, and Kindra wanted one similar to hers. Embroidered in the center in gold was Kindra's personal symbol. Along the edges in a silver-colored thread were the symbols of every Valkyrie who fell to the Norns.

Attached to her belt was her dagger inside a sheath crafted from the leather of a dragon's wing. Over Kindra's left shoulder, opposite the pauldron, was the compact shield ready to slide into place on her forearm if needed. Kindra found the Midgard Stjarna in the depression where she fought Urd and realized it was the well of the Norns only buried under the surface. So she filled the well with dirt to keep their private quarters away from mankind out of respect. Then, rather than carrying the powerful weapon with her, Kindra sent Stjarna to soar the skies until called upon when Kindra needed her once again. And for Hildr's ax. Kindra held the large weapon on her back, carrying a piece of Hildr everywhere she went.

Shuffling in the right pocket of her backpack was little Bjorn, blissfully taking in the sights with his tongue hanging out of his small mouth.

"Couldn't you … have flown us … closer to our destination?" Anna asked, sounding winded as she strolled behind Kindra, doing her best to keep up.

"And miss the fun of this? Besides, this will help in your conditioning for training," Kindra replied.

Anna groaned but kept moving at Kindra's pace.

When Kindra returned to Midgard after escorting her sisters to Valhalla, she first asked Anna if she would be interested in becoming a Valkyrie. At first, Anna seemed hesitant to accept Kindra's offer but was happy to support her after what Kindra had done for the world. Kindra did admit Anna may not be the most confrontational person. However, Kindra was not looking for someone exactly like herself. Anna could offer wise counsel and advice to Kindra, which was more valuable than strength. Once Anna could fend for herself, perhaps her confidence would increase. For now, Kindra wanted to get Anna into better physical condition to handle the level of training she would endure. Anna was given something new at every opportunity to learn about Kindra's culture and lifestyle as a Valkyrie.

There was nothing but pure excitement filling Kindra's heart for putting her apprentice through training. She wonders if this was what Hildr felt throughout her time when Kindra was under her instruction. It was a glamorous sensation that was its own reward.

As the world gradually rebuilt itself after the calamity caused by the Norns, there was a rude awakening for mankind to deal with the creatures that remained and the reality of what truly existed from the stories told. So naturally, many attempted to seek Kindra out for answers for everything that had transpired, but thankfully, after making amends with Chris, he offered his assistance in keeping her away from all the prying eyes by relocating her and Anna to a quiet spot outside the city. It was his way of thanking Kindra for saving the city and his compatriots, not to mention getting information from her about the whole incident. However, Chris was patient with Kindra since she was also settling back in the aftermath of her battle.

Reaching the summit of the hill, Kindra gazed at the small island where the council once stood. Now it rested as a dismantled lump of rocks and overgrown vegetation. Anna reached the peak, taking a moment to catch her breath.

"There it is," Kindra said.

"That's the council?" Anna asked.

"It was, for a time, where the great Valkyries once convened. And I stood trial to become one of them," Kindra said, with her voice shifting into a sentimental tone as she ventured into nostalgia.

Anna adjusted the straps of her backpack over her shoulders, then said to Kindra, "Then what are we waiting for? Let's go check it out."

She stepped off to lead the descent, bringing a smile to Kindra's face.

After reaching the bottom of the hill and crossing the shallow creek, that was once a mighty river, they step onto the council grounds. Kindra pushed the large, crumbled rocks that were the pillars that held the stone ring above the thrones where the Valkyries at a time convened.

Standing in the middle of the platform where Kindra fought Rota and Kara, the wind seemed to have stopped, and everything became silent just for her.

Anna stood beside Kindra, taking in the once glorious site. "So, this was where you had to prove yourself. What was it like?"

"It was painful. I remember the fire burning in my chest and the heavy fatigue in my muscles. I was beaten, stabbed, and broken, yet I did not yield, not even against two Valkyries. That was when I proved myself that I was worthy to walk among." Kindra pointed to the crumpled pile of stones in front of her. "Herja, our leader, sat there and was the one who decided on the outcome." She then pointed to the right of Herja's seat. "And that … is where Hildr sat to observe the trial."

Even in its current state as only ruins, Kindra could still see Hildr sitting on her throne, watching Kindra battle against Rota and Kara. Hearing the clanking of their weapons and the grunts from every hit made that morning. It was a memory that would never be forgotten, no matter how many years pass by.

"Are you okay?" Anna asked, disrupting Kindra in her reverie.

"Yes, Anna, I am fine. Thank you. Please, take Bjorn for a moment."

Anna plucked Bjorn out of the pocket, clutching him close to her chest and taking a few stepped back from Kindra.

Holding out her shield, Kindra slammed the metal into the slab floor, easily fracturing the center. The large fragments were lifted out of the crater and tossed aside. Despite witnessing Kindra in battle, Anna was still amazed at this woman's strength and how effortlessly she appeared to move several hundreds of pounds of rubble.

Once Kindra had uncovered the last of the fragments, a wool cloth lay flat underneath the platform. With a quick swipe of the fabric, Kindra and Anna were instantly gifted with light reflecting off the mass collection of gold and silver items.

"Oh my god," Anna said, shocked at the sight of the treasures.

"So, this is where they kept them," Kindra muttered.

"You know what this is?" Anna inquired.

Kindra picked up a few coins in her hand. "These were offerings given to the original council when Freya was in command. Armies would come to make offers to gain favor in battle, leaving piles of gold for them, but Freya hid their offerings and forbade all Valkyries from accepting bribes as it may influence their decision."

"Then what do you plan on doing with it?"

"I plan to share its wealth, starting with you." Kindra handed the gold coins to Anna.

"Kindra, are you serious?!" Anna exclaimed.

"Yes, I am. You have given me so much in my time of need that I am compelled to return the favor."

With this treasure and Anna's help, Kindra could rebuild the Council of Valkyries. They could continue their legacy with new blood and a fresh purpose for this realm. Kindra owes them for their sacrifice and honor. And Kindra had the promise to keep.